Cary grew up in the UK, but now lives in Sweden. After a varied career that saw her tap-dancing in pantomime and selling towels on shopping channels, she settled down to write contemporary fiction. She swims in the Baltic year round, stands on her head once a day and enjoys Merlot over Shiraz.

For more books and updates visit:

www.caryjhansson.com

A Midlife Baby

CARY J. HANSSON

Cover design and art direction by Berenice Howard-Smith, Hello Lovely. Illustrations by Amy Williams, Beehive Illustration Ltd.

Typesetting by preparetopublish.com

For my children

Part One

1

You have reached your destination.

Helen leaned forward to look out at the drab brick building across the drab grey car park. 'You sure?' she said.

'It's the sat nav,' Lawrence muttered. 'Of course it's sure.'

'Not the oracle then?'

'The what?' He squinted at the screen in the centre console. 'This is it, Helen! This is St Stephen's Wellness Centre.'

'Right.' Sitting very still, Helen stared straight ahead. Well then. Marriage guidance. Here they were.

She'd left the arrangements to Lawrence. Weeks of pointless discussions since that magical week in Cyprus had worn her down. So much so that, at times, she struggled to believe it had ever happened at all. But it had. She had been away for a week with her oldest friends, Caro and Kay. She had met a marvellous man called Kaveh, and they had made love on the beach, the cold-warm waves of the

Mediterranean tickling her toes. Her *From Here to Eternity* moment that should have propelled her, rocket like, towards a whole new solar system. Should have left her lighter and bolder and ready to reclaim her life. And it might just have done, had it not come up against Lawrence's granite-hard resistance. Her husband was, after all, a man who had, literally, just climbed the highest mountain in the world. For the first time in her life, Helen felt she was beginning to understand the tenacity this required, because although there was no doubt in her heart that her marriage was over, and she had said as much many, *many* times, she'd come to the conclusion that it didn't matter. It didn't matter what she thought, or what she said, Lawrence would simply never hear her. The irony! Just as she was preparing to leave him, she was beginning to understand him. And so, unable to find a way around the impasse, she had conceded to this surprising suggestion of his with a resigned *we'll go if you think it will help.* But the emphasis had been firmly on the *you* and she'd been secretly confident that a man who had longer conversations with his Garmin gadgets than he did with her would never get around to making an appointment.

Except he had.

And when he'd presented her with a time and place it was like a little slap, waking her up to a fuller comprehension of how much he didn't want what she did. D.I.V.O.R.C.E. Even so, the idea of Lawrence in counselling was preposterous. Like making a fidgety toddler sit through a quantum physics lecture.

Face as blank as a wall, she stared across the car park,

at the inaptly named St Stephen's Wellness Centre, thinking two things at once. First, the miracle required to save her marriage wasn't going to be found in this two-storey paean to suburban banality, and second, why was it that a man capable of climbing the tallest mountain in the world couldn't drive from one part of a small market town to another without the help of sat nav? She closed her eyes. How long had she been back from Cyprus? Too long. Far too long.

Lawrence took the keys out of the ignition, and they sat, silence ringing.

How sad, Helen thought, how sad. 'So!' And, with the kind of forced jollity she'd always used at the beginning of parents' evening, opened her eyes, turned to her husband and said, 'Shall we get it over and done with?'

'Over and done with?'

'Sorry. I meant… Yes…' She was opening the car door, grabbing at the straps of her handbag. 'I meant, let's get on.' And as she closed the door, the wind caught it, slamming it shut.

Inside they were greeted with a room so bland it had to have been designed this way. Boring everyone who had to sit in it into a numb submission. The walls and carpet were beige. The large central coffee table was empty. Around the sides of the room stood chairs with padded seats in a colour that was either blue or smudged green, so undecided was the final effect. To the right were three shut doors, with ugly, brushed-nickel handles and framed A4 signs. There was nothing to distract and nothing to do, except take a seat and begin an inevitable spiral of introspection. Helen smiled. The room was a triumph. Ten minutes waiting here, and you'd be more in need of therapy than when you'd walked in! Except... she turned, one of the doors was open, ever so slightly open.

Beside her, Lawrence checked his watch and nodded at the door. 'Think this is us,' he said, striding towards it.

'Lawrence,' Helen hissed. Sixty seconds in and she'd already skim-read the A4 signs. Lawrence, obviously, hadn't. But then he *never* read instructions, and he *never* asked for directions. And he *never* stopped, so she could ask for directions. She stood watching his back, the hulk of his shoulders in his Alpine Trek shirt. She could, she supposed, tell him what the sign next to the partially open door said...

'Oh.'

... or she could leave it, because the door had already been pushed open and Lawrence was already halfway across the threshold.

He stopped short.

Helen sighed. She was thinking of that track in Wales, which despite her protestations, Lawrence had insisted was a scenic route back to the campsite they were holidaying at. It wasn't. It was an access road to Craig Goch Dam. And peering out of the Volvo window at the 150-foot sheer drop, her children Libby and Jack squealing in the back seat, Helen had experienced a strange out-of-body experience which felt every bit as real every time she remembered it, right down to the question she'd asked herself as she'd squeezed back against her seat and closed her eyes on the vertiginous view. Was she woman or lemming? Even now, in this brutally bland room, she found herself gripping the

4

strap of her handbag as the memory took hold. Well, what was she? Cyprus had answered that question, hadn't it? Or, more to the point, Kaveh had. Allowing herself the briefest moment of Kaveh-shaped indulgence, her fingers loosened their grip and she watched as a few feet away Lawrence stood swaying in the doorway. She sighed again. Cyprus was over and she had to keep moving forward, no matter how hard the terrain. Besides, she was, at the very least, curious. She shrugged her handbag over her shoulder and walked across to join her husband.

Standing in the doorway, a head and a half shorter than him, she peered past his shoulder. The room ahead contained a large spa-bed, strewn with balls of tissue and crumpled towels. Behind stood an apparatus not so dissimilar from a portable oxygen machine. Clear plastic tubes led up to a holding tank that… Helen's eyes narrowed. The contents of the tank were horribly fascinating, brown-coloured stew-thick liquid that she couldn't stop staring at. It was like passing an accident, you know you shouldn't look and yet can't do anything else *but* look. Her nostrils caught up with her eyes. The room smelt like their en-suite after Lawrence had been through what he called his daily *routine* (which was daily and was very much a routine). All this she had time to process before a door at the back of the room that she hadn't noticed opened up, and a young woman wearing the white coat of a therapist came in and said, with perfectly manicured eyebrows, 'Oh?'

'Oh.' Lawrence mirrored. He too was looking at the sludge in the holding tank. He hadn't, Helen knew, worked it out.

'I think…' One hand on Lawrence's arm, Helen was already backing out. 'I think we may have the wrong room.'

The woman smiled. 'I think so too. This is colonic irrigation.' From behind the door through which she had just come, a toilet flushed.

'Colonic what?' Lawrence barked.

'Irrigation.'

'Lawrence.' Helen tugged his sleeve. 'We're in the wrong room.'

The toilet flushed again and for a moment they all looked at the closed door.

'Sorry!' Helen smiled and gave Lawrence's arm such a hard yank he had no choice but to turn and follow her out.

Behind them the therapist closed the door.

'What the hell is colonic irrigation?' Lawrence said.

Helen looked at him. Where to start?

'Mr and Mrs Winters?' And from the other side of the reception room a voice saved her.

Relieved, she looked up to see a slight young man, clutching his mobile phone.

'I'm Simon,' the man said.

And she tried to smile. She really did. But Simon looked as if he'd just left sixth form, plus he was wearing a nylon sweater with a huge shiny iron mark across it. Hadn't he checked in the mirror before he left the house?

'Come on through.'

She lowered her chin. Lemming or woman? *Woman,* she whispered to herself. *You're a woman, Helen!*

*

Smiling broadly (which seemed a little inappropriate), Simon placed his phone on the table next to a small black clock. 14.04. 'So,' he said and leaned forward to turn the clock to face him. 'Have either of you had any experience of counselling before today?'

Helen didn't speak. Simon was still looking at the clock and she wasn't sure if she should wait until he looked back at her before she answered. Or was he waiting for her to answer so he could start the clock? Was that how it worked? 'No, we haven't,' she ventured, smiling herself.

He smiled again and she had the distinct feeling that a box had just been ticked.

'Mr Winters?'

'Sorry?' Lawrence jerked his head up.

He'd been fixated on and completely distracted by an ornamental stone cairn sitting on a sideboard across the room. The only dressing in what was otherwise another fanatically neutral space. The only dressing, that was, except for an artificial orchid at the other end of the sideboard, which immediately had Helen thinking of Marianne, the receptionist at the hotel in Cyprus, and then of course of Kaveh, *again.* How, she thought as she shifted her weight on the cheap plastic chair, was she going to get through the next fifty-six minutes of this session? She wished she could see the clock face, at least count it down. And then was glad she couldn't. It would be like the clock on the treadmill at the gym she used to occasionally visit, the smug little display she threw towels over so she couldn't see that she still had 13:30 minutes out of 15:00 left. She glanced up at Simon. Did he ever feel the same? In his worst sessions did he ever feel like draping a tissue over his tiny clock? 14:08. 14:19. 14: 36…

'What was the question?' Lawrence said.

'Counselling? I was asking if either of you have previous experience.'

'Of counselling?'

Helen sighed.

'Yes.'

'No.' Lawrence turned to her. 'We haven't, have we?'

Helen looked at him. A brief moment in which to wonder again at the compartmentalised manner in which her husband seemed to live his life. How on earth was he going to cope without her?

'No,' she said. '*We* have never had counselling.' What was the point of reminding him? Twenty-four years ago, after she'd laboured and delivered their dead son, Lawrence had carried on as if it had never happened, while she had just carried on. She'd had counselling then, and it had helped and she had told him, but all that was as lost to him as yesterday's sunset.

Simon nodded. 'Well first of all,' he said, 'I'm not here to tell you what to do.'

Good, she didn't say. He seemed, Helen thought, to have grown in confidence in the last few seconds, as well he might, finding himself with two such counselling novices.

'My role is first and foremost that of a listener.'

And at this, much to her surprise, Helen found herself nodding, enthusiasm opening her face like sun on a flower. A listener? That was exactly what she needed. *All* she needed! A listener would be great! Perfect! If she said *divorce* once and someone in the room actually heard, that alone would be worth the cost of the session.

'So,' Simon continued, oblivious. 'I suppose you could say that my main role is to help you communicate.' He paused. 'How does that sound?'

Again, she nodded. It sounded fair enough. Doomed to fail, but fair enough.

'I presume—' Simon glanced from her to Lawrence. 'That's an issue?'

An issue? Helen looked down at her hands and smiled the smallest wry smile. Communication between them had gotten to the point where if she said *up*, her husband would hear *down*. If she said right, he'd go left. Maybe it hadn't always been that bad, but it was now. And whose fault was that? She folded one hand over the other and stared at the floor. Once, many, many years ago, they'd had dinner with a French couple. The woman's parents were English although they had lived in France for decades. What Helen had always remembered was that she had asked which language they used when they were all together, and the woman had turned to her husband and said, *It's a mix isn't it?* To which he had responded, with eyes as clear as a spring sky, *I don't know. Oh, don't ask him,* Helen had quipped, *he's never listened!* How they'd all laughed! Oh yes, how funny it had been! And how hilarious (not) that for years now she'd been living the same situation without even noticing. *What's water?* the goldfish once said. Well, yes! Lawrence and she had gotten through at least the last ten years swimming around each other without communicating anything beyond the quotidian fill of each day. A hybrid lemming/

9

goldfish. 'It's an issue,' she murmured. 'Communication.'

Lawrence coughed.

'Right.' Simon too cleared his throat. 'Well, I think then that we'll start with a few questions about your relationship. Are we alright starting there? Lawrence? Helen?' He made it sound like they were a couple of toddlers being talked down from the naughty step.

From the corner of her eye Helen glanced at Lawrence, his huge frame hunched in his cheap chair. It was too small for him. But everything in the room was too small for him, as it would be for a man who, a few short weeks ago, had been clambering vertical rock faces. He didn't need this. Especially when, in the smallest pocket of her Russian-doll heart, she knew it wasn't going to work. Because if what she had first said to him in Cyprus, and since repeated over and again, was true – then there was nothing to be done. What had changed in their marriage was her. And a snake cannot slip back into its discarded skin. A sheep cannot re-fleece itself. She had changed and she liked it and there was nothing this young man could do or say that was going to alter that. She glanced at Simon now, earnestly studying his blank page.

He had no idea.

The broken lines of communication that she really needed help with, that were really breaking her heart, were those between her and her children.

Jack was barely speaking to her. The boy who had inherited both her sense of humour and her thick, dirty-blonde hair. The child with whom she would sing 'Knees Up Mother Brown' to dry him off after a bath, the boy who (for one brief summer) had loved nothing more than to peg out washing with her left a room now if she entered it. Yes, he still ate the food she prepared and wore the clothes she washed, but he'd get up and walk out when she came into the living room which, although she didn't show it, was a fresh wound every time.

And Libby? Away at university Libby had been through cycles of grief and anger and was currently in a wise-elder advice mode. The problem was Helen hadn't asked for advice and Libby wasn't her elder. Had she said this? No, she'd held the phone at her ear and sipped her wine quietly and said nothing at all knowing that there was something unusually fragile about her daughter right now, the source of which – she couldn't quite believe – was her Cyprus fling. Cyprus, Cyprus, Cyprus… The memory had her lips curling into a smile. Like she could still taste the salt on his skin. The man was a god. A Greek god, or a Cypriot god. Either way, briefly, in her arms, he had been a god and if she lived to be a hundred she wouldn't regret it. Not unless it really had hurt Libby as much as her subdued calls home seemed to suggest. And then what? She could hardly turn the clock back, and anyway she didn't want to. The Helen she'd discovered in Cyprus was a Helen who'd existed long before Libby. B.C. Before children. Wasn't she allowed to see if there might be an A.C. as well? An after children?

'You have two children?' Simon asked, the dullness of the question clubbing her back into the present.

'Yes, two,' she murmured.

On he continued, with what she supposed were the usual questions. How long had they been married? How did they meet? Immediate family backgrounds… 'So.' His page was now a quarter full. 'What would you both like to get from these sessions?'

Neither of them answered.

Simon glanced at his clock and, looking up, met her eye. He gave a wan smile and went back to his notes, which Helen could see had been bordered by curly doodles.

What could she say? She knew what she wanted. She wanted out. She wanted a chance to explore the second half of her life unattached to Lawrence. To shed her lemming skin and discover what water really was. On her own! She wanted to buy a backpack and take her twenty-five-year-delayed gap year! She didn't say this and as it turned out, she didn't need to. Because –

'*The problem is,*' Lawrence exploded, *'that after twenty-five years of marriage, my wife went on holiday and shagged the first man who crossed her path!*'

Helen almost ducked. Lawrence's anger was like one enormous fart, which is, she supposed as she looked at him, what happens if you hold it all in too long. *The first man who crossed her path? My wife?* He was talking about her as if she wasn't in the room. Like she was a thing, a suitcase who'd gone and messed things up by putting herself on the wrong flight and she couldn't… she couldn't take it seriously. Leaning away, as if he emitted radiation, she watched him fidget under the onslaught of his own words. He was the only one in the room hurt by them and seeing his white lips and his fisted hands, she felt the kind of helpless sorrow one feels for a bird with a broken wing. He was beaten and he could not and would not admit it. For weeks he'd been trying to stick a lid back on Cyprus, refusing to utter a single word about it and choosing instead to steamroll discussions of cruises and fire off over-the-top compliments about her cooking. Well, at least it was out now.

'Ok,' Simon managed, looking a little windswept. 'Umm, Helen? Is there anything you'd like to say in response?'

Helen shrugged. 'It's true. I went on holiday and I had an affair. Although I'm pretty sure there was a male taxi driver and a border control guard who crossed my path before—'

'This isn't a joke,' Lawrence seethed.

Simon nodded.

Helen pressed her lips together.

Simon drew a long straight line down the side of his notes. For something to do? Emphasis? A secret code? He turned to Lawrence. 'And before this happened,' he said seriously, 'did you have any suspicions, Lawrence, that something wasn't right with your sex life?'

'What? Wait a minute!' Lawrence sat upright. 'This isn't about me! Everything was fine.' He looked from Helen back to Simon. 'Everything was fine!'

But Simon was already turning to Helen. On a roll. 'And how does it feel, Helen, to understand that your husband was so unaware of your sexual needs?'

Helen's lips twitched. It was like a script. He didn't have a clue.

'I mean!' Lawrence waved his hand at the ceiling. 'I was prepared to put it behind us. That's what I wanted to do. I've booked a cruise—'

'I don't want to go on a cruise, Lawrence,' she said calmly. 'I've told you that.'

'You said you did.'

'Once upon a time, yes, I may have said I did.'

'There's no *may* about it! You said you did!'

'And you said you'd fix the back fence.'

'*That's completely different, Helen.*'

'*No. It's not.*' Was it? Or wasn't it? She leaned back and folded her arms. She really didn't care. They were arguing semantics.

Simon pressed air down with his hands. 'Let's try and keep our voices calm.'

No one spoke and Helen stared at Simon's hands. Perhaps there was a sign-language script that had to be memorised as well.

'What else would you say you've changed your mind about, Helen?' Simon asked.

'Sorry?'

'You were just saying, how you'd changed your mind?'

'About the cruise, yes.'

'So my question is, is there anything else you've changed your mind about?'

She put her head to one side. The charade was ridiculous. 'What else?'

'Perhaps you could give us an example?'

An example? She tipped her chin to the ceiling. 'I've changed my mind about ironing. I now consider it a complete waste of time.'

'Oh… that's not quite—'

'And socks! I don't bother my arse matching them up any more.'

'Do you have to be so vulgar?' Lawrence muttered.

Helen turned to him. She was thinking about that 150-foot drop over the side of Craig Goch Dam. Why the hell hadn't she spoken up before he put them all in that life threatening situation? *Yes*, she had to be so vulgar! *Yes*, she was going to have to scream and shout it, literally bang it like a nail through the wood of her husband's head, if she was ever going to be heard. She turned back to Simon. 'You asked us what we wanted from this session?'

Simon blinked. 'I did. Yes.'

'Nothing. I don't want anything.'

'I—'

'What I want,' she said, 'is a divorce. And I don't think that's going to happen in…' She leaned forward and turned the little clock around. 14:27. 'Thirty-three minutes. Is it?'

As the St Stephen's Wellness Centre receded in the rear-view mirror, Helen leaned back, exhaling all the air she didn't know she'd been holding.

Something had shifted. It was tangible in the shape of the space between herself and Lawrence. What had once been rigid, was softer. What had been flat, felt rippled. Like a stone thrown into water, Lawrence's involuntary outburst had broken the smooth surface of his resistance. After his explosion and her flat announcement, the counselling session had drizzled to a close. And although she'd always intended taking another sneak peek at Simon's clock, in the end she hadn't because standing to leave, Lawrence hadn't been able to resist taking one of the two stray stones at the bottom of the ornamental cairn and placing it on top. The action had sent Simon into a paralysis of fear.

'Please don't!' He'd trembled, one pale hand thrust forward just as the tiny cairn had toppled.

After which they had left as quickly as possible, with yes, something changed.

Was it the conspiratorial smile they'd shared getting into the car? (It had been hard not to giggle over Simon's attempts to put the stones back together again.) Or just the relaxation of the force-field they'd been operating in for weeks now? Either way, as she unwound her scarf and pulled the passenger mirror down to check her face was still on, Helen felt sadly optimistic. She could almost feel the change pulsating towards her. Was this the beginning of the end of his resistance? 'Well,' she breathed as the car came to a stop in front of a red light. 'That was that.'

Lawrence leaned forward, craning his neck at the traffic light as he always did, as if watching would make it change faster. 'You really mean it, don't you?' he said to the red light.

Helen nodded.

And when he turned to look at her, she was still nodding.

'I do,' she murmured. 'I'm sorry, but I do.'

The lights changed. Lawrence sat back, arms stretched to the wheel, and the car gathered speed. On they went, past the old stocking factory that was now a Tesco Extra, past the primary school gates she'd once walked through twice a day and never would again. Past the bakery, where the hawthorn blossom was going over and where she used to sit counting red, blue or green cars, Libby on the bench, Jack in his pushchair, strawberry jam over their faces. Days, more distant than stars, that produced such bittersweet nostalgia. She turned her head to the window and watched the town flash past, the sky above grey as unwashed socks. It was hard to believe how quickly this part of her life had passed. Gone now, all gone.

'What is?'

The question startled her. Had she spoken out loud? 'The clouds,' she said quickly. 'It's the middle of June and the sun's gone. All gone.'

Lawrence glanced upward. 'Storm clouds,' he said and when he inhaled, his chest swelled like a balloon. His knuckles shone white against the black leather of the wheel.

Helen looked at them, the hands she knew so well. 'I suppose you learn to read them. Clouds, I mean.'

'Of course,' he murmured, eyes fixed on the road.

She brought her elbow to the rim of the window and leaned her chin in her hand and all along the high street memories unfolded like pop-out greeting cards. The butchers, queuing in the semi-dark of a December morning for a free-range, locally reared turkey. The town hall, scuffing dirt waiting for Brownies or Scouts or tap class to finish. The post office, queuing in the semi-light of a December afternoon to post Christmas cards to Lawrence's parents. The health centre (she checked her watch) where even now her colleagues Daisy and Tina would be arguing over whose turn it was to put the kettle on. Where she'd spent eight years treading the water of missed appointments and ear infections. Was she really ready to leave all this behind? Ready to embark on the second half of her life based upon nothing more than a shift-shaping, nebulous idea of travel that *would not* go away. The answer slipped into her mind, seamless as dawn. Yes, she was.

Lawrence flicked the indicator and the car turned into Station Road. Within another minute they were pulling into the driveway of home.

'No one,' Lawrence said, 'wants to get caught in a storm at thirty thousand feet.' He switched the engine off.

Helen looked at him. Thirty thousand feet was as high as a jet plane. 'Were you scared?' she whispered. Hadn't she asked him this before? So why, suddenly, did it feel like she hadn't?

He didn't answer. His jaw worked side to side as if he was having to chew the words before voicing them, a reverse digestion process.

She didn't speak. She was still looking at him, only now she was thinking something she knew she'd never thought before. That filled her with sudden and profound sadness. The great void at the centre of their marriage was as much her creation as it was his. *Were you scared?* She *hadn't* asked Lawrence this. Ever. What she'd always said was: Was *it* scary? And that was something else altogether. Her eyes pricked tears. It was true. She'd laid as many bricks between them as he had.

'Sometimes,' Lawrence murmured, and his head moved up and down. 'Sometimes, I was very scared.'

Again Helen didn't speak. Once upon a time this would have been the cue for her to reach across and put her hand on his knee. Such a shame. It was all such a shame.

'Sometimes,' she said quietly, 'I was too.'

His jacket rustled as he turned to her.

'Sitting at home,' she continued, 'trying to imagine where you were, or what you were doing... Sometimes I was terrified.'

They sat in silence, no hands on knees. It was too late.

Outside the first heavy spots of rain tapped on the windscreen. Helen leaned her head back against the headrest. What she had said was true. Sometimes she had been terrified. His adventures had left her lonely and afraid, but what she had always known was that the fear wasn't so much about losing Lawrence as of having to cope without him. And with that fear gone, because it had, so very little seemed to be left. A companionship maybe? Someone to sit alongside and watch the latest Netflix with? If that was what she was willing to settle for. Her head moved in tiny side-to-side shakes, involuntary movements as if her body was stepping up to persuade her mind. After Kaveh? After everything Cyprus had revealed about herself? *No.* It wasn't enough and this much she knew like a desert knows rain. Her marriage had been a cushion. A great soft armchair that she had sat in for so long, bits of herself had gotten lost, like pennies between the folds. Cyprus had made all that clear and the only thing she was unclear about, as she sat watching fat raindrops hit the windscreen, was if this new awareness, the understanding that she had been equally complicit in the breakdown of her marriage, should make her feel guilty, or sad? She didn't know, she just knew that it was true. And because she couldn't tell Lawrence any of this, but because she had been married to him for twenty-five years and shared two children with him, she reached out and covered his hand with hers. 'I'm not scared any more,' she said. 'And I do want a divorce.'

Lawrence nodded. 'I know you do.' He looked down at their joined hands, one wedding band on top of the other. 'I won't stand in your way.'

Her fingers squeezed his. 'Thank you,' she whispered, and wondered at how alive she felt, her heart strangely vibrant with this kaleidoscope of emotion.

'But I want to ask you one thing? Can you wait until after Libby's graduation?'

The question surprised Helen. 'Wait for what?'

'Before we start with all the practical stuff.'

She frowned as she looked down at their joined hands. Practical stuff? She hadn't given any of that a thought. An idea revealed itself, clear as the sun breaking through cloud. Lawrence was already there. In the space of twenty minutes, he'd both resigned himself and begun preparing himself. How different they were! And how much she could learn from him. Box it up, put it away, move on. She looked up. 'Will you stay in the house?'

Lawrence frowned. 'Maybe.'

'I think it would be good for the kids.'

'Do you?' He leaned over the steering wheel. 'I'm not so sure. It would feel very different.'

Helen turned and looked at their house. The home they had bought right at the beginning of the marriage. Of course, it would feel different without her. As far as Libby and Jack (and Lawrence) were concerned, she and the house were integral. This house, as a home, was her creation. So what had she imagined would happen? That she would sneak out one morning, a photo album under her arm, suitcase wheeling behind? She bit down on her lip; this was the brutal reality of divorce. Never mind that Libby had already to all intents and purposes left home, never mind that Jack would soon be doing the same. It was going to be hard. For everyone. So on this, she knew that Lawrence was right. Practicalities must wait.

'Of course, Libby must have this summer,' she said, her voice cracking. 'Of course.' And as she spoke the front door opened and there was Jack, standing on the step, his face drained. For the first time since she'd come home from Cyprus he didn't look away when she met his eye.

Something was wrong.

'Just don't go off the handle, Mum. Promise?' Jack stood one step higher than his mother, hands pressed together as if in prayer. He was wearing the shorts he'd slept in and a t-shirt fresh from the floor.

Helen looked at him. *Just don't go off the handle, Mum.* That was the longest sentence he'd deigned to say to her in weeks. 'I won't go off the handle,' she said and moved forward to pass because she knew what and whom he was trying to protect.

He cut her off. 'Promise?'

Helen held his eye a long moment, then looked past him into the gloom of the hallway. By the kitchen door a bulky dark shape had been propped up against the wall. Libby's rucksack. Something about the sad, slack shape of it confirmed in Helen all the nagging fears that had tiptoed around the edge of her mind these last couple of weeks. Libby was home. Libby, who, right now, should be up to her eyeballs in parties celebrating the end of her finals, thus completing an education process that had spanned a decade and cost a fortune. And Jack's policeman act wasn't about protecting himself. He was here for his sister. Her face softened as she turned back to him. 'I promise,' she said. Then, 'Where is she?'

'In the living room.'

Gravel scrunched behind as Lawrence caught up. 'What's going on?'

Helen nodded at the rucksack. 'Libby's home.'

Lawrence peered into the hall. 'I thought… She wasn't due back yet.'

'No,' Helen sighed. 'Not yet.' It was clear by the tone of his voice that he didn't suspect a thing.

He moved to pass her, but from behind it was Jack who stopped him. 'Let Mum go first,' he said and turned to look at Helen. 'I think it's better if you go first.'

He didn't look away and in the moment that passed between them, Helen sensed her son's surrender. She was still his mother and she was going to be allowed to retain the role. She felt a tender relief, nodded, turned to go, paused, then turned back to Jack and gave his shoulder a squeeze.

From the open doorway, the living room at first seemed empty. The coffee table still held its pile of good intentions, exactly as she'd left them: *Brain Training, Sudoko for Beginners, The Fast Diet*. And the elegant straight spines of her dining room chairs were undisturbed. The only thing that seemed to move in the room was a column of dust motes dancing across the French windows. Then, from the furthest corner of the furthest settee, a tiny voice said, *I'm here.* Helen turned.

There was Libby, curled into the corner of the chesterfield, cushions propped around her for all the world like a toddler's play-fort. She was almost completely obscured by shadow, which was, Helen understood, the point.

She dropped her handbag on the nearest armchair, walked over and sat down on the far edge of the settee, careful to leave a large space between them. She didn't speak.

The clock ticked, the dust motes danced and as Libby lay with her face half hidden, Helen ran through every dreadful explanation possible for Libby's unscheduled return home.

Libby was pregnant (laughably unlikely).

Libby had been raped (unbearable, unlikely, but possible).

Libby had been caught cheating and thrown out (impossible).

Libby had had some sort of breakdown (Helen's greatest fear and most likely of all. Didn't she take to her room for two days when she failed her Brownies crafting badge?).

'Libby,' she murmured and inched her hand across to her daughter. Her sweet, serious daughter who had been born with an expression of consternation that had never quite left. Libby, who would quite happily have carried the world, never noticing how her own back was breaking. What on earth would have caused her to come home so unexpectedly like this?

Libby looked up. Her face was covered with red and white splodges, like she'd been tie-dyed. 'I have to tell you something,' she croaked.

Helen shuffled closer. 'OK,' she murmured and put her arm across her daughter's shoulders, and as she did, she saw.

Option Number One.

Which was laughably unlikely.

So laughably unlikely, she laughed. Libby? *Pregnant?*

'I'm pregnant,' Libby said, and she wasn't laughing.

Helen pulled back. Not only was Libby pregnant, she was *heavily* pregnant. Huge. Now they were arm's length away, looking back at each other in shock and confusion and, from Libby's side of the chasm, terrible fear.

'I'm sorry, Mum.' Great tears fell down Libby's cheeks. 'I'm so, so sorry.'

Lips tight, head tight, fists tight, Helen nodded – tightly.

'It doesn't mean I won't finish,' Libby blurted. 'I've deferred. I'll still finish, I promise.'

Helen brought her hand to her mouth and pressed it there. 'You didn't take your finals?' she managed.

Libby looked down at her stomach, one trailing tear on her cheek. She brushed it off with the back of her hand. 'I couldn't concentrate, Mum. I'm so sorry. I couldn't do it.'

'Oh.' It was the only sound she could manage. She sat looking at her daughter. The clock, as ever, ticked, and in the kitchen a tap was turned on. Moments passed. Slowly Helen set her mouth free to let her hand rest at her chin. 'When…' she started and the word stuck, yanked back by a mob of panicked thoughts. Never mind that *when*. How about another *when*. Like, *when* was the last time she'd seen her daughter? And *why* hadn't she noticed? And shouldn't she have known? Or was this her fault for not being there?

For going to Cyprus? And what about a *who*... 'When...' She forced the sound out. 'When is it due?'

'September,' Libby whispered.

Weeks away! Not trusting herself to speak, Helen took Libby's hand and squeezed it. It was cold and stiff with fear. Her child. Her beautiful, bright child, who hadn't even started yet, who was still a child herself... There was so much she wanted to say, nearly all of it beginning with *why?*... But before she could get any further, she saw Libby's bottom lip break into a tremble and she knew what was coming. Like the distant rumble of an avalanche she could read these signs from the grave. Any mother could.

'*Oh, Mum*,' Libby wailed and threw herself against Helen's shoulder. 'I'm so sorry,' she cried, snot and tears once again, soaking Helen's blouse.

Helen leaned back and opened herself up, one hand patting Libby's hair, the other holding her hand. 'It's OK,' she whispered and felt the wetness of her own tears. 'Everything's going to be OK.'

Was it? What had Lawrence just said? *Give her the summer?* She would, of course she would. And the autumn and the spring that followed and the summer after that. As long as Libby needed... Still, it was there, the thought that she couldn't help thinking. When? When was she, Helen, going to get her summer?

2

'Come on in, Kay,' Nick drawled. He didn't look up from his phone and his gangly six-foot-three frame had slid down his chair, presenting her with a suit-clad bundle of pointy limbs – all knees and elbows. If this had been her classroom she'd have barked at him to *sit up… and put that thing away!* But it wasn't her classroom; it was his office. And he wasn't her student, he was the headteacher and her boss.

She slipped into the seat opposite.

'Won't be long.'

'No problem,' she lied, letting her handbag drop to the floor.

'My wife,' Nick muttered, managing to look at her. 'Need to let her know I'll be late or I'm in trouble.' He smiled.

Kay managed something like a smile back. Nick went back to his wife and she turned to look at her bag, squinting at it as if it was a puppy who might yet disobey. She'd forgotten something, something that she should be doing right now if she hadn't had to come to this meeting. The clue was in her handbag, that much she felt sure of. But the handbag sat smug and silent as a sphinx. Turning away, she tilted her head to the ceiling. No, the clue wasn't there either.

Nick was still tapping. Tap tap… tap tap tap…

Kay closed her eyes. *Relax, Kay, and breathe in and out, in and out, in and…* She tried to let the words flow, but they stuttered and stuck like a shopping trolley with a wonky wheel. Her fists balled and her jaw clenched and hell, she knew, would freeze over before she relaxed, which was so ironic considering that up until yesterday (when Nick's email had pinged into her inbox), she'd been bowling along quite nicely. The week's holiday in Cyprus had changed things. Caused if not a seismic shift, then a gentle tilt in her world and for the three weeks since she'd been back, she'd felt as if she'd been walking on air, clean and fresh as a drain after a slug of Mr Muscle.

Because while she was away Alex, her grown son, had coped brilliantly. He'd managed his meals and the house and his job in a way that had Kay, for the first time since his childhood diagnosis of Aspergers, believing in a different kind of future for both of them. It seemed that Martin, her ex-husband and Alex's dad, had been right all along. Alex could cope on his own. More than that, he would, she conceded, probably thrive in his own little flat. His needs were simple and as long as they were met, he was happy. It was time, long past time, that she finally released all those dreams she'd held on to for so long. Let them, like feathers on water, drift away for some other mother to pick up. Her son would never be a doctor, or a solicitor or a teacher. He'd probably never travel, or even marry. And the irony of her week away from him, the only time in her life they had ever been apart, was that in leaving him, she had enabled him to leave her. An emancipation that left her both heartbroken and excited. How impossible motherhood was.

And how ironic that the same situation was also being played out with her own parents. Because while she was away, her mother, deep now in the grip of dementia, had gone into a nursing home. And in that one week, her father had been out of the house more times than he had in the last twelve months. He'd always turned down the respite care offered, preferring instead, as he explained, to keep it in the family, which of course meant Kay. She hadn't argued. Because wasn't that what families did? Take care of each other? Except after seeing Alex cope so well, it was becoming clear to Kay that the orthodoxies she had accepted without question were vulnerable after all. In other words, she might be wrong. She'd been wrong about the best way forward for her son, refusing to cut the apron strings, using (yes it was true) his diagnosis as an excuse. And now it seemed that the best way forward for her mother might also be an option that neither Kay herself, nor her father, would have considered before. A permanent place in a nursing home. Thinking this, she squinted and turned again to her handbag. What she'd forgotten to remember was something to do with her mother. She was getting warmer, definitely closing in…

'Thank you for coming, Kay,' Nick said loudly. He laid his phone on the desk and whatever it was she had come so close to remembering scurried away to the shadows. Lost amongst the fluff and the debris of her overworked mind.

Kay made a half-nod. *Thank you for coming?* The idiotic things people said these days, as if attendance had actually been optional. Unintentionally she glanced at the clock and then back at her bag. Was the clock a clue?

'Good.' Now Nick was looking at her bag. 'Well,' he started, 'as far as—'

'Excuse me.' And like a struck bowling pin, Kay suddenly tipped sideways to sweep her bag up, part the depths of its contents and yank out an empty packet of incontinence pads. That was it! She needed to stop at the chemist's and pick up some more for her mother. 'I'm sorry,' she muttered, stuffing the packet into her cardigan pocket. 'I just remembered. Need to pick some up on the way home.' She patted her hip. 'If I hear it rustle, I'll remember.'

Nick flexed an eyebrow. 'Well, obviously I'll keep this as short as I can.'

'It's OK.' And even though she could feel herself flushing, she gabbled on. 'There's a chemist on Park Road, open late. I'll pop in there. It's not that far out of my way.' Why was she doing this? Why was she explaining herself to a man, who had a wife to do chemist trips? A wife who would, right now, be cooking his dinner, pairing his socks, changing the nappies of any family members that needed changing. Nappies? That felt like a clue... She looked at her handbag again. Hadn't she already solved the puzzle?

'Or.' Leaning back in his chair, Nick nodded at her cardigan pocket. 'You could always pop a reminder in your phone calendar?'

'I could, couldn't I?' Kay smiled. Of course she could!
If she ever found herself at the end of the day with forty
minutes spare to work out how to affiliate all the calendars
of her life she could just pop a reminder in! If she wasn't
wasting precious time watching *Real Housewives of Beverly
Hills* (which was very relaxing), she could do that!

'Shall we start?'

'Of course,' she beamed.

Nick leaned to his computer. 'Right. Well as I hope I
made clear in the email, Kay, regardless of the fact that this
is now—'

'Official?'

He looked at her. 'Yes, unfortunately, that is the right
word.'

Her lips pressed to a thin hard line. She would not cry.
She would not... A tear sneaked out. A great fat disobedient
glob of wetness. Fuck it! She patted her pocket, pulled out
the empty packet of incontinence pads, stuffed it back in
and searched the other pocket until, finally, she found a
scrag of tissue.

'Kay.' On the other side of the desk, Nick waited. 'This
is still resolvable on an informal basis,' he said gently. 'And
that's how I would like to manage it.'

Kay blew her nose. What did he expect her to say? Me
too? She didn't say anything. She was twenty years older
for God's sake and, after this stupid shaky start, determined
to retain her dignity. Thirty years of teaching with an
unblemished record and now this *official* complaint that
could *never* be erased. Because no matter how it was resolved,
whichever way Nick spun it, the slur would remain.

'Let's start at the beginning,' Nick said. He peered at his screen. 'Mrs Woods first made contact back in May. And I forwarded you her concerns—'

'You did,' Kay said and before she could stop herself, added, 'Friday before half term.' Friday afternoon? Who forwards that kind of mail, on a Friday afternoon, before a week's break?

'Ah.' Nick glanced at her, a flush of discomfiture crossing his face. 'Look, Kay.' He leaned his elbow on the desk and rubbed at his chin, which was pale and smooth as a teenager's. 'You're a good teacher.'

I know – she didn't say.

'You know it.'

I do – she didn't say.

'The whole school knows it.'

As it should – she didn't say.

'But—'

She raised her chin and watched him.

'We have to take parents' concerns seriously. And despite the fact that a formal complaint has now been recorded, that is still what we're terming it. A *concern*. You can understand that?'

'Of course,' she lied. Oh, to go back to the last century! To when Lizzy, the headmistress then, simply told the caretaker to switch off the lights when parents' evening had gone on too long, had threatened to get stuck in the bog of parents' *concerns*.

'Good.' Nick glanced back at his screen. 'How was your holiday? I hear you went to Cyprus.'

So – he wasn't even going to apologise for the timing

31

of the email. She shifted her weight and scratched at the itchy point on her neck. The *always* itchy point. For nearly a month now, this parental *concern* had been squatting like a sulky child in the corner of Kay's mind. The mother of one of her year ten pupils had become convinced it was Kay's personal dislike of her son (and not the boy's lousy attitude) that was responsible for his poor grades. The week in Cyprus had kept the issue in the shadows, and since she'd been back Kay had done her best not to think about it. Which had been surprisingly easy. Nick had promised the parent in question, Mrs Woods, that he would investigate, which he had with what Kay considered to be a long and productive chat between the two of them. Most importantly, she'd felt a real improvement in her relationship with the boy himself, Zac. Which is why, last week, she'd felt confident enough to ask him to step up and swap roles with her for a few minutes. A light-hearted challenge to keep him engaged in the class, that Zac had embraced with enthusiasm and thoroughly enjoyed. So how, in the name of all that was sane, that five minutes of laughter and good-humoured repartee had been twisted into this official complaint, stating that she had forced Zac into a situation whereby he was humiliated and embarrassed and left feeling *unsafe*, Kay had no idea. An official, unmovable, indelible complaint: she still couldn't quite believe it was true. After thirty years! 'The holiday was lovely,' she answered perfunctorily. The sooner this was over the better.

'Great.' Nick nodded. 'And your mother? How is she?'

Kay's mouth widened in surprise. In five years of his headship, she hadn't had a single personal conversation with him.

'Emma was telling me.' He indicated the door, on the other side of which, during school hours, sat Emma, the school secretary.

Well, that made sense. She did talk to Emma, who talked to everyone else.

'I understand,' he said quietly. 'You have a lot on your plate right now.'

A lot on your plate? Kay looked at him. It wasn't that she didn't like Nick. True, he was no Lizzy who finished off half and full terms with drinks to 70s hits in the staff room, rather than emails that outlined *concerns*. No, it was more that he was a different generation with different ideas, some of which she could accommodate and some of which she couldn't. The isolation room for example. Whenever she passed and saw the row of small heads, spaced in their blank cubicles, her gut rolled like a barrel. That wasn't teaching. But then again, she couldn't deny the success of the Friendship Bench he'd introduced, a simple idea where kids feeling lonely or left out might sit and wait for someone to notice and then include them. She'd witnessed its modest methodology time and again, marvelling at the innate goodness in children. So, although for better or worse it did increasingly feel to Kay that the terrain of her professional world was transforming so fast she could barely stay standing, she was, she knew, still a good teacher. Regardless of what went on outside the classroom, inside it she remained in control, respected. She could still do it. So, if Nick was now trying to imply something else… If he was insinuating… Her thoughts crashed aground. 'No more than usual,' she said, tight-lipped, a little depleted.

Nick nodded. 'My wife's grandmother had dementia. It was… it's hard.'

'Fuck-a-duck!' Kay slapped her hand on the desk.

'Kay?'

The dementia team! That was it. That was what she *really* needed to remember! The phone call they were due to make, which was the first tentative stage in the process of, perhaps – because she wasn't quite there yet – admitting her mother into the nursing home permanently. It was today at six. 'I'm sorry,' she said and shook her head. She *had* to get back. Her father needed to be with her to take the call, even though she hadn't even told him the call was happening yet! And how had that happened? How was it that in the time between she and her mother's carer Craig deciding upon this first step, she hadn't found an opportunity to sit down with her father and say: *You're not to worry. Nothing's decided. It's just a phone call. This is what I'm thinking… This is what is needed, Dad… This can't carry on, Dad… I can't cope any more, Dad…* Because it was too hard, that's why. Because it would break her father's heart clean in two, that's why. 'I'm sorry,' she mumbled, burning up with a heat that could have come from the guilt she felt, or the shame she felt, or even the hormones she was shedding through menopause. Take your pick. 'I just remembered something,' she added quietly. 'Something quite important… yes…'

Nick was watching her, studying her actually.

Her eyes half closed. This *too much on your plate* conversation had reached a dead end she couldn't see a way out of. She was trapped, because it was true. How could she have possibly forgotten something so important? Too much on her plate? It was heaped, overflowing. Starters, main and dessert all lumped together. Alex. Her mother, her father. Her job. The cat. Her weight. These flushes. The dragging fatigue. The washing machine spin cycle not working, the leak at the back of the kitchen sink. Portion after portion after portion... Unable to extricate herself from Nick's questioning stare, Kay fell back on the only thing in her life that had never failed her. Her humour. 'The funny thing is,' she said lightly, 'The carer that my mother has, he went to this school. I used to teach him maths.'

'A him? Really?'

'Craig Taylor. Before your time.'

Nick nodded. He was stuck on the *him* part, exactly as Kay knew he would be.

'Of course my mother gets his name wrong.'

'She does?'

'She calls him Tony,' Kay said. 'Tony Blair.'

Nick's eyebrows shot up.

And suddenly Kay realised why she remained so ambiguous about Nick. It wasn't just the generation gap. It was the sense of humour gap. Tony Blair? It was funny. My God, when did it become necessary to get permission to laugh at something so obviously funny? 'It's good actually,' she added.

'Is it?' Nick floundered.

'Oh yes. My mother always had a lot of respect for Tony Blair, so at least she's stopped hitting him. Craig, I mean. Not Tony. Obviously not Tony.'

'Right.' Nick's jaw remained slack.

Kay looked at him. No more *too much on your plate* bullshit again – she didn't say.

35

'Right.'

'So! I suppose we'll be needing to fix a time for us all to meet?'

'Er… yes.' Nick held her glance half an uncomfortable moment longer, then palpably relieved, turned to his screen. 'Mrs Woods has suggested next week.'

'Fine.' Kay waved her hand at his screen. 'Just go ahead and schedule something. I'll make myself available.'

'You don't want to discuss it further…' He trailed off, because she was shaking her head.

'No.' She absolutely didn't.

'OK… Well, I'll need your account in writing before…'

'Of course.' Kay heaved herself to her feet. 'Was that it? Because, if you don't mind, I do really need to get on. I'll have something with you by tomorrow.'

'Kay.' Nick too was standing. He opened his palms. 'Are you OK?'

'Absolutely fine,' she said and swung the door open.

3

Kay drove home in a blur of tears, made worse by the steady rain. Everything was a fog. The whole world was a soupy thick fog, grey outside, grey behind her eyes. Craig had arranged this call a week ago and immediately she had let it slip to the back of her mind. More and more she seemed to do this. With sauerkraut and red cabbage, with odd-shaped walking shoes that were meant to burn twice as many calories and with books that had *How to... Why your... Learn the...* in the title. Bottom shelf of the fridge, back of the wardrobe, all her good intentions, all the things she found too difficult to face. Tucked away for another time.

Only the dementia team weren't quite as inanimate as a jar of sauerkraut. So now she had precisely twenty-three minutes to get back, park the car and warn her father that a stranger was going to be ringing and asking a lot of personal questions about his wife of sixty years. More personal than he'd ever dream of asking himself.

At least the gods were on her side. The parking space

outside her parents' house was free. Reversing in, she sat for a moment staring at the back windscreen of the car in front. When things were a little calmer, she would get to the doctor. HRT had worked wonders for Helen... well HRT and an extra marital affair... Still, she had nothing to lose. The constant forgetfulness, the fatigue... Yes, she'd get herself an appointment as soon as possible.

The idea was a pocket of energy. She jumped out, bounded up the drive and opened the porch door, managing to get a hand on the door handle of the inner door before it swung back to reveal Craig, who hissed, '*Where have you been?*' and took her handbag, even though she hadn't offered it.

'You were meant to be back half an hour ago!' he seethed. 'Your mum's had her dinner. Haddock and peas. She left the peas. She's in the living room, with your dad. They're watching *Countdown*, well he is. Your mum wants to know why her auntie Shelia is on the telly.'

'Her auntie Shelia?'

'Anne Robinson. Have you told your dad? I can stay until quarter over—'

'*Craig.*' Kay surrendered, hands up, palms open.

Clutching her handbag at his chest he stopped talking.

'What time are they ringing?'

'Six.'

'Right. We've got time.' And edging past him she made her way along the dark hallway, towards the kitchen.

'Kay?' Her father's voice travelled along behind her.

'Just popping to the loo,' she called back. 'I'll be right in, Dad.' Then she stopped in the kitchen doorway, turned back to Craig and waved him towards her.

'To the loo?' he stage-whispered.

'No,' she stage-whispered back. He never had been the sharpest tool in the box. 'Kitchen. *Now!*'

'Ah… right.' And silently Craig followed along to the kitchen, where they stood either side of the table looking at each other.

'I was thinking—' Kay began.

'You haven't told him, have you?' Craig put her handbag down, right next to the vinegar.

She looked down. The table was still set from her parents' dinner. Salt, pepper, Sarson's vinegar, HP brown sauce, and now her handbag. She reached out and moved the vinegar six inches to the right and then back six inches to the left.

'I said you should tell him straight away,' Craig scolded.

She moved the vinegar pot to the right again.

'*Mrs Patterson!*'

Now she looked up. 'Would you stop calling me that! I haven't been your teacher for years. And I've been divorced for decades!'

'I can't help it!'

'I couldn't do it,' she whimpered and collapsed into the closest chair. 'I just couldn't do it.' Aware of Craig watching her, Kay felt self-conscious. It was funny how this oh-so-young man, with his hard-headed shell and his soft centre, made her feel. He couldn't determine a fraction from a decimal and yet he was emotionally more competent than almost anyone she knew.

For a long moment Craig continued to watch without speaking. Then he pulled his own chair out and sat down opposite. 'I wasn't going to tell you this,' he said.

Kay raised her chin to meet his eye. 'What?'

'I...'

'Craig?' She sat up, a trickle of cold running down her spine. From the look on his face, she knew what he was going to say. 'Has she hit you again?'

He glanced down at his hands.

'Craig, has my mother hit you again?'

'Not me.'

Kay's heart shrank, she actually felt the fibres contract with fear. If not Craig, who else? She knew who.

'Dad?'

Craig nodded. 'He has scratches all down his arm. I saw them a couple of days ago. Your mum threw her lunch and some of it landed on your dad's shirt. I saw, when he was changing.'

'Oh, Craig.' Two words that held an infinite weight of sadness.

Craig looked back at her and smiled and the wonder of it, for Kay, was how capable he was of bearing all the sadness his working days must bring him. He was still so young. His face retained the fullness of youth and no one could ever have described him as athletic. In fact, there in her kitchen, with his pale arms and his wispy hair and clean nails, he looked as harmless and inconsequential as a portrait from another century. And perhaps that was the clue. He was light as a watercolour, still a feather in the world. Weightless, untroubled, care-free. He'd yet to reach where she was at. This strange time of life, midway, when she could still remember those fresh-air days of her own, and at the same time understand how few were left. 'What a topsy-turvy world,' she murmured. 'What a topsy-turvy world.'

He frowned.

'I think you're the teacher now, Craig. You're the one speaking sense and I'm like the child... running way.' She leaned forward, her hands covering her eyes. 'You're absolutely right. This cannot go on.' And she stood up. 'I'm going to get Dad now.'

He nodded. 'And I'll go and start getting your mum ready for bed. Give you some space.'

'I still don't understand why it's necessary,' her father said for the fourth, or fifth time. She'd lost count.

'Dad.' They were sitting side by side at the kitchen table, her mobile phone like a hand grenade between them. From out in the hallway, behind the closed bedroom door, she could hear Craig's voice, talking and cajoling her mother into bed. Kay looked up at the clock. The dementia team were now eight minutes late in calling, which wasn't a bad thing at all considering how difficult it was proving getting her father to understand the implications, the general direction in which this was all heading.

Sighing, he rose to his feet, picked up the vinegar and the salt and shuffled across to the cupboard. 'We can manage, Kay,' he said. 'We're managing fine.'

'Dad.' Kay turned in her chair. 'You're not.'

'Craig comes in, three times a day. That's enough.'

Kay dropped her head to her hands. Word for word, this was how the conversation had started ten minutes ago.

41

We're fine. We have Craig. Twisting around, she watched as her father put the condiments on the workbench and with a shaking arm reached up and opened the cupboard. The salt went in first, then the vinegar. He closed the cupboard and stood with his back to her, looking at it.

'When I was in Cyprus,' she said, launching into this pause of a moment, 'you had a nice week, didn't you? When Craig took you down to the Rose and Crown. I heard you saw a couple of people you haven't seen in ages. Alan Watts is still the landlord, isn't he? Craig said he was delighted to see you.'

'We did.' Her father turned. 'It was pleasant to get out, yes. We should do that more. Your mother and I—'

'Dad.' It was almost a plea. She'd never expected this to be easy; even so, the reality was harder than she'd attempted to imagine. Why couldn't he see? The last thing she'd wanted was to pressure him into taking this phone call, but now it had become imperative that he did. If she'd been tentative before, she could feel the change within. An incremental hardening of her heart. The sensation turned the corners of her mouth down, but it didn't stop her saying, 'You know that's not possible.'

'Your mother has the chair—'

'And how is Mum going to get into the chair, Dad? And then get from the chair to the car? And then out of the car?'

'Kay—'

'*Dad.*'

For a long moment they looked at each other.

Kay shook her head. 'Before I went to Cyprus, when was the last time you left the house?'

'Well,' her father said and took a tissue from his trouser pocket, dabbing at his nose.

Kay watched him. She knew the answer, but she was waiting for him to say it.

He didn't. He dabbed at his nose and shuffled across to the bin.

Dropping her head to look at her hands, she said, 'It was March. When I took you both out for Mother's Day lunch, remember?'

'That's right.' Her father nodded. 'That's right.' And again, they looked at each other.

'Well, that's enough,' he said. 'Every now and then, when you can manage it. That's enough.'

Her shoulders slumped, she leaned back in her chair and closed her eyes. March. The daffodils had been out. It had been unseasonably warm and by the time Kay and her father had struggled her mother into her wheelchair, and into the car and out of the car and into the chair, Kay had been soaked with sweat and useless with fatigue. *This* was how she had spent Mother's Day. Lifting her mother, feeding her mother, wiping her mouth. Not so dissimilar from when Alex was small. And what for? Not once had her mother been aware of where she was, or who she was with. So, what was it all for? And suddenly she understood that what was *enough* for her father was too much for her. Far too much. *I want some time,* she didn't say. Because a Mothering Sunday bled into an Easter Sunday, which overflowed into Christmases and summers, all lost now. Every one of them. And if there was one thing Cyprus had taught her, it was to turn her face to the sun while she still could, and now she remembered Helen, how she glowed, how alive she was! *I want some time,* the voice inside her head cried. *While there is still time, I want some time!*

'We'll manage, love. Don't worry.' Her father had moved to stand next to her chair. He patted her arm. 'Tell this girl when she rings that we'll be happy to look at the respite care.' And he turned to leave. 'I'll go check on your mum.'

Kay snapped her head up. 'What about your arm, Dad?' she said, and her voice was louder than she'd intended and nearly all of her wanted to drag the words back and bury them, but they were out now. 'Your arm,' she repeated sadly. 'Craig told me.'

Standing in the doorway, her father sagged, just a little, like dough punched.

'Craig said that—'

And whatever she was going to say was cut dead by the sound of her telephone ringing. She looked at it. Unknown number. She reached out and picked it up with an arm that felt as if it didn't belong to her at all. 'Dad,' she pleaded. 'Please come and sit down. We're going talk to them.'

Head bowed, her father moved across and sat down.

Kay sighed. She put her phone on speaker and answered it. She didn't look at her father. She couldn't bear to see the expression on his face.

'Hello,' the voice said. 'Am I speaking to Kay Burrell?'

'Speaking.'

'Hello, Kay. My name's Angie, I'm with the North Herts dementia team.'

'Thank you,' Kay managed. 'Thank you for calling.'

And as Angie talked on, Kay sat listening, imagining

a large-boned, well-fleshed woman, halfway through life. A woman, it soon became clear, with a keen humane intelligence that allowed her to rephrase, skip over and generally articulate the most intrusive of questions, and no doubt draw conclusions, so her words rang with the tone of nothing worse than a catch up over a cuppa. She had both Kay and her father if not at ease, certainly not on guard, within minutes, her voice floating between them like a calm and friendly spirit.

What she would be asking, Angie explained, were questions about Kay's mother's specific needs. The help she needed to get out of bed, get dressed, eat, take her medications. Is she for example, Angie asked now, able to take care of her own personal hygiene?

Beside her, Kay's father tapped his nails against the table, his hand bunched and jointed as a spider.

As a working woman in the seventies, her mother had never left the house without her shoes polished and her rayon blouse starched. The smell of her perfume – Avon's 'Roses' – was the pervading scent of Kay's childhood. 'No,' Kay answered quietly. 'Not really.'

'Not really?'

'Not at all.'

At the other end of the line she heard Angie pause. 'And how is she able to manage toilet visits?'

Kay glanced up. Her father had squeezed his eyes shut.

Ninety-nine per cent of her wanted to stop the world, let them both climb off. What kind of a daughter, she thought, puts her father through this humiliation? 'She isn't,' Kay whispered. 'Not alone.'

'Craig comes in three times a day,' Angie said. 'Is that right?'

'Yes.'

'So…' Angie paused. 'How are you managing… between times.'

Kay pressed her lips together. 'Best we can,' she said and left it at that, understanding that Angie would hear what wasn't said.

Which she did. Because after that the call began to draw to a close. Angie was promising to get in touch with her parents' GP. Between social services and the GP, she was telling them, a care plan would begin to be formulated. Another assessment would have to be made, this time in person, but considering all the information she already had from the carer's reports, she didn't see any hurdles and she expected the timescale to be reasonably quick.

And then Kay made her mistake. 'What,' she asked, 'does *reasonably quick* mean?'

'A couple of weeks,' Angie replied. 'There's no waiting list at Ashdown House. And considering that your mother recently had a week there and is familiar with the place it seems like the sensible choice.'

A couple of weeks. The words resonated through the silent kitchen. Kay looked at her father. But he still had his eyes closed and in that moment all that Kay wanted was to close her own and sit with him and, like a child, wish it all away.

4

Walking home, which was only a hundred yards, lumpy great sobs racked her frame, so by the time she reached her own door Kay was so blinded by tears it took her three attempts to get the key in the keyhole. Her father hadn't banished her, but he had suggested in the gentlest way possible that he needed a little time and space, and as she'd gotten up to go, her legs had almost given way, so weakened was she with shame and guilt and remorse.

She managed three mouthfuls of her microwaved dinner, which was three more than she'd expected to. She slung the carton and its contents into the bin, and turned for respite to what never failed. A cup of tea and the *Real Housewives of Beverly Hills.*

One housewife was designing her ex-husband's mansion, another was having a coming-out party for her new nose and everyone was drinking rosé in the sunshine. Squeezing away the image of her father as she'd left him, sitting alone at the kitchen table, Kay dropped into the nearest armchair, stretched out her legs and raised a mug to the screen. Relax, relax relax... Her phone rang. *Helen Helen Helen* flashing across the screen.

Just what she didn't need.

She pressed her head back against the cushion and stared at the ceiling. The last time she'd spoken to Helen was over two weeks ago, when she'd rung to talk through the implications of Caro's positive pregnancy test. Yes, Caro would be fifty-one (and a half) when the baby was born, yes nearly seventy by its eighteenth birthday. But they already knew this, and with everything feeling so much more manageable in her own life, Kay had made it crystal clear that she didn't want to re-hash things. At which Helen had taken offence, retreating into a sulky terseness which, perhaps for the first time ever, Kay had ignored. She'd been a sounding board for her friends for so long, they'd battered her paper-thin. It was beyond time that she put her own needs first. So the conversation after had been brief, and only now did she remember that it had ended with Helen telling her that Lawrence wanted to try marriage counselling. Sitting up, Kay took the remote, paused the TV and picked up her phone. She was emotionally exhausted, as wrung out as a flannel, but the image of an all-cycling, all-climbing, all-action Lawrence wedged into a counselling session had been impossible for her to imagine then, and could be just the distraction she badly needed now.

As soon as Kay answered, Helen's voice blew into her living room, as loud and clear as if she were standing outside the front window.

She was. Almost.

'*Kay!* I'm outside your house!' Helen babbled. 'But there's a parking cone in the only parking space!'

Confused, Kay heaved herself out of the chair and went to the window, pulling the net curtain aside. Yes, there was Helen, sat in her car, blocking the road, pointing at the parking cone.

'Can you move it?' Helen mouthed.

'Do you have an appointment?' Kay said into her phone.

'Move the bloody cone,' Helen answered with such a tone of weariness that, watching through the window, Kay's smile died. 'I have news,' she finished.

'OK. OK.' Dropping her phone onto the chair, Kay hurried to her back door. She didn't have shoes and she couldn't find shoes and a man in a white transit van behind Helen was now blasting his horn as if Helen wasn't aware he was there, as if he and his van were cloaked in invisibility and hence the horn was the *only* way of attracting Helen's attention. '*Men,*' Kay muttered and set off down the narrow passageway that led to her road, stones pricking, damp seeping through her socks. At the pavement, she tiptoed into the road and picked up the cone.

Helen reversed into the space and hopped out in one swift move. 'Asshole,' she muttered, waving cheerily at the man as he screeched past. 'Where are you parked?' she asked, still waving.

'Outside my parents'.'

'Right.' Helen nodded. 'How's things?'

'Fine.' Kay's voice choked as she turned away and put the cone on her gatepost. She wasn't ready to try and explain what had just happened. Right now, she wasn't sure she ever would be. 'So,' she said cheerily, busying herself with brushing non-existent dirt from her palms. 'What brings you here on this fine evening? Let me guess. Marriage counselling was a huge success and you've decided—'

'Libby's pregnant,' Helen blurted.

'Li—'

'I just got back to the house, and she was there—' Helen stopped, because for the first time she was now looking at Kay directly. 'Your eyes?' she whispered. 'What on earth has happened?'

'Libby?' Kay pressed her hand to her cheek. 'Pregnant?'

'Yes.'

The ground scooped away. Kay felt light-headed and fragile. Libby? The gorgeous little girl, who Alex had always been in awe of? Sleepover Libby, with Alex, the two of them tiny dots in her double bed, munching on popcorn, watching *Dora the Explorer* on the bedroom TV? How could that child be…? A square-shaped sob forced its way into the round of her mouth and she couldn't swallow it down. 'Libby's pregnant?' she managed.

'Please don't cry.' Helen reached out, took Kay's hand and squeezed it. 'Please… or I will and if I do I won't be able to stop.'

But it was too late. Already huge tears rolled down Kay's cheeks, one after the other after the other.

And now Helen's eyes too had filled. She opened her mouth but no words came out and so they stood together on the pavement, crying.

*

'How long?'

'I'm not sure exactly,' Helen sniffed. 'She says it's due in September. So, seven months?'

They'd retreated to the kitchen, backs against the counter, waiting for tea to brew.

'Seven months!' The teaspoon Kay held fell from her hand, clattering against the counter. 'God, Helen!' Her face was chalk white. 'When you said pregnant, I thought…'

Helen shook her head. 'It's too late. Far too late.' And it was. Her child was going to have a child before she'd ever had a chance to grow up, and the stark truth of that was a spear in Helen's gut. It physically hurt, so much so that she put a hand on her stomach and held it there.

Neither of them spoke. Kay reached up to get a cup. Holding it to her chest she said, 'I'd offer you something stronger, but you're driving.'

'Yes.' Helen sighed. 'I'm driving, and Lawrence has gone on a bike ride! Can you believe that?'

'Perhaps he just wanted to clear his head.' Kay's hand shook as she took the handle of the teapot.

'And perhaps he just didn't want to miss his Tuesday training!' She was looking at Kay's trembling hand. Kay, who would have loved a daughter, who had always had the softest spot for Libby. It was horrible, just horrible to upset her like this. Especially as there was obviously something else going on.

'Helen…' Kay let the sound drift. 'I'm sure he's… He's probably shocked.'

'He is,' Helen said quietly. 'But the difference is, Kay, he's unaffected. This won't make a jot of difference to him. You know Lawrence.'

'I do,' Kay answered, equally quietly. She poured the tea, added milk and handed it to Helen. 'Where's Libby now?'

'Asleep,' Helen whispered, as softly as if her daughter were asleep upstairs, rather than three miles away. 'Jack said he'd call when she woke, but I could see how exhausted she was so… I didn't know what to do… Except come here.'

'Of course.'

'She'd caught the train. God knows how long she's been hiding it… I didn't notice anything at Christmas, and she didn't come home for Easter.'

'Didn't she…?' Kay paused. 'She must have known…'

Helen shook her head. 'She said she thought her periods had stopped because of stress. I think it was more like denial.' Helen sighed. 'Then she said she just wanted to get through her finals, which she hasn't. *Why? Why didn't she talk to me, Kay?* I could have helped her. I…'

'I don't know.' Again, Kay's eyes filled with glassy tears. 'I don't know.'

'Just…' Helen put her cup down. 'I feel so guilty. Like I've let her down. Perhaps if I hadn't been so wrapped up with my own unhappiness… If I hadn't gone to Cyprus…' Her head dipped and she pressed her hands to her eyes.

Silently Kay moved across to the roll of kitchen paper sitting on the table, tore two sheets off and handed one to Helen. 'There's only so much we can do, Helen. They're not children any more. That's the problem,' she added sadly.

In unison they blew their noses and dabbed their eyes, and as they did Helen saw such a clear mirage of a sunny afternoon years and years before it made her wobble, had her putting a palm flat on the counter for balance. Tears and nose-blowing, here in Kay's kitchen the day that Alex and Libby had had a fight and fled to their mothers for comfort. She remembered it so clearly. Kay and she looking at each other over the tops of their sobbing children's heads, utterly secure in the knowledge that they could make it alright again. Which they did easily – a pat on the bottom, a beaker of juice and a cartoon. And it felt to Helen as she stood now in the same spot, barely fifteen years later, as if she were experiencing the cruellest evolutionary trick in existence. The understanding that motherhood was a state that only becomes less powerful, that indeed, as the love grows, the ability to protect the child fades. She held the tissue at her nose and shuddered. Mother Nature was one heck of a bitch.

And beside her Kay shook her head, as if she too was coming to exactly the same conclusion.

'So,' Helen breathed, 'that's my news.' She gave a weak smile. 'Your turn.'

'My turn?' Kay shook her head. 'Stuff,' she said unconvincingly. 'Just stuff.'

'Your mum?'

Kay nodded.

'Is she OK?'

'We just took a call from the dementia team.'

Helen frowned. 'Not to be confused I suppose with the A team.'

And beside her Kay tipped her chin to the ceiling.

'I'm sorry… that was a stupid weak joke that…' Helen put her hand over Kay's. 'What's going on?'

'I have to…' Kay stopped talking, shook her head at the ceiling and turned to Helen. 'We… Dad and me, we have to decide whether to put Mum into a nursing home… permanently. And this is the first step.'

'Oh.' Helen pressed her lips together. Kay's mother should have been in a nursing home a year ago. The strain, for anyone on the outside looking in, was obvious. She'd said as much to Caro many times, but never of course to Kay. Still, this was a start and for the first time since learning Libby's news, Helen felt a pang of soft relief. If Cyprus had helped Kay come to this decision, she was pleased for her friend. Pleased and relieved.

'And…' Kay said falteringly, 'if we do decide… it could go very quickly. A couple of weeks,' she whispered.

Helen didn't speak.

'My poor dad! I feel like I've betrayed him. Both of them. I feel awful…'

Nursing the cup at her chest, Helen's mouth turned down. 'You're not betraying them, Kay,' she said firmly. 'What else can you do?'

'I don't know. Something? There must be something else.'

Blank eyed, Helen stared across the room. 'We put Mum in a hospice at the end and she didn't want to go.'

Kay turned to her.

Helen shook her head. 'She didn't say as much, but I could tell.'

'You never said, Helen.'

Helen nodded. It was true she'd never talked about this, either with Caro or Kay. Sometimes, some things are just too hard to hear. 'What was I going to say, Kay? That I forced her?'

'I'm sure you didn't—'

'But that's the thing. In a way, I did. My brother and I persuaded Dad, and he persuaded Mum.' She blinked hard, her eyes smarting, the memory tender.

Kay pressed the back of her hand to her nose. 'I'm sorry. I didn't realise.'

'Don't be.' Helen managed a smile. 'Please don't be. In the end it was the right decision, and I don't regret it. The pain Mum was in couldn't have been managed at home. That's what I hang onto.' She smiled again, easier now, a door gently closing on those half- remembered, always unbearable conversations. What she'd said was true, she didn't have regrets. She had experience, which was just as heavy, and like a weary pioneer raised its head now to point the way forward. She'd been here, done this; she knew the way. 'Your mum will be fine,' she said. 'She'll be well looked after, and it will be better for everyone. I really do believe this, Kay.'

'I think so too,' Kay sighed. 'I do. It's just my dad. He's adamant he can manage, with the carers, and me of course.'

'And what do you think?'

Kay turned back to the cupboard, took the sugar out and piled a teaspoon into her cup, stirring noisily. 'I think…' she began, and stopped stirring. 'I think I want my life back, Helen. I think I'd quite like to join that tap class on Tuesday evenings, instead of stopping in at my parents' house every single day.' She scooped another spoonful of sugar.

'Kay, one is enough—'

'I saw you in Cyprus,' Kay interrupted. 'You were so alive, Helen! And I just want some of that before it's too late. Is that wrong? I want my mum in a home, so I can go to a tap class!' She picked up her cup and immediately put it down again. 'What on earth is wrong with me?'

'*Nothing!*' Helen's voice was loud. 'Nothing, Kay!' She looked down at her own mug and then across at Kay's. And without saying a word, she tipped her tea down the sink, did the same with Kay's and stalked across to the fridge. 'I'll get a bloody taxi,' she said, as she opened the door. 'You…' she continued, scanning the inside of Kay's fridge.

'Bottom shelf,' Kay said flatly.

'… Are just about the most selfless person I know, Kay Burrell.' Bottle in hand, Helen slammed the door shut. 'There's nothing wrong with you for wanting some time back.' Elbows wide, face flushed with emotion, she opened the bottle and sloshed a couple of generous inches into two glasses. 'You know what I thought when I heard about Libby? Of course, I'm devastated, but you know what else I thought Kay? I thought about me! I don't want to be left looking after a baby.' She handed Kay a glass. 'So, if there's something wrong with you, then there's double the amount wrong with me!'

Taking the glass, Kay said, 'Are we selfish, Helen?'

'Yes,' Helen answered decisively. 'I think for the first time in our lives we are! And I'm not sure there's anything wrong with that.'

For a long moment Kay didn't speak, then she raised her glass, knocked it against Helen's and said, 'Well cheers to that!' in a voice as grim as a January Monday.

From the living room a burst of excited voices bubbled through. Kay turned to the sound. '*Real Housewives of Beverly Hills*,' she murmured.

'Which season?' Helen too had turned to the voices.

'Six.'

'Mind if I join you?'

'Why the hell not.'

As Helen sat herself down in the armchair closest to the window, something hard pressed against her spine. She picked it up, saw it was Kay's phone and squinted at the screen. 'Caro's texted.'

'Has she?' Kay was moving piles of schoolbooks from the settee to the coffee table.

'Have you spoken to her lately?' Helen passed the phone across and leaned back. 'I always wanted to get my nose done,' she said and nodded at the TV.

Kay looked from Helen to the screen and then back to Helen. 'There's nothing wrong with your nose,' she said, then, 'I rang to say congratulations. Not since.'

'Me neither.' Helen pressed her finger to her nose. 'It could do with being flatter here.'

'Oh,' Kay said. She had her reading glasses on, scrolling through Caro's text.

'Caro had hers done, didn't she?' Helen said. 'You've got to hand it to her, Kay. She always has just gone out and gotten what she wanted from life. And I know you said you didn't want to talk about it—'

'She's on her way.' Kay looked up, her glasses tipped right to the edge of her nose. 'Caro.'

'Where?'

'She wants my advice. Something to do with the baby...
She says it's urgent.'

'Not here?' Flustered, Helen inched to the edge of her
seat. 'She's not coming here?'

Kay didn't answer. She fell back in the settee and took
her glasses off.

'She's barely a month gone, Kay! What could be so
urgent?'

Kay shrugged. 'Stick around and find out?'

But Helen was already on her feet. 'I can't,' she said,
halfway to the kitchen. 'It's not that I don't want to see her,
but I can't. Not today. Not today of all days.' And standing
at the sink, swallowing back a mouthful of wine, Helen
could think only one thing – she *must* leave. Because how
could she tell Caro about Libby? After everything Caro had
gone through to get where she was, all the soul-searching
that had gone on to get to this odd and tentative place (that
even now Helen wasn't entirely comfortable with) – how
could she possibly sit there and tell her about Libby, who
obviously hadn't searched further than her knickers...
Libby. Her little girl... Her head dropped quicker than a
clipped rose. She turned the tap on, squeezed a drop of
washing up liquid into her glass and swished it out, rubbing
at it as if it had been filled with blood, not wine.

How could Libby have been so bloody stupid...?

'Helen—' Kay was right behind her. 'I'll do that.'

'I have to go, Kay,' she muttered, her voice thick with
tears. 'I have to—'

'*Hello the house!*' And up the passageway and through

the open door of Kay's kitchen, Caro's voice swept in like a tsunami. *Hello the house! Hello the flat!* Their old calling signal from the flat-sharing days of university. Used to signal an arrival, the starting gun on what inevitably would turn out to be an evening of laughter and gossip. Where on earth had all that gone? The sublime confidence that everything would be fun – the evening ahead, life in general. Where had that certainty gone?

Kay, who still had her phone in her hand, glanced down at it. 'The text was sent twenty minutes ago,' she whispered.

'Kay?' Caro called, sounding *very* close.

'You *have* to stay,' Kay mouthed.

'Don't say anything,' Helen mouthed back.

And Kay was still shaking her head as less than half a moment later, Caro stuck her head around the open back door and exclaimed, 'Helen! What are you doing here?'

Helen opened her mouth, shrugged and closed it again without managing a word. Caro looked amazing. They hadn't seen each other since Cyprus and the sight of her now, dressed in a neatly tailored trouser suit and gorgeous emerald-green polka dot blouse, stunned her. She'd always had a fantastic wardrobe, but this wasn't about clothing. Yes, the holiday tan helped, but added to that was a peachy softness that had settled all over Caro's cheeks and lightened her eyes, that had melted the hard-set line of her jaw. She looked as if she'd been dipped in happiness.

'What's wrong?' Caro turned from Helen to Kay.

'Nothing!' she managed, then, 'You look great, Caro. Doesn't she?'

Beside her, Kay nodded vigorously.

Caro dumped the pile of brochures she was carrying onto the closest counter top. 'What's wrong?' she said again.

'How's everything? Is everything OK?' Helen stammered. 'With, umm…'

'Everything is absolutely fine,' Caro squinted, pacing her words like they were coded instructions. 'Now, *what is wrong*? Your eyes are like raisins, Helen.' She turned to Kay. 'And yours are no better.'

'Helen came to help me,' Kay said quickly. 'It's…' she waved a hand. 'I had some news, that's all.'

'What news? What do you need help with?'

Back to the sink, Helen took a tea towel and began drying her glass. There would be zero chance of bluffing Caro. Her stomach twisted like the cloth in her hands. She wasn't ready, she'd barely processed it herself. Telling Caro was going to be like announcing an engagement at a wedding. She wasn't ready.

'My wardrobe!' Kay blurted and the tea towel fell limp in Helen's hands. Wardrobe? Kay didn't have a wardrobe. She had a built-in cupboard in which fabric went to die. Why on earth would she need help with that?

'I need help with my wardrobe, and Helen came to help me.' This time, Kay's voice was steady. She nodded at Helen. 'Didn't you?'

'Wardrobe?' Caro said and the three of them looked at each other incredulously.

'I have a meeting at school next week.' Kay went to the fridge and took out the wine. 'You remember that thing I told you about?'

'The thing you thought had gone away?' Caro said crisply.

'Well… it hasn't.'

Helen switched a glance at Caro. She looked back at Kay, who was making urgent eye signals at her.

'What does that mean?' Caro frowned.

'It means… that what was a concern, is now a complaint. It's on my record.'

'On your record!' Caro gasped.

'Forever.'

Helen dropped the tea towel. She pressed back against the counter for support, hands spread. All the way over, the image of Libby's swollen stomach had blinded her. It was there huge in her mind and she couldn't get past it, huge in the empty passenger seat and she couldn't see through it. Low as a rain cloud, impenetrable as a wall, and yet, already the first person she'd told was facing problems of her own, equally daunting, easily tragic. Life goes on. Like a sulky teenager it just keeps stomping on! She shook her head. 'How can you stay so calm?' she said, and she meant it. Swollen eyes aside, Kay was already back at her swan act. Calm exterior, furious paddling underneath the surface.

Kay shrugged. 'I may look calm, but I don't think I feel it.'

And how many times, in thirty years, had she heard Kay admit even this much? Helen stared at her.

'So,' Kay said. 'I just wanted some advice on what to wear. When I meet this boy's mother.'

'The mother?' Caro looked as if she were trying to frown. 'The one you told us about?'

'Yes.' And Kay's head wobbled, halfway between a nod of affirmation and a shrug of distress.

'The bitch has made it official now?' Helen said, grateful and relieved to be off the hook, but also newly enraged on Kay's behalf and… she glanced at Caro whose forehead hadn't really moved, even though her eyes had narrowed. Botox. Definitely Botox. 'So it's on your record?' she said, turning back to Kay. 'Permanently?'

'*Yes*, Helen,' Kay said tightly. 'As I told you? *Remember?* Before Caro arrived?'

'Yes… Of course.' Helen's jaw fell slack. She was having trouble keeping up. So much so that Libby's pregnancy actually fell out of view, just for a moment.

No one spoke.

And then Caro said, 'Have you started?'

'What?' Kay said. 'Started what?'

'Picking something out?'

'No. I… We were—'

'Good.' Caro picked up the brochures. 'Because if there's anyone who knows how to dress for success, it's me. Let's get going.' And she went to the cupboard, pulled out a glass and handing it to Kay said, 'Orange juice for me.'

5

Upstairs in Kay's bedroom Caro pulled a gauzy lilac curtain aside and, nursing her orange juice, looked out of the window. In the garden below a man had crouched over the metal frame of what was almost recognisable as a motorbike. She watched as he operated a welding machine, fireworks of white-hot sparks dancing around his hands. His face was masked by the thick goggles he wore, still she recognised him. 'Is that the guy with the funny name?' she said, watching.

Kay came across to join her. 'Shook?'

'Shook, yes. What are they doing?'

'Building a motorbike.'

'A what?' Caro laughed.

'I told you,' Kay said. 'Remember at Helen's lunch? Alex has been working on it for months. Shook's helping.'

'Oh...' Caro turned back to the window. 'That's right, I remember now.'

'Is he still planning on racing, Kay?' Helen put her glass down on the bedside table and climbed onto the bed, reaching behind to puff up one of the many pastel cushions scattered there. She hadn't been upstairs in Kay's house for a long time, not since the days when Libby and Alex had played together. It hadn't changed much and, looking around, she was surprised all over again by this soft side Kay kept hidden away. She leaned back against the thick padded headboard, stretched her legs out and crossed her ankles. The patches of flaking pink varnish on her toenails were all that remained of the pedicure she'd had done for Cyprus. Cyprus... Right now, it was as out of reach as a half-remembered dream.

'Yes.' Kay answered Helen wearily. 'He's adamant. It doesn't matter what I say, he's absolutely set on it. I'm just glad Shook's involved.'

'Why's that?' Caro murmured. She was watching the welding.

'Because,' said Kay, 'that man can do anything. He'll make sure the bike is put together properly. That it's as safe as—' She stopped talking, shook her head and turned away from the window. 'Anyway,' she said, 'let's get started.'

Caro and Helen exchanged a brief glance. Kay, Helen knew, wouldn't be pushed. She was obviously more than worried about the motorbike, but the years had taught both her and Caro that Kay never really offered up more than a small taster of the Alex-shaped fears she carried. Maybe, back in the beginning, they had both tried to extract more from her in the hope of offering solutions and reassurance. Now, and this was something Helen was sure Caro felt as well, she knew that because there were no solutions, all Kay needed, and probably all she would ever have, was the reassurance of friendship. Which she had, in spades.

As if, somehow, Helen had communicated all this telepathically, Caro put her glass down and went across to Kay's wardrobe where she flung the doors open. 'First of all,' she barked, 'what kind of a meeting are we talking about? Formal? Semi-formal? What time of the day, Kay? And who's going to be there?' She reached up and pulled out a hanger draped with something navy blue. But whatever it was had slipped to the floor before Caro could look any closer, beaten without even trying. 'You should organise by colour,' she said.

Helen glanced at Kay who had come across to join her on the bed, so they were sitting now like schoolchildren, side by side, knees aligned, wine glasses in hand. She wanted to giggle. Despite everything, despite the whole shit show of today, she wanted to giggle.

'I do,' Kay muttered. 'Navy blue or black. Take your pick.'

'What kind of meeting, Kay?' Caro turned.

'Mediation. It's called a mediation meeting.'

Caro shook her head. 'Typically vague humanities-speak.'

'And the boy's mother?' Helen asked. 'She'll be there?'

'Amanda Woods. Yes, she'll be there. And the head and me.' Kay yanked her blouse open at the neck and fanned air. 'God, it's warm in here. Anyone else warm?'

'Not me,' Helen smiled. 'A dose of oestrogen a day, keeps sweaty armpits away.'

Caro laughed. 'It's working then?'

'Very well.' Helen smiled. A month into HRT and she

definitely felt more energetic. And maybe it was the after effects of Cyprus and maybe not, but up until this afternoon she had been riding a wave of renewed enthusiasm that had sustained her through the last few weeks. So it couldn't be more ironic, could it? Just as she had finally broken through the solid mass of Lawrence's resistance, she'd come crashing up against something far more formidable. Libby. She picked up one of the cushions, her finger tracing the bumpy silken path of embroidery. Was that how she thought of Libby's news? Well… yes. Libby's news felt like a huge brick wall that now had to be scaled.

'So what about you, Kay?' Caro said. 'Perhaps you should try it?'

'I will.' Kay scratched her neck and got up off the bed, moving to the window to open it a few inches. The whirr of the welding machine floated through. 'I was thinking that earlier and I will, as soon as this thing is over. Right.' She turned to her wardrobe. 'It's a mess in there, Caro.'

'I can see that.' Caro dangled a shapeless navy t-shirt.

'That's quite smart,' Kay offered.

Helen and Caro looked at each other. The chances of Caro finding anything suitable were going to be less than slim. Kay had always had about as much interest in fashion as Caro had for equations. All through university, she'd worn a uniform of Doc Martens, duffle coat and jeans. Swap out the Doc Martens for Hush Puppies, and the duffle for an M&S anorak, and nothing much had changed for Kay.

Caro shook her head. 'Amanda Woods – from what you've said – wouldn't be seen dead in a t-shirt.'

'You're right.' Kay shrugged.

Caro stuffed it back and pulled out a grey shift dress.

'Is that mine?' Kay frowned.

Helen tilted her head. 'Might work. What does this woman do?'

'I'm not sure. A lawyer I think.'

'Fat? Thin?' Caro asked.

'Thin. From what I remember of parents' evening.'

'Absolutely not then,' Helen said.

'I agree.' Caro stuffed the dress back.

'What then?' And Kay's voice was so forlornly small it had Helen turning to her, and Caro pausing, hands on her slender hips.

'Kay?' Helen said softly.

Kay's hand was at her mouth, chewing down on the already chewed skin of her thumbnail, her eyes wide as a child's.

'You're really worried, aren't you?'

Kay nodded. She managed a tiny smile.

'You're going to be fine,' Caro said firmly. 'You're a great teacher. Everyone knows that.'

'Is there something more?' Helen frowned. The expression on Kay's face was so extraordinary she realised she might never have seen it before. Ever. Thirty years of friendship and she could probably count on one hand the number of times she'd seen Kay let her guard down to show this degree of vulnerability. It left her cold, the back of her neck tingling.

And Kay managed another tiny smile. 'She's used the B word. Zac's mother.'

'The *b* word?' Helen asked. 'What's that?'

'Bullying,' Caro answered, tossing the word over her shoulder like a weed.

'Bullying!' Helen laughed. Kay? A bully? The suggestion was as ridiculous as it was unbelievable. In another place and another time, they would have laughed themselves silly over it. She glanced across at Kay, still standing by the window, at the lumpy middle-aged spread of her back and the freckles all across her neck. Kay had been dealt a hard enough hand as it was with Alex. Diagnosed just as he was setting off on the big adventure of school, Kay had done nothing but work at making that hand play as well as possible, when, with other cards, she could have been anything. She could have been head of a thousand schools, minister for education, she was that smart and that committed. Instead, she'd settled for a career that was one rung up a ladder she could and should have scaled without breaking sweat. And she'd made it work. Everyone who knew her, who'd ever had a kid taught by her, couldn't say a good enough word. So it was just wrong that an accusation made up of nothing but fresh air could take away (was already taking away) her impeccable record, causing her so much stress, *hurting* her. Helen looked down at the cushion in her lap. She'd squeezed it to half its size. All the intricate, delicate stitches squashed and flattened. Like Kay's life. Squeezed. Pressed in from all sides. The outrage surging through loosened the knot of anxiety Libby's appearance had tied, and again she forgot. She completely forgot that her daughter was asleep at home, seven months pregnant. She turned to Caro. 'That's not fair,' she managed through a jaw rigid with anger. 'In fact it's ridiculous.'

'I agree,' Caro said and turned back to the wardrobe, staring at it as if it were a foe to be vanquished.

Caro versus the wardrobe. The idea calmed Helen. The cushion in her hands expanded. Caro would know. Caro thrived on pressure. Depended upon it.

'You need to be ready,' Caro said, hands on hips, bony elbows wide.

'With clothes?' Kay said, her voice thick with emotion.

'Yes. With clothes.' Caro had her back to them. 'Never *ever* underestimate the power of appearance.' And she began riffling through Kay's hangers.

Kay forced a laugh. 'I could always fish out my Doc Martens. I think I still have them. Then again,' she murmured, 'maybe not. Considering…'

'Bullying!' Shaking her head, Helen snorted in derision, but neither Caro nor Kay responded. The smile left her lips. That other place and time, where they would have laughed all this away, was long gone 'For fuck's sake, Kay!' she muttered.

And Kay shrugged.

'Right then!' Caro said to the hangers. 'No. *No. No!*' she scolded, sweeping aside blues and more blues, navy blues, blacks and greys. 'For God's sake!' she cried. 'Have you got *anything* that's got a bit of colour?'

'Maybe.' Kay rolled her eyes. 'Towards the back…'

And Helen was relieved to see Kay's smile. It made her own mouth turn up. They both knew how single-minded Caro could be.

'It's no good,' Caro called. 'I'm going to have to go in.'

She stepped into the void of the wardrobe. 'I may be some time.'

Still smiling, Kay waved down to Alex and Shook as she closed the window. They didn't see her, engrossed as they were with the bike. She walked across and flopped back down next to Helen. 'Good luck,' she murmured and raised her glass to Helen's.

Helen cheered back. She squeezed Kay's hand. 'Everything will be alright,' she whispered.

'Will it?'

'Of course. We'll make sure.' The blue skies of Cyprus seemed a universe away. Those last few days of the holiday when a thousand plans had paraded across her mind. Plans for the second half of her life. And Kay too, with her tiny burgeoning hopes... But what else could she say?

'*What on earth!... I don't believe!... Why would you even keep...*' Caro's muffled mutterings reached them like waves lapping their toes. They looked at each other and smiled and sipped their wine and enjoyed the moment for what it was.

'I think...' Caro exclaimed, and re-emerged holding a fold of ivory, pure as fallen snow, and a box, from which trailed a tail of scarlet.

'That's my beachwear box!' Kay laughed.

'Exactly!' Caro smiled. 'It's probably the least worn clothing you have.'

'She can't go in a bikini, Caro.'

'Not if I want my pension,' Kay quipped.

'No, but you can use this.' And triumphantly Caro tugged at the scarlet tail which twirled upward like a gymnast's banner, revealing itself as the sarong Kay had

70

bought for Cyprus. She turned, stretched the chiffon out, swung it in circles until it had rolled like a pipe cleaner and bent to knot it loosely around Kay's neck. 'This, along with this!' Now Caro held up the ivory blouse. 'This is your response. Your *fuck you* response!'

'I like it.' Helen nodded approvingly.

'Me too,' Kay said. She was looking at herself in the wardrobe mirror. 'And when it's over, how about we all just bugger off back to Cyprus? I'm friends with Marianne on Facebook now.'

'From the hotel?' Caro asked.

Kay nodded.

'Well,' Caro beamed. 'It was a lovely place, wasn't it? I wouldn't mind going back perhaps, after…' And she stopped talking and placed her hand gently on her stomach.

And looking at Caro's still-flat stomach, at the radiant expression of joy and happiness on her face, Helen burst into tears.

'Libby's pregnant,' she blurted. 'And it's far too late to do anything about it. My baby is going to have a baby!'

'I just can't believe it,' Caro said *again*. 'Libby?'

They were back in Kay's living room, *The Real Housewives* frozen in a flurry of hair and lipstick.

And because for Helen Libby's pregnancy had already lost its opening shock, she nodded and said, 'It's true. Libby is pregnant.' The words didn't stick any more. She could think it without her stomach somersaulting. It was there as a black shape in her mind that she was already becoming accustomed to.

But of course, for Caro it was horribly novel.

Helen watched. Perched on the edge of Kay's armchair, Caro was polished as a sideboard, manicured and styled, the image of a woman in control of her life... except for her eyes which had gone wild with disbelief and her face which was very pale. The rawness of this reaction touched Helen. Kay's reaction had been the same and it was only as she thought this through that Helen understood how much her friends had invested in Libby. As the only girl in the next generation, they had, she realised, placed a little of their own hope in her. A tiny torch to pass on, fuelled by collective experience and goodwill. And for what? For Libby to fail at the first hurdle? To fall for this trap, old as time itself?

'Who's the father?' Caro asked, interrupting her thoughts.

Helen startled. Kay hadn't asked this. She'd barely given it any thought herself, which struck her now as more than strange. And then struck her as not strange at all. It was only that initial part that took two, another truism as old as time. 'An American boy,' she answered. What did it matter where he came from? Who he was? None of that would make the slightest difference now. 'He was over on an exchange year. He's back now.'

No one spoke. The TV sprang back into life.

Are you bleep bleep crazy? someone yelled.

Kay grabbed the remote and turned it off. 'I don't know why it does that.'

And still no one spoke.

'What are you going to do?' Caro stared at the blank dark screen.

'There's not much I can do.' Helen sighed. 'Like I said, it's far too late not to go through with it. We'll just have to—'

'I didn't mean Libby.' Caro turned. 'I meant you. You and Lawrence.'

'Me and…' Helen looked at her.

'In Cyprus you talked about travelling. Selling the house, buying somewhere small, and travelling.'

Helen shook her head. She had talked about these things. About her tiny, tentative plans. But that was then and this was now, and she couldn't understand why Caro was bringing it up. 'I can't do that now, can I?' she said helplessly.

'Why not?' Caro's response was blunt and swift as a boxer's jab.

'Well…' Helen faltered. 'I…'

'If it's still what you want to do, Helen – then why not?'

She looked to Kay. 'I… I can't leave Libby. Not now—'

'You're not leaving, Libby,' Caro interrupted. 'You're leaving Lawrence.'

Kay nodded. 'She's right, Helen.'

'Even so.' Helen fell back in her seat, tears burning. 'Even so.'

'Helen?'

She closed her eyes, as if that might shut out what she knew Caro was going to say.

'I know it's a huge shock.'

Was that it? If so, it was a mercifully short response.

'But you mustn't let this stop you living your life.'

That wasn't it. Irritated, she opened her eyes again.

Caro might be pregnant, but she had no idea yet of what it was to be a mother. The lifelong commitment, the permanent switch of the self from *No 1* to *No 2, 3* or *4*. 'It's not as simple as that,' she said tightly.

'Caro,' Kay said. 'Libby's going to need her mum.'

'I'm not saying she isn't.' Caro sighed. 'I'm saying…' Trailing off, she leaned across the arm of her chair, toward Helen. 'All I'm saying is, try to remember, Helen, this isn't your baby. Libby will have to take responsibility—'

'I know that!' Helen snapped. 'Don't you think I know that?'

'OK.' Caro put her head to one side. 'You know that, but it might not stop you—'

'What?'

'You were happy in Cyprus. I thought…' And again, Caro trailed off, waving a limp hand. 'It doesn't matter,' she said. 'Forget it.'

Helen closed her eyes. It wasn't like Caro to back down like this, as if the cause she was trying to champion was so hopeless it wasn't worth the bother. Was that it then? Were her plans so lost and hopeless that Caro had already given up on her? Caro, who at fifty was expecting her first child, who turned her own hopeless causes into real heart-beating possibilities. And anyway, wasn't Caro getting to the heart of what she'd been unable to stop herself thinking and had just confessed to Kay. *I don't want to be left looking after a baby.* 'What do you suggest I should do?' she breathed. A tear escaped her eye and ran down her cheek. 'It's so ironic. We went to counselling today and on the way home, Lawrence actually agreed to a divorce.' Now she opened her eyes. 'We had the first productive conversation since I got back from Cyprus and then… then Libby was there.'

Silence fell. Outside Kay's living room window, someone passed along the pavement whistling. It sounded ridiculously cheerful.

'Nothing's changed, Helen.'

Helen looked up. She wasn't sure she had heard Caro right.

'Nothing's changed,' Caro repeated.

'Everything's changed,' she whispered.

'You just asked me what you should do.'

'Did I?'

'You did,' Kay gave her a knowing smile.

'Keep moving forward, Helen,' Caro said. 'Get a solicitor. Give the ball a push, set it rolling. Get the house valued. Work out what you've got to play with, for when you're ready.'

Helen sighed. 'I don't even know where to start.'

'Well,' Caro leaned across the arm of her chair. 'What's the mortgage?'

'I've no idea.'

Caro's jaw dropped.

Over the top of her dipped head, Helen could sense messages of astonishment passing between Caro and Kay, feel the buzz of the zipwire. But she didn't know what the mortgage was. She didn't even have her own bank account.

'You need to find out,' Caro said. 'Get busy with the practicalities, Helen. You have to.'

'There's no harm in that,' Kay agreed.

Practicalities? Helen ran her hand up the stem of her

glass. Wasn't that what Lawrence had mentioned earlier? Practical stuff? Not for the first time Helen thought how similar they were. Caro and Lawrence. Maybe they should have gotten together all those years ago at uni. It was certainly what Caro had wanted. She'd always known that. The thought effected a wry smile, which seemed to energise Caro.

She sat up. 'And Libby? Well, look at it this way. At least she won't end up like me. Well, she won't, will she?' She looked from Kay to Helen.

Helen opened her mouth, but Caro cut her off. 'She won't have to do yoga every morning just to make sure she can bend down and pick up her baby. And she won't need reading glasses for medicine bottle instructions. And...' She smiled. 'She won't ever get confused for the baby's grandmother, will she?'

Now Kay smiled.

'Plus,' Caro shrugged, serious now. 'Her baby will actually know its grandparents.'

And at this, Helen too managed a smile. It was true. Libby's baby would know her.

'Libby can always go back and re-take her exams, Helen. She's so young. She can wait until the baby is at school or day care. Try to think of it as a positive, Helen. I mean it.'

Helen frowned. She understood what Caro was saying, of course she did, but Caro was still at the betrothal stage of motherhood, blithely unaware of all the many maternal responsibilities that alight one morning like spring birds and *never, ever* leave. That perch on a mother's shoulders for life, always there in peripheral vision, distorting the view, bending it slightly, like so many heat-rays. It was over for Libby. That wide-open sky of no responsibilities had clouded over, and this, more than anything, she realised was the real source of her grief. The idea of her girl, striding off into the world as a young woman with a bachelorette flat, full of IKEA prints and smart dresses to wear from the office to the bar, weekends away with which to forge her own female friendships. Plus, Caro was right. Hard as it was going to be, Libby would have to step up. Because she wasn't leaving her children; she was leaving her husband. Practicalities? Well, there was no point in waiting for graduation ceremonies or summers to end now. Caro was right again. Nothing had changed.

'All this money I've spent,' Caro was saying. 'Don't get me wrong. I'm extremely happy. Right now, I think I'm happier than I've ever been. But I'm lucky. All those millions of women like me, freezing eggs, having IVF – what about them? And there's something else I've been thinking.'

Slightly dazed, Helen turned to her.

'What about the men who created this business?'

'The men?' Kay said.

'Yes. Baby-making is a very lucrative business. You know it's mostly created and run by men?'

'What are you trying to say, Caro?' Kay asked.

Warming to her theme, Caro inched forward on her seat. 'I've been thinking about this a lot recently. What if all that money and time and energy was pumped into subsidised childcare instead? And we all just accepted that babies are a part of life, and that men and women will *both* take time away? Couldn't we all then have our babies when nature intended us to?' She looked first to Kay. 'Don't you think?'

'I do.' Kay nodded. 'I always have done.'

Encouraged, Caro turned to Helen.

But Helen didn't answer. She felt stunned, caught off guard by Caro's speech. Was there any upside to the fact that her daughter was going to become a mother at such a young age? Every nerve and sinew strained in denial, and yet there was one thing Caro had said that Helen could not deny the truth of. She wouldn't, not for anything, have wanted Libby to go through all that Caro had gone through. To find herself at fifty, pregnant with a child to whom she had no genetic connection.

'Actually—' Caro stood up, calling back over her shoulder as she went out to the kitchen. 'That's why I'm here.' When she came back she was carrying the brochures she'd come in with.

Kay looked up at her. 'You said it was urgent?'

'Well, it kind of pales considering other news.' Caro shrugged. She sat down, the brochures on her lap. Her cheeks coloured and she looked almost coy. 'Umm… I wanted to ask, Kay. You sent Alex to Little Bird Nursery which is still going. I consider that a really good sign, if a business has lasted that long.'

Kay frowned. 'Nursery? Isn't this a bit early Caro?'

'Yes. And no. Believe it or not, the waiting list is nearly a year. Plus I'm off to New York next week and then another week in Hong Kong. I wanted to grab the chance to talk to you.'

'May I?' Helen leaned across and picked up the top brochure.

'Those are long plane journeys—' Kay began.

'First class.' Caro smiled. 'Don't worry, I'm taking good care of myself.' And she glanced down at her stomach.

'Twelve hundred pounds a month!' Helen's jaw fell slack with astonishment.

Caro nodded. 'It's crazy, isn't it?'

'Crazy,' Helen repeated. She turned back to the brochure. Over a grand a month for day care? Her heart dropped all the way through the fat cushion of Kay's sofa. Libby wouldn't be re-taking her finals any time soon, not at these prices. Not until the child was in school, walking to and from by itself, making its own dinner. Her mouth hardened. What on earth were they all going to do?

The thought had her slapping the brochure shut. Libby was going to have to step up. Lawrence was going to have to accept the fact that she was leaving, and she was going to have to get practical. Very practical, if she didn't want this next half of her life slipping away like the first.

'So,' Caro was saying. 'When is Libby due?'

Helen shook her head. 'She thinks she's around seven months. But until she's had a scan…'

'Well.' Caro smiled. She looked from one to the other. 'I thought that when I get back we could have lunch in town and…' Her face coloured slightly, almost shy. 'And I wanted to ask if you'll come with me.'

'Where?' Kay said.

'Shopping. Well, window shopping really. Helen's birthday lunch was such fun. I thought that we could do something similar, and after take a little browse for…'

'For baby stuff?' Kay finished.

'Just a browse. It's far too early.'

'Of course. Helen?'

'Of course.' Helen looked down at the dregs of her wine glass. Browsing for baby stuff? It wasn't what she'd had in mind this summer of her fiftieth year. Lately it had been rucksacks spinning through her mind. She'd been determined that with Jack leaving in September and Libby… well. Yes, it was rucksacks she'd begun to think about shopping for. That, and a new life.

'Great. So,' Caro turned. 'When is this school meeting, Kay?'

'Next week,' Kay said flatly.

Pushing her own thoughts aside, Helen also turned to Kay. 'What's the worst that can happen?' she said cheerily, because poor Kay really did look washed out.

'The worst, Helen?' Kay looked at her. 'I lose my job.'

Part Two

6

Back from her receptionist job at the health centre, Helen dumped her handbag on the kitchen table and stood staring at her fridge. Something was missing but she couldn't think what. She was full to the brim from an afternoon of ingrowing toenails, mucus-encrusted noses and her co-worker Daisy's home-made tiffin cake. She narrowed her eyes. The dried-up painting Jack did at primary school was still there, and the chipped London Bridge magnet. But *what* was missing?

She couldn't think so she walked over to the sink, leaned across the drainer and stared at her garden instead.

Can we wait until the scan?

That had been Libby's response to her first tentative questions. *How, Libby? What will you do Libby? What will we do? Why didn't you...?*

So she'd stopped asking and started waiting, and the prickly tensions of the house had bubbled away under a shaky lid that prevented discussion of everything that might have needed discussing. Her daughter was in shock, she needed time, that's what Helen kept telling herself. Either that or wilful denial.

Still, the scan had come along, and with it a due date and, helpless, Helen had felt the mood of the house shift again. Into this present becalmed period of nest building. A state of being that seemed to Helen to have been woven from thin air and yet was as sticky and stealthily inescapable as a spider's web.

Nappies, for example. No one had asked her, but suddenly she was buying nappies again. Emptying drawers, moving furniture. Trawling the baby aisles of the supermarket and reading the small print on bottle teats, moving through a world that she had become glued to – each attempt to free herself with a quiet half-hour looking at houses she might be able to afford was an exertion of ever-decreasing will.

And it wasn't until twenty-four hours ago, when she'd finally battled her way up the ladder into the attic to look for all sorts of half-forgotten baby paraphernalia, and glimpsed instead her hopelessly old-fashioned rucksack, that, standing there on the top rung, she'd thrust her head back, broken the thick sticky surface of this world, and gasped for air!

The sight of it had slapped her awake. Produced tears. Her poor old rucksack! Bought with the proceeds of a summer job in Woolworths, it had once had so much hope invested in it. It should have spent a gap year trekking the beaches and deserts of Australia. Her father had scoffed all that into oblivion. Her husband had never wanted to go any further than the next mountain and, for reasons that were now as lost to Helen as size eight jeans, she had allowed it to sit up here, in the dust and dark of a rarely visited attic.

Because where had it ever gone? One week in Cornwall and a series of weekends in wet and windy western Scotland, where she'd traipsed along behind Lawrence, pretending to enjoy herself. Oh, and that wonderful weekend at Stonehenge, the last year of uni with Caro and Kay. That one weekend of her life when she'd felt closer to breaking free of all the expectations that bound her than at any other time in her entire life.

She hadn't intended to bring it down and dust it off, but leaving it up there was suddenly not an option. So now here it was, propped up against the side of the tumble drier. Where it was going from there, she didn't know.

She straightened up, dragging her hands through her hair. The lawn needed mowing. Pink carnations and peonies bloomed. The lupins were out and the poppies, and ever reliable Hebe: all the colours of an English summer.

From upstairs came the soft whomp-whomp of a drum beat, otherwise the house was silent. Helen folded her arms, turned back to the kitchen and looked again at the fridge door. What *was* missing?

Can we wait until after?

That had been Lawrence's response, when she'd ambushed him in the kitchen last night, with the suggestion that they *really* needed to talk. *Now. Today.* The rucksack and all its dusty memories galvanising her.

After?

After Libby has the baby.

At which point, Libby and her hugely swollen belly

had appeared in the room silencing all discussion.

So here they all still were. Waiting, waiting, waiting... All of them bound up in this web of a house, navigating directional lines that hummed with tension. Lawrence to work, cycling or running, anything that needed a Garmin gadget. Helen to work and the garden, where she mostly just stood, hijacked by memories of Kaveh. Jack to school and Libby, the spider in the middle. Waiting, waiting, waiting.

Sighing as loudly as she possibly could, she went to the fridge, pulled out an open bottle of wine and took a glass from the dishwasher. As the bottle glugged out a cold inch she sighed again. The drumbeat from upstairs was getting louder. First, she glanced at the clock, then she tipped her head to the ceiling. The sound, now she listened, was coming from Libby's room. She sighed again, and this time her sigh was loud enough for her mother to hear it in her grave. *But really?* She'd been at work all day, and now there was a dinner to be made, and Libby was sat up in her room playing music?

She banged her wine glass on the drainer and walked back to the fridge, opened the door and stared angrily at the contents. Salad. Potatoes. A bowl of cooked rice, at least a week old. There was always a bowl of rice at least a week old. She took it out and banged it into the compost bin. Bang... *Bang, bang, bang.* So where was Libby? Where was the mother-to-be, if not here in the kitchen learning to be a mother? She threw the bowl into the sink and went through the motions of preparing a meal for her family.

Lawrence came home, unstrapped his Garmin watch and laid it ceremoniously across the dresser.

Jack came home, dropped his rucksack in the hallway and put his phone on charge.

Libby came downstairs, yawning.

'Dinner,' Helen announced, 'is ready.'

At the table a subdued Jack ate with his head down. He hated fish. Poor Jack. He'd looked, Helen thought, perpetually bewildered since Libby came home, like he'd wandered into the wrong house. She watched him fork reluctant mouthful after reluctant mouthful. Libby had been his hero. And, three years older, she'd been his protector, bossy, confident and always right. Talk about a fall from grace. Added to this of course was Helen's own recent fall from the pedestal of motherhood and so yes, poor, poor Jack. The sight of his bowed head and stooped shoulders squeezed her heart. Her boy had always been chilled and loose as a hand-knitted cardigan, easy as a Sunday morning and, she realised, wholly unprepared for a life that was going to have plenty of rainy fucked-up Mondays. The lump of fish in her mouth dried up. She forced it down with a gulp of wine as the understanding of the precious little time left to get him ready stuck in her throat.

It was mere weeks now until he left for university. So how to prepare him? How to prevent him from making the same stupid and fundamental mistake as his sister? What must she get through to him before he left? And how to do it? From nowhere a cold, tripping panic began, flinging open thought after thought like so many kitchen cupboards. Her fingers drummed the table. Where to start? Jack couldn't even do his laundry, and he had about as much ambition as a sloth. Whereas Libby. Libby had been pairing socks since she was eight (and look where that had got her). Libby had led the successful charge that *Yes, Disney Princesses Set Harmful Stereotypes* in her sixth form debating competition (useful as a chocolate teapot when it came to insisting on contraception). Her fingers stopped drumming and clamped themselves around the stem of her glass instead. What the hell did she need to get through to Jack before he walked out of her door almost forever?

'I had an answer from the English department today,' Libby said. 'I'll be able to take my exams in January.'

And all her mental cartwheeling came to a shuddering stop. Helen put her glass down. 'January?' she said as lightly as she could, a speeded-up film of nappies and pink, baby limbs whirling through her mind now. 'The baby will be less than six months old in January, Libby.'

Libby shrugged. 'It's OK, Mum. I've done all the revision and everything. It'll be like a week, that's all.'

'A week?' Helen swirled the contents of her glass. 'And who's going to have the baby then?'

'I was thinking...' Libby paused. 'I was hoping,' she began again, 'that maybe...' And quite suddenly she trailed off.

You, Mum.

Those were the missing words, and everyone at the table knew it, although of course no one would actually say it. The conspiracy of it all enraged her! Lit her up, like paraffin on a bonfire. 'What about after your finals?' she said tightly, because arguing against a week was hopeless, and of course she wanted Libby to take her finals and of course she would look after her grandchild, but that wasn't really what this conversation was about. Suddenly, and it felt strangely exhilarating, Helen understood that all the waiting was finally over.

'I had some ideas. About the masters programme, but...' And again, Libby trailed off as if what she was going to say was far more difficult than she'd anticipated.

Now Lawrence looked up. 'What about if you were to cut back?' he said.

'Me?' Helen blinked, trying to look surprised, trying to look as if she hadn't been expecting this every single day since Libby came home.

'You've been there so long. I'm sure they'll be willing to find something that works for everyone.'

'Everyone?' she mouthed, holding Lawrence's eye.

'It's just a suggestion,' he said and went back to his plate.

Helen looked away. The emotion she felt now wasn't even hot enough to be anger. It was more of a lukewarm resigned sludge of *whatever*. Twenty years of climbing every mountain in the world to escape the daily drudgery and slug of parental responsibility and now her husband was oh-so-casually dumping someone else's responsibility on her doorstep. *This isn't your baby, Helen.* Who had said that? No one had said that! No one was in her camp, aside from Caro and Kay.

A great tuning fork of truth banged down on her head and she turned to look at Jack, who, head down, was emulating his father. *This.* This is what she needed to teach Jack. She needed to show her son exactly where the buck stopped, in a way she obviously hadn't with Libby. *Exactly* where. And if necessary she'd get a stick out and draw the line at his toes. *Here, son.* This is where it starts and ends. And suddenly she was thinking of Kay and how wagons of responsibility had circled around her life and how Kay had done nothing but rise to the challenge and then, looking from Jack to Libby, it felt entirely possible to Helen that both her children were actually capable of growing into people she could find it possible to dislike. It was a stunning, dreadful idea. And it was her fault!

And Lawrence? Well, what was the point of including him in this parental day of judgment?

Her eyes narrowed to slits. She loved her daughter. God knows she loved Libby, but this baby wasn't her baby, and she had no intention, not even for a moment, of allowing Libby to make the mistake of thinking that it was. 'What were you thinking?' she asked. 'That I would look after the baby?'

Libby nodded.

Jack bit down on his lip.

Lawrence folded his hands into his chin as he leaned his elbows on the table.

Helen didn't speak. She picked up her glass and looked up to the antique-copper lampshade overhead, dull from lack of polishing, and across to the hand-painted tiles behind the butler sink and the duck-egg-blue Roman blind, which had cost nearly five hundred quid (and that was twelve years ago!). She looked past her daughter to the massive pine dresser, where a large collection of spotty Emma Bridgewater crockery sat unused, and beyond, to the Aga, cluttered with pans, and the fridge... And suddenly she knew what was missing from the fridge door! Her magnetic pad with the picture of the kingfisher. Her £2.99 pad that was hers and hers alone – because no one uses notepads any more. Two bloody pounds and ninety-nine pence! Where had it gone? Was nothing sacred? She turned back to the table. The solid oak table Lawrence's parents had bought them as a wedding present, which had seen ten thousand breakfasts and ten thousand suppers, and she knew what they were all waiting for. Her family with their ten thousand needs. They were waiting for her to commit to ten thousand more! She took a sip of wine and Cypriot flavoured memories flooded back. *Kaveh.* Sea and salt. The boy's dusty limbs outside the taverna. Postcards of her life. The trail of gold-dust that had been her stillborn son's eyebrow came back to her.

'I'm sorry, Libby,' she said as she put her glass down and shook her head. 'But this baby is your responsibility. I'll help. But it starts and ends with you. This is your life now. Not mine.'

Because suppers weren't postcards. And if this wasn't quite the last one, the last one was now in sight.

7

Kay leaned forward and glanced through the partially open door of the headteacher's room. Nick was on his phone, all knees and elbows again like a suited-up stick insect. Even though everyone else had loosened ties and rolled up sleeves and generally begun that delicious slide into summer.

He'd invited her in to wait, but as Amanda Woods wasn't due for another five minutes, Kay preferred to wait in the cool of the corridor. *I just need to answer someone,* she'd excused herself with, and settled into the small chairs lined up outside, like a naughty child.

A week before term finished and the best part of being a teacher unrolled itself out into the sun-lounger of a six-week summer break. Which wasn't quite true. Because as equally as she loved the break, Kay loved the work. Or until very recently she'd loved it. The last week or so, it had felt that every move she made was being watched, everything she said recorded. It hadn't escaped her attention that she was never on her own in the classroom any more, her teaching assistant didn't seem to leave her side. And when she passed Zac in the corridors, or in the playground, all she detected was embarrassment and she didn't know how to respond to that. With anger that she'd been placed in this position? Or pity for the boy who was so obviously uncomfortable?

She brought her hand to her face and fanned herself. God it was hot. The back of her neck was going mad with itchiness and she still hadn't gotten anywhere near a doctor to talk about HRT. When this was over, which would hopefully be soon… the first thing she would do was make that appointment. And join that tap class. If there was anything spare that was, after the care home bills. The plan that her mother's GP and the dementia team had configured was indeed that her mother should be admitted into a nursing home as soon as possible. But the costs! They were eye-wateringly high. And the weight of sorrow her father now bore was unbearable to witness. Remembering again the terrible resignation he seemed to be displaying toward life in general, Kay unknotted the scarlet sarong masquerading as a scarf, and let it slip from her neck to her lap. It made not a jot of difference. She was still sweltering.

'Nice scarf.'

At the sound of the voice, she looked up. It was Emma, the school secretary. She had her cardigan on, and her bag in her hand.

'Oh…' Kay looked down at the snake of chiffon in her lap.

'You should wear colour more often.' Emma smiled. 'It suits you.'

'Does it?'

'Yes it does.' She opened her bag and took out her car keys. 'I'm sorry I can't wait any longer. Nick will buzz Mrs Woods into school. I told him I couldn't stay past six.'

'No,' Kay said. 'Of course not.'

Emma crossed the small foyer and stopped at the front door, one hand on the handle. 'It'll be alright, Kay,' she said. 'Nick knows what a great teacher you are.'

Kay managed a nod. Or she thought she did. Emma's words were like a quiver of tiny arrows; they punctured her paper-thin bravado without even trying.

'Take care. See you tomorrow?'

'See you tomorrow.' And she watched as the door swung shut and Emma walked across the wide-open empty playground.

Mechanically her fingers twisted through the soft chiffon. Was it going to be alright? Yes, she was a good teacher, but in this last week of waiting she'd travelled long past the point of believing that would be enough. It didn't seem to matter nowadays what reputation preceded you. The *b* word had been used and nowadays that was often all it took. What would she do if it stuck? If this allegation became her downfall? What would she do if she actually lost her job? And more than that, how would she face her colleagues? Or the kids, present and past, of whom she'd always been inordinately fond, and who seemed to respond in kind. *How are you Mrs Burrell? You were always my favourite, Mrs Burrell, even though I hated maths!* That's how they greeted her in the supermarket, with wide-eyed kids of their own.

Swallowing hard, she leaned back against the wall, the

curled-up corner of a piece of year seven artwork nestling into her hair. Emma had disappeared, the school corridors rang quiet and although Amanda Woods should be here in… she glanced at the clock… two minutes, there was no sign of her. So unless she was going to miraculously transport herself into the school, the woman was going to be late. Why didn't that surprise Kay? More to distract herself than anything else, she reached into her bag and took out one of the thirty-odd maths books she'd be marking later on. Turning to the blank pages at the back, she drew vertical lines down the gridded paper, and then slashed across with several horizontal lines. Almost as an afterthought, she flipped the book over to see whose it was, and the name made her smile. Rosie Milford. Well, this was the last assignment of the school year. And Rosie wouldn't be needing her year seven exercise book in year eight. And going by this year's effort, Kay wasn't convinced that Rosie would be filling many pages in year eight either. Anyway she'd rip out these few back pages she'd used. Rosie would never notice.

Pen in mouth, she stared down at the table of lines she'd just constructed. What would happen if she did lose her job? She still had sixteen years until retirement. She scribbled a series of figures down one column. Income as it stood now. Income as it might stand, based upon the pension calculator she'd Googled at 2am. There wouldn't be anything left from her parents, that was clear. Right now, because her father was still living in the house, they wouldn't have to sell it to pay for the nursing home. But their savings would be used, and then when and if her father also went into care… well that would be the house sold too. She'd be on her own, with her truncated pension and Alex's garden centre salary.

Teeth biting the sour plastic, she chomped down on the biro and made a monumental but easy decision. If this next half hour went badly, she'd quit before she could be pushed, and she'd move to Cyprus. Marianne was always sending her pictures over Facebook, and it always looked beautiful. Her pension would go a whole lot further over there than it would here, and she could always wait tables, or maybe teach privately.

A brush of fresh air fanned her face, cooling her Cyprus daydream, and as she turned she saw Nick standing in the doorway to his office. 'That was Amanda Woods,' he said, holding up his phone. 'She'll be here in two minutes.'

Kay nodded, the pen stuck like a forgotten cigarette. So maybe she did have a transporter?

'Maths problem?' Nick smiled, gesturing at her page of criss-crossed columns.

'Nothing,' she murmured, scrabbling to hide both the scribbled calculations and the fact that she was using a pupil's exercise book.

'I use this.' Nick waved his phone. 'Got everything on it nowadays. Calendars, calculators, alarms…' He stopped. 'What am I saying? Maths teacher like you doesn't need a calculator.' And his laugh was a little too loud and a little too forced.

The smile she gave back was more of a grimace. But bugger him! Nothing about this situation was funny. She looped the sarong back into its long roll and folded it around her neck. 'No,' she said as she stood up. 'I certainly don't.' By God, if she was going to go down, she'd go down fighting! 'I'll wait in your office,' she said, 'if that's OK.' And heart hammering but head up, she walked in and took her seat.

A few minutes later (definitely more than two), the first thing Kay thought when Amanda Woods walked through the door of Nick's office was how young she looked. Because investigating her nemesis on LinkedIn she'd been surprised to discover that Amanda was fifty-nine, which meant she would have had Zac at forty-four. At the time it had made Kay think of Caro, and for weeks after she'd had the strangest dreams. She was at a parents' evening and all the parents were in wheelchairs, holding old-fashioned hearing aid trumpets. She'd had to lean over the desk and shout into them. Louder and louder; still they couldn't hear.

But this older parent was nothing like that. No wheelchair... no trumpet... not a grey hair in sight and suspiciously few wrinkles. Amanda Woods was dressed in a pencil-slim shift dress, accessorised with a shiny black handbag the size and shape of a large clipboard. Her cheekbones were high, her earrings subtle and her hair drawn back into the kind of sleek obedient ponytail Kay had always envisioned for herself, on the very few occasions she had tried, and failed, to grow her own hair long.

'Amanda,' Amanda Woods said and stretched out her hand.

'Kay,' Kay said, offering her own hand, just as she had on the previous three parents' evenings when they had met. Maybe this time it would stick? She flicked the tail of her scarlet sarong-scarf into place and thanked God that she hadn't squeezed her sausage torso into her own shift dress. That she'd taken Caro's advice: loose blouse, elasticated trousers, slash of colour.

'Please… take a seat.' On the other side of his desk, Nick pointed out the fairly obvious free chair.

Kay resumed her own seat and watched as Amanda reached into her handbag and took out her phone. The handbag retained its shape, becoming neither slimmer nor smaller. Was that the only thing she had in it?

'I hope you don't mind,' Amanda said as she laid her phone on the desk. 'I thought I'd record the meeting.'

Smooth as silk Nick smiled. 'Absolutely. No problem. That's OK with you, Kay?'

As she leaned back in her chair, Kay nodded, folded one hand on top of the other and breathed in through her nostrils. For a fragment of a moment she thought she'd seen a conspiratorial light flare in Nick's eyes, a moment in which their mutual shock at this opening salvo from Amanda had instantly transformed into mutual resolve. Perhaps he was wary about his own position? The thought hadn't occurred to Kay, but already she sensed that Amanda Woods wasn't the sort to take prisoners. They needed to be on the same team here, that much at least was obvious. She breathed out, two thin streams of air, mouth tight. She wouldn't let him down.

Amanda pulled a sheet of paper from her bag. (So there was something else in it.) 'If perhaps we can start with some background information,' she said and whipped the paper through ninety degrees so it was facing Nick. 'This is a copy of Zachery's last maths paper.'

Squinting, Kay leaned forward.

'I wonder,' Amanda smiled, 'if you could tell me if you understand it.'

Now Nick squinted.

As well he would, Kay thought. Nick came from humanities. He wouldn't understand a year ten maths paper even if it set about explaining itself in an email with the subject line: *Things to Focus on Going Forward.* The kind of mail, Nick himself sent (always) on the last day of term.

'Zachery got a C minus,' Amanda said.

Kay glanced at her. He did. And she'd been generous with that. If she remembered rightly, he deserved a D.

'Now,' Amanda's voice was unnaturally light. 'I'm full of understanding for the fact that teachers can on occasion become... How shall I word this?'

Kay shrugged. There were plenty of words she could have supplied...

'Less than motivated in setting homework assignments?' Amanda finished.

Less than... Her fingernails dug into her palm, five pink crescents of frustration.

'But frankly I don't think I've ever seen such a poorly worded paper.'

'It's a series of division problems,' Kay said and didn't add, how many *words* are necessary?

Amanda turned. 'I'm aware of that. I work in law.'

Kay stared, her lips twitched, and she almost wanted to laugh, so preposterous was the statement. Working in law had nothing to do with how a maths paper was set out. And thinking that it did was like Sarah Palin thinking she understood Russia because she lived in Alaska. Genuinely perplexed, she frowned. 'There's really only so many ways of wording the problem, Mrs Woods.'

Ignoring her, Amanda turned to Nick. 'I would like it re-marked.'

'What?' Slack-jawed, Kay too turned to Nick. In thirty years of teaching, not once had this happened.

He was nodding seriously, his head wobbling.

'Another thing,' Amanda continued. 'Since he has been in your class, Mrs Burrell, my son has missed three tennis lessons because of detentions.'

'Zac—' Nick started.

'Zachery,' Amanda snapped, cutting him off like a praying mantis with a fly. 'His name is Zachery.'

Slightly stunned, Kay leaned back. In all the years of teaching Zac, she had never once heard him call himself anything other than Zac. And she'd never heard his friends or his teachers refer to him as anything other than Zac. Did his mother even know this? Or did she know it and not care? 'His behaviour,' she said carefully, 'has been challenging.'

'It's not at home,' Amanda retorted.

'But it has been in the classroom,' she fired back, sweetening the bullet with a smile. Because honestly, how many times had she heard this? Parents always had difficulty understanding that once out of their sight, their children behaved differently. Why would Amanda Woods be any different? And for the first time since she had entered the room, Kay felt a smidgeon of sympathy for her. For the idea that she obviously held sacred, the absurd notion that she could and would be able to predict every nuance and turn of her son's character and behaviour.

'The problem is,' Amanda said, turning to address Kay directly, 'we pay a lot of money for his extra-curricular activities, and we really don't expect to see them disrupted because of petty disciplinary matters that could probably have been quite easily resolved with better classroom management.'

'I wouldn't call them petty,' Kay said and stopped, her mind stalling as it caught up with Amanda's last three words – *better classroom management.*

'Well!' Sensing a lull, Nick leaned forward. 'No need right now to get into the ins and outs of...' He trailed off, pulling a sheet of paper towards him. 'Perhaps though, it might help to go back a few months. It might be useful to go though some of the umm... some of the incidents—'

'He comes in late,' Kay interrupted, any sympathy she might have momentarily felt vanishing in a puff of exasperation. *Better classroom management?* This woman was making her classroom sound like a corporate board room. She didn't need to go back anywhere! She didn't need a printed list of *incidents.* Kids like Zac stood out. *Incidents* that disrupt a class and send a teacher's blood pressure through the roof get remembered and what was more... There was nothing wrong with the way she managed her classroom. Nothing at all! 'He chews gum,' she continued, 'which I have to ask him *repeatedly* to remove. He doesn't have his textbook with him, so he has to share, which disrupts the kids around him. During class I've found him playing on his phone—'

'Why,' Amanda tilted her head, 'is his phone even accessible in the first place?'

The comment knocked Kay off balance, stuck a foot out and tripped her up. 'It shouldn't be!' she blurted. 'That's the point!'

Amanda Woods shrugged. 'Well, exactly,' she said. 'Management.'

Stunned, Kay stared at her. Amanda Woods, she realised, had an answer to everything. And *nothing*, it was clear, was going to be either her, or her child's responsibility. She was the very embodiment of what the younger teachers labelled *uber parent:* a scary new cross of life experience meets success meets money. She wasn't the type to be fobbed off with the usual *we will endeavour* or *we're keeping an eye* blandishments. This woman wanted *proof.* Expected her son's education to run as tick-tock smoothly as she ran her life (and her hair). She'd invested and she expected a return, and again, Kay thought of Caro. Could this also be Caro? That it could, that she was so easily able to imagine Caro, in place of Amanda, demanding and expecting, physically upset her. She pushed back in her chair and looked across the small room. The expectations! Why? Why do people bother having kids, when all they're looking for is a copy of themselves?

'Anyway,' Amanda shook her head, her pony tail swinging like a metronome.

Kay watched, her fingers twitching with the urge to reach out and yank it. HARD!

'As you're probably aware, my husband and I lead very busy lives. Sending Zachery home with extra assignments to make up for work that should be taking place in school is *not* helpful. We have neither the time nor the...'

And here Kay switched off. Pressed pause. Busy lives? Three nights ago, her mother had gotten up and fallen in the hallway. Her father had found her soaking wet, freezing cold, sound asleep. He'd thought she was dead. He couldn't lift her and he couldn't help her and he'd rung Kay at three in the morning because he thought he'd found his wife of sixty years dead in the hallway... *Can you come? Shall I call an ambulance? Can you come... now.* She looked up at Amanda. Time? She wanted to say. What the fuck is that?

'And then,' Amanda continued, 'we come to this latest incident. Which I have to say really fuelled my suspicions and has led us to the unfortunate position we find ourselves in.'

Kay's mouth flattened to a long flat line. Stick a moustache on her, and Amanda Woods could be Poirot. With Nick and she the suspects, awaiting the denouement. She should loosen up. Try a bit of *Real Housewives of Beverly Hills.* The thought had her suppressing a smile.

'Indeed.' Nick looked down at his papers.

'I find it totally unacceptable,' Amanda seethed, 'the way Ms Burrell forced my son to participate in an exercise designed solely to embarrass him.'

Kay held her chin up and shook her head and in the moment that followed, no one spoke.

And then Nick nodded. 'Kay, would you like to say something?'

Yes, she bloody well would! She sat up, tucked her sarong-scarf into place and said, 'This latest *incident* as you call it. I asked Zac—'

'Zachery.'

Waiting a beat, she paused. 'I invited Zachery to come

up to the whiteboard, because he was asking questions about stuff we hadn't covered.'

'Zachery is gifted. He can't help that.'

'And he has private tuition.'

'Your point is?'

That he's privileged, not gifted. She didn't say this. What she said was, 'It can sometimes place him ahead, as it did on this occasion. I considered that it would be a good way to stop him getting bored, keep the class on track and keep him engaged.'

'By dragging him up in front of the whole class?'

'I didn't need to drag him. It was meant to be a bit of fun. Switching roles.'

'So you could then humiliate him? By asking questions he couldn't answer?'

'No!' Kay snapped. But by God, she'd had enough! She was a teacher. She wasn't Amanda Woods' cleaner, or her au-pair, or her birthday-cake baker, or her secretary, or anyone else on her payroll. She was a teacher! 'That wasn't the point at all. And actually Zac... Zachery *could* answer some of them. Those that he couldn't, I phrased the question so the answer was in it. So the whole class, including Zachery, could learn. And what's more, as far as I could see, he enjoyed himself.'

'He did not enjoy himself,' Amanda said primly. 'He was embarrassed and humiliated and he felt unsafe!'

'Unsafe?' Kay paused. Zachery Woods was taller than her. Unsafe? The word was used in such strange contexts these days. 'No one,' she said quietly, 'was carrying a concealed weapon, Mrs Woods.'

The joke fell flat.

Nick cleared his throat. 'Did Zachery use those words?'

'He didn't need to,' Amanda answered.

And astonished, Kay turned to Nick as if she'd almost forgotten he was there. His face had frozen in panic. It was, she knew, that word: *unsafe*. Thrown as randomly and thoughtlessly as confetti. The corners of her mouth turned down, as clink by clink, muscle by sinew she felt an internal armour fastening into place. Nick might be cowed, but she wasn't. Zac hadn't felt unsafe in her class, and no one was going to strong-arm her into believing that he had, especially someone who'd never set foot in a classroom. She crossed her arms and looked at Amanda. How, she considered, would the woman react to her, Kay, striding into Amanda's office and offering an unasked for, uneducated, irrelevant opinion? In a cool, composed voice she said, 'Mrs Woods, the boy I saw in my classroom that day wasn't humiliated or embarrassed. And there was nothing about the environment that I could, in any sane situation, describe as unsafe. In fact, in thirty years of teaching, I don't think I could ever have used that word to describe either a student or a situation.' She paused. 'Although once we had an accident with a banana, left in someone's rucksack so long it might possibly have fallen into that category. But Mr Hodges is pretty handy with Domestos and it was dealt with long before the lesson in question.'

Neither Amanda nor Nick responded, and somewhere way back in a dusty corner of her mind, she could hear a voice calling, *Stop with the jokes, Kay!* But she was fifty and her mother was hitting her father, and Helen's child was

CARY J. HANSSON

having a child and her own precious son was embarking on motorcycle races and on the verge of moving out and jokes were about the only thing left to hang on to, a reliable raft in this maelstrom... She looked at Nick's fingers pale and hairless stretched out like beached starfish. Then, slowly she turned to look up at Amanda Woods.

Who was staring at her in disbelief.

So Kay stared back. She was beyond caring. In total kamikaze mode.

'I want,' Amanda said imperiously, 'the paper re-marked, before the end of term.' She turned to Nick. 'It's very clear to me that Mrs Burr—'

'Ms,' Kay clipped.

'I'm sorry?'

'It's *Ms* not Mrs.' She smiled. 'If we are aiming to get names right.'

Amanda scowled. She turned back to Nick. '*Ms* Burrell has a bias against my son, in all probability because of the colour of his skin. He's aiming for Oxbridge. He needs at least an A in his GCSE next year, and this... this is a question of fairness.'

'A bias?' Kay repeated.

'That...' Nick began, glancing at Kay. 'That's quite a serious allegation—'

'Which isn't true.' Blunt as a hammer, Kay cut him off because like a sudden shift in winds, Amanda Woods' words had produced a sea change in the atmosphere of the room, charging it with tension, which to her surprise, only left her calm, as detached as if she were watching a storm from a very safe harbour. She had, she realised, been expecting

106

this. Zac's father was black, and from the moment Amanda Woods' complaints had started, Kay had found herself on high alert with regard to her interactions with him. No, she didn't like the boy, but these last few weeks she'd put that aside and concentrated on trying very hard to like him, testing herself, trying out the sobering possibility that there might be a truth in what she'd seen coming. How hard she had tried! Including him in discussion more often, laughing at his unfunny jokes, praising his successes. To which, surprisingly, he'd responded. So much so that, together, they had been bumping along much better, quite nicely in fact, which had left her feeling relieved and happy and ready. 'It's just not true,' she repeated, with a pronounced confidence. 'I—'

But Amanda was reaching for her phone. 'After the re-mark, I'm prepared to let the matter be closed... with one further suggestion...'

Kay's eyes widened –

'...Ms Burrell attends unconscious bias training...'

– and widened. She looked first at Amanda, then at the phone which was still recording.

'Well...' Nick looked from one to the other. 'I think...' He pulled Zac's test paper towards him and picked it up. 'I think a re-mark is... well it wouldn't do any harm. Kay?'

Did she answer? Kay barely noticed. In fact she barely noticed anything about the rest of the meeting, how long it lasted, or what was conceded, agreed, disputed. She didn't really come round until Amanda Woods had left the room and Nick had re-seated himself opposite her, an expression of shameful contrition slapped and stretched across his face like a wet flannel. As if he knew it was all bullshit. As if he knew that what he was selling wasn't decent wool-pile carpet, but a threadbare doormat. And even then, it wasn't enough. His obvious empathy wasn't enough to help her wound. Thirty years she had given, in fair and dedicated practice, in the face of abuse from parents who couldn't be arsed to put a clean t-shirt on for parents' evening, parents who did their kids' homework for them and said as much… And all of that was better than this. Having her integrity judged. Having to endure the humiliation of having someone else check her marking.

'I'm sorry, Kay,' Nick started. 'For what it's worth—'

She held her hand up to stop him. She felt sorry for him but whatever he was going to say wasn't worth anything – not under the shadow of such unfounded and dangerous allegations. 'Ask Annie to re-mark it,' she said flatly. 'The paper's on… It's maths,' she shrugged. 'It's pretty black and white.' And couldn't help adding, 'Although that's probably not the best metaphor.'

Nick ran his thumb along the edge of the paper. 'Would you go on a course? If this goes to the governors,' he added softly, 'it's out of my hands.'

Kay looked at those pale, unlined hands, soft as sponge. Did she really want her professional future nested in them? 'Of course,' she said, because what other answer could she possibly give?

8

Helen stuck a leg out from under the duvet, feeling the relief of cool fresh air on her ankle. Her t-shirt was soaked with sweat. How on earth Kay coped without HRT was beyond her. If she could, she'd sleep naked, but the marital bed had become disputed territory and she couldn't risk so much as a brush of her pyjamaed leg against her husband's, let alone the frisson of bare skin. Such a misunderstanding could wipe out the minuscule progress she'd made, if she had actually made any progress. Judging by last night's dinner table conversation and Lawrence's blithe assumptions about the way she might put her life on hold, she wasn't sure she was a centimetre further along.

She folded her hands over the top of the duvet and stared at the ceiling. Her mind had already sprung clear from the starting blocks and begun its now daily exhausting sprint: *How to… Where would… What if…* All those practicalities she knew she must start getting to grips with. It was halted only by a message pinging through on her phone.

Can we put lunch back half an hour? Have to fit in a quick meeting. Kay can't make it. She'll meet us after. Problem with Alex. Caro x

Helen frowned at the message, momentarily confused, before instantly remembering the lunch and shopping trip planned. Her phone pinged again.

I'm not going to buy anything, I just want to look, it's way too early to get excited.

So a shopping trip that wasn't even a shopping trip. And no Kay for lunch. Helen yawned. At least it would give her a chance to talk to Caro, seriously, get some one-on-one advice, some indication of how to get this practical-shaped ball rolling. Caro would be able to help and yes, after last night's dinner this was exactly the impetus she needed.

Her phone pinged again.

V. excited! Caro x

Well so was Helen. Just not about the same thing. She let the phone drop and rubbed her eyes. Babies. They were like buses. No sign of one for decades, then suddenly too many to cope with. Beside her, Lawrence's arm flew out and slapped her shoulder. Gripping the duvet, Helen sidled away. This could not continue. She slept so close to the edge nowadays that two nights ago she'd fallen out. Silently she slipped out of the bed, padded her way to the bathroom and greeted herself in the bathroom mirror.

Helen, Helen, Helen, she whispered and the woman in the mirror, the woman with tractor lines between her eyes and droopy jaws echoed it back. *Helen, Helen, Helen.*

*

Ten minutes later she was in the kitchen, hands on hips, watching the garden and listening to the kettle, which as well as its customary whistling seemed to be making an odd shuffling sound. Helen flicked it off. The whistling piped down, but the shuffling continued and now that the sound was isolated she could hear better. It wasn't the kettle, it was the utility room. 8:25am on a Saturday morning and someone was doing laundry? Either that or someone had broken in. It was crystal clear which scenario was the most likely and without thinking, she grabbed the bread knife and strode to the door. Something about the utter stupidity of breaking and entering on a Saturday morning filling her with unquestioned courage. Heart pounding, she flung the door back and there was Jack kneeling in a sea of clothes. He had a bottle of fabric conditioner in one hand, the cap in the other, like a novice priest about to perform Holy Communion. Relief made her legs wobbly. She blinked.

Jack?

Doing Laundry?

At 8:25 on a Saturday morning?

Helen clamped her mouth shut. *Just throw it in!* she would have barked to literally anyone else on the planet naive enough to think that fabric conditioner actually needed to be measured. To Jack she smiled, lowered the knife and said, 'Want a cup of tea?'

'She's really fucked things up, hasn't she?' Jack was leaning against the oven.

Helen was leaning against the sink.

'Don't swear,' she said, but she didn't mean it and he

111

knew she didn't. For the first time since she came home from Cyprus, her son was actually trying to have a conversation with her, and she understood how fucking difficult that was right now.

He dipped his head to the floor. 'I want you to know something, Mum,' he said, his voice hoarse.

'Jack—'

'No, Mum, listen. Please?'

'OK.' She clasped her mug to her chest and nodded and willed herself not to move across and hug him. He looked so forlorn. The face of a child, the six-foot frame of a man.

'I want you to know,' he whispered, 'that I won't let you down.'

Helen gasped. The words sounded so cruel. 'Libby hasn't let me down,' she managed, but even as she said it, she didn't really believe it. 'She's...' Flustered, Helen looked across the room. What had Libby done, if not let her down? All those hopes and dreams she'd nurtured for her daughter. They were impossible now. 'This is life, Jack,' she sighed. 'This is what happens. You know... stuff happens.'

'Like in Cyprus?' Jack mumbled and lifted his chin to look at her from under the flop of his dirty-blonde hair.

Helen's shoulders rose, tensed and then dropped again. She wasn't being attacked. There had been no accusation in her son's voice and there was certainly none in his stance. 'I suppose so,' she said. 'It's complicated, Jack.'

'Are you and Dad getting divorced?'

And what could she do but nod a silent yes, watching as he turned away, face flushing. It was like ripping a plaster off his scratched knee, only much, much worse. She was tearing her boy's soft untried heart and in doing so, tearing her own. Hurting your children, it was true, was the most brutal kind of torture. For one blow landed, two came back. After all these weeks, just as he was turning toward her again, she was making him turn away. Her throat was hard and it hurt to force the words out, but she did. 'I don't want you to worry, Jack,' she said. 'About me, or your dad. We're always going to be your parents. We'll always be there when you need us and… You have your own life now. You'll be off soon—'

'That's what I said to Libby,' Jack whispered as he turned back to her.

Helen stared at him.

'Last night,' he pushed through, his voice scraping and his eyes shiny with tears. 'After you'd gone to bed. I told Libby that it wasn't fair of her to expect you to look after the baby. That you have your own life.'

'You said that?'

'Yes, Mum,' he mumbled. '*I* said that.' He blew his fringe clear from his eyes and as he did a tear escaped, wiped clear with a swift embarrassed movement.

Helen didn't speak. She couldn't. Her throat was raw with the concrete sob she was trying not to let out. It had been such a long time since Jack had revealed this much to her. Memories flooded back. He was still there. Under the hormones and the unspeakable debris of his room, her tender-hearted, good-natured boy who held the pegs while she hung the clothes was still there. And the idea that she was the source of his pain wasn't something she could even look at. How could she ever have known? And if she had, if she'd known that she was capable of hurting her children so, would she ever have started this journey?

For the longest time they both stood, sight-lines like laser beams, crossing but never meeting.

'I'm always going to be your mum, Jack,' she whispered finally. It was all and everything she could offer. 'Wherever I am, is your home.'

'I know,' he whispered in response, lip trembling.

She hesitated half a moment before saying, 'Do you want a hug?' Her whole world pinned upon him saying yes. That he would give her permission to hold him, like she used to.

He didn't move, but his head bobbed a tiny movement up and down.

She was barely as tall as his shoulder, her hands not quite meeting around his back. The baby she'd strapped to her chest for months and months, the tiny tot who sat on the counter while she buttered toast soldiers.

'Everything's going to be OK, Mum,' he whispered, as he hugged her back, those same words she'd comforted him with so many times before. 'Everything's going to be OK.'

Later, with one child showering, and another child (with child) sleeping, Helen set about the kitchen. She emptied the dishwasher and re-filled it, cleaned the sink and sorted the recycling, swept the floor, fed the cat, cleaned the sink again. Wiping benches, her pace slowed and she leaned back against the counter to look around the room she had spent such a large part of her life in. What would she take? The clarity of the thought surprised her. It's clean practicality, a cool relief. Her nose wrinkled as she squinted up to the top shelf of the dresser. Obviously, the rose teapot that had belonged to her grandmother. And that pottery pencil holder beside it that Jack made at school, and the set of…

With zero warning Lawrence materialised in the doorway, splintering her chain of thought into useless pieces. He was dressed in neon green cycling shorts and an orange and green lycra top. In one quick movement he was at the fridge, pouring a glass of juice and knocking it back. 'I'm going for a ride,' he said, lowering the glass.

'Really?' She nodded at his shorts. 'I thought you were on your way to Tesco.'

But Lawrence had already turned to the dresser and was fiddling with a watch or a sat nav, or a heart monitor thingy. She didn't know if he'd even heard her joke, and what she noticed was the vacuum of emotion she felt. It didn't matter. Suddenly it didn't matter any more that he didn't listen to her jokes, or that he didn't find them funny, that he was and always would be hopelessly absorbed in his own Lawrence-centred world. She watched him strap the thingy on and make his energy drink – 500ml of water, three scoops of (very special) powder. God, once upon a time she used to stand and make the mix up for him.

'Lawrence,' she said, turning her head sideways to look at him. 'I think we should start things moving.'

'What do you mean?' The pointy point of his helmet was like that huge pointy finger on those war posters, accusing. She wanted to laugh, but now was absolutely not the right time to laugh. With effort she continued.

'I think we should start sorting things out. You know, financially at least.'

Lawrence snapped the lid of his sports drink shut. 'We're not doing anything until Libby has had the baby,' he barked and shook the drink violently.

We're not doing anything. We're not... The words winded her. So much so that unconsciously she took a step sideways, away from him. He'd grabbed the reins again. Taken control, when it was her life too. *Her own life* as Jack had said less than ten minutes ago. She swallowed hard. 'What I'm saying,' she began in a voice that sounded oddly loud, 'is that I think we should start getting the finances straight. Separated. Get the house valued.'

'I can't believe you!' Lawrence spun to face her, his face as orange as his sports drink. 'What kind of a mother are you, Helen? You'd see your daughter homeless, when she needs you the most? You... you're...God, Helen!'

Helen's jaw dropped. Half shock, half disbelief. *What kind of a mother was she?* A good one, she thought. A devoted one if the last two decades were anything to go by.

And with another two enormous strides he was out of the kitchen.

She didn't move. Back to the counter, she stood and stared across her empty kitchen for long and silent minutes. The clock ticked on, its brassy hands showing IX something and outside of the window the forsythia swayed, flashes of vibrant green scratching at the window, the flowers long gone. Helen turned to the sound. So what kind of a mother was she? The kind with a teenage son who still talked to her! The kind with a grown daughter who still sobbed on

116

her shoulder. She was every kind of mother, depending on the time of day and the state of their rooms and the last row, but most of all, she was the kind of mother who was *there*. She had been present and no one could take that away from her. Especially the one person who had, so often, been absent! It wasn't fair of Lawrence. But then nothing about the way he ran his life, she understood now, was fair. He went whenever it suited him and always had. A month here, two months there. Weekends year round. Helen pressed her hands to the counter, leaned forward and closed her eyes. If she did wait, how much longer *could* she wait? Another six months? Because that's what it would be with a baby coming. The chaotic aftermath as everyone found their feet. Could she go through all that with no light at the end of the tunnel? Or was it more likely that she'd lose her way again, give up, allow herself to fall between the cushions once more? The weight of the stone at the small of her back was as real as it had been on that day, on that beach with Kaveh. And the moment of level-headed clarity she'd experienced a few minutes ago felt suddenly as rare as a completed to do list. One of those precious light-filled moments in which she could see beyond the landscape of this house. She turned back to her kitchen, went to the dresser and took down the little rose teapot. Then hugging it close to her chest, she ran up the stairs, two at a time.

Straight into the small walk-in cupboard – home to the most precious and the most useless objects in the house. Dusty photo albums, where her mother lived again as the first woman in Whitley Bay to wear a bikini. Red booklets that spelled out in centimetres and kilograms Jack and

Libby's first twelve months. An ice-cream maker, whose duplicate sat in a kitchen cupboard, equally unused. A set of cut-glass whisky tumblers, next to her wedding album. And there, the grey box file labelled in her own hand. *Important Things*. She pulled it down, took out her passport, and what else? Marriage certificate, that should do. She slapped them onto the bed and stood looking at the open file, struggling with the temptation to pick up the Certificate of Stillbirth, which lay on the top of the pile. Resisting the urge to carry it across to the bed, curl up under the duvet and allow herself to once again become submerged in a quicksand that was equal parts nostalgia and grief. Her hand reached for the certificate, memories flooding back. Caro was there. It was Caro who had held her hand as she went through her first labour, with her first child, who had already died. And it was Caro who just last week at Kay's house was telling her to *get busy*.

With infinite care she ran the tip of her finger across the printed name, whispering it aloud: *Daniel Andrew Winters*. A calm settled, silent and fragile as the first snowfall. She'd been every kind of mother she could possibly be, to *all* her children.

Courage, Helen, she whispered as she pressed her finger to her lips and touched it once again to the first name, of her first child.

Then she threw off her dressing gown and stepped into the shower. If she left soon enough she'd have time to get at least one ball moving before catching the train. One ball to push down the hill, after which everything else would follow.

9

Caro picked up the jacquard cushion, plumped it fat again and pushed it back into the corner of the chair, shuffling herself comfortable. As this meeting with Danny Abbot had been scheduled pre-lunch, she could easily get away with ordering a non-alcoholic drink. Danny would barely notice, which was good, because no one knew yet (except Kay and Helen) and she hadn't even begun to work out how to expand that circle of knowledge.

She picked up her lime and soda and leaned back. A few hundred yards away, framed by the clean blues and whites of an English summer sky, Tower Bridge rose magnificent. With the glass at her lips and the cushion at her back, Caro felt the measure of this perfect moment. She was eight weeks pregnant. Her baby was the size of a kidney bean, its tiny limbs already forming tiny fingers and tiny toes. Ears had budded and eyes too. The formation of another person, in this most ordinary of miracles that she couldn't quite believe and yet knew from the nucleus of her being was true.

And it was a source of wonder for Caro how, from the very beginning, she had felt those physical changes. How, from the outside, she could feel the miniscule and precisely calibrated alterations, how all those years of controlling and silencing her body through decades of birth control and dietary discipline had melted away in the face of these strange but most welcome upheavals.

In the beginning there was the tingling pins and needles of tender breasts, soon after a dragging fatigue thin as a bridal veil that she just couldn't shake. And then for weeks the swell of nausea whenever she passed the roasting chicken spit in Sainsbury's. And coffee. On her first day back at work she'd had to leave her CEO Matt's office because of the overpowering smell of it.

Still this wasn't enough. All her life, the only thing Caro had ever really placed her faith in was the tangible proof of her own endeavours; a sudden dislike of roasting chicken wasn't going to convince her that this latest and most hard-won dream might be accomplished. So the steely will that had steered her career kicked into action and for the first time in her life she had ignored her symptoms. Coming back from Cyprus, fourteen days passed and she wasn't even tempted to take a test. Then, on the morning of the fifteenth day, she had stood in her bathroom and watched the stick perform exactly how she had been expecting it to. After, it was with a sense of serenity that she had dressed and gone to work. It had all come together. All the decisions and choices Caroline Hardcastle of Artillery Terrace had made over the last thirty years slotting into place now like a celestial jigsaw.

But telling Matt, her CEO? Or her team? She wasn't quite sure how that fitted. Let alone her mother. No, she wasn't sure at all.

She turned her head to the sun and closed her eyes. She would just have to be open and honest. Why not? Sunlight seeped through the thinly porous skin of her eyelids as she took a deep breath. Worrying about other people's reactions was like trying to shut out the sun and why would she try to do that? On a day like today, why would she do that? She lifted her chin higher, kept her eyes closed and soaked up the moment.

Looking around at the primary-coloured furniture and the huge blue *Welcome* sign in the bank entrance, Helen had a wobble. She hadn't been inside for years. It looked more like the Holiday Inn than a place to do business. On the far wall stood a row of sleekly curved ATMs, framed either side by displays of brochures. Straight ahead, guarding a corridor that obviously led into the bank, stood a young girl dressed head to toe in navy blue and clutching a blue clipboard.

I'd love to help! read the blue sign next to her. And obviously she did love to, because despite the increasing irritation in the face of the customer she was currently helping, an elderly man in a lemon-coloured short-sleeved shirt, the smile never left her face.

Helen wandered over to the brochures, idly reading through the titles: *Protect Yourself, Your Money, Reach Your Goals.* Nothing as exciting as *Learn to Sail* she considered with a smile as she picked up the *Reach Your Goals* leaflet. It seemed the most appropriate.

'I would prefer not to discuss that here!' The customer in the lemon shirt grumbled and he turned around and glared at Helen.

Startled, she stuck her nose in the leaflet.

'Certainly, sir,' the *I'd love to help!* girl said, 'but if you could just tell me how much you were looking—'

'Young lady!' the man snapped. 'I've been banking here since before you were born. When I say I have no wish to discuss my financial affairs in front of every Tom, Dick and Harry that is what I mean!'

Still pretending to read, Helen took a step back. Any further away and she'd be through the window. As the only other customer in the place, she was obviously Tom, Dick and Harry all rolled into one, but she wasn't offended. On the contrary, the wobble she'd experienced coming through the door evaporated. And having no wish either to discuss her financial affairs in front of Toms and Dicks, she was now keenly interested in where this conversation would go. The whole forced make-yourself-at-home, let's-all-discuss-it-together vibe 21st-century banking had obviously adopted wasn't helpful. Confessors got more privacy.

'Is it too much to ask for a little privacy these days?' the man huffed.

Hallelujah, Helen thought. He'd read her mind.

And the girl looked at her clipboard. 'There's… I…' Then, 'I'll just go and see if anyone's free to help.' And she turned and hurried off down the corridor.

*

Three minutes later, with the lemon-shirted man whisked off down secret passageways, and the *I'd love to help!* girl back on guard duty, it was Helen's turn.

'I want to set up a bank account,' she said quietly. Behind her the Holiday Inn was filling up with Toms and Dicks and Harrys.

'Certainly, madam,' the girl said, one arm already raised to guide Helen to a computer perched atop a high desk next to the ATMs. 'I can assist—'

'Not here,' Helen said firmly. 'I'd like to do it in person. With someone.'

The girl stared at her.

'*In person*,' Helen repeated.

'I understand, but it's a very simple—'

Helen shook her head.

'But it's very simple,' the girl said hopelessly.

'In person.' Helen smiled. 'Could you see if someone is free?' *If someone's free!* Now that she'd gotten this far she could see further down the corridor to where at least two staff members sat staring at screens. On Facebook probably.

'We even have an app,' the girl tried. 'All you need to do is take a selfie.'

Helen smiled.

'No?'

'No.'

The girl turned and headed away down the corridor. Helen watched her go. It wasn't that simple; she didn't have the app and the very last thing she needed right now was for her financial laxity to be hung out and displayed in front of Toms and Dicks and Harrys and *I'd love to helps!*

and everyone else who happened to be strolling in off the high street.

'*Caro!* You star!' The voice that boomed across the terrace was so loud it created a shadow.

Startled, Caro opened her eyes.

And there was Danny Abbott, looming over her in a blinding white shirt and mirrored sunglasses that reflected back her own startled expression.

'Danny.' Instinctively Caro sucked her stomach in as she stood up. Why was she doing that? She wasn't even showing.

'Caro! Blimey, you look well.' Danny grabbed her shoulders and landed a smacker either side of her face. 'This is Emir,' he said and turned to a man standing behind him.

'Emir.' Caro swallowed down her surprise. She knew Emir was coming, that was the whole point of the meeting. And she knew he was young. But *this* young? 'Pleased to meet you,' she said and held her hand out, wincing as Emir shook it firmly. His jaw was so square it could have been cut by a laser machine. He was wearing a leather jacket and jeans that screamed £££.

'Shall we…?' she said, indicating the sofa and chair opposite.

Emir took the chair and Danny fell back into the low sofa without even checking it was there, which reminded Caro of the trust exercises she'd played as a child – lean back, eyes closed, arms crossed and hope the group will catch you – the exercise she'd never been able to do without cheating. Because what if no one was there?

'Another one, Caro?' Danny said. He'd turned to wave down a waiter.

She mouthed a *no* indicating her still full glass.

'Really?' He turned to her. 'Not like you,' he smiled and a huge dimple in his right cheek seemed to wink at her.

Caro smiled back, small and tight. 'I'm meeting some friends for lunch,' she said. 'Need to pace myself.' She was long practised in the little white lies needed to keep her clients happy.

'Amongst them your friend Helen?' Danny asked.

Caro nodded.

'Sailing Helen?'

'Sailing?' Caro frowned.

'I spoke to her on the phone, remember? When you were away. Cyprus, was it?'

She nodded.

'That's right. She told me all about a sailing lesson she'd just had, and,' he turned to Emir, 'gave me a right bollocking.'

Emir laughed. 'I can't imagine that.'

'She did. Very protective she was about you, Caro.'

'Well…' Colouring, Caro reached for her briefcase. The memory of that day, coming back from the fertility clinic full of fragile hopes, was raw. She'd felt so protected, by both Helen and Kay. Perhaps more than at any other point in her life. It still moved her.

'Anyway!' Danny stretched back, one leg swung over the other, the embellishment on his black Hermes loafers shining like fresh liquorice. 'It's good to see you looking so well. That holiday must have worked wonders.'

Caro smiled. Yes it had: the biggest wonder of all. 'Shall we get started?' she said, and pulled out a file of papers. She wouldn't have scheduled this meeting if she'd had any other choice. Saturday meetings weren't normal at all, but Danny Abbott was notoriously hard to pin down. For three weeks now, she'd been trying to fix this introduction to his friend and possible new client, Emir. She didn't need long. A quick elevator pitch before lunch. Time enough to whet Emir's interest and get him committed to a more detailed presentation later. Quality time that is, with no distractions. Specifically, no Helen-shaped distractions. She felt her stomach fold over itself, soft dough under strong hands. Danny, Helen, the pregnancy, it wasn't a combination she felt comfortable with.

'Why not?' Emir shrugged now and all the buttery softness of his expensive leather jacket shrugged with him.

'Are you meeting here?' Danny drawled.

Caro nodded. 'So,' she said, her voice tight. 'Shall we—'

'I have to meet this woman.' Danny had turned to Emir. 'She's the reason I bought my yacht.'

Emir nodded, weaving his fingers together. '*The Catalina?*'

'Yep!'

A waiter arrived, bearing mineral water for Emir and a Pilsner for Danny.

Danny leaned forward and scooped a handful of the accompanying bowl of nuts into his palm. 'Best thing I've done in years,' he said. 'I'd like to thank her.'

'Shall we?' Caro said.

And Danny tipped his chin to the sky, elbows and knees wide as a starfish. 'Off you go, Caro. Stage is all yours.'

'You do realise you could have done all this online?'

Helen nodded lamely. What was the point of arguing? Besides, she was past the gatekeeper, had been ushered down the hallowed interior, into a nearly private cubicle, and was face to face with a real person. Well, semi-real. The young woman she'd been assigned had the usual high-gloss finish once only seen on cinema screens. Blown-out lips, marker-pen eyebrows, foot-long lashes. Willing herself not to stare, Helen opened her handbag and took out her passport and her marriage certificate and three Marks & Spencer bills in her name. Better to be safe than sorry.

The woman stared at them. 'You won't need them,' she said archly. 'You're already a customer. You have a joint account with your husband.'

Helen flushed a deep red as she inched her documents back into her handbag. Superfluous. Not needed. Of course not. Why would she need to provide proof of who she was when she'd been banking with this bank for the last twenty-five years? She hadn't felt this stupid since she'd once tried to do a run on the gym treadmill using the app Libby had installed on her phone. *It's a GPS-based app,* the gym instructor had informed her, when after an exhausting four minutes her tiny little avatar still wasn't off its starting mark. *You haven't actually moved.*

'It's really very easy to do all this online,' the woman intoned. She turned to her screen and began tap, tap, tapping.

Isn't everything, Helen thought as she sat, sat, sat. And

this was why she needed privacy. *This* was her confession. Because how to explain that somehow, she'd gotten herself into a situation where it wasn't going to be easy at all, a situation where only her husband knew the passwords to their account. That *she*, in fact, hadn't been banking with anyone for the last twenty-five years. Lawrence had. On her behalf. That she'd washed her hands of all of this, way back in the previous century. So no, it wouldn't have been easy to do this online. It would in fact have been impossible. Unless she'd rung him and asked him for the passwords for their joint account, so she could go in and open a new personal account. And she wasn't about to do that.

The woman opposite tapped away and the more she tapped and moved the mouse and made neat little notes on her neat little pad, the more inadequate Helen felt. Like she'd been asleep for twenty years and was only just waking up. She glanced up at the clock. The train left in twenty minutes. Her nails dug into her palm. This much she *had* to get done. One step forward, one ball rolling...

'Right.' The woman looked down at her sleeve, brushed a tiny thread clean and turned to Helen. 'That's all set up for you then.'

'It's done?'

'All done, yes.'

The immense relief of achieving something had her beaming. It was done! The very first step.

'Is there anything else I can help you with today, Mrs Winters?'

Mrs Winters. Her married name, the sound of it when here she was, beginning the process of loosening and teasing the threads of her marriage apart, focused her attention. 'I'd like to make a transfer,' she said. 'From the joint account.'

'That shouldn't be a problem,' the woman said, quite cheery now. She turned back to her screen and as she did a single fake eyelash detached itself, floating down to the desk, graceful as a disembodied insect wing.

Helen stared at it.

The woman reddened. 'How much would you like to transfer today?' she said, with an involuntary glance at the rogue lash.

'What's the balance?' Helen answered, suddenly and serenely calm. Like she'd been handed the steering wheel and was finding that she could, in fact, drive.

The woman leaned into the screen. Tap tap. Tappity, tap. 'Four hundred and three pounds seventy-five pence.'

'I'm sorry?' Helen shook her head. She hadn't heard right.

'Four hundred and three—'

'Four hundred and three pounds?'

'And seventy-five pence.'

'Are you sure?'

'Yes.'

'*Absolutely* sure?'

'Yes, I'm sure…' And the woman once again leaned forward and read through the amount, this time silently, her lips moving.

Helen's brow furrowed. Numbers tumbled. She'd always been quite good at maths, never in Kay's league, but good enough. Lawrence earned (in the region of) £60,000.

Which was, very approximately, three and a half thousand a month. Her own wage, after tax, was nearly five hundred. Four hundred and three pounds didn't make sense. Four hundred and three pounds wasn't possible. Four hundred and three pounds was nonsense. 'Can I look?' she asked, dumbfounded.

This time they both leaned in, the eyelash like a tiny black smile on the desk between them.

Helen pointed at the screen. 'Can we go to…'

'Transactions?'

A few more taps and again they were both peering.

'Shall I scroll?'

She nodded, the screen unfolded back to May and April and March and the cosy booth in which they sat grew snugger, cloaked as it was now in a degree of mystery highly unusual for Saturday mornings. The woman, Helen knew, for as long as this appointment lasted at least, was now on her side.

'What's that?' She pointed to a sum going out of the account on 4 February. The same figure she'd glimpsed in March and April.

'Two thousand, one hundred and nine? That's…' The woman's hands flew over her keyboard. 'That's a regular payment to… us actually. It looks like your mortgage.'

'Our mortgage!' Helen gasped. 'Our mortgage isn't that big!'

The woman frowned. 'It's definitely a payment to'… She tapped a little more. 'It's a mortgage payment.'

'Can we go further back?'

'To…'

130

'I don't know.' Helen pressed her lips together. The mortgage wasn't two thousand pounds a month. She didn't know much, admittedly, but she did know this, because she remembered Lawrence telling her a while back how it was under a thousand. Buying the house had been a stretch, but that was twenty-five years ago. He'd been earning less, she'd been earning more, and together they had made it work. They'd paid it back; they should be sitting quite comfortably. Certainly she was. Every time she'd put her card in, money had come out. And it wasn't as if she was running around buying designer handbags and having expensive facials, but she didn't blink at the price of unfiltered olive oil and she never allowed herself to run out of Clarins Day Cream. Four hundred pounds? Had it ever been lower than that? How close had she come to handing her card over and having it refused? Her fiftieth birthday lunch had cost the best part of a hundred pounds. And Cyprus? Yes, Caro had paid for the hotel, but her flights had been nearly two hundred. So, *how close had she come?* And how hadn't she known? She'd been blind. Walking along the precipice of a vertical drop, blindfolded. Swallowing down the angry confusion she was feeling, she said quietly, 'How about this time last year? Can you go back that far?' Because an idea was forming. Just a little niggle of a thought, standing on the horizon of her mind, waving its tiny arms determined not to be ignored. Well, it needn't worry, she was past the point of ignoring niggles. They only grew up to become loud insistent scolds.

'Yes. Of course.'

And a few taps later...

'There!' Helen cried. 'That's the mortgage! That's what it should be.' She was pointing to a figure less than half the amount of what had been going out of their joint account for… For how long? She had, she realised, no idea. The last five months at least.

'Yes,' the woman tapped away. 'Yes, it seems to be.'

Helen leaned back in her chair. 'So when did it change?'

'I'll find out.'

But she already knew. Or she could give a pretty close guess. Everything was slotting as neatly into place as the clicks on a Rubik's Cube.

'The first time I can see the increase is the eighteenth of November last year.'

Helen nodded. 'So how much has my husband re-mortgaged our house for?' She watched as a strange expression flowed across the woman's face, a mixture of surprise followed by astonishment, which was immediately shut down by something else. Sympathy? Probably. Wouldn't she herself, after all, feel sympathy for someone who'd been docile enough to get into this position?

The women looked at her screen and then back to Helen and then back at her screen. 'The mortgage wasn't in your joint name?' she said, unable to meet Helen's eye.

Chin set, head high, Helen shook her head. Like bubbles escaping a bottle, she could see the next question already forming on this smart young woman's lips. The question that would never be asked. *Why?*

And the answer, of course, that would never be offered, was because she had allowed it. That's why.

The woman picked up her pen and tapped it against

her lip. 'I can't access that information she said, but –' and she glanced at Helen – 'I can use our mortgage calculator if you like? It might give you a rough idea.'

Helen smiled. 'Yes, please.' But she had the feeling that her own internal calculator would be more accurate. The amount Lawrence had taken would be in the region of a hundred thousand pounds. As the woman tapped at her keyboard, Helen glanced up at the clock and looked away again without registering what the time was. A hundred-thousand-pound re-mortgage. A loan, using *their* biggest asset as collateral because on paper it was only *his* biggest asset. Without even mentioning it to her? Her intestines shredded to confetti. So did her mind. Like looking through a kaleidoscope, she couldn't get two single ideas to hook together. So as the woman tapped, she began to lay it down brick by brick, measuring out each thought with her fingers on the table. One finger: their joint account had barely four hundred pounds in it. Two fingers: this was because the mortgage repayments had doubled. Three fingers: this was something she'd known nothing about. Four fingers... So where did that leave her now? And why hadn't she known? Or more to the point, why hadn't he told her? Or even more to the point, why *why why!* hadn't she made it her business to know!

'It could be as much as—'

'A hundred thousand,' Helen finished.

The woman nodded. 'If it's been a fairly short-term loan. Which given the age of...' She stopped talking and pressed her pen to her lips and looked at her screen. 'I have a friend,' she said, 'who once saw her house for sale in the paper.'

Helen looked up.

'She was a bit surprised.'

'Who?'

'My friend. She thought they owned it. But it turned out it was rented all along.'

Helen blinked. She felt like a Polo mint, punched out in the middle by the demands of a day which had barely past its eleventh hour.

The woman put her pen down and pressed her fingertip over the fallen lash. 'My friend's husband used to drive around in Porsches, BMWs, the lot. We all thought he owned them as well, but he was just picking them up and delivering them from A to B.' She shrugged, made a small turn and wiped the lash clear, letting it drop into the bin. 'I suppose,' she said, 'there's a lesson in there somewhere.'

'My husband's not into cars,' Helen said dully. She looked at the single lash in the otherwise clean bin. 'Are they fake? she asked.

'Extensions.'

'Right.'

The woman raised her hand and touched a finger to her lashes. 'They fix them to your own lashes.'

Helen nodded...

'Instead of mascara.'

... and kept nodding.

'So... Is there anything else I can help you with today?'

'Mountains,' she said.

'I'm sorry?'

'Mountains are my husband's thing. The thirty-three-thousand-foot-high, one-hundred-thousand-pound type of mountain.'

10

Oh, but she was good! So good that as she leaned back and opened the calendar app on her phone Caro allowed herself an imaginary pat on the back and a small smug thought: how was Matt ever going to manage without her?

Because anyone else on the team would have flunked this pitch.

Because if she was good, Emir was equally as good.

She should have known. The persona he wore, easy as a hat, was exactly the kind of exquisite display of ethics and personality, income and political affinity that could only be achieved by minute attention to detail. Everything about him – the sneakers, the iPhone case, the pause before he spoke – was calculated to the nth degree. He had about as much spontaneity as her Facebook feed. Twice, her pitch had wobbled dangerously, under the pressure of that microscopic attention to detail and had, in fact taken three times longer than she'd been expecting. Nervously she glanced at her phone. Danny was nearing the end of his second beer and Helen was due any minute.

'A week next Tuesday?' Emir said, glancing up from his open calendar app.

'Sounds good,' Caro answered. He was definitely one of the most astute investors she'd ever had to persuade, crossing every *t* and dotting every *i* of his Due Diligence. And if she hadn't been equally as assiduous with her own preparation, they would not now be discussing an initial position of two hundred thousand. (A little more than she had been aiming for, twice as much as Matt had guessed.) She looked across at him. He reminded her of herself – this young man, groomed to within an inch of his life, meticulously prepared. So much so that watching him on his phone, Caro experienced a moment of clarity. What could she tell him? What advice would she give him, for those moments in life that cannot be prepped in advance?

Suddenly, he lifted his face and smiled at her and in a moment of light, she saw just how young he was. Her shock shocked her. The office was full of a younger generation for heaven's sake. And even though neither Mel her secretary, nor Matt, had any living memory of Live Aid, even though for them 9/11 wasn't much more than a big news day, somehow the link had still been tangible . But this smiling boy-man? Emir? In that moment, it felt to Caro as if he'd fallen to earth from a whole other place, shiny and perfect and young enough to be alien. Thrown, she dipped her head to type in the appointment and to conceal an odd surge of feeling. How long could she continue doing this job? How long did she want to continue doing it? How on earth was she going to connect with a baby, who would be a generation even younger?

'Tuesday, Caro!' Danny turned, palm raised ready to high-five.

Caro braced herself, felt the sting of Danny's hand and looked up just in time to see Helen, appearing at the far end of the terrace.

'You'll never guess what that bastard's gone and done now!' Face flushed, hair flying, Helen was already halfway across the terrace, passing a waiter, who looked up from the glasses he was polishing in mild astonishment.

Danny turned, 'This sounds like her!' He threw his head back and laughed.

Caro stood.

'No, don't get up!' Helen said and lunged forward, wrapping her arms tight around Caro's neck. 'You are not going to believe this!' She tugged her top back down over the slab of still tanned midriff that was on show. 'I'm not even sure I believe it myself! I was—' Suddenly she stopped talking and looked at Caro's stomach. 'How are you?' And without waiting for an answer flung her handbag behind her. It landed on Danny's lap. 'Everything alright? I thought you were in a meeting.'

'I am,' Caro said pointedly. She indicated the settee behind where Helen stood. '*This* is Danny and Emir.'

'Oh!' Buttons of pink appeared on Helen's cheeks. 'I didn't see you.'

'Camouflaged,' Danny winked and stretched his hand up to the tall upright terrace of vine which backed the sofa.

'Want your handbag back?' Smiling, he handed the bag to Helen, whose buttons of embarrassment had bloomed to dinner plates.

'We were just finishing,' Caro said, sitting down. And she squeezed her eyebrows together and shook her head in a tiny *no one knows – don't mention it* kind of way.

Helen fell into the seat next to Danny. 'Thanks,' she said, retrieving her handbag. Then glancing at Caro made a *don't worry, understood* face back.

In response, Caro pressed her lips together. Helen was flushed and breathless and at least, she suspected, one alcoholic drink down.

'Danny Abbott,' Danny offered.

'Emir,' Emir said.

'Helen Winters,' Helen answered. She raised a conciliatory hand to Emir. 'Sorry if I'm interrupting.'

'Helen!' Danny laughed as he turned his palms to the sky. 'You're hurting my feelings here. Don't you remember me? You're the reason I just splashed out fifty thousand on a yacht. Mind...' He pointed a finger at her. 'I don't want you capsizing this one any time soon.'

Helen frowned.

'You spoke to Danny in Cyprus,' Caro said tightly.

'I did?' A tide of crimson rose up her neck. 'Oh I did, didn't I?'

'Yes, you did!' Again Danny threw his head back and laughed. 'And I hadn't been spoken to like that since... well a long time. Anyway.' He leaned forward, his eyes dancing. 'I'm delighted to meet you at last. What's your tipple?'

138

Helen's blush ebbed away. 'I don't want to interrupt anything…'

'You're not!' Danny answered. 'We're good, aren't we?' And he looked first to Emir, who nodded, and then to Caro.

'Are you sure?'

'It's OK. We're finished,' Caro said, and her voice was a degree sharper than she had intended.

'OK.' Pushing her hair back from her face, Helen shrugged. 'Well, after the morning I've had, I think a large G&T is called for.'

Caro flinched. A large G&T type of lunch wasn't what today was about. Helen knew that.

'Caro?' Danny asked.

Tight lipped, Caro shook her head. 'I'll stick with this,' she said, indicating her lime and soda.

'Emir?'

Emir too declined.

'That's the trouble with the younger generation,' Danny laughed. 'They're far too sensible. I'll join you, Helen. That's if we're not interrupting anything by hanging around a little?' He looked at Caro.

She shrugged. 'Not at all.' Hanging around? Danny Abbot meetings were passing trains. She got to spout as much information as she needed before he steamed on past to another destination. Now he was hanging around? Like a teenager at the chip shop?

Danny leaned forward and with both palms on the glass coffee table he patted out a drumroll. 'Now,' he said, grinning. 'Why don't you tell us all about what that bastard has gone and done now!'

And wearily Caro leaned back. It had been like this from the very beginning: whenever Helen appeared, Caro became invisible. She felt a little dull inside. As if someone had come along and removed the sunshine from this perfect afternoon that she had been looking forward to for so long.

With the help of a G & T served in a glass large enough to house a small fish, Helen's encounter at the bank spilled forth. Even as she told it, she didn't believe it. It sounded so cliché, something that had happened a million times before, to a million other people. But not her. That kind of thing would never happen to her. Still, she slurped on her straw (which was paper and kept sticking to her lipstick) and pressed on, faithfully relaying the ridiculous conversation with the bank clerk almost word for word. 'Mountains,' she finished on. 'That's his thing.'

Danny's mouth had dropped open.

Emir, silently handsome as a Greek statue, sipped his expensive water.

And Caro leaned back, her expression inscrutable.

'So that,' Helen said as she threw the straw on the table and swallowed the last icy sludge in her goldfish bowl, 'is that.' She turned to Caro. 'I didn't know what to do with myself. I grabbed a can of one of these from M&S and hopped on the train.'

'Excellent idea,' Danny said, 'in the circumstances.'

'You think so?' Helen held up her empty glass and pretended to study it. 'Whatever happened to highball glasses?' she said. She felt light. Light as the bubbles in the tonic, and Caro's face was odd. What must she think of her?

'Let me get this right.' Emir clasped his hands together. 'You didn't know about this re-mortgage?'

Head shaking, she lowered her glass.

'Wait a minute.' Danny waved his hand. 'Why didn't you have to sign?'

Helen opened her mouth to answer, but before she could say anything Danny had lowered his chin.

'*Hel-e-n*,' he drawled. 'No, no, no. Don't tell me your name isn't on the paperwork?'

She didn't answer.

'Don't tell me this, Helen.'

'My name isn't on the paperwork,' she said finally.

There was a short, odd pause and then Emir said, 'Did you know that?' And his eyes were dark pools of astonishment.

Helen looked back at him. He was so handsome, this young man, so together and so cool... 'Yes,' she shrugged, every last shred of dignity shredded. 'I knew that.'

Beside her Caro had lifted her chin and closed her eyes and was now shaking her head in the kind of tiny imperceptible movements not meant to be seen, but which were as visible as clouds to Helen. She looked down at her empty glass.

And all around the table astonishment fizzed like an electric current.

Or was that just Helen? She didn't know. All she knew was that sitting there, on a chic city terrace surrounded by all the financially astute, fiscally responsible people of the world, she had never felt more stupid in her whole life. If the floor had opened up, she would have gladly slithered down into a black hole of mortification. A warmth swelled behind her eyes. This was her fault. That's what they were all thinking. Caro definitely. And they were right. Her longstanding acquiescence in all things financial had been more complete than she'd ever admitted – to anyone. Lawrence earned it, she spent it, and that had been the roomy and comfortable shape of their finances. *She thinks you have it easy,* Kay had once told her about Caro. Well, there wasn't anything easy about what she was feeling right now. Exposed. Humiliated. Ashamed. And what exactly had she done to deserve that? Trust her husband? The buttons of pink rose again in her cheeks, only this time they tingled with defiance, even anger, and from the corner of her eye she saw Danny nod at her glass. She nodded back. Fuck it. From the corner of her other eye, she saw Caro bristle. She ignored it.

Danny turned for a waiter.

'Can we get a menu as well, Danny?' Caro called, a right-angled edge to her voice. 'Let's eat?' she added, addressing the question to Helen.

Helen shrugged. 'I'm not that hungry.'

'You need to eat.'

'OK,' she breathed, and tipped her head back and breathed again. What she needed, what she really needed to do, was open up the steam valve in her chest with another large G&T, not stuff it down with an overpriced posh burger and chips. Especially considering the grave state of her bank balance.

A waiter approached trailing a cloud of pungent aftershave.

Numbly Helen took a menu. She had about as much

interest in eating as she did in Lawrence's heart-rate monitors that *always* littered the kitchen dresser. Added together, over the years, how much had they cost? 'I'm really not...' But she was saved from any further feeble explanation by another waiter arriving with refills for her and Danny, and a bowl of crisps for the table. She slapped the menu closed and picked up her refill.

'You're not going to order, Helen?' Caro asked without looking up from her own menu.

Helen shook her head. Why was it that Caro could always make her feel like a child?

'Do you think he did it to fund the Everest thing?' Glass in one hand, Danny had spread his elbows across the back of the sofa. He looked as if he'd settled in for the afternoon, which was exactly what Helen felt like doing, which was a problem given that they were due to meet Kay in the baby department of Selfridges in just over an hour. Baby department! How was she going to get through the afternoon? She nodded at Danny.

'I know he did,' she said flatly.

'How do you know?' It was Caro. Her first words on the matter.

Helen looked at her. 'Well, I don't know a hundred per cent, but where else has it gone?'

'I thought you said he sold some stock.'

'That's what he told me.'

Caro nodded. Her lips were a thin line.

'That's about the cost,' Danny said. 'I had a mate do it three years ago. Cost him the best part of eighty grand back then.'

'Exactly.' Helen eased back herself. She didn't want to encourage Danny… She shouldn't encourage him, but with the freshness of the first sips of her new drink she could feel muscles relax that hadn't relaxed in weeks, and it felt good. All she wanted was to keep that feeling going. Never mind that beside her, in a complete reversal of sensation, she was aware of Caro closing up like a clam. Well, there would be time for all that Caro had to say on the matter after. But right now, right here, the spotlight of Danny's attention was a warm and comfortable place.

'Man, that's impressive though.' Emir shook his head. 'Everest.' He'd stretched his arms forward, nursing the glass in his hands.

Impressive? Helen looked at him. Emir was square jawed, with a rack of visible abdominal muscle under a top that masqueraded as a casual t-shirt, but was really an exquisitely styled, cost-enough-for-a-lifetime item of clothing. His hair had been shaved at the sides in a ruthlessly clean line, and his nails showed perfect cream half-moons. In fact, the level of personal grooming he displayed required the kind of sustained sense of self-absorption Helen knew she hadn't possessed since she was seventeen. That season of her life when, locked in her bedroom, plucking her eyebrows and shade-testing lip-gloss to the backdrop of Stevie Nicks' *Edge of Seventeen*, she could let a whole day slip by. So fast forward a few decades, years in which every hair follicle in her body had been allowed to run wild and nail-files were rusted in place on the edge of the bathtub, and, compared to this magnificent young man, what was she but a middle-aged, fluffy, flabby, flushed mess?

On her third G&T, while he calibrated his sips of water to exact hydration requirements. *Impressive,* he thought. And who was she to disagree with that? She took another slug. Resentment bubbling. A mother, that's who she was. A mother who had kept the fort safe and the knickers clean while her husband, every inch as disciplined as Emir, had re-mortgaged the house and buggered off to climb a mountain. Which was criminal and selfish and not impressive at all. She reached forward and took the largest crisp in the bowl, stuffing it sideways into her mouth. 'That,' she crunched, 'isn't really the point, Emir. The point is, what am I going to do now? He's got his *I Climbed the Highest Mountain in the World* certificate, but what have I got? How's he going to buy me out when he's mortgaged up to his eyeballs? And how am I, on a part-time doctor's receptionist wage, going to be able to buy my own place?'

Danny turned to her. 'You're a doctor's receptionist?'

'I am,' she said and took another three crisps.

Caro snapped her menu shut.

'Oh, it all makes sense now!' Danny laughed. 'Remember Caro? How she put me in my place?'

'I do.' Caro was on her feet. 'I'm just going to order some food,' she said and looked meaningfully at Helen.

'OK.' Helen took another crisp and then another. 'I'll just snack a bit,' she said, turning away from Caro. Yes it was Caro's day, yes, they were here to look at prams and cots and... *good grief!* Were they really going to do that! The three of them, one hundred and fifty-one years between them, browsing Moses baskets, like dewy-eyed newly-weds!

'You should eat something, Helen,' Caro muttered.

'I've lost my appetite,' she muttered back and sucked at her paper straw.

'My mum was a doctor's receptionist,' Emir smiled. 'She hated it. Couldn't wait to quit. She said the patients were too rude.'

Surprised, Helen looked at him. She couldn't have found a single way to connect this specimen of humanity to her world, and here he was doing it for her. Unpicking the straw from her lips, she said, 'Well your mum's right, Emir. They can be rude bastards.'

Danny laughed. 'Don't mince your words, Helen.'

'I don't mince anything these days, Danny,' Helen slurped. She looked at Emir. 'Is that why your mum quit?'

'No.' Emir leaned back and crossed one leg over the other so his thighs made a wide denim triangle. He scratched his chin. 'She stopped because I bought her a flat in Malaga. For fifteen years, she worked two jobs to raise me and my sister. My dad bailed when I was two. Bought a one-way ticket back to Dominica along with all her savings.' He gave Helen a rueful smile. 'I get it,' he said. 'She trusted him. She didn't do anything wrong either.'

Salt on her tongue, Helen lowered the crisp she'd been about to eat. She wanted to cry.

Sensing this, Danny tilted his head at Emir and said gently, 'Self-made millionaire here, Helen. And he's right. You didn't do anything wrong.'

Caro came back, slipping into her seat. 'I've ordered,' she said but no one seemed to hear.

'Millionaire!' Helen whispered, caught in a gin-befuddled mix of astonishment and self-pity. 'What do you do?'

'I trade. Markets. Short-term stuff mostly.' Emir smiled.

'*Financial* markets,' Caro added.

Helen eased back in her seat. Now she really did want to cry. This lovely young man, buying his mum a flat as soon as he could.

'He can turn a fiver into five hundred in twenty-four hours,' Danny laughed.

'No!' Helen looked around the table. 'Really?'

'It can be done,' Caro said stiffly. 'Sometimes.'

Helen raised her glass. 'I think I need your number,' she said.

'It takes a lot of skill, Helen,' Caro said lightly. 'Emir's been doing this for a long time.'

And the lightness of Caro's voice was like a little whip, startling her back to life. Emir couldn't be more than a day over twenty-five-ish. And he was a millionaire? Buying property for his mother? She'd passed the train journey up engulfed in a maelstrom of emotion. How stupid she'd been! How blind! And until this moment not a single patch of clear or positive thought had emerged, an idea that might carry her forward and out of the storm. She leaned forward and slapped her glass on the table. 'I have a savings account my grandmother started for me when I was eleven.'

Danny was laughing.

Undeterred, she grabbed her handbag. What did it matter? She had nothing to lose, no dignity left to salvage. 'Last time I checked there was about three thousand. I have to try and do something. It's either that, or staying where I am. In the house, I mean, with Lawrence – and with Libby

147

now—' Abruptly she stopped talking. Pregnancies, she remembered, were not to be discussed here and now. From out of her handbag she pulled a packet of tissues and a foil sleeve of Ibuprofen, the top of an eyeliner pencil and a copy of *The Big Issue*.

'Three K will get you started,' Emir nodded.

Helen leaned back and pulled out the sleeve of a pop-up umbrella.

'You can lose money, Helen,' Caro said. 'Very easily, if you don't know what you're doing.'

Defiantly, Helen looked at her. 'Well, it's time I learnt, don't you think?' And finally she pulled out her phone.

'I can give you some tips.' Emir too had his phone out. 'What's your number?'

'Me too,' Danny held up his phone.

Helen shook her head and smiling, turned to Caro. 'Can you believe this?' she said. 'Me? Interested in investing?'

But the smile Caro managed barely reached her lips.

11

'So,' Helen said through a mouth stuffed with pizza, 'that's more than enough of my problems. We need to know about the meeting, Kay. What happened?'

'Amanda Woods?' Kay pushed her plate aside and picked up her coffee. Helen was more than tipsy and less than drunk. And her slurred-at-the-edges bank story was astonishing and outrageous and inconvenient. Kay's allegiance was, once again, split. Across the table Caro had almost frozen with impatience. She already knew the bank story and they shouldn't be here now, watching Helen eat herself sober. The day had been hijacked. And it wasn't just Helen, because, with the motorcycle built, Alex had taken it for a test drive early that morning and crashed it. Not badly. Just the tiniest of scrapes, and Shook had been driving behind to sort him out. But it was enough for Kay's blood pressure to hit the roof and for her to need to see her son safely back home before she dared leave the house, which had resulted in her missing the riverside lunch. Not that she minded. If she were about to lose her job, expensive lunches would be the first thing to go. And even though that wasn't a hardship, even though she'd always preferred pizza to pretentious pasta, Thursday's school meeting reverberated loud as an electric drill in her head. She'd been shaken. So much so that she'd called her ex-husband, Martin. Divorce had separated them only as man and wife. As friends, Kay knew, they would never be estranged, and talking to him she'd felt a sad and questioning nostalgia resurface, as it sometimes did. What would have happened to their marriage, if Alex hadn't been how he was? (The idea was destined to remain embryonic. Alex was Alex, and her love for him simply couldn't comprehend any variation.) Martin had been cheery, brushing off the training session as a box-ticking exercise that she shouldn't be in the slightest bit worried about. But she was worried. More than she wanted to admit. What she had been accused of was no less than racism. And because she was pragmatic to the bone, and notwithstanding the improvement in the relationship with Zac, Amanda Woods' words had re-started her own internal enquiry. *Was* she? *Had* she been biased? Past episodes of Zac's behaviour replayed again and again. Followed by her response. Followed by a relentless self-interrogation. Had she behaved as she would have with any other pupil? It was an exhausting process that she hadn't been able to switch off. So now, the last thing in the world she felt like doing, the *very* last thing, was traipsing around looking at prams and cots.

Caro turned to her. 'How did it go?' she asked.

'Oh... you know.' Kay shrugged. She swallowed a

mouthful of coffee and put the cup down. 'The mother has asked for a paper to be re-marked, and then... I think it will be OK.'

'How do you feel about that?' Caro asked.

How did she feel? Humiliated. Furious. Embarrassed.

'What a cow,' Helen whispered, mopping her mouth with her napkin. 'Why are people such bastards to each other?' And she stood up, her chair scraping loudly. 'I'm going to get another coffee. Anyone else?'

Kay shook her head. Watching Helen's unsteady gait as she walked across to the counter, she turned to Caro. 'Why don't we get started?' she said. 'Helen can join us when she's finished.' She nodded at the slice of pizza left on Helen's plate. Caro might explode if she was forced to wait any longer, Helen needed more starch to sober up and, until she was more sure of herself, until she'd finished her self-imposed investigation, she wasn't ready to share what was really on her mind.

'Good idea,' Caro answered briskly.

They were out of the restaurant and in the baby department with minutes.

'So?' Stopping at the side of a large, expensively dressed and exquisitely detailed cot, Caro trailed her fingers along the polished rail. 'What *was* she like? This Amanda Woods? I'm curious.'

Kay frowned. 'Oh, you know,' she sighed. 'Well groomed. Slim. Exactly as we guessed.'

'And did the scarf work?'

'I think so,' Kay smiled. Nothing had worked. She

151

reached across the cot and flipped the price tag over. 'Bloody hell, Caro!' she gasped. 'I didn't pay that for my bed!'

Caro slipped her glasses on, leaned across to read the tag and without comment let it slip and walked around to the headboard. 'What happened?' she said, tapping the rail with her fingertips. 'I mean what *really* happened, Kay?'

'I said—'

'Kay,' Caro interrupted. 'Helen's the one in shock. Not me. I'm sober, remember? And I've known you long enough to know—'

'I have to go to unconscious bias training.'

From over the top of her glasses, Caro looked at her.

'You're not surprised?' And now that it was out, now that she'd said those words out loud, she understood what had been holding her back. Shame. The shame of the accusation. The shame of the possibility of it being true. She felt very cold and very sad and very vulnerable.

Caro was shaking her head. 'It's a thing nowadays, Kay. Everyone does it. Whatever you do, don't take it personally.' She paused. 'You're not, are you?'

'I don't think so.'

'Really?'

'Oh, who am I kidding!' she cried. 'I'm taking it very personally, Caro. How can I not? What if it's true?'

And to her surprise, Caro laughed.

'Caro!' All around Kay's tired eyes, fine lines of worry rose and settled like shifting lines of sand. 'If there's a part of me that's been holding that boy back because…' She shook her head, her voice dropping to a whisper. 'Because of the colour of his skin… It's devastating. *I* would be devastated.'

And again, Caro laughed. 'Kay, you married a man who's a quarter Nigerian.'

'Please,' Kay said softly. 'Whatever you do, don't laugh.'

And instantly, Caro stopped. 'Don't you see?' she said. 'You're the only person I know who would do this. Only you would be prepared to string yourself up like this.'

'Is that what I'm doing?' Kay said, knowing of course that was exactly what she was doing.

'Kay, I can't seriously entertain the idea that you haven't done your absolute best for any of the kids you teach.' Caro smiled. 'And I think that you think the same.'

Kay didn't answer.

'When is it? The training?

'I'm not sure. Maybe not until next term.

'Right.' Caro smiled again. 'So, for now, put it to the back of your mind. Please? Cyprus did you a lot of good. You got a lot sorted, didn't you, with Alex and your mum?'

She nodded.

'So don't slip backwards. Don't lose all of that, Kay, based upon something that someone else might or might not believe of you.'

'I—'

Caro reached across the cot and grabbed her hand. 'Kay,' she said urgently. 'Do you think I'd be standing here now, if I'd given any weight to what everyone else was saying about me?'

Kay's smile was weak. She turned to look along the row of cots. It was still quite unbelievable that Caro was expecting a baby. That she had in fact carved herself a solid future from thin air. And even though, like Helen, she was unable to decide what she thought about it (and perhaps never would), the commitment Caro possessed, in living her life, on her terms, was undeniable and admirable. It took a degree of self-belief, Kay knew, she should cherish a little better herself. Because she *was* a good teacher. An excellent teacher. The training would show up what it showed up and she would not be cowed. 'I'm sure,' she murmured, fingertips trailing the deliciously smooth wood, 'that I have Alex's old cot in the attic somewhere.'

'Do you think, after, she'll be satisfied?' Caro had her palm flat on the headboard, as if she were divining its quality. 'The mother?'

'I hope so.' Kay shrugged. 'Then again I thought she'd be satisfied by asking for her son to be moved to a different class, even though it will probably make him miserable and embarrassed.'

With a sudden movement, Caro broke free of her cot-spell. Turning to Kay, she said, 'And can't she see that?'

'No.' Kay frowned. 'I really don't think she can, Caro. Some parents don't,' she added. 'Some parents just aren't capable of understanding that their kids are separate entities, that…' And she trailed off because Caro, she could see, had stopped listening and was now staring at a point halfway across the cot, her face busy with emotion. 'Caro?'

'Do you think I'll be like that?' It wasn't more than a whisper.

A whisper that it took Kay long moments to respond to. 'No,' she began. 'No, Caro I—'

'But you'd tell me? Wouldn't you?' Caro pressed. 'If I

started behaving like... If I was making his... or her... if I was making my child unhappy?'

Kay looked at her. Was it just Thursday that she was sat in Nick's office, comparing Amanda Woods to Caro? Right now, they couldn't be further away from each other. She reached across and put her hand on top of Caro's. 'Of course I would. You're going to be a wonderful mum.'

'Am I?'

'Yes. You are.' Again, she frowned. Her thoughts were too slow, spinning in the tailwind of this unexpected moment. 'Yes,' she said again and because she simply couldn't manage anything more, she squeezed Caro's hand. She didn't know if Caro was going to make a good, bad or indifferent parent. Who did? The journey, for everyone, was almost impossible to predict. What she did know was that in all the years of their friendship, she'd never heard Caro express such sincere doubt.

With trembling hands, Caro picked up the quilt from inside the cot. Her forefinger following a line of delicate embroidery, she whispered, 'I just don't want to get it wrong.'

Mesmerised, Kay watched Caro's shaky hands as they carefully placed the quilt back in the cot. 'Caro,' she said with quiet command. Because the plinth of self-belief upon which her friend had built her life was cracking apart in front of Kay's eyes. Caro, it was clear, needed a safety net – her tall, broad-shouldered, expensively clad friend needed something to fall back upon. Who else but a friend? 'You're about to enter a foreign world,' she began.

'I know—'

'No.' Kay smiled. She shook her head, leaning her elbows forward on the cot rail. 'This is something you *don't* *k*now. And no matter how well you prepare, or think you've prepared, you will sometimes get it wrong. There's nothing you can do to avoid that.' She let her head drop to one side. 'Do you remember that story Helen used to tell? About driving Jack to nursery?'

Caro frowned.

'You should do. We've both heard it loads of times.'

'I do remember.'

'Good, so what do you remember?'

'About what happened?'

'Yes.'

'That Jack wouldn't get dressed? That in the end she put him in the car half naked and told him that's how he'd go to school?'

'Nothing else?'

Caro shook her head.

'Nothing at all?'

Again, Caro shook her head. Her eyes went glassy. 'What am I missing?' she said. 'I'm missing something, aren't I?'

Kay looked at her. Every time Helen had told them this story it had squeezed Kay's heart and left it limp as an old dishrag. Not the story itself, Helen's reaction. This was what Caro was missing.

'Tell me, Kay. *Please.*' Caro's whisper had an echo of panic to it.

And smiling back at her friend, Kay wasn't at all surprised by Caro's bewilderment. To her, the point of

Helen's story had always been clear as the nose on her face, but that was because hearing it had always reminded her of her own ghosts, her own past failures in the never-ending and never-complete role that was motherhood. It was different for Caro, she hadn't yet made any ghosts to come back and haunt her. With a rueful smile, she took Caro's hand again. 'What I remember,' she said, 'is the part where Helen cries. She starts to cry, her heart breaks when she tries to describe how Jack was crying. *Always.*'

Caro closed her eyes.

'You're going to get it wrong, Caro. We all do. And when you do it will haunt you, like that story haunts Helen. There are no guarantees but… that's life. You'll be fine and you'll be a wonderful mother.'

'Will I?'

'I wouldn't have asked you to be Alex's godmother if I had any doubts.'

'That's not—'

'It is the same,' Kay finished.

Caro took a tissue out of her bag, blew her nose and dabbed at the flakes of mascara under her eyes. 'I'm scared,' she whispered unfolding the tissue and folding it again. 'I think I'm actually scared.'

'I know,' Kay whispered back. Poor Caro. She had everything, and nothing. And the kind of support she was going to need was the kind that money can't buy. She leaned her weight further forward, across the side rail of the cot. 'I'll be here,' she said. 'When you need me, I'll be—' And the rail dropped, shooting Kay face first onto the little embroidered quilt. 'Bloody hell,' she muffled through a wadding of cotton.

Caro stared, put a belated hand out to help and then seeing Kay straighten up, threw her head back and laughed. 'Ouch!' Her hand went to the small of her back.

'You OK?' Kay said, straightening out the quilt.

'Muscle twinge. From laughing.' Caro pulled the rail back up again, her head bent as she tried and failed to fix it into place.

'And that,' Kay laughed, 'is something else you're going to get wrong. Again and again.'

'It should just slot in I think. Here.' She tried again.

'Car seats, stair gates, cupboard locks, prams, rain covers... Shall I continue?' Kay was still laughing.

'No.' Caro smoothed her blouse down. 'But thank you,' she whispered. 'I mean it.'

Kay shrugged. 'You will be fine, Caro. I'm going to be here and so is Helen.'

Nodding, Caro stared across the shop floor. 'She had two G&Ts at lunch. Another on the train.'

Kay followed Caro's gaze. 'I think, under the circumstances, I might have done the same.'

'Me too.'

Kay's mouth turned up in a discreet lopsided smile. Was Caro already softening?

'Well.' Caro took her handbag. With her other hand she held her back. 'I suppose I'll get used to the mechanism.'

'Are you going to buy this?'

'It's lovely, and I'm only going to do this once.'

'That's true.' Kay glanced at the others. This was indeed the nicest and the biggest and by far the most expensive and Caro could afford it. And if she had her time over again with Alex, perhaps she'd do the same. The baby years were butterfly brief, why not indulge every last thing about them? She turned back to Caro. 'I think you should,' she declared. 'It's beautiful and—'

'Not too early?'

'It is a little,' she said and watched as a shadow crossed Caro's face. 'Then again, it can take quite a while before it's delivered.'

'It can, can't it?' The shadow lifted.

'So why don't you just go and have a chat?'

'Good idea…' Caro turned to look across at the cash desk. 'Just a chat. That's all.'

'Go on then.'

'This is so silly. I'm nervous.'

'*Go.*'

Caro nodded and set off, all bubbling excitement and shy doubt, like a child on the first day of school. Helen, Kay thought, should see this. And she took out her phone.

Finished?

On my way down.

Good. Caro is ordering a cot! It's beautiful!

Turning away she slipped her phone back and meandered towards where a young couple stood in front of a changing table. The woman, heavily pregnant, was opening drawers, turning over a ribbon-threaded basket. Kay smiled. Three weeks in, she wanted to say, and you'll be using any old towel, slung over a bed, or a kitchen table or just the carpet. As the woman bent to put the basket back, the man took it from her, his hand protectively placed on her back. Kay moved on. This place, this whole room, was a place of dreams, and who was she to trample all over them? Why not buy the most expensive cot in the room, why not buy every last ribbon-threaded basket and every last teddy-bear-embroidered towel to wrap around your precious child! Why not? Soon enough they'd be grown and out of the door, falling off motorbikes and getting themselves pregnant and there was nothing – *nothing* – in this room, nothing in the world, to help then.

Slapped into reality by her own thoughts, she stopped walking and turned. She was standing in front of a baby swing that someone, moments before, had obviously set in motion. Kay watched as the tiny swing creaked back and forth, playing a tinny tune. It took her less than half a moment before she'd recognised it.

Lullaby and goodnight, thy mother's delight, bright angels around, my darling shall guard…

A mangled electronic version, but still the lullaby her mother had once sung to her, and she in turn had sung to Alex. Warm tears sprang, too fast, too many to stand a chance of blinking back.

'Kay!'

With a clumsy arm at her face, she turned.

From across the shop floor, Caro called, 'They're just going to find out about delivery times!'

'OK.'

'I'm going to take a look at the rockers.' Caro pointed to the row of chairs further along the room.

Kay nodded, swallowing back the grief in her throat. Baby years, intense as a blizzard, as transient as the flakes themselves. Alex grown and on the verge of leaving. Her own mother unable to recognise her. So where did that leave Kay? Neither a mother. Nor a daughter either. Life was terribly cruel sometimes.

She leaned forward and switched the swing off. Just as the lullaby died away, Helen appeared, cheeks full of colour, a hand on her stomach. 'I ate so fast,' she gasped, 'I've got wind at both ends.' She put a hand to her mouth and burped. 'Where's Caro?'

Kay nodded across to the rocking chairs. 'She's waiting to hear about delivery times for a cot.'

'She's already bought one?'

'Maybe not bought. Getting organised though,' Kay said. 'You know what she's like. This baby will want for nothing.'

'Except a father,' Helen said, beat perfect, like a drum-roll at the end of a gag. 'Sorry,' she said. 'But it's true.'

'So is evolution, Helen.' Kay's return riff was equally swift. Still, she wasn't in the mood for this discussion. 'It's a tough one. You'll have to learn to live with it.'

'I am. I am…' Helen's answer was half-hearted. The real truth was that she had no energy left to expend on the subject. And it was, as Kay had so adroitly put it, a done deal. With an air of dejection, coloured by the after effects of gin, she looked down at the circle of child-sized furniture. Tiny tables and tiny chairs, stools and desks and matching plates, bowls, spoons and forks. Perfect little kitchens. 'I think I've accepted it more than Libby's situation actually,' and she took a breath deep enough to fill the sails of a galleon. It didn't work; she was, she felt, still sinking.

'Are you OK? You look odd.'

'Do I?' Helen shook her head. 'I just need to sit down.'
And without thinking she dumped her handbag on the
nearest tiny table and sat down on the nearest tiny stool.
Chin in hands, elbows on knees, she nodded at the nearest
perfect kitchen. 'Libby had one of those,' she said sadly.

'I remember.'

'Not that it did her any good. She couldn't find her way
around a life-sized kitchen now even if her life depended
upon it. God knows how she's going to cope, Kay.'

'You've had a shit day, Goldilocks.'

'I have, Mummy Bear.' Helen laughed. 'How did her
story end? Death by housework?'

'Get up,' Kay scolded, but she was still smiling. 'You'll
break it.'

Helen shuffled her bottom across the stool. 'It's pretty
sturdy,' she said. 'Here.' And she reached out and pulled a
chair for Kay. 'Sit down.'

'No. I'll definitely break it.'

'You definitely won't! Actually, I think you've lost
weight.' Helen put her head to one side. Kay did look
slimmer. The holiday had done her so much good. 'Are you
dieting?'

'Stress,' Kay said, and inched her way onto the stool.
'Best diet in the world.'

'Now, that *is* true.' Helen picked up a child-sized fork
and turned it over. 'Did you get all this for Alex?'

'Not me.' Kay picked up the matching spoon. 'Martin's
parents did though. They bought a Peter Rabbit set. I've
still got it somewhere. Never used.'

'No?'

'No. Alex point blank refused. He had to have this old fish fork I'd had forever. I'm sure Martin's parents thought it was my doing.'

'Oh, Kay.' There were a million different ways in which Kay's experience of motherhood differed from her own. A myriad more difficult and sadder episodes, and if they had another fifty years she guessed she'd never hear all of them. That was Kay. She kept it to herself, let it slip now and then (like now) and got on with it. Helen's eyes smarted. What did she do when shit hit her fan? Get drunk and spill it out to any passing stranger. She felt Kay's hand on hers. 'Is the school thing really going to be alright? You'd say, wouldn't you?'

'I'll say,' Kay smiled. 'If and when the time comes, but right now, you have enough going on.'

Helen shook her head. And although she suspected that Kay wasn't telling her the whole story, she didn't have the storage space to process any more information. Lawrence's deception sat like a grand piano in her head, plonking out base notes that boomed and echoed and...

'How is Libby?' Kay said gently. 'I wanted to ask earlier, but... you know, with everything else.'

'All my other news you mean? Libby's fine. Blooming as they say.' And this too was true. In the ten days since Libby had been home, she had blossomed. Fed and watered, back in her own bed, looked after and mothered, the soon-to-be-mother had grown beautiful and more pregnant, it seemed to Helen, by the minute. As if, once the dread of letting the news out had passed, her baby had stretched itself out and relaxed. September, Libby had said. But beginning of August, the obstetrician had confirmed. So a couple of weeks then. A couple of weeks before she became a grandmother. 'Lawrence,' she said bluntly, 'has suggested I give up my job.'

'What?'

'Last night. Libby was talking about taking a masters'.'

'What did you say?' Kay turned, her eyes wide.

'I said no, Kay.' Helen turned her hands over and looked at them. 'Do you think that's selfish?'

For a moment Kay was silent. Then slowly she looked up, and across at Caro. 'No,' she said. 'But I think it's very hard to put yourself first.'

'Sometimes,' Helen whispered, and she too was now looking across at Caro. 'And I'm ashamed to say this, Kay, but sometimes I used to think Caro was the most selfish person I knew. She always put herself first and I couldn't understand how she did it. Until now. Now, I get it.'

'Caro has lived and worked in a man's world for a long time,' Kay said, her voice flat. 'They're much better at it.'

'Why is that? It's true, but why?'

'Oh, Helen.' Kay sighed. 'You know why. It's biology. Someone *always* has to take care of the baby. That's just the way it is. And after that I think it becomes a habit.'

'Except this time, it's not my baby.'

'Another truth, Helen. This time it's not your baby.'

And together they sat, two middle-aged Goldilocks looking across to the rows of rocking chairs and gliders, where Caro sat, one hand on her stomach, chin tipped back to the ceiling.

'So… What are you going to do?'

'I'm not going to give up work, that much I know.' As Helen stretched her legs out her knees popped.

'Ouch!' Kay winced.

'Oh, that's nothing.' Helen smoothed her hands over her jeans. 'Since HRT I can actually walk across the floor in the mornings without sounding like a shipwreck. I really think you should go to the doctor, Kay.'

'I will, when everything has settled down, I will.'

'Good.' Helen took her handbag. 'A hundred bloody grand,' she muttered. 'I still can't believe it.' She stared down at her legs. Sitting on her tiny chair, Helen felt tiny herself and everything that she was facing that would have to be faced felt huge. How was Lawrence going to be able to buy her out now? And if she had to stay, how was she going to do that? And Libby? Where on earth were Libby and the baby going to live? And should she just stay, to keep everyone happy? To keep it simple? She ran her palms along her shins and let out an enormous sigh. Far bigger than the sighs her mother used to make. 'I don't even know where to start,' she said, hopelessly.

In response, Kay lifted her hand to Helen's back and rubbed it in a small circle. 'You'll find somewhere.'

'Will I?'

'Yes, because you have to.' She nodded to Caro. 'We should go over.'

Her knees creaked and her back felt stiff but eventually Helen got to her feet. 'Hangovers start earlier these days, don't they?'

Kay laughed. 'I wish I knew.'

Helen hitched her handbag up her shoulder, went

to follow and then stopped. 'Just give me a minute,' she said, half turning. 'I'm not going to let Caro down. I'm coming, but I just need a moment.' And she hurried back around the corner and out of sight, back to the department entrance and the stand of white-as-snow, perfectly formed baby-grows she'd passed on the way in. Riffling through, she found what she was looking for. Baby-grows with a lemon trim. A neutral colour. Holding the hanger at arm's length, Helen stood looking at the tiny empty baby shape a long moment. Then she took another one, exactly the same, folded them both over her arm and sneaked across to the nearest till to pay. One for Caro and one for Libby, because Kay was right. She had to start somewhere.

12

Caro pushed back against the cushion of the glider chair, trying to get herself comfortable. Across the floor she could see Kay and Helen squatting down on the baby stools like a couple of giant children. They were chatting away, just like little girls. She smiled and turned back to the rows of cots opposite. Of course, Kay's initial reaction was right. Nine hundred pounds for a cot that one baby would use, for one year, was an outrageous expense. But so was her hair every six weeks and her Botox every six months. And she could always sell the cot afterwards, or pass it on to charity. She stretched her foot out and slapped it down to stop the glider mechanism. The movement was making her feel dizzy and it was slightly reminiscent of the water-bed one of her exes had had. What was his name? She couldn't remember. A person to whom she had once attached so much importance and she couldn't even remember his name? She tapped her fingers lightly against the polished wood. So much about her life that had once seemed desperately important was sliding away, crumbling like a landslide under the force of Teutonic and welcome change. She was ready; it was coming and she was ready. She glanced up, saw Kay and spread her hands on the arms of the chair ready to stand. The cot, yes. This chair, no.

'Helen's just coming,' Kay called.

'Where's she gone?'

'Not sure, but she's on her way.'

'Fine.' Caro pinched her lips together, still visibly annoyed. Helen was probably in the toilet *again*. Hardly a surprise given the amount of alcohol she'd knocked back. Lawrence's behaviour was outrageous, but having spent the best part of twenty years watching the men she worked with dot every single *i* and cross every single *t* making sure their financial backs were covered, Caro wasn't even surprised by what had happened. She'd witnessed even the most (outwardly) devoted of husbands nesting secret eggs. It didn't shock her. It made her more thankful than ever that she'd never handed the financial reins of her life over to someone else. And surprised, all over again, that she had, for so long, envied Helen. Well, that was all over.

'Here she is!' Kay called.

And from nowhere, Helen appeared, holding out a small carrier bag.

'What's this?' Caro looked at Kay.

'Don't ask me,' she said.

'It's just a tiny, tiny thing.' Helen offered a placatory smile.

'Helen.' Caro took the bag. 'I said we weren't—'

'*You* said you weren't buying anything. That doesn't mean that I can't. Does it, Kay?'

168

'Course not.' Kay glanced down at the other small carrier Helen had stuffed in her handbag. 'Of course not,' she repeated.

'Go on.' Helen grinned. 'Open it.'

'OK.' Despite herself, Caro smiled. She eased the bag open and pulled out the baby-grow and as she did huge hot tears popped. The baby-grow was snow white, tiny and perfect and real. So very real. 'It's beautiful,' she whispered, her fingers tracing the delicate lemon trim. 'Thank you. Thank you.'

Helen stepped forward and put her arms around Caro's neck. 'It'll be alright,' she said.

And that was the last thing Caro heard. As she leaned into the embrace a bright needle of pain speared her from the inside out, clean as a surgeon's knife, blinding as the sun.

'Caro—' Helen gripped her shoulder.

But the blade of pain sliced again and sent her sideways, half on, half off the glider where she hung, suspended in a spasm of pain, hands clutching her stomach.

'Caro.' Kay bent.

And then Caro fell, and the baby-grow dropped from her fingers and landed beside her in a tiny crumpled heap. In her head voices echoed. She could see feet, feel the salt of sweat on her top lip and all the time, needles punched away at the soft, soft lining of her belly. Kay's face appeared. *What's the matter?* she thought she said, but at the same time was aware that her lips remained pressed tight together. She felt pinned to an apex of pain, more dazzling than the sun. And then somewhere, far away at the edge of being, she felt a thick wet warmth between her legs, and everything went black.

'Sorry, love. Family only.' The paramedic seated at the head of Caro's stretcher looked up at Helen and shook his head.

'I have to,' Helen pleaded. She had one foot on the back step of the ambulance, could see the top of Caro's head, a patch of forehead glistening white above the sickly pale blue of the stretcher blanket. '*I have to come.*'

'She's in good hands.' A second paramedic, who had been strapping Caro in, jumped now from the ambulance to the pavement. As he did he brushed against Helen's shoulder. 'We'll take care of her,' he said. 'Don't worry.' And he began unlatching the door, getting ready to close it.

'But…' Helen spun to Kay. 'One of us has to be with her! One of us has to go.'

A step behind, clutching the carrier bags of baby-grows, Kay nodded. Her face was as white as Caro's.

The driver shut the first door, locking it into place. He shook his head.

'Please,' Helen urged. They were less than a foot apart. 'Please.'

Again, he shook his head.

Helen dropped her chin. Defeated, she stepped back straining to see through the gap to where Caro lay.

I'm sorry, Mrs Winters. There is no heartbeat.

The years collapsed, slick as a card trick in a gambler's hands. The knot in her stomach tightened, goosebumps sprang, her mouth dried. In panic, she turned to the paramedic and although her voice was hoarse she managed to get the words out. 'She's losing her baby. *Please...* please don't let her go through this alone.'   From behind, a hand slid into her own and squeezed it. Kay.

The paramedic's face softened. He put his hands on his hips and looked down at the pavement. 'OK,' he said. 'Just one though.' And he turned to Kay. 'I can't take you both. Just one.'

Kay released Helen's hand. 'Go on,' she urged. 'I'll meet you there. Go on.'

'Are you sure?' Twenty-four years ago, Caro had been by Helen's side. Of course, she should be the one. She didn't even know why she was asking.

'Mind now.' And the paramedic swung the second door across, Helen slipping into the ambulance just before it closed.

'Look after her.'   As the door swung shut, Kay's voice fell away.

Helen inched her way to the flip-down passenger seat, her lips pressed tight together, a slow churn of terror in the pit of her stomach.

'Seatbelt.' A voice called and she turned. She'd almost forgotten he was there, the first paramedic at the head of Caro's stretcher. Hands trembling, she reached for her buckle. The engine started, loud vibrations rattling through, and slowly the ambulance moved off.

The siren was on, but like a shadow lifting, the sound was always ahead, slightly out of reach, and possible therefore for Helen to imagine that it wasn't meant for Caro at all. Not really. In fact the only indication of speed and urgency was the fact that she had to plant her feet firmly on the floor and press down, as if she were in a waltzer at the fairground.

Caro, veins full of painkiller and sedative, didn't stir.

Helen leaned back against the cold leather of the passenger seat and closed her eyes. It would be better if it stayed that way. If Caro slept through all that was coming. Because, for Helen, what was coming was clearly remembered.

The bright red splatters on the floor of Selfridges, and the dark ground-coffee smears left across the delicate stitching of that glider chair had signposted in as brutal and visceral a way as was possible *exactly* what was coming. The ordinary path of miscarriage, as bloody and tragic as any celebrated battlefield, immediately recognisable to a veteran like Helen.

Silent and ashen faced they had crouched either side of a barely conscious Caro and said nothing. Either to Caro, or to each other. What was the point of words?

'Is there supposed to be this much bleeding?'

Startled, Helen opened her eyes, willing herself back into the moment. The voice in her head was horribly loud. As if it were only yesterday. *Is there supposed to be this much bleeding?* She'd asked over and over again. Pleading with any medical professional who had crossed her path, the same question over and over.

'Try to relax,' the paramedic said.

And a drench of ice cold goosebumps showered down Helen's spine. *She* hadn't asked the question. It hadn't been *her* voice. It hadn't been *her* memories.

It had been Caro.

She leaned forward. Caro's hand, on the black buckle of the strap that crossed her chest, had clenched so tight the knuckles were white. She wasn't asleep. She was awake. Awake and holding on with every sinew to something that was already gone.

'Caro,' she whispered and put her hand over the top of Caro's. It was rigid and cold.

Caro made a strange low sound, a mix of groan and vowels as her head twisted left to right.

'Caro.' Helen tried to stand.

'I feel sick.' Now Caro stuck her neck out and tried to raise her head.

Helen undid her buckle.

'*Sit.*' The paramedic snapped his head at her and glared at the buckle.

Hastily Helen refastened it.

'Sick,' Caro mumbled, blue deltas of veins panning across the paper-thin skin of her forehead.

The paramedic leaned forward. 'Can you turn onto your side?'

'Ohh…' And already Caro was on her side, knees folded up in the blanket. 'Ohh…' she called again, loud, long, wobbly. Her head went back, her teeth bared and a thin *sorry* seeped through and then the paramedic was on his feet and moving around the stretcher and lifting the blanket and such a stench of shit and iron-rich blood filled Helen's nostrils that she gagged and the only way to stop herself from puking was to slap her hand across her mouth. And from deep within her handbag, she thought she heard a low humming sound. Her phone. Someone was ringing her phone.

The paramedic was between her and the stretcher now, his gloved hands smeared with blood. Again Helen undid her buckle and this time slipped quickly across into the next empty chair, closer up to the head of the stretcher where she leaned forward and took Caro's hand and pushed Caro's hair back from her brow. 'It's alright,' she whispered, tears streaming down her face. 'It's alright. You're going to be alright, Caro.'

Her phone had stopped humming and immediately started again.

'The baby,' Caro whispered, eyes shut. 'Is the baby alright?'

Unable to answer, Helen nodded. With clumsy hands, she reached for her phone. 'Kay,' she whispered, 'it's—'

'Mum!' Libby's voice spiked with fear. 'It's coming…'

'I'm sorry…' Caro moaned.

'The baby…' Libby gasped. 'It's coming.'

And by the foot of the stretcher, the paramedic unwrapped a kidney bowl.

Helen went limp with panic. 'Lib…' Her voice broke. Inches away she could smell the dry starch of the paramedic's uniform. He had tongs in his hands and she could see his concentrated expression, the movement of his arm, scooping and scooping and then a wad of white paper blotting and blotting.

Caro's lips moved but no sound came out.

'Mum,' Libby whispered, 'I'm scared.' And her daughter's voice burned like a flame against her skin.

'I'm here,' she answered, watching as the paramedic took a strip of gauze and lined the kidney bowl as carefully as if he were preparing it to receive a gift for the gods. 'I'm here,' she said.

'I doubt you're in labour, dear.'

Two taxis, one train, uncountable texts and an hour and forty-three minutes later, Helen hurtled through the doors of the maternity unit just in time to hear the sturdy, red-faced midwife make her pronouncement.

Not in labour? The words reached her like a white flag. Thank God! But, not in labour? So she could have waited until Caro had been admitted? At least until Kay had arrived? Because leaving as she did, with Caro pale and sedated on a stretcher was the worst thing she thought she'd ever done.

Go, Kay had urged over the phone.

She won't know, the paramedic had said, with a short blunt tap on Caro's vein and another vial of painkiller going in.

Still…

Panting and stooped, handbag swinging, she put a hand on her beating heart and tried to catch her breath. Libby had needed her, Libby had cried. How could she not have left? But not in labour! Shredded by the journey and the stress, she looked across at Libby, who stood by the admissions desk, supported by Lawrence. Her face glistened with sweat. One arm cradled her bump, the other clutched a square of pale yellow material that Helen recognised immediately as the comforter she'd snuggled Libby in as a baby. That Libby had snuggled herself against as a child, left close by enough to reach as a teenager and had now fallen back upon as a mother-to-be. The sight of it pierced Helen. Threw into sharp focus once again how much of a child her child still was.

Seeing her, Libby gasped. 'Mum, thank—' But her voice was felled by the spasm of pain that pulled her head back. '*Oh God!*' she gasped. '*It hurts.* It…' And her shoulders dropped, her legs buckled. Lawrence scrambled to keep her upright.

Not in labour? Helen found her breath and pulled it in, deep and steady, right to the bottom of her lungs. If her daughter hadn't had her father to support her she'd have collapsed on the spot. Not in labour, my arse! She dashed forward.

Lawrence's face had frozen into a cartoon expression of fear and bewilderment, still, together they manoeuvred Libby to a waiting wheelchair and managed to get her into it.

'Three minutes,' Libby gasped. She peered up through curtains of hair. 'The gap was three minutes.'

'Okey dokey, then!' The red-faced midwife said cheerily and bustled Helen aside to grab the handles of the wheelchair. 'Let's get you admitted. Grandma can follow!' she called over her shoulder and was gone, with just the brush of the swinging doors as evidence she'd ever really been there.

Standing in the sudden silence, Helen watched the doors swing themselves shut.

'Are you going?' Lawrence asked.

She looked at him.

'You can go. She just said.'

Helen startled. The midwife had said *grandma can follow*.

Grandma. She hadn't even twigged that was her role now.

'What about you?' she answered and something sashayed to the front of her mind. Sly and self-conscious, but determined to be seen. Something £100,000 shaped. Her eyes narrowed.

'I'll umm…' Light on his feet, itching to move anywhere but the direction in which his daughter and soon to be grandchild were heading, Lawrence ran his hand through his hair. 'I need to re-park the car?' he said, cloaking the statement as a question they both knew he'd already answered.

'Of course.'

And for a moment they stood looking at each other. *Not now, Helen. Not now.* It wasn't hard to listen to, this whispered internal entreaty. Libby needed her mother. Everything else must and could wait. So, she thought as she turned to follow, nothing new under the sun then.

There was no need to ask for directions. No need to stop any of the blue scrubbed doctors or nurses, or stand and try to decipher which way the yellow arrows on the polished hospital floor might lead. Oh no. Helen could hear Libby the moment she stepped through the doors.

'Mum, *Mum, MUM!*'

She was in the room and by her daughter's side, squeezing her hand, and easing Libby's sweat drenched hair back from her forehead in moments. And despite the mounting terror that stirred and crawled inside her like a furry black spider, somehow Helen managed to keep her voice steady and her face calm.

'Libby,' she whispered. 'You're—'

Another contraction exploded, silencing Helen and wrenching her daughter's body apart, and in the face of it, Helen felt herself slipping into the jaws of fear. Her hand on Libby's went limp. Nausea balled in her throat. Paralysed and helium-light she floated, and for a brief helpless moment the awesome terror of childbirth, the unnatural meta-physicality of it, struck her hopelessly dumb.

Until Libby moaned her name, *Mum*.

And Helen came to her senses.

Once again, she grabbed her daughter's hand, a strength back in her limbs, warmed by love. This was *her* baby. *Her* child, and there wasn't anything in this world, or the worlds above, that could stop her from fulfilling her maternal role. The pain of childbirth may have been God-sent, but the ability to endure it was a woman's creation. She could get Libby through this, she *would* get Libby through this.

'I have to push,' Libby panted.

'Not yet, dear.' The midwife, who had been taking notes on the other side of the bed, put her hand on Libby's shoulder. 'Baby's not ready yet.' She peered down at her watch and as she did her face drained.

'I'm pushing.' Libby was scrabbling at the bedcovers. 'Help me, Mum.' And before Helen could get to her feet, Libby had twisted herself onto her side, was on her knees, and grabbing at the bedrail, head down, teeth bared.

In a flurry of movement, the midwife lifted the back of Libby's gown and bent to look. 'Baby's crowning,' she said, turning to Helen, with as much surprise in her voice as if she'd been offered full-fat rather than semi-skimmed in her tea.

'Should she push?' Helen asked.

'I have to push,' Libby cried.

'Push,' the midwife demanded.

'Push,' Helen urged, bending low. 'Libby. *Push.*' Everything felt outside of her now, even her heart, which was so huge and so loud it couldn't still be inside her chest. This was it then. They were, all of them, past the point of no return.

But in response Libby twisted her head and whispered, 'I can't do this, Mum. I can't…'

'Push, Libby.' Was all she said. 'You have to push. *Now.* push. *Push. Push…*'

The air was thick and heavy with oxytocin and like an eager passive smoker Helen sucked it in. She was in love. Once again, she knew she was in love, and it was the most intoxicating feeling in the world. She looked down at her grandson. Seven pounds, four ounces. Gorgeous, scrumptious, mouth as clean as a cat's with a teeny-tiny pinky-wink tongue. She was so in love.

The soft brush of footsteps stirred her and as she looked up, she saw Lawrence standing in the doorway. From deep inside her rosy glow, she watched as he drew up a chair and sat down, her eyes lazily flicking up to the clock. Fifty-five minutes he'd been re-parking the car.

'How is she?' he asked in a low voice, nodding at Libby.

Helen looked at her daughter. Libby was propped up by pillows, softly snoozing, exhausted and irrevocably changed in ways she hadn't yet even begun to imagine. 'She's fine,' she said smiling, and watched as relief softened the line of her husband's jaw. 'Did you find a parking place?' she murmured, looking back down at her baby grandson.

'Helen…' Lawrence shook his head. 'This is… it's not… You're better at this…' he finished helplessly. A lump had formed in his throat.

As Helen looked at him, she felt the weight of his words settle on her like protective padding. Of course she was better at this, just as he was better at other things. They were, or had been, a partnership. 'Would you like to cuddle your grandson?' she said.

And with glassy eyes, Lawrence nodded.

Helen settled the baby in his arms and sat down, half watching Libby, half watching Lawrence, half watching a silent reel of this extraordinary day play back in her mind. And despite the heady atmosphere, despite the sweet relief that flowed through every vein in her body, details of that conversation with the bank clerk filtered into her mind. She couldn't help it. The words that she didn't want to say had already duplicated themselves many times over, and were pushing through, rising up. They would be heard.

She leaned back, pushed her hands through the mat of her hair and held them at the back of her head. 'Why did you re-mortgage the house?' she said and even she could hear the note of sadness in her voice.

Lawrence glanced up.

'I was at the bank earlier,' she continued. Earlier? It felt like a century ago.

Lawrence didn't answer. He dipped his head to the baby in his arms.

Did she see a flush of discomfiture? She would never

know, because almost immediately he raised his head again and said, 'Now isn't the time, Helen.'

And this time, she didn't answer because of course he was right. She pressed her lips together and sat and told herself that it would come. Her time would come.

Part Three

13

A month later

'And the share price barely moved!'

'Because the news got buried! The market was down three hundred points that week but Andy released the report anyway. He was told not to, but Caro wasn't here and...' Matt turned, his broad forehead furrowed in irritation. 'Do you need to take that?' he said, then, '*Caro?*'

Caro stared at him. Like a child blindfolded and spun around, she wasn't sure where she was. She blinked as the room settled back into focus. A long polished oval table, three windows, outside of which she could see the unmistakable shape of the Gherkin and beyond it the rounded benign dome of St Paul's. She was at work, in the boardroom.

'Do you need to take the call?' Matt repeated.

Everyone at the table was looking at her, but she couldn't for the life of her remember who they were. One, two, three... Her heart picked up and she felt a tingling at her fingertips. The beginning of an overwhelming panic, something she'd never suffered from, but that had in the last week or so found a space to settle inside her and was only growing more confident with each foray. Steeling herself, she pressed her nails into her palm, and the sharp pinch of skin was an anchor tethering her in place. 'No,' she said and pushed her buzzing phone away.

'Right.' Matt turned back to the faces at the table. 'It got buried, Danny. That's all.'

Danny. Of course. Caro looked down. She felt squeezed in by the coldness of her panic. How could she not have recognised Danny? Or Emir, sitting next to him? When she glanced back up again, she saw that they were both watching her.

'You OK?' Danny mouthed.

'Fine,' Caro mouthed back and dug her nails in harder. Less than two hours ago she'd answered her phone to a delivery company trying to deliver a cot that was no longer needed. The last nail in the coffin of a dream that was dead as a dodo. Apart from that, yes, she was *fine.*

'The last FPO sold out in three hours. Minimum you're looking at, minimum, is a four hundred per cent return. That's more than feasible in my opinion.' He turned to Caro.

Who nodded.

Matt frowned gently at her.

'Yes, more than,' she offered.

'Jeez, Caro.' Matt shook his head and turned back to the table.

And Caro looked down at the empty sheet of paper in front of her and drew a tiny circle in the margin. A four hundred per cent return was feasible because it existed in a way that another pregnancy, for her, would never exist. Was in fact impossible.

Kay had explained. Poor Kay, left to deliver the news. After losing the baby – foetus, as everyone had referred to it – she'd undergone a scan, which had revealed uterine tissue growth in the intestines. *It wasn't worth the risk. Not at her age,* the doctors had explained. It would only grow back and then there was the possibility of acute obstruction, of further serious complications. No, not worth the risk. But Caro had been numbed by shock and painkillers, she wasn't sure what they were talking about, she wasn't sure what she'd said. Either way, twenty-four hours later she'd woken up, having undergone a full hysterectomy, her uterus removed, the problem solved.

Gone. All gone. And poor Kay, red eyed and white faced and stumbling out the news that Helen couldn't come because Libby had had her baby on the same day that… Thinking this, Caro's head dropped as it always did when the truth hit her. Libby, who had spent most of her pregnancy trying to wish it away, and she who had counted and treasured every last minute of it.

Unconsciously her hands settled on her stomach, a habit she had so easily acquired and now couldn't break, as if her body remembered, which of course it did. Every fibre of her being remembered.

'So,' Matt was saying. 'The order sheet doesn't lie, Danny.'

Emir shrugged. 'I didn't realise Caro wasn't in when the report was released. That explains it.'

'Timing was shit.' Matt held his hands up. 'No argument there.'

'But she's back now,' Danny grinned.

Caro smiled, and although the men continued talking,

she didn't hear a word that was said. She was back. She'd been back for three weeks now. And on that first day, it had been like stepping onto a lifeboat. No one had known. She'd been able to slip back into her role seamlessly, passing off her hospital stay as *women's problems*, two words, about as popular a subject matter in the office as tax and audit. But with every passing day, the men and women with whom she spent the best part of her week had seemed increasingly alien to Caro. And the value of what they valued increasingly worthless. Overseeing investments worth millions of pounds, she'd felt numb, as if she was a child in a sandpit, mindlessly moving spadefuls of sand from A to B. So that now the lifeboat she'd jumped onto gladly felt more like the *Starship Enterprise*, with everyone around her hellbent on going somewhere and going somewhere boldly, and Caro wholly unable to name any destination that she might even want to journey to.

'Caro!' Matt threw himself back in his chair, arms wide in a gesture of impatience. 'If it's not important, do you mind?'

And again, she felt herself snapped back into the room.

'Your phone,' Danny said gently.

She looked at her phone. It was buzzing away on the table in front of her.

'Just answer it,' Matt said, his voice heavy with irritation.

'OK.' Caro pushed her chair back and picked up her phone. But the name that flashed up sent a powerful wash of cold through her legs, and it was with visibly shaking hands that she swiped to answer, moving away to the window as she did so.

14

In a long-practised move, Helen wedged the front door of her house open with her shoulder, manoeuvring herself and the shopping sideways, like a crab – if crabs shopped in Sainsbury's.

'Hello the house,' she muttered.

The house didn't answer, but her phone did, pinging deep within her handbag. She stumbled into the kitchen and banged her funny bone on the dresser. A card fluttered down from the top shelf and her elbow throbbed in pain. Dumping the bags on the table, she picked up the card.

Congratulations Grandma.

Well there she was! (According to Hallmark.) A rounded old woman with a cardigan, glasses and grey hair. Seriously? Daisy from work had given it to her, but then it was Daisy who, a few short weeks back, had given her the Kissable Body Powder for her fiftieth. Daisy, Helen decided as she dropped the card in the bin, obviously approached the marking of momentous life events with all the discernment of a fox approaching a chicken coop. In, out, grab what you can. Anyway… Turning her back on the bin, she stood in the middle of her kitchen, ran her hands through her hair and tried to remember what had caused all the hurrying and bumping and throbbing.

To remind her, her phone beeped again.

With boxing glove hands, she scrabbled through her bag. It might be Caro.

It wasn't. It was a text, from Libby.

⬤ *Shhh! Ben is sleeping! Finally.* ◗ ◗ ◗

⬤ ◗!? Helen threw the phone on the table. After three (well, very nearly) years at university and another eleven in the education system before that, that was the extent of Libby's vocabulary? With the enthusiasm of Sisyphus preparing another roll of the ball up that interminable hill, she put the carrier bags on the table and set about unpacking. Quietly.

Milk, juice, nappies, the nursing mother's supplement Libby had asked for. Yogurt, bread, more milk, chicken, frozen beans, frozen peas, potatoes… And so on… and so on…

And although she didn't intend it to happen, thoughts of Caro once again slipped beneath the surface of Helen's mind, forgotten under the rising swell of her heart when she pictured her grandson's face, and completely swept away by the eternal, unanswerable question that had haunted her most of her life: what to make for dinner.

Finally, when nearly all the groceries were out, she folded her reusable bag in half and held it pressed against her chest and waited, not knowing what it was she was waiting for, until it resurfaced. Caro.

It had been a month now.

One whole month.

Cyprus was even longer back. The cool breeze rising off the ocean to tickle against her naked body, her stomach. God, would she *ever* experience anything like that again?

Behind her, the phone pinged again.

Did you remember the supplement?

She didn't respond. Instead, she turned to the last bag, and unpacked a family-sized lasagne for those days when she couldn't be bothered (which was most days), a family-sized packet of cornflakes that Jack would eat in twenty-four hours, baby wipes, cotton wool pads that Libby had asked for, and a Rapid Rehydrate mix for Lawrence, as per his note this morning. Plus a bag of dried pellets for Libby's rabbit. Poor Sasha. He didn't eat much else. And didn't she read recently that the secret to longevity was a near starvation diet? Something like five hundred calories a day? Thousands the survey had cost! Helen snorted as she scooped up the rabbit food and put it away. Whoever commissioned that survey could have saved themselves a fortune and just asked her. Rabbit pellets were obviously the secret to longevity and she'd have been happy to supply the answer for a fraction of the price.

Her phone pinged again.

What about the cotton wool pads? Did you get the round ones?

This time Helen banged out a *Come downstairs!* and moved onto the next stage of manoeuvres. The manual transference of groceries into cupboards and fridge. And how could that be, she wondered? In a world where scientists had discovered water on Mars, why hadn't someone invented a machine or an app that moved groceries from grocery bags into fridges and cupboards?

Behind her – oh, yes – her phone pinged *AGAIN,* so that now, staring at the white light of the fridge interior, milk in one hand, juice in the other, her shoulders tensed to doorknobs. She threw the cartons in, banged the door closed and stalked back to the table, where she stared at the text…

Can't come down just now. Ben is sleeping. Remember?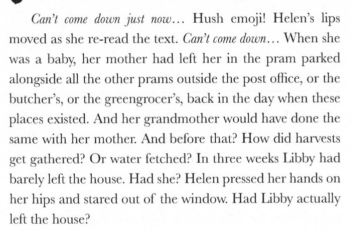

Can't come down just now… Hush emoji! Helen's lips moved as she re-read the text. *Can't come down…* When she was a baby, her mother had left her in the pram parked alongside all the other prams outside the post office, or the butcher's, or the greengrocer's, back in the day when these places existed. And her grandmother would have done the same with her mother. And before that? How did harvests get gathered? Or water fetched? In three weeks Libby had barely left the house. Had she? Helen pressed her hands on her hips and stared out of the window. Had Libby actually left the house?

Why not? she jabbed out a response. Libby needed to start moving.

Mum!

Helen sighed, a huge, enormous sigh, exactly the shape and sound her mother used to make. Arms folded, she leaned against the counter and looked around. The kitchen, *her* kitchen, was chaos. A battlefield of strewn and stained baby-grows and spit-bibs. Newly opened packets of nipple shields and bottles filmed with milky residue. A bouncy chair on the table, in place of the fruit bowl (were they all to eat the baby?), a bin stuffed full of mulchy plastic yellow parcels that *stank*. Lawrence, this was Helen's theory anyway, simply didn't see the mess. Jack she knew was using all his strength to ignore it, pinching his nostrils together every time he passed the bin. He had the same look when he came out of the bathroom these days, which wasn't surprising given the fat, rolled wads of bloody sanitary towels and cotton wool pads smeared with baby-shit that greeted him every time he made the mistake of pressing the pedal bin open. It made her smile, his terrified expression. Yes, water on Mars or not, it was still only women who retained the ability to deal with these animalistic aspects of life. One whole month of the shit, if not quite hitting the fan, then certainly splattering everywhere else (and with Libby's movements wholly synchronised to a baby that seemed to sleep twenty-three hours out of twenty-four) she was, she knew, the only person capable of cleaning up the mess. A metaphor for her life.

She looked up at the clock. Ten past one. Seventy minutes past midday, almost the same age as she was. Time was running away from her, had turned its back without a second glance and was sprinting off. How the hell was she going to catch up with the rest of her life?

She didn't know. So she did what she always did in times of crisis; she made herself a coffee, picked up the newspaper from the hall floor and went into the living room.

*

The first thing she did was turn to the property pages; a habit acquired on the back of her conversation with that bank clerk. Because if Lawrence had been deceitful enough to re-mortgage without telling her, it wasn't beyond the realms of possibility that she too, might one day open the paper and find her own house for sale. Conversations these last couple of weeks had proved impossible. Lawrence was either avoiding her or cradling the baby. A deliberate tactic, Helen suspected. Plus, she was exhausted. And where would it leave her anyway? She only had so much room in her head. Lawrence's deceit seemed (ironically) like a mountain too many. Libby obviously still needed a lot of support, Kay had been on the phone just yesterday with the solemn (but in Helen's mind, sensible) news that her mother was going to be admitted into the nursing home today. Gosh... It was happening today! The paper slipped from Helen's hands, floating to her lap as if her arms were too weak to hold it. There was a time when the three of them, Kay, her, Caro, were so tightly entwined nothing slipped by, like this barely remembered but oh-so-big event had almost done. But that was life, wasn't it? If they'd started out as swift and conjoined as a mountain stream, it was sadly inevitable that they would diverge, that the rivers of their lives would separate as surely as a delta on a flood plain.

Caro, for example, was already back at work. She had obviously moved on. And if that was the case, well... Helen didn't know what she thought. Was she impressed by Caro's invincibility? Her determination to keep pushing forward? Yes... with reservations, yes, she was, but there was something else. Something so ugly Helen knew it could never be revealed. She was jealous. After everything Caro had been through, she was actually jealous because Caro was back at work, back at life and, according to Kay, had even been to New York. And where, despite all her half-fledged but earnest ideas in Cyprus, had Helen managed to get to? Suspected hernias from the patients and the brain numbing office chat of last night's TV. Oh, and Sainsbury's. Twice a day – that's where.

She didn't like this Helen. This person who stood on clifftops sullenly watching other people's ships depart. But what could she do? How could she possibly set her own sails? The cliff felt too high and the other ships were too far away and all she could do was watch this glittering armada that was supposed to be the second half of her life ease further and further out of sight.

With all sorts of sighing going on and very little attention being paid, she picked up the paper again and scanned through. At least the house wasn't up for sale. So far. She continued flipping through until, at the bottom of the last page, her eye was caught by images of a smart block of flats. Neat balconies and even neater communal gardens, filled with an unlikely number of people enjoying them on an unlikely fine day. An advertisement for a new development on the other side of town.

Helen read through the details, and then read through them again. The development was to consist of one- and two-bedroomed apartments with Juliet balconies, mostly facing south or south-west. As if the descriptions were a puzzle she needed time to contemplate, she lifted her chin and frowned and sure enough the answer came. Yes. Yes, she could picture herself on a Juliet balcony. Every morning with a cup of tea and a face to the sun and no winsome Romeos below buggering up the view. She smiled. Was it a glimpse of a ship within reach? Maybe.

Upstairs the bathroom door banged against the wall. (Jack approached doors as if they didn't exist). The baby let out a loud cry, Libby hissed and Jack snapped back. All as predictable as the clock on the wall. Sighing, Helen folded the paper and stood up. She hovered a moment, then went to the bookcase by the patio doors and tucked the paper between her recipe books. For later. For when she could think about a Juliet balcony undisturbed.

The catastrophic stroke her mother had suffered, the news that Sean had interrupted her board meeting with, hadn't killed Caro's mother, but it might as well have. No one could say if she would wake again. And worst of all, Caro could not decide if she should. Because wouldn't it be better if they never had to face each other? Wouldn't it be easier?

Thinking this, and damning herself to all kinds of seventh circles of hell for doing so, she bent down and reached her hand underneath the white stone that sat by the back gate. She knew exactly where to find it, tucked into the back-right corner, propped up against the fence. In fifty years the hiding place had never changed, like a little door that had been left permanently ajar. One through which she might slip back in. Not as Caro, of course, with a slimmer, straighter nose and a six-figure pay packet. But as Caroline. Her mother's daughter, with whom on a fine Sunday morning she might once again share time peeling potatoes.

What ifs, and what might have beens… She swept the key clear from the stone, pushed back on her heels and straightened up. Sean, her brother, hadn't needed to tell her where to find it but Caro had let him anyway. It was the least she could do. He'd never stopped coming back home. Hadn't in fact gotten much further than Kay in terms of moving away from where he'd grown up. So she'd stayed quiet on the other end of the phone, and allowed him to describe the stone, the colour of it, the way it was half hidden by the snow-in-summer that smothered the rockery. It had felt like an impertinence to do anything else.

She leaned forward to brush the dirt from the knees of her trousers, feeling the cold weight of metal in her hand. As she straightened up, her fist uncurled to reveal an old-fashioned brass skeleton key attached to a faded red leather Stonehenge key fob. It was, she considered, before she'd had the chance to stop herself, not so very different in length from that of the baby.

The baby. She was incapable of saying *mine* or *my* because on a fundamental level it had become clear to Caro that it had never been hers. If it had, if she'd had even the smallest stake, the tiniest genuine, authentic claim, her body, she was convinced, would not have betrayed her like it did. It would have fought harder. *She* would have fought harder, as she had for everything else in life. She would never have let it slip away.

Her fingers curled over the key, covering it, and deep in her heart a door closed quietly. She took a deep breath, walked across the garden, put the key in the latch and turned it.

Inside, the house was as cool and dark as she had anticipated. Despite the fact that it was August, the air was chill. And stale. This back entrance opened straight into the kitchen, where immediately Caro saw the single plate, knife and fork neatly stacked, sitting by the sink waiting to be washed. Exactly as her mother would have left them. Feeling like an intruder, she left her handbag next to the kettle and tiptoed through to the front room.

The smallness of it took her breath away. She stood in the doorway, one hand on the frame, almost swaying. When had she last visited? She couldn't remember. Five years? Maybe even six? Either way, it was long enough for an estrangement to have formed. For her to be able to look at the room she had spent the formative years of her life in with new eyes. Three strides and she'd be at the front window. The front door was only another stride beyond, and in turn opened straight onto Artillery Terrace. How had they all managed? Still holding the doorframe, she looked around the gloomy room. From the bookcase, to the dining table in the corner, to the electric fire in its cheap wood surround. How had the four of them, her brother, her father, her mother, herself, lived in this tiny house? Releasing the frame, she pulled the corner of her cashmere wrap tighter, wrapped her arms across her chest and hugged herself. How had they eaten and slept and entertained themselves? How had they found the room to dream? Or the space to fall in love? (Which she had, at least once, in the third year of secondary school, and which her brother had, several times.) Or fall out of love, for that matter? As her parents so conspicuously had. Where had Sean and herself raged through toddlerhood? And adolescence? And where in God's name had her mother gone to cope with the crushing disappointment of her own life?

Caro turned back to the cramped narrow kitchen and then back again to that single front-room window. Dreams? There had been no room in this house for dreams. And as she stood and looked out at the pavement beyond and the row of identical terraced houses opposite, what she couldn't understand was why she hadn't understood before. No wonder her father had retreated to the armchair in the corner – which was still there. No wonder Sean had become a walking, talking carbon copy of him. How could you not, in such proximity? And... In a swift decided movement, she went to the window and pulled the net curtain back, craning her neck to see along the road to the junction, the corner where for so many years she had waited for the bus to take her to school. No wonder her mother had seemed to reserve every last ounce of energy she had to push Caro away. Out the door, up the street, onto the bus. If she hadn't, was there a chance Caro too would have stayed?

Again, she turned back to the tiny front room. It was, as always, neat and tidy. The ceramic cats, her *whimsies*, were dust free on the window ledge, and behind the dark glass of the tall cabinet unused crystal glasses stood in neat rows. On the coffee table was a copy of the *Radio Times*, the remote control and a leather glasses case. The carpet had been recently vacuumed, the mirror above the mantle was smear free, and, looking at all these familiar yet strange objects, suddenly Caro was remembering something. Helen had said it, about a school reunion she'd attended. It had been like meeting a bunch of strangers she knew intimately. She smiled. Coming home was exactly that. Take out the people and replace them with ornaments and she was in a strange place that she knew as well as her own heart. So would... *could* this really have been her?

Polishing, dusting, standing on the front doorstep to wave the teenagers off to school? She thought of her own apartment, clean, white, light, airy. The clever electronic door lock she could activate with her mobile while still in the lift. And then she thought of the baby, and perhaps for the first time since it had all happened, the memory softened. It was still brutal, still a great soft wallop through her guts that weakened her knees and made her lumpy with dullness, but now she sensed something beyond the blow. Briefly felt, but there. A glimpse of a place she might one day get to? Her head dropped as if it had suddenly become too heavy for her neck to support it, and for a moment she stood in the middle of the room, seeing nothing, hearing only a low hum. Then from the street outside a woman's shout cut through and Caro looked up. No. She shook her head. This couldn't have been her. She couldn't have stayed and this, she understood, was the glimpse of that somewhere she might get to. That gently sunlit upland of no regrets. Because if she'd stayed, she wouldn't have lived the life she had. Even if it had led to where it did.

The thought was a quiet little engine. It had Caro moving to the front door and unlatching it, wedging it open with a dining chair that still had her mother's apron hooked over. It had her filling the house with sunshine and light.

An hour or so later, she'd stripped the bed in her

mother's room, washed the sheets and had them hanging on the line. She'd poured away the milk in the fridge and re-stacked it with the groceries she'd brought from her apartment. And she'd unpacked her bag. It hadn't taken long. This time was only an overnight visit. She had to be back for one last presentation she'd promised Matt, the day after tomorrow.

The next few hours loomed before her like a tsunami.

Was she mad? Shouldn't she have just booked into the Holiday Inn, at least to ease herself in gently? Or going further, asked Matt for an extended absence instead of... Unable to decide and unwilling to consider it further, she went down to the kitchen, made herself a cup of tea, took it into the front room and sat in her father's armchair.

Relax, she whispered, and turned to look at the front door. Her father had been dead for nine years so it wasn't like she was expecting him to walk in and yell: *Up!* Scattering her with the shotgun of his voice out of *his* chair. And yet that's exactly what a part of her was expecting. A little numb, she turned away from the door to the bookshelf tucked away in the alcove. On the bottom shelf were a row of photo albums. She took one out and began leafing through.

Sean, herself, her mother and father. Tansy, the cat... She'd almost forgotten they'd once had a cat. Summers and winters, herself as a Brownie, Sean in his new school blazer, her father in the garden, and, very rarely, her mother, in the kitchen, or hanging washing, or back in the kitchen. *There,* like the wallpaper was *there.*

She kept leafing through until she came to a page of photos taken at Stonehenge. The photo that she couldn't stop staring at, that she pulled free of the plastic film, was that of Sean, herself and her mother. Two small children, bucket fringe haircuts and tiny shorts. Suntanned slim limbs, swinging loose from the ancient stones. And behind them her mother, in a brightly flowered sundress, with a smile as wide and easy as her children's.

Who had taken it?

Not her father. She didn't have a single memory of her father outside of Artillery Terrace. And the day trips that her mother had taken them on were few and far between. But, yes, occasionally they had made it to Stonehenge. It was, after all, only a few miles up the road. And going by this photograph, they'd had fun. They'd been happy.

Caro stared at the little girl in the photograph. Was that really her? It didn't seem possible, and she couldn't find a way of tracing the thread back, connecting these two people again.

Until, staring at the photograph, the answer to the question she'd been torturing herself with ever since she'd heard, crept up and wrapped around her heart, squeezing like a bear, cutting off her breath, sending tears streaming down her face. No, it wouldn't be easier if her mother never woke, if they never had to face each other again. Despite the fact that she *knew* the stroke was her fault, she *knew* it was the shock of the phone call from the hospital requesting, as next of kin, her mother's permission to go ahead with the hysterectomy, explaining the aftermath of the miscarriage…The photo slipped from her hand. What had her mother thought? What on earth had gone through her mind? Caro folded her arms and shook her head furiously. It didn't matter. Nothing mattered except that her mother woke again. And to make that happen, she'd stay as long as it took, and somehow find her way back.

Taking refuge from the squabbling of her almost adult children upstairs, Helen stood in the middle of her garden looking at the rabbit hutch and the boundary of the pen. Poor Sasha. Ten years stuck in that space. Ten years hemmed in by chicken wire. Without stopping to think, she strode across, unlocked his cage and carried him out to the wide-open expanse of the lawn – where he froze, his body trembling. *Come on, Sasha,* she whispered. But Sasha didn't move. *Just a peek,* she coaxed, but even his eyelids remained frozen shut. He was, literally, petrified. Disappointed, Helen scooped him up again and popped him inside the pen where he came back to life, sniffing the grass under his nose as if it had just materialised. 'Sasha.' Helen shook her head. 'You need to be brave.' In response the rabbit darted underneath his hutch where he sat looking at her with empty black eyes.

'Don't look at me like that,' Helen said. 'I was only trying to help.'

Sasha didn't respond.

Sighing, Helen walked across to the patio chair, stretched her legs out and pulled the straps of her top down from her shoulders, soaking up the sun. She still had tan lines from Cyprus which, as she twisted her head to look, felt so ridiculous it made her chuckle. She'd gone to Cyprus as a married mother of two, and now she was a (hopefully) soon to be divorced grandmother. Her tan lines were older than her grandson. Yes, it was almost funny. Tiny gorgeous Ben was younger than her tan lines.

Four weeks. Already? Helen pointed her toes and lifted her chin to the sun. Love, she thought, dismantles time. Takes it apart quicker than an Allen key on an IKEA table. Hours become specks, because every time Libby had handed the baby over, she had simply sat with her nose pressed against his chubby thigh, or his arm, or the top of his soft, soft head and passed away speck after speck after speck. And in this pleasant way four weeks had flowed past easy as silk.

Horror, on the other hand, freezes it. She sat up, suddenly cold. Horror superglues itself into consciousness, so it sticks like a lid on a half-used paint tin. You never get past it and you can never confront it, not without damage, even though it wasn't as if she hadn't tried.

In moments when she could be absolutely sure that Ben would not be heard in the background, she had gone to pick up the phone and call Caro. More than a thousand times it seemed. But their timetables hadn't coincided. When Ben was sleeping, Caro had been working. She'd been in New York when Helen had been in Sainsbury's buying nappies. Just like old times, really.

She understands, Kay had said. *Things are busy for you.*

But is she alright? Helen would ask.

She says she is, Kay would answer.

Well she must be, if she'd been to New York.

Above her head, from the open window of Libby's bedroom, Ben's cries rose. He was getting louder. In fact, he was getting louder every day. He'd found his lungs. She got up and went inside.

Libby came down the stairs and instinctively Helen held

her arms out. The baby was handed over, Libby tugging her saggy pyjama bottoms up. Her stomach looked like a deflated balloon. She was young, it would work its way back, but it would never be the same. Helen averted her eyes. This was just one more thing Libby would have to find out for herself.

'Jack woke him,' Libby sulked.

'Why don't you take him out?'

'Where?'

'For a walk. Get some fresh air. I'm sure he'll drop off again.'

'I'm knackered, Mum,' Libby whimpered. 'I can't.' And she brushed past Helen, collapsing onto the sofa in the living room.

Concentrating on her grandson, Helen shucked him into the crook of her arm. His little eyes were red rimmed. 'He needs to sleep,' she murmured.

'So do I,' Libby grumbled, flat out on her back, hands flung over her eyes.

'I'll take him for a walk then. You have a shower.' The day was glorious but more than that, sixty seconds in her daughter's company and already Helen was irritated.

'That would be great,' Libby said through her hands. 'I think I'll go back to bed.'

Helen didn't respond. She stood in the doorway, swaying Ben, occasionally glancing across at Libby whose hair was greasy and whose pyjama top was buttoned wrong. 'There's half a quiche in the fridge,' she said tersely. 'Heat it up and have some lunch. Then take a shower.'

Libby took a cushion and balanced it on her chest. 'I just want to sleep.'

And Helen turned away. She pressed the pad of her finger on Ben's button nose and cooed at him. 'It'll get easier,' was all she trusted herself to say. 'But you have to start moving, Libby. It's time.'

'I am moving, Mum.'

'From the bedroom to the kitchen.'

'What's that supposed to mean?'

Helen switched Ben into her other arm. (He smelt so good.) 'It means,' she said, 'that you have to get up. Face the world again. I mean, if I wasn't here you'd have to go out and buy the nappies yourself.'

Libby turned the cushion over. 'But you are here,' she said quietly.

So quietly, without a trace of resentment, that Helen's irritation evaporated.

Libby had the cushion over her face now, as if she was hiding herself.

She was, Helen realised with a sudden clarity, scared. As well she might be. Having a baby was scary. The sudden, absolute, constant responsibility of keeping another human alive was terrifying. And her daughter was still so much a child herself. So how fortunate that she was here to help. How wonderful that she was right here beside her. She took Ben's finger and shook it, a *How-do-you do?* shake. 'Why don't you start with a shower?' she said. 'And some clean clothes. I promise it will make you feel better.'

Slowly Libby came out of her hiding place and lowered the cushion to her chin. 'OK,' she said. 'OK.'

*

Feeling as if something had been achieved, Helen left Libby on the settee and went out to the front drive where Ben's pram stood sheltered against the wall. She tucked him in, released the brake and rocked the pram back and forth. He opened his eyes once, flung up a tiny fist of resistance and then fell, loose as water, into sleep. The day was warm and sunny, all along the front border the roses were in full bloom and here she was with her grandchild, deftly steering her daughter though these difficult first weeks. It was all good and she should have been feeling all good… except this Helen, grandma Helen, felt as far away from sailor Helen, sex-on-the-beach Helen as the Helen who had once walked up the aisle to meet Lawrence. All these Helens, she thought. One would be enough. To make a decision and move forward, one would be enough.

'Stay simple,' she whispered at her grandson. 'Stay just as you are. Baby simple.'

'Mum!' Behind her the front door slammed.

Helen turned to see Jack standing on the doorstep, a flushed, excited look on his face. 'Can't you ever just close a door, Jack?' she said.

'I just did, didn't I?' Jack glanced back at the front door. 'Where are you going?' he said, walking across to her.

'I'm taking Ben for a walk.'

'Where?'

'I don't know where, Jack. Just a walk.' There was a nub of irritation in her voice. Did it matter where? And when were her children *ever* going to stop asking questions?

'Well do you want to come with me?' Jack offered. He had his head down, shy.

Helen frowned.

'It's results day.'

'Jack!' Helen's jaw dropped. She'd forgotten. How could she possibly have forgotten? His A level results were out. The day his future was decided. (Which was rubbish of course, but was how teenagers weaned on a diet of *The X Factor* viewed life.)

'All or nothing.' Jack shrugged.

Helen smiled. 'Of course I want to come. Let's go.' What else could she say? Jack had all his hopes pinned on this flag of achievement. Which of course could get blown over or trampled on at any time. Libby, after all, got it all. Two A*s And an A. And where had that landed her? Supine on the sofa, unable to button her pyjamas. Life was a slippery eel. You might grab its fat belly one day, only to watch helplessly as it slipped free the next. A level results were only A level results. Life was sudden and people were as many segmented as a citrus fruit. And if she knew only one thing, it was this – the good-looking, slim-hipped, smooth-skinned Jack of today was going to be a different person to the Jack of tomorrow and would need a whole lot of other things besides A levels. Just as the Jack of yesterday had once only needed a red elephant called Efant and wouldn't have known what A levels were if she'd cut them up into soldier-sized pieces and served them with dippy egg.

The truth of this made her eyes sting. Nothing stayed. Everyone left. She looked down at tiny Ben sleeping peacefully. Life. Who would possibly believe that it becomes so complicated?

15

'Here? Are you sure?'

'Here is fine.'

Kay looked around. The park bench which her father had directed them to faced east, up toward a small green hillock framed by beech trees.

'It's not much of a view, Dad.'

It wasn't. Behind the hillock rose the brick rectangles of a retail estate. B&Q, Poundland, Burger King. 'Are you sure you don't want to sit there?' She indicated a bench further along. A bench that faced the opposite direction, towards the lake where shouts of excitement from the nearby playground floated towards them like seeds through air. If her parents sat on that bench they might catch one. Imagine that? A seed of childishness to reinvigorate them. Wouldn't that be lovely?

'Here is fine, Kay.' Her father turned to Craig. 'Would you wheel Val around?' he asked, waving his arm, signalling the wheelchair around to the end of the bench.

Kay jammed her hands in her jean pockets and watched

her father first settle himself and then reach across to help Craig smooth the blanket over her mother's legs. She was under no illusions. This would be her mother's last trip out in the world. Ever. An ambulance had been booked for this afternoon to take her to Ashdown House. And with her behaviour now so unpredictable, it was unlikely that she would ever see beyond its manicured lawns again. So why not take the other bench? Why sit and look at the back of B and fucking Q? As if he had read the waves of frustration she emitted, Craig looked up and smiled.

Kay nodded at the other bench.

He shrugged, offered his palms to the sky and bent to finish tucking the blanket around her mother's back.

'Thank you,' she mouthed when he had straightened up.

'Right then.' Her father laid his stick on the bench. 'You two young people make yourself scarce.'

'Young?' she managed and was overwhelmed by an odd tight feeling.

'Scram.'

She didn't move.

'Kay,' Craig whispered.

Still she didn't move. Her hands were stuck fast and her veins filled with floating pins and needles and although she could see her legs, she couldn't actually feel them, let alone move them. A psychological paralysis gripped her. A state of being she was almost accustomed to. Because this wasn't the first time. Or the third or the fourth. Over the last few weeks her mind had decided that only by standing still could this end game be stopped from starting. In her parents' bedroom trying to pack her mother's suitcase (one suitcase for the rest of her life?), frozen in place holding a nightie. At the dining table filling out forms about food allergies, the pen suspended above the page. Odd moments of stillness that were the physical embodiment of magical thinking when every neuron in her brain and every fibre of her being had pushed back against this relentless march of time… and failed. Like now. 'We'll be back in twenty minutes,' she croaked, her voice raw with grief, her legs heavy with all the blood that had once again filled them.

'Make it half an hour,' her father answered.

'Dad—'

'I have my phone, Kay. Half an hour.'

'OK,' she said, and bent and kissed her father's dry cheek.

Straightening up, she scratched the back of her neck. The heat only seemed to make the irritation worse. 'We'll go and sit over there,' she said to Craig, indicating the bench that faced the lake.

'*We will not.*' Craig walked over and looped his arm through hers. 'You'll give your parents some privacy,' he hissed and steered her away in the opposite direction.

She didn't resist. The only thing she felt as Craig manoeuvred her away was that at last someone was taking the lead. Someone other than herself was making the decisions. They had walked only fifty yards before the path turned a corner. As they disappeared out of her parents' sight Kay took one last look over her shoulder and saw her father reach for her mother's hand. Privacy. Of course. She'd forgotten what Craig instinctively knew. Her parents had had a relationship long before she'd come along, just as they still had one now.

They kept their arms linked and walked in silence through late-summer borders that made the only noise necessary. Through a thousand salvia that boomed explosions of orange-red, and elegant fuchsia scaling spikes of coral-purple. Past notes of echinacea tinkling delicate daisy heads across the pathway and bursts of tall goldenrod, backlit by sunlight, humming, vibrant lemon. They were caught in a crescendo of colour, one last swell of summer vibrancy before the deeper, more sombre tones of autumn crept in. And thinking this, Kay stopped, her arm slipping free from Craig's. This, of course, was why her father had wanted to sit facing the back of B&Q. She clasped her hands under her chin. 'There used to be a bandstand,' she whispered.

Craig frowned.

'That rise up to the industrial estate? That was where the bandstand was!' She turned to look back along the path they had just walked. 'They took the railings away during the war, but the stand was still there. And that's where he asked her to marry him. Under the bandstand.'

'Under it?'

Kay nodded. 'It was raining.' And she burst into tears, ugly lumpy sobs that shook her shoulders and had her scrabbling in her pockets for a tissue. 'She's never going to come home, is she?' she gulped, folding the tissue in half.

'Mrs Patterson.' From his back pocket Craig pulled out a neat packet of tissues.

Swallowing hard, Kay took the offering. 'Burrell…' She

waved her arm. 'Oh, it doesn't matter! Why am I doing this, Craig?' she whispered.

Very slowly she unfolded the clean white paper.

'Mrs Pat... I mean Burrell. I mean—'

'Can't she just stay at home? Where we can look after her?'

'No.' He was shaking his head.

'Why not?'

'Because you can't look after her,' he said kindly. 'And we both know that you know that. She needs twenty-four-seven care.' He paused. 'You have your own life, Kay.'

'But it feels so wrong. Shouldn't I be looking after her, the way she looked after me?'

Craig sighed. 'The kind of care your mother needs would finish you off. Do you think she'd want that?'

'I'm not sure she'd want to go and live with strangers either.'

'It's not the same.'

Kay looked down at the square of tissue in her hand. She was stuck again. She couldn't take a step forward, and she couldn't take a step back.

And once again, as if he'd read her mind, Craig linked his arm through hers and said, 'Let's walk.'

This time he steered her around to the playground, and they found a bench where they could sit and watch a girl in daisy-patterned shorts cross a swinging rope-bridge. Occasionally the girl would stop and shout over to where her mother sat at a table, spoon-feeding a pushchair. And occasionally the mother would wave back and call encouragement and just as occasionally she would sigh with impatience instead, wipe the pushchair with a wet wipe and call, *I'm coming,* or *Just a minute.*

It was instantly engaging and welcomingly calming. So on they sat, not talking, just watching, until Kay looked down and scuffed a line in the sand-gravel with her trainer and voiced the thought that had been plaguing her ever since this decision had been made. 'I think we've become crueller,' she said. 'I mean, as a society, we're crueller.'

Craig stretched his arms back, resting his weight on the heels of his hands. 'What do you mean?'

'A hundred years ago,' Kay said, 'there were no care homes. Now it's a huge, lucrative industry. Three thousand a month it's going to cost.' She shrugged. 'But a hundred years ago we just looked after our own. And I... I don't know why I'm not doing that now.'

'Right.' Craig looked down at his arm to where an ant crawled across the bumpy contours of his skin. He dipped his head, pressed a fingertip down and watched as it crawled onto his nail. 'Can I be frank?' he said, lowering the ant to the ground.

She nudged his arm. 'No, you can't. You're Craig, not Frank.'

But for the first time ever he didn't take the bait and when she looked at him his face was dark and it almost scared her. Never had she seen him look more serious.

'I thought you were smart, Mrs B?' he said, and although his intonation made it a question, he didn't wait for an answer. 'A hundred years ago,' he continued, 'people didn't get old. Not like this. They didn't live for years and years, with medicine and stuff. They had like… what? Walking sticks? Now we've got chairs and stairlifts and hoists and…' He waved his hand. 'And anyway, if they did get very old, they were mostly still standing and there weren't that many of them.'

Kay smiled. 'You make people sound like bowling pins.'

'I know one woman,' Craig sighed. 'She's trying to juggle caring for both her parents – who are divorced by the way, so don't live together – with caring for her aunt *and* her mother-in-law. And she works full time.' He leaned his elbows on his knees and shook his head at the ground. 'That's fucking crazy, Mrs B. I'm sorry to swear, but it's nuts! Four to one? Her husband's a useless arse as well. I mean he earns a shedload and he pays for everything but the way this woman runs around, she'll pop her clogs before any of them.'

Kay tipped her head back and laughed. A ripple of a chuckle that felt so welcome, breaking through the clouds of her mind. Everything Craig was saying was true. Of course it was impossible. Her mother's needs were beyond what she could meet, so why was she still trying? And not just her; hundreds, probably thousands of women trying to live up to unrealistic ideals that had been dropped into their laps. Dropped? *Or willingly received?* Who'd asked her to take on the full-time care of her parents? They certainly hadn't.

'And I'll tell you something else.' Craig said. 'I've never once heard anyone's son talking the way you are now. It's *always* the women who are willing to give everything up.'

She turned to him. 'Really?'

'Yes, really.'

'Oh. Well, I'm not sure I'd say willing to give—'

'No,' he interrupted, 'neither would I. Obliged then?'

'Obliged... yes.' Kay nodded as she looked at him. At sixteen he still hadn't known his times tables, but he had the emotional intelligence of Ghandi.

'Mrs B?'

'Craig?'

'Mothers don't want their grown sons checking under their boobs for sores. And men don't want their daughters washing their penises and rinsing their catheters.' He shook his head. 'It's not the same as changing a toddler's nappy. You said you wanted to look after her the way she looked after you? But it's not the same. Will you take my professional advice on this?'

'I'm trying to,' she whispered. And as she breathed in, her chest felt painfully tight. Everything she was being told was both uncomfortable and true. Helping to change and wash her mother had been awful for them both, and the one blessing of the fact that her mother didn't recognise her any more was that as far as she was concerned, it was now a stranger that wiped a flannel between her pale and spindly legs. Which didn't, of course, ease Kay's own discomfiture. And as for her father, how could she care for him, like that? When and if the time came? The thought warmed her with embarrassment and shame and guilt. An overwhelming, impassable minefield of emotion. She turned to Craig. 'I'm really trying to.'

'Good.' Craig folded his arms, nodding as he shifted his weight. 'Because there's more to this job than people think. Much more. We don't just wipe arses and slap ready meals in the microwave, you know.'

'I know. I—'

'No… you don't.' A shy smile spread across his face. 'Sorry, Mrs B, but you know as much about this as I know about fractions! Ever sat all night with someone who's too scared to sleep in case they never wake up again?'

The warmth of emotion that she had been feeling drained away. *Never wake up again?* Suddenly, under the August sun, Kay was cold. She shook her head.

'Or cleaned shit off wallpaper?' Craig continued.

'No,' she whispered.

'Or spent half a day reminding someone every three minutes that there are no car keys, cos they don't have a licence any more, let alone a bleeding car? And I do mean *every three minutes*, all afternoon.'

'Craig—'

He raised his hand to cut her off. 'We stay awake when they can't sleep, and we comfort them when they wake up. We sit with them on the floor, to wait for the ambulance. We manage tantrums and fire hazards and all kinds of abuse and we still treat them with the respect they deserve.'

'I know—'

Again he cut her off. 'And I can do that, Mrs B. I can do that, because it's my job. I get to go home, stick a pizza in the oven and open a bottle of wine. People caring for elderly relatives in their home can't do that. It's full time. So – all respect and everything, cos you were my teacher…'

'I was.'

'But you don't know.'

She didn't answer. She lifted her chin and looked across at the mother and the pushchair. Now it had been turned she could see the baby. Another mouth to feed, bottom to wash. 'How much do they pay you?' she asked.

'Not enough.'

'Well...'

'It doesn't matter how much. I love this work. You know I wasn't any good at school, but now I've found something that I love and... Well, what I've seen... I could write a book.' And he stopped talking and looked down at his hands.

Across the park, the mother kicked the brake of the pushchair free and called across to her little girl. *Time to go home.*

Kay watched them leave. Home. For tea and bath and story and bed. Those days, those halcyon days that encompassed a child's every need and wish and desire, and that ended so perfectly with tea and bath and story and bed. Slowly she turned to Craig. 'Let's get back. It's time.'

They walked back slowly and silently, and as they walked Kay thought of the daisy shorts the little girl was wearing. Alex, she was remembering, had had similar shorts. Train patches on the pockets. Red trains, blue track. As they turned the corner of the pathway, past the last burst of salvia, the back of B&Q rose into sight. Where were Alex's shorts now? On another little boy? Or rotting in landfill? She looked up. There were her parents, sat in exactly the same position as she had left them. 'This is the price we pay,' she murmured.

Craig looked at her.

'For love,' she said. 'Everyone grows up and leaves, and everyone grows old and dies, and this,' she said, 'is the price we pay for loving them.'

16

'Here's to Jack,' Lawrence said and lifted a glass full to the brim of sparkling champagne.

'Thanks, Dad.' Jack returned the gesture, his face bright with happiness and, looking at him, Helen realised just how much of a strain the last few weeks had been. Because here was a glimpse of the old Jack, looking like his young self again. Handsome and lean. Clear skin, shiny hair, bursting to set sail upon his own personal epic. Her boy, the tiny boy who had once tripped down the stairs, half asleep, re-living his dreams of golden dogs and racing chickens between mouthfuls of cornflakes. She lifted her own glass, blinking away the tears that threatened. Two As and one A* he'd achieved. So he was off. In a few short weeks, he'd be off. Those cardboard boxes they'd picked up on the way back from their walk, filled with all he was going to need for his new life. And how was she ever going to bear him leaving? Then again, how could she bear him staying, with his huge hairy feet on the coffee table and his habit of drying hair-gelled hands on clean towels. 'To Jack,' she managed, caught up in the paradox of reconciling herself to something that she would never be reconciled to.

'To Jack.' Libby echoed quietly.

Helen turned. Libby wasn't drinking champagne. She was drinking water, from a squat tumbler, and thinking perhaps of the day they had celebrated her results, in exactly the same spot, almost exactly three years ago. Helen held her glass at her lips, acidic bubbles tickling the inside of her mouth. *Don't think about it,* she willed. *Don't think…* But there it was! An image of Jack, trundling up the front path, a baby swaddled in his arms. Beaming. *Look, Mum. Look what I've brought you.* Imagine! And to stop herself imagining, she swallowed another mouthful of champagne. But the idea was so horrifyingly ridiculous it almost made her laugh and in trying to suppress the laugh she snorted, which drew a stream of bubbles up her nose, tickling all the tiny hairs, making her sniff and then sneeze and shoot nasal bubbles all over her plate. A wholly physical response to the idea of another baby in the house.

Across the table Lawrence glared. As if she'd done it on purpose.

She wished she had. 'Inhaled it,' she explained. 'By accident.'

He shook his head in profound dismay. (He did that a lot lately.) Then he raised his glass again and said pointedly, '*Anyway*, I'm very proud of you son. I always knew you wouldn't let us down.'

Ignoring him, Helen slugged back another large mouthful. What Lawrence meant was, you haven't let *me* down… Unlike herself, of course, who having let the whole family down didn't deserve an iota of sympathy. Well. She might have had a brief (and wonderful) affair, but she hadn't secretly re-mortgaged the house... She stopped thinking, shifted her eyes left to Libby and instantly slapped a lid down on the pot of sour irritation Lawrence had stirred.

Because Libby's head had dropped and no one had noticed. Her chin was on her chest and she was making a show of smoothing out Ben's spit-bib, but her lips were thin with the strain of emotion and she was blinking furiously. Trying not to cry.

With dagger-eyes Helen turned back to Lawrence. She didn't care what he thought about her, how unsubtle his subtle digs were. But to tar Libby with the same brush, or even for a moment to allow Libby to think she was being tarred... She sat there willing him to turn and face her, but he was still jabbering on to Jack, and Libby still had her head down. 'Lawrence,' she hissed through bared teeth.

Lawrence looked up.

She jerked her head an inch to Libby and to her immense relief Lawrence put his glass down.

And for a long awkward moment no one spoke.

Then, in a show of emotional intelligence that warmed her heart, Jack lined his knife and fork together and dipped his head, giving his sister all the time she needed to compose herself.

'We need to forge a plan here,' Lawrence said and leaned his elbows on the table, hands cupped.

Helen glanced at him, that *we* again. Never mind, *they* did need a plan. Or Libby did, and at least he'd gotten her hint.

'Libby.' He frowned at his glass. 'You said before the… um, before… Yes, before everything happened.'

'Baby?' Helen offered. 'Before the baby?'

He glowered at her and turned back to Libby. 'You mentioned re-takes in January?'

Libby nodded. She was holding Ben's hand in her own, his tiny finger wrapped around hers.

Ah… A rush of bubbly champagne love swept over Helen. She wanted to scoop them both up and pack them somewhere safe and warm. Like her pocket. Libby and Ben. They were both babies, the pair of them.

'You see.' Lawrence nodded. His features were heavy, as if his face was having trouble supporting them. 'You see,' he repeated. 'That sounds achievable to me.'

No one answered.

Libby glanced at Helen. She looked anxious. The last time this conversation had been raised it hadn't ended well.

'Don't you think?' Lawrence said, looking at Helen.

Wary, Helen narrowed her eyes. It did sound achievable, of course it did. But then Lawrence was good at making everything sound achievable. Everest for example. What he wasn't so good at was spelling out the price. Everest, FOR EXAMPLE!

Circling his glass on the table, he said, 'I think you should aim for that. It's always good to set yourself a goal. Get it done while the material is fresh in your mind. Do you think you could cope?'

Libby made the smallest of nods. 'I think so.'

'Your mother and I will support you.'

Again, Libby nodded.

'I think that's reasonable. Helen?'

'That's reasonable,' Helen agreed. What else could she say? It did sound reasonable and after so much work, it would be ridiculous not to help Libby get past the finishing line.

'What do you think, Libby?' Lawrence pushed.

'If Mum agrees?'

Tightly Helen nodded. She knew where this was headed and, once again, she had no idea how to stop it.

'Good!' Lawrence raised his glass. 'So let's get the resits done. We'll wait until that's all out of the way and then we'll go from there. All of us. Little Ben as well!'

The net of tension that had so suddenly enfolded them had loosened. Libby smiled and raised her tumbler. The first time she'd smiled all through the meal. And Jack was smiling and everything was alright again and, not trusting herself to speak, Helen flashed a smile back at her family and reached across to begin scooping up their empty plates. *We'll wait until that's all out of the way… We'll wait until Libby's had the baby… We'll wait and wait and wait…* Dot after dot after dot. If it was left to Lawrence, he'd lay out enough dots to take them all up to Ben's eighteenth birthday. Enough dots for that Juliet balcony she hadn't stopped thinking about to crumble to dust. And actually, maybe even enough time to pay back the money he'd taken.

At the dishwasher, she dropped the knives in blades up. At the hob, she collected pans and lids and grease-splattered spatulas.

'I'll help,' she heard Libby say, but she waved it off.

So Libby stayed seated. And with her back to the

table, scrubbing fat from the saucepan, Helen listened to her family discuss their futures. And it was fine. It really was. Jack, so excited to be arranging a weekend to check out accommodation, Libby tentatively putting forward a schedule that would take her to the re-sits. Every now and then she padded back to the table and topped up her glass, ignoring every attempt by her husband to make eye contact. Eventually the chat died away. Libby went upstairs to bath Ben. Jack went out to celebrate and Helen picked up a tea towel and dried her hands. Where was *her* future in all of this?

Jack stuck his head around the door. 'You sure there's nothing I can do to help?' he said, looking at an almost cleared table and an almost full dishwasher. (An old trick of his.)

'We're fine,' Lawrence said.

No she wasn't. She wasn't fine.

'Go and have some fun,' Lawrence said. 'We'll sort it.'

We… *we, we, we.* That was it! The way that when it suited, he kept fusing them together like wire. She put the tea towel down. On one hand what Lawrence had suggested made perfect sense. On the other hand, it was pissing her off no end! *Your mother and I will support you…* Which she would. In her own time, in her own way and with her own choice of words.

Behind her, she heard a scrape as Lawrence pushed back in his chair. 'I know what you're going to say,' he said.

(Even now! Even now, deciding her language.)

'And I understand your frustration. But this is something we need to face as a family, Helen. I think *we* should—'

And because she couldn't bear to hear another *we*, she twisted to him and snapped, 'When are you going to tell me why you re-mortgaged the house, Lawrence?'

He blinked.

'How about now? Is now the right time for you? Because it certainly is for me!'

His mouth drew itself closed, like a small pink drawbridge. Everything else about him stayed rock still. It reminded Helen of Sasha earlier, petrified by his freedom.

She leaned back against the dishwasher and released her arrows. Precise, measured, very cold, as they should be, having had to wait in the freezer section of her mind these last few weeks. 'I went to the bank,' she said, 'as I told you. The day Ben was born and Caro…' Catching herself short, Helen drew a deep breath.

'Why?' Lawrence asked, his face open with confusion. 'Why were you at the bank?'

Looking straight at him, Helen said calmly, 'To open a personal account, Lawrence. To start the process of separation.'

His left eye made an involuntary squint. Like she'd hit her target.

Helen pushed back against the sink. She didn't like doing this, she didn't like hurting him. An image of that morning at the bank re-surfaced, the eyelash sat on the desk between her and the clerk. The £100,000 Lawrence had taken. Without so much as a word. She continued in a low voice, 'When I tried to make a transfer, the balance was too low. So we went through the last twelve months' statements. Me and a very helpful young lady.'

Lawrence's squint became a spasm.

'And of course it wasn't hard to discover.' Helen shook her head. 'You re-mortgaged the house, Lawrence. Without even telling me, you re-mortgaged this house.'

'Have you ever been short of money?' Lawrence said calmly.

'What…?' She was too surprised to finish.

So he jumped right in. 'I'll put it another way. Have you ever *not* been able to buy exactly what you needed? When you needed it?'

The air seemed to leave Helen's chest, which didn't matter because she was speechless anyway. She literally couldn't find any words to answer him. Probably because it wasn't a question that should have been asked. Her mind caught up with what he was doing. 'This isn't about me!' she gasped. 'Don't turn—'

'Have you,' he interrupted gently, 'or the kids, ever gone short of money?'

Helen didn't speak. She picked up the tea towel and twisted it into a tight snake. How, in the course of micro-seconds, had she lost grip of the conversation?

'Exactly,' Lawrence said. 'So what is your problem?'

His voice was cold and, suddenly, so was she. In the heat of an August evening, Helen felt herself chill, as if she'd opened the freezer door to a blast of frigid air. He wasn't even sorry and that lack of contrition had her doubting what had actually happened. Because wasn't it his money anyway? Didn't he earn it? 'You used it for Everest,' she said. 'Didn't you?'

He lifted his chin. 'Yes.'

Her lips flattened out in disgust. At herself? Or him?

'There's a window of time in which I could have done it, Helen,' he said, and his voice regained a transparent layer of warmth. 'I can see why that might be difficult to understand. The climbing... And I agree, it's an obsession. I tried to explain it in Cyprus, remember?'

She did. But hadn't she also tried to explain something in Cyprus? And wasn't there a window of time also for her? A window which right now felt as if it were closing fast. 'You told me you'd sold shares, Lawrence. That's what you said.'

'Well...' Lawrence leaned forward, twisting the stem of his glass. He shrugged. 'Obviously I didn't.'

And watching him, Helen took a much needed breath. Her whole body shuddered. Right now, in this time and this place, there wasn't anything about him that she even liked. This man she had spent half her life with. 'Why did you lie?' she whispered. 'I'm your wife. Why did you lie to me?'

He laughed. A low chuckle, reserved for harmless disbelief. As if a child had told him that reindeer definitely can fly. 'Honestly?' He looked up. 'Not telling you was easier than having to explain it to you. You're not exactly Caro are you, Helen? I didn't expect you to understand the ins and outs of what at the time was the most financially astute decision. Especially when you didn't need to know.'

Helen stared at him, such a storm of emotion going on she could not have grabbed any one feeling and pinned it down long enough to name it.

But he did. 'Don't look so outraged,' he said gently. 'You would never even have found out if you hadn't...'

And here he trailed off, his hand releasing his glass as it fell back into his lap.

'What?' she said, and it was like poking a bear. A bear that had lied and deceived her. 'What wouldn't I have known… if I hadn't *what*?'

'If you hadn't gone and shagged that… that person,' he spat. 'If you hadn't gotten all these stupid ideas into your head!'

'Stupid ideas!' And Helen nodded. *His* stupid ideas meant *her* life and her finally making a pro-active choice about how she wanted to spend it! She shook her head. How foolish she'd been. How utterly inept at playing this game between them. Thinking that he'd fall in with the flow, that they could be civilised, that he'd hand over the keys of this supremely comfortable prison that she'd allowed herself to be held in. 'Stupid ideas,' she repeated. 'Is that what you think all this is?'

Now he looked at her. 'It's so incredibly selfish, Helen. Breaking the family apart like this.'

Her mouth fell open. *Selfish?* She couldn't even get the word out. Of all the ways she might have imagined this conversation going, this wasn't one of them. Lawrence *defined* selfish. Lawrence had selfish running through him like everyone else had blood. Months away climbing mountains, cycling the length and breadth of countries, while she waded through the long grass of domesticity, waiting years… no, decades, before she could even get five minutes to address her *needs*. And beyond that, was there any one thing they had done in the whole course of their marriage that had been Helen's idea? That had been based on her *needs*? She gripped the bench. Was there any one thing in the course of her whole life that had been solely her idea? 'What's selfish,' she said, faint with the realisation that it had taken fifty years for her to even acknowledge that she might try to live her life based upon her needs, 'is *you*, re-mortgaging our biggest financial asset without telling me.' Because she *had* to get a grip on this, she *had* to keep this on track. 'Just because you earn the money, doesn't mean you get to control my life, Lawrence,' she said, each word a glowing coal. 'Not any more.'

'That's a bit dramatic,' he said and laughed again. That same self-satisfied chuckle.

Helen stared at him. Now she was numb – with disbelief. Thirty years ago, she'd fallen in love with a man who would, one day, *laugh at her.* 'Is it?' she said, feeling dull as a dishrag. 'Is it really, Lawrence?'

He didn't answer.

'How can you buy me out, when you've already climbed the money away? How can I leave?'

Still he didn't speak.

'It wasn't your decision to make,' she finished, turning back to the sink, because really, what was the point?

'*Whose was it then?*' Lawrence's voice was so loud and so angry it had Helen turning back to him. 'If it wasn't my money, Helen, whose was it? And this has nothing to do with control. So don't try and spin some sort of equality slant to this because I know one woman, for a start, who wouldn't stand for anyone telling tell her how she should spend *her* money. Caro!' Lawrence finished, as if he'd just produced a Royal Flush. 'Caro wouldn't let anyone tell her how she should spend the money *she* earns.'

Helen's felt her shoulders fall slack. The depths of misunderstanding between them were suddenly fathomless. Wholly un-navigable. Who was this man in front of her? Why was he saying these things? 'What are you talking about?' she said quietly. 'Caro's never been married.'

'I can see what's coming next,' Lawrence sneered. 'You'll be demanding half my pension next.'

Like a whip had been lashed across her toes, she flinched as she stared at him. Her husband, the stranger. 'Yes,' she said slowly. 'I will. And you know who advised me to make sure I do? Caro!'

The smile dropped off Lawrence's face.

'Do you know why, Lawrence?'

She didn't wait for an answer.

'Because,' she continued flatly, 'you're right. The only one who spends Caro's money, *is* Caro. So she knows how much it all costs. She's paid a cleaner for decades. She has her groceries delivered, her windows cleaned and her suits dry cleaned. When she's away, she pays someone to water her plants, when she had a dog she paid someone to walk it. At her last apartment she even paid an interior designer to design it! She even,' Helen leaned forward, her face red, 'has someone jet-spray her sodding bins.'

Lawrence shook his head. 'Why do you have to be so vulgar nowadays?'

'Maybe,' she hissed, 'I've always been vulgar and you just never noticed. And imagine, Lawrence. Imagine the cost if there were children involved. Or half an acre of garden. Dogs. Cats. Even a fucking rabbit! Imagine all those extra man-hours, the emotional energy of it all, never mind

230

just the finance. Imagine that. So yes actually, that's exactly what I'll be instructing my solicitor to do. Because after all my unpaid work I deserve just as much of a sit down as you do. Although I won't even need to bother doing any instructing. It's standard practice this century.'

Lawrence's face coloured several different shades – red, a blotched maroon-purple mix, then pale grey-white.

And if she'd had any energy left, if she'd felt she could get through to him, she might have screamed. Might have lunged forward and kicked the legs from under his chair. But, no. If she'd had any energy left she'd turn back, race through the decades and find her twentysomething self, shake her by the shoulders and tell her. Tell her that it's OK to put herself first. That she should follow her dreams and everything else would surely fall into place, and if it didn't… well, then it wasn't meant to be and that was alright as well, because life was long and oceans were wide and there were so many more fish in the sea and the only person with the key to her happiness was her. She was the riddle-master, the knight in shining armour, the captain of her life. Utterly wrung out, the only thing she felt was a bedrock of sadness. Twenty-five years together and she'd had no idea how deep her husband's vein of selfishness ran. 'You *went out* to work,' she sighed. 'And I *stayed home* and worked. It's what you…' She stopped talking, folded her arms and looked down at the floor. 'It's what *we* both wanted, Lawrence.'

Lawrence was silent. His fingers twitched as he brought his hands to the table and folded them together. 'I can afford the extra payments,' he said. 'On the mortgage. You don't have to worry about it.'

'But how can you afford to buy me out?'

He looked at her.

'You're still not hearing it, are you? I want to leave, Lawrence. I want—'

'But Libby.' Helpless Lawrence looked towards the kitchen door, out to the hallway. 'We said we'd—'

'You.' Helen said. 'You said, *we'd* wait. And we did. But it's time to stop waiting. Jack will be gone in a few weeks.'

Lawrence blinked.

'I'm sorry.'

And he lowered his head and blinked again, his jaw held tight.

Helen pressed her arms against her chest, a self-imposed barrier to stop herself from breaking free and going to him. She was breaking his heart and it was happening right in front of her, in real time, close up. And the effort not to comfort him was superhuman. To inflict this pain on someone she had once loved and now didn't was the cruellest thing she thought she'd ever done. No wonder women stayed. 'Well,' she whispered, her voice hollowed out with emotion. 'Maybe you could stay and then the kids can also stay, as long as they need to. And in the meantime, you'll have to somehow buy me out. Sell the shares you said you were going to sell for Everest.'

'I can't.' Lawrence let his head fall to one side. He was staring off, midway across the kitchen.

'Why not?' she said. But already she knew why not. She wasn't that financially inept.

'They've... they're not worth—'

And Helen thrust her palm up to stop him from saying

anything more. What was the point? The room fell very quiet as she stood, arms still crossed, processing and not processing what this meant. 'I'm leaving,' she said finally, because it was the only way out of this conversation. 'One way or the other, Lawrence, I'm leaving. There's a new development on the other side of town that I'm interested in. With my share of the house, I can afford a place. Libby… until she's gotten sorted, can choose between us.'

Lawrence turned the fork over one last time. 'Is that what the boxes in the hallway are for? For you to start packing?'

Boxes? A frown bloomed. Those boxes were for Jack. 'Yes,' she said. 'That's exactly what they're for.' And there it was – the ball pushed, just as Caro had said. The rolling started.

The sound of a marriage falling apart could be heard throughout the house hours after Libby had retreated to her bedroom with Ben, and Jack had come home, heard the echo and, like Libby, closed his door on the corrosive aftermath.

Lawrence occupied the living room. Helen staked her ground in the kitchen, trying first Caro, and then Kay. Neither of them answered. Three hours passed with her padding between the fridge and the table, filling her glass an inch, scrolling through Rightmove, scrolling through *stocks for beginn*ers, scrolling through YouTube videos of Stevie Nicks and eighties hits and Live Aid. Crying for Freddie Mercury, crying because she couldn't stay and crying because it was so hard to leave. Crying for Caro and crying for her children, the baby that never lived and the young adults, upstairs, barricaded in their bedrooms. And crying also for a man she'd once loved who was now shuffling around the living room.

Why was it so hard? She scrolled through to Coldplay and as Chris Martin sang his mournful best, set about unloading the dishwasher.

It was gone midnight by the time she went upstairs, straight into the spare box room that doubled as an ironing room. It took the last of her strength to yank the sofa bed out, throw a sheet down and collapse, half undressed, eyes as swollen as grapes.

The next morning she woke late, her mouth dry, her heart heavy, every muscle in her body stiff. The sofa bed was as comfortable as cardboard. From the kitchen she could hear the sound of someone moving around and when she tiptoed out to the landing, it was Libby's soft voice that floated up the stairs. She was humming to herself. Helen turned away. The bedroom door, the room that until yesterday she had shared with Lawrence, was open. He was obviously up.

'Libby,' she whispered as she leaned over the banister.

No answer.

Cautiously she went downstairs. The hall cupboard was open, and looking inside she saw that Lawrence's cycling shoes were gone. So he was out. A huge wave of relief swept through her; tentatively she made her way to the kitchen. She didn't know what Libby had heard last night, but whatever she had was too much. Two or twenty-two, in this situation Libby and Jack were innocent bystanders.

Easily bruised, in need of shelter, not stray bullets. It was hers and Lawrence's battle.

Libby was at the sink.

'Good morning,' Helen said, almost shy.

Turning, Libby smiled. 'Ben's still sleeping,' she said and nodded at the baby monitor on the table.

'Oh.' Helen stood listening to the raspy little breaths the monitor emitted.

'I've got to get on. I've been expressing and I want to get it frozen.' Picking up the kettle, Libby poured an inch of boiling water into a row of bottles.

'What are you doing?' Helen asked, a little dazed. The kitchen, her kitchen, seemed to be a hub of organised activity that for once she was not the centre of. Libby was.

'Sterilising.' Libby turned the tap on and refilled the kettle. 'Do you want a cup of tea?'

'I do,' Helen murmured. 'I would love a cup of tea.' And she went to fetch cups. Autopilot.

But Libby was already there. 'Sit down, Mum,' she said, pulling out cups, easing back a chair.

Helen sat watching. And although Libby was humming again, she could tell now how forced it was. As if something had happened to set her daughter's senses on red alert. Which of course it had. Last night, she'd had to listen to the sound of her parents hurting each other. She frowned. Was that it? Was it her presence now that had Libby so nervous? 'Libby,' she said. 'What's the matter?'

'Nothing,' Libby answered and flushed bright red.

'Something is.'

Libby shook her head. 'Nothing,' she managed again,

through tightly pressed lips. But her eyes were glassy as a mountain lake.

'You heard, didn't you?'

This time Libby nodded.

Helen's heart folded over. She dropped her head into her hands, her hair falling like loose straw. 'I'm sorry,' she whispered.

'It's OK, Mum,' Libby whispered back. 'Don't cry.'

Libby the busy bee, the little mum, playing mum to her own mum now was all Helen needed to come to her senses. She stood up, went over and threw her arms around her daughter, holding her tight, pressing her into her chest. '*It's not alright.*'

Libby couldn't have answered if she'd wanted to, Helen was holding her so tight.

'I don't want it to be like this,' she continued. 'Stupid arguments and rows. There's no need for it and I promise you…' She pulled back, holding Libby's face with both her hands. 'We won't do that. Last night won't happen again. Me and your dad will get through this and somehow, we'll stay friends. OK?'

Looking straight back at her, Libby sighed. 'Are you going to tell Dad that?'

'Of course I am! He won't want—' She stopped talking. 'Why?'

'The living room.' Libby shrugged. 'You should look in the living room.'

And because Helen didn't know at first what she was looking for, she didn't at first see. She stood in the doorway, like a cat at a window, scanning the room. And slowly they came into focus. One… then two… and then three, four, five, six. Like early primroses on a spring walk, with each one discovered, more and more came forward. Except she wasn't looking at the yellow of spring flowers, she was looking at post-it notes, stuck to various ornaments and items of furniture. One word scrawled across each: *Lawrence.* Her initial reaction was to gasp, a reflexive response made up of equal parts astonishment and amusement that flowed seamlessly into a concentrated frown of such deep curiosity she had an instant in which to be grateful that she never had got around to Botox. What *had* her husband set about so fastidiously to claim? What, in Lawrence's mind, remained, *his*? She was suddenly and keenly interested.

The French carriage clock on the mantle that had been his grandparents' own wedding gift. Fair enough, family heirlooms are family heirlooms.

On the top shelf of the display unit, the commemoration medal (mounted and framed) for his Five Countries, Five Months All-Road Cycle Challenge. Helen shook her head. Why would he think she had any intention of taking that? And anyway what about her commemoration medal? For twenty-five years of keeping-everyone's-knickers-clean-challenge? What else?

She walked across to the window and turned to face the room. The very expensive painting they'd been given for their tenth anniversary. *Mmm.* It wasn't that she wanted it, but it was valuable and why should Lawrence take it? Was that mean of her?

His favourite armchair. Fine, although the post-it

note there had almost given up, hanging as it was by a curled-up corner.

And books… Lawrence seemed to want every book on the shelves. Fine. It was mostly a collection of books on mountain climbing anyway and she might have laughed! If what this sad display revealed wasn't so bleak she might have thrown her head back and enjoyed the best laugh of the day. He was like a child, her husband. A child, hoarding the last of the sweets. He'd obviously done this last night. All the shuffling and moving of furniture she'd heard from the kitchen. Was this what was paramount in his mind? After everything that had been said?

And because she still couldn't quite believe what she was seeing, she turned and took the stairs two at a time, up to *the most useless and most precious things cupboard.* It was a post-it note free zone. Of course it was. Helen leaned back against the wall and tipped her head to the ceiling. She would have walked out of her marriage with nothing more than Daniel's birth/death certificate and the envelope that contained Libby and Jack's baby teeth, which wouldn't, when seen with a clear head, have provided her with much shelter. *Time to get going, Helen,* she breathed. *Time to get busy.*

She went back downstairs, peeled the post-it note off the tenth-anniversary painting, grabbed her handbag, and called to Libby, 'I still want that tea! I won't be a moment, then let's sit down.'

'That'll be nice,' Libby called.

And again, Helen took the stairs two at a time.

*

Emir's number went straight to voicemail, with a message saying not to bother leaving a voicemail.

Danny Abbott answered on the first ring. 'Helen!'

'Danny...' she said and failed to find an end to the sentence.

He chuckled. 'What took you so long?'

Helen walked across to the bedroom window and closed her eyes. Danny was fun but this wasn't a time for fun. This was a time for growing her building society nest. That little flat she'd seen? With the Juliet balcony? And if she wanted him to take her seriously, she had to keep it serious. 'I've been trying to get hold of Emir,' she said. 'I was wondering if you knew if he was around.' *If he was around.* She sounded like a teenager ringing for a date.

'Funny,' Danny said. 'I could say the exact same thing about Caro.'

'Caro?'

'Yep. You're looking for Emir and I'm looking for Caro. Maybe we should get together and make up a search party?'

'We...' Helen paused, looked up and out of the window and frowned. 'You're looking for Caro?'

'Yes. All joking aside,' Danny said, 'how is she? I don't mind admitting, I'm a little worried.'

Helen gripped her phone. She had no idea how much Danny knew, *if* in fact he knew anything. It wasn't her place to... and she wasn't going to... 'Caro's fine,' she managed. 'She's fine.'

'Really?' Danny fired back.

'Yes!... Well, the last time I saw her. She's fine, yes.'

On the other end of the line she heard Danny unpack

her mumblings. Underneath his jovial exterior, she knew, worked a shrewd and diligent mind. She didn't speak, and for a long moment, neither did he.

'If you say so, Helen,' he said finally. 'It's just I've known Caro for ten years and I did not see this coming. Not. At. All.'

The words thumped into her. *He knew.* She hadn't imagined Caro telling *anyone*, let alone Danny Abbott. But maybe with the time off, she'd had to explain herself. And then again, maybe it was a sign of just how recovered she was. 'Well,' she breathed, 'to be honest, Danny, I didn't either. When it first happened.'

'So what's she going to do now?'

Do? Helen stretched her phone away from her ear and looked at it. *Do?* Why was he asking her this? And what was it to him anyway? *Do?* Kay and she had discussed this just once. What was Caro going to do? Adopt? Try surrogacy? Forget the whole idea? The subject was a wounded bird that they had tentatively placed in a darkened box and tucked away, fearful of opening the lid and hurting it again, deciding without ever saying so that it was best left to recover on its own. So. *Do?* Regardless of what Caro might decide, or had already decided, she wasn't about to start discussing it with Danny Abbot. 'I really don't know,' she said, truthfully.

Danny sighed. 'Well, she blindsided all of us I can tell you, Helen. I mean, we all knew something was going on, that much was obvious yesterday. I don't know what planet she was on, but it wasn't Earth. Matt is fuming.'

'Matt?'

'Her CEO. She's given him a week's notice. She didn't give me any! I found out through Mel.'

'Mel?'

'You sound like my echo,' Danny said drily.

And Helen didn't speak. She felt a little disorientated, as if she'd been led to the edge of a precipice and left there.

'Melanie,' Danny said, laying emphasis on the name, interrupting her thoughts. 'Caro's secretary?' He sighed. 'Seriously though, Helen? I understand the news about her mother was a shock, but to quit? I thought Caro was a lifer.'

Slowly Helen lowered herself onto the marital bed she had so recently vacated. 'What are you talking about?' she whispered, and goosebumps raced along her arms.

'Caro. Quitting.'

'Her job?'

'*Of course her job!*' And finally Danny paused. 'Wait a minute, wait… What are *you* talking about?'

He didn't know! He didn't know and she'd nearly told him and…

'Helen?'

'She quit?' Now Helen was back on her feet. 'When?' Caro *was* her job, how could she quit when she was her job? 'And what did you say about her mother?'

There was a long silence in which Helen heard Danny put two and two together and come up with four. But she wasn't about to confirm it for him, so she made a fist of her hand and waited… Firstly for him to forget what she might just have been about to tell him, and secondly to tell her what the hell was going on.

'OK,' he said. 'Obviously there's other issues—'

'I can't—'

'I wouldn't want you to, Helen. I'm just worried for someone I consider a friend.'

Helen was silent.

'Her mother, apparently, has had a stroke. Caro got the news yesterday during a meeting, so obviously she left.' Danny gave a dry laugh. 'Not that anyone noticed – she was pretty spaced out... anyway, yadda yadda and then, next thing anyone hears, she's rung Matt and told him she's quitting. No explanations, no notice... *nada!*'

'A stroke?' Helen managed, grasping onto the only thread of Danny's speech that made any sense at all.

Danny waited a beat. 'Yes. And of course, in those circumstances, she'd want to take some time out. But she quit. And...' Danny's voice dropped a tone, becoming darker and slower. 'The thing is, Helen, no one can get hold of her. Mel's been trying every half hour since yesterday. She's not answering her phone. I mean I'm sure she's fine. I'd feel a bit easier if she checked in, that's all. Know what I mean? As I said, she was definitely a bit off yesterday.'

Palm pressed to her cheek, Helen leaned against the bed. She knew exactly what Danny meant, times a hundred. Suddenly it was overwhelmingly clear that she too needed to speak to Caro. Yes, check in with her. Set a tab up and keep it going. Danny didn't know the half of it and it was all too obvious now that Helen didn't either, which made her feel ashamed in a way that was becoming all too familiar in this long friendship. What she did know was that Caro wasn't OK, she wasn't back to normal, she wasn't over it, and now, her mother had had a stroke?

'I'm sorry, Helen,' Danny said, reading her silence. 'I didn't realise you didn't know. I just assumed... You being friends and...'

As if he were in the room with her, Helen waved his words away. 'Even friends,' she croaked, 'don't tell each other everything.'

17

'And that's why they gave me the hysterectomy. They said I had no choice. That at my age…' Caro stopped talking and sat very still, the last words she'd spoken visible as the vapour trail from an aeroplane. *At my age…*

Caro eased back in her chair, her hands spread along its tastefully upholstered arms. Along with the bed, side table and washbasin, the chair was the only furniture in this private room her mother had been moved to. It was spacious and clean, with a window that mostly overlooked adjoining roofs, but also included a triangle of blue sky. The walls were a soft white, the floor a smooth vinyl that squeaked under pressure. All in all, a huge improvement from the understaffed ICU ward. So, along with the private nurse she'd hired to fill in the gaps, Caro had done as much as she could. Not that her mother was aware. It didn't matter. It wouldn't matter if her mother never opened her eyes again (which she wasn't expected to) – she would still have spent the money. It was the least she could do.

'I know,' she whispered, 'you know all this already, don't you?'

All around the air was vibrant with the sounds of life support machines. In the midst of them, her mother lay silent as the grave, her face whiter than the pillow upon which it lay, her mouth forced into a silent and gaping O by a clear breathing tube.

'There isn't anyone else though.' Caro turned the corner of her mouth up in a wry smile. 'Kay was ringing every day at one point, but she's got problems of her own and I had to tell her. *I'm fine.* And Helen?' Caro looked off to the side, her eyes briefly closing. She tried again. 'I... It doesn't compare to what she went through, I know that. She had to deliver Daniel, and I can't imagine...'

The IV monitor bleeped.

Caro stared at it. 'I just can't do comparisons,' she said finally. 'Even if they're only in my head.' She looked down at her hands. 'But I'm not fine, Mum. I just can't find a way of saying that. Do you understand?' she whispered, and looking back up at the monitor, gave a weak smile. 'One for yes, Mum?'

The machine stayed silent.

Slowly she got to her feet, linked her hands together and stretched them forward. She was stiff, from sitting too long in the hospital chair, and from sleeping in her mother's bed, which was so much softer than her own. Nearly forty-five minutes she'd been here. Plus two hours yesterday, without a flicker of a response. She went across to the bed and re-tucked the corner of an already neatly tucked sheet into place. 'You always liked Kay, didn't you?'

she said. 'I remember you saying so on the drive home from graduation.' Caro leaned forward to push thin grey strands from her mother's liver-spotted forehead. 'In fact,' she said, her voice no more than a whisper, 'Kay's mum was about the only person you spoke to all day.' The sheet fixed, her mother's hair smoothed, Caro stood looking down at her. 'I do know you were very impressed with her being a deputy head, but…' She sighed. 'She has dementia now, Mum. She's going into a nursing home. Today I think. Or yesterday? I should call,' she murmured, looking out of the window and the thought slipped away as swiftly as it had arisen.

From the outside corridor the sound of footsteps slapped past, and she turned in time to see, through the small glass window, the blue shoulders of a passing nurse. She walked back to the chair and sat down again, chin resting in the palm of her hand. This was what she mostly remembered from her own stay in hospital. The uniforms. Blue scrubs, white coats, green masks, the rub of disposable gloves. Squeaked on, squeaked off, clang of the bin as they were thrown in. She leaned forward, elbows on knees. 'I remember the doctor saying, *the worst of it is over now.*' And from underneath quizzically raised brows, Caro looked at her mother. 'What do you think of that, Mum? *The worst of it is over.* What a funny thing to say.'

The room hummed back its ICU tune.

Again she shook her head. 'I knew she was wrong, but I didn't say anything. *The worst of it is over?* It hadn't even begun. I knew that. It hadn't…' And her hand flew to her mouth, made a fist and stayed there. 'Sorry,' she blinked, her

246

voice splintering. 'I'm so sorry that you found out like that, Mum. I wouldn't have had them call you… if I'd known. If… But I couldn't tell you. I couldn't find a way of…' A sob forced itself out from behind her fist, and then another and another. Shoulders rising and falling, Caro shook her head furiously. 'I told myself I wouldn't cry. Not here. Not in front of you. I promised myself that. I did.'

Moments passed. Moments spaced and counted by the rhythmic mechanical suck of air and high-pitched, precision-coded chimes.

Eventually her sobs faded and her fist relaxed and she leaned over to smooth out non-existent creases in her trousers. 'Anyway,' and she heaved a breath in. 'That's all for me to work out and if… Well, if you wake up, I will explain it. I promise that too because Kay's mum doesn't even recognise her any more and Helen's mum died five years ago and…'

Caro leaned back in the chair and turned to the window. This was a promise she would keep. If her mother ever woke up, she would find a way of talking to her. Because if there was anything at all to be salvaged from this, she knew she must find it. Outside, a flock of birds flew past. A small V-shape, black specks, with one lone speck, some distance behind, struggling to keep up. Caro watched. The V disappeared, so only the straggler was left in sight, its jagged flight path a sign, she imagined, of panic. How easy, she thought, it is to get lost. How easy to be lost. 'Do you remember,' she murmured, 'that hat Helen's mum wore to graduation?' She was still watching the window, the small patch of blue, the lone and lonely bird. And as if Helen's mother's long-ago hat was up there in the sky, Caro smiled. 'It was rose pink, with a matching feather. I remember it well.'

Turning back to her mother, she continued. 'In fact there are a few things I remember about that day. The hat. Dad, stubbing his cigarette out on the grass outside the marquee. And you, Mum. You, standing on the steps outside the main hall. I was a little bit behind and I'm sure you didn't realise I was there, because I heard you. You said, *I wonder if I could have done something like this?* You said it out loud, even though you were talking to yourself. I was closer than you knew, and I should have answered, but I didn't. I was too embarrassed. By everything. Your outfit. Dad throwing his stub like that, the way you couldn't, or wouldn't, mingle. Helen's mum was like the queen. Floating around the quadrangle in that hat, talking to all the professors, while you and Dad sat at that table by the stone lion. Three statues. You, Dad and the lion. Except you moved your hand to cover your mouth every time you took a bite of sandwich. Champagne and strawberries, pavlova, scones, *vol au vents*, pastries… and you managed half a ham sandwich. Everything was a source of embarrassment for you. And me. But the thing was, I was graduating with a better degree than Helen. Not as good as Kay, but better than Helen and we didn't need to be embarrassed. About anything.' As suddenly as she'd started, Caro stopped talking. In her lap her hands had curled to fists. She sat up and put her hands to her face. It was soaking wet. 'Why?' she whispered, looking at her mother's pale immobile face, '*why* were we always so embarrassed by ourselves?'

248

18

Ten am on a Saturday morning and Kay stood in her lovely floral bedroom, hair dripping, tea cooling as she looked out of the window, thinking the same question she'd been thinking for the last few days. Since she'd found a space, that is, to resurrect this particular worry, dust it off and hang it out again. Caro seemed to be fine, Helen was headily in love with her new grandson of course, her mother was finally in a safe place, her father... resigned, and Amanda Woods (she'd heard via an email from Nick, who couldn't resist violating even the sanctity of the summer holidays) had been happy with the new (inflated) grade that Zac had earned from the re-mark. Plus, her place on the unconscious bias workshop was booked for September. At last! Time to spare for her to start again with all her Alex-shaped worries. Which always began and ended with, *why?* Why hadn't she learned to understand that when Alex set his mind to do something, he did it.

She wrapped her hands around her mug and held it at her chin, the steam damp on her lips. There he was now, in the drive with Shook. Together they were fixing heavy-duty straps over the trailer, over all those boxed up bits that had arrived throughout the spring and were now transformed into a contraption Evil Knievel would have been proud of.

And she'd laughed? When, at the end of another mind-bogglingly boring episode of *Rust to Riches,* he'd declared his intention, she'd laughed? She took a sip of tea, head shaking in disbelief.

When Alex was two, he could spend an entire nursery session threading paper loops, an activity the other children tired of in ten minutes. And at five, when she'd popped up the road to the Khans to see how their new driveway was coming along, Hassan had let Alex sit in the mini digger. Five minutes – while the adults went inside. An hour and ten minutes later she'd had to come and fetch him, after he'd worked out how to move the digger forwards and backwards, thus digging a strip of the Khans' front garden. (Which needed doing anyway, but that wasn't the point). So why the hell had she laughed at those boxes? Because if there was one person in the world with the patience and tunnel vision required to re-build a motorcycle from scratch, it was Alex.

As if he had heard the frenetic thrum of her thoughts, Shook looked up and waved.

Kay waved back. What a good and kind man he was. Always helping her and Alex. Never wanting or expecting anything in return. This was why she would never move. The neighbours on her street, the old timers she'd grown up with and these newcomers, were like extended family. She held her cup up and pointed at it, mouthing *Tea?*

Grinning, Shook gave her a thumbs up.

They'd be leaving within ten minutes and then she needed to fill her day. She'd already rung her dad who'd told her to stop worrying and *do something nice.* Her mother was fine. Confused, but fine. And no he didn't need a lift because he wasn't going today. Lindsey from Ashdown House had already rung and advised him to leave it twenty-four hours to help her mother settle. Bemused, Kay had ended the call wondering, not for the first time, at her father's readiness to acquiesce in the decisions of the professionals. *Leave it to them* had always been his mantra. He was of that generation who thought doctors were gods. And although she wasn't entirely convinced that not visiting was the best way to settle her mother, she wasn't going to go against her father either.

So what would she do? She turned to her wardrobe. Sort it out? The idea wilted before it had even begun blooming. She just didn't have the stamina. Even after a good night's sleep, she seemed to wake nowadays with energy levels already drained to half empty. Doctors, Kay, she whispered. You must make a time.

Two minutes later she was dressed in her uniform of leggings and t-shirt and on her way downstairs to make more tea.

In the kitchen Shook was washing his hands at the kitchen sink. He looked over his shoulder and nodded at her phone. 'Been ringing non-stop,' he said.

Kay picked it up. There were five missed calls from Helen who would, Kay knew, be ringing to discuss Caro. *Again.* As if constantly recycling the story was going to effect a different ending. It wouldn't and the only person who seemed unable to accept that was Helen. Which was ironic, given that Helen had had the strongest resistance to Caro's pregnancy in the first place. The episode had been awful and sad, but Caro seemed to have moved on and Kay had enough on her plate with her mother's move and her job situation. She put the phone down and handed Shook a tea towel.

'He's a good mechanic,' Shook said, drying his pink, scrubbed hands. 'Who taught him?'

'Alex?' She handed him a cup. 'He taught himself.'

'No one showed him?'

'No. I certainly didn't, and his father couldn't tell one end of a spanner from the other.'

'Well, he knows what he's doing. It's impressive.'

Kay sighed. She looked out through the open kitchen door to the drive where her son stood, hands on hips, broad shoulders, surveying the trailer. 'Yes,' she said quietly. 'I suppose it is.' How tall he was, her boy. Her man now. 'Alex? Tea?'

Alex shook his head. 'We need to be leaving soon.'

She nodded. Of course they did. A cup of tea wasn't going to stop him. Nothing was.

'Better get on then.' Shook winked and gulped his own tea back, wiping his mouth with the back of his hand. He started towards the door and as he did, her phone started ringing.

Helen.

Again.

Six calls now, which even for Helen wasn't right. Kay picked it up and turned to Shook. There was something she wanted to say before he left. *Needed* to say. 'Wait a minute?' she called and into the phone said, 'Helen.' Then, 'What—' Frowning, her hand went up in a stop sign, both to Shook in the doorway, and Helen across town. 'Slow down,' she said.

Shook slowed to a standstill. At the other end of the line, Helen rushed on.

'Helen! Slow— *Helen!*' Kay glanced at Shook. 'You're not making any sense. *Slow down.* Start again.'

And as Helen finally slowed, and Kay listened, her hand came to her brow. 'She just quit? Well, how bad? How bad was the stroke?… No…' She spoke slowly now. 'I agree,' she said. 'I think we should… We can go in mine… *Helen!*' Again her palm went up and she almost had to shout. '*I'll* drive. I can pick you up in ten.'

'Trouble?' Shook asked as the call ended.

Kay nodded. 'Caro's mother has had a stroke and… well, no one can get hold of her, Caro that is. Helen's car is in the garage,' she said vacantly. 'Helen thinks we should go down. Check she's OK.'

Shook frowned. 'Is there anything I can do?'

'I don't think so,' she said and stared at her phone as if she'd forgotten what a phone was. 'The thing is, she's quit her job.'

'Doesn't sound good.' Shook stuck his lower lip out.

'It's not.' Kay paused. 'Caro… I can't imagine it. Caro loves her job.'

'Is this the Caro who was here when I did the electrics in the bedroom?'

'Yes.' Kay looked at him. When did Shook put the extra socket in her bedroom? Before Cyprus? It seemed odd to her that he should remember. 'Yes,' she said again. 'That was Caro.' And without stopping to think, added, 'She's just lost a baby and now she's quit her job.'

'Baby?'

'I don't mean lost…' Kay blurted. 'I mean… I mean she was expecting… and now she isn't. She had a miscarriage. It was quite bad. There were some complications and she had to have a hysterectomy…' If Kay could have stopped talking, she would have. If a celestial hand had appeared and slapped it across her wide open mouth she wouldn't have resisted. *Why* did she keep going? Because it was clear by the mix of emotions passing through Shook's face that she should have stopped three sentences ago. Sometimes that happened though, didn't it? Words just came out. Fell… spewed… To avoid adding to Shook's discomfiture, she looked at her phone again.

His face a deep red, he nodded.

'We're… Anyway, my other friend thinks we should go and try and find her…' And again Kay trailed off to study her hand, as if it wasn't her phone she was holding but a tiny Helen calling out instructions.

'Are you worried?'

Kay looked up. 'Yes,' she answered. Caro quitting her job, not answering her phone, were so far out of character as to be… worrying. Her legs went airy and her stomach went cold. She'd known Caro for many years and through some awful times, the worst of which was so recent, but Caro had never gone AWOL like this. She always responded to a text or a missed call. It wasn't in her nature not to, she was too diligent. Even the night before her ex, Mike, had got married, when she'd shut herself away for the weekend, she'd still responded to Kay's text: *Are you alright? Fine, just need to be alone.* And just a couple of weeks ago, when she came out of hospital, *I'm fine, Kay. Honestly, I'm fine.*

'You should go then.'

Shook's calm voice stirred her. Kay looked at him.

'It sounds like she might need her friends,' he said. 'You should go.'

Lips pressed tight together, Kay turned the phone over. Shook was right. Caro, who had never admitted to needing anyone in her life. Who had never really *had* anyone in her life, needed her friends now like she never had before. Even, Kay decided, if she didn't know that herself.

'We need to be going as well.'

'Shook?' There was a note of pain in Kay's voice, as if it had been pinched. This was it. This was what she needed to say before they left. 'You'll look after him, won't you? Alex? He's all I've got.'

Shook smiled and all the cragged lines of his face folded upward like a pleated fan. 'Like he was my own, Kay,' he said.

The pressure eased, her voice softened. 'Thank you,' she said. 'Thank you.'

19

'Anyway...' Caro rose, walked across to the window and unlatched it. 'Things haven't worked out so brilliantly for Helen either,' she said, easing the window open an inch. It was stiff and she had to cup both hands underneath the rail and jerk it up, but instantly a wave of fresher air swept in, cooling her cheeks and her mind. What was the point of trawling over the hot coals of painful memories? The shame she felt at having let her mother down, at not having the courage to speak up, would stay warm, Caro knew, until the end. Slipping it away under a thousand other thoughts, she turned back to where her mother lay. 'She's getting a divorce,' she said, and looked at her hands, sticky with flecks of paint and dust. 'From Lawrence.' And she walked across to the basin and turned the tap on.

'You probably won't remember her husband,' she continued, rubbing her hands together under a trickle of water. 'They met at uni... well, we all did, so he was at graduation too. Very tall. Good looking. He came over and said hello but…' Caro shrugged. 'It was very brief, and I can't imagine…' Caro stretched her hand out and turned the tap off, holding it there in place. She looked up, and in the small mirror above the sink her reflection looked back. 'Very brief, under the circumstances,' she murmured, watching as her mouth turned up at one corner. It wasn't a smile, more a belated acknowledgement of the outstanding unimportance of something that for far too long had pretended otherwise. A recognition, finally, of just how trivial it had all been and how far away from it she was now. The privilege of maturity of course, with its top-floor view. And looking at herself, for a moment, Caro had no idea who had come to this conclusion first. Herself, or her mirrored reflection. 'Here's a secret, Mum,' she said, smiling for real now. 'I'd lost my virginity to him the week before. She turned to her mother. 'Are you shocked?' she whispered.

Her mother was silent. Her eyes stayed closed, and her mouth gaped open to accommodate the ventilator tube. Against the white of the pillow, her thin curls lapped like sad grey waves.

Caro tore a square of paper towel. Twenty-nine years had passed! Twenty-nine years in which she had never dared breathe those words out loud. Decades of scientific progress, of technological wizardry increasingly at her disposal, undreamt of back then, and yet she had never dared ease this self-imposed burden, had allowed instead these words to nestle in her conscience, stone-heavy, dull, immovable. She tipped her head back to the ceiling and laughed out loud and the stones rolled free, smooth and soundless as bubbles on a stream, and all she could think was how ironic life is. How ridiculous that the first time in twenty-nine years she'd felt safe enough to make this most mundane of confessions was in front of her mother, the one person in the world whom she absolutely couldn't talk to. She pressed the towel against her wet hands and held it there. 'Three years at university, Mum,' she whispered, shaking her head. 'Supposed to be having the time of my life, watching Helen *actually* have the time of her life, and even Kay – she had her share of liaisons... And me?' Caro smiled. 'All I had was headaches and 2:1 essays which I never did get up to a first.' Pressing her foot down on the pedal of the bin, the lid flipped open. 'So,' she sighed. 'It could have been anyone really, and with hindsight...' Her hands worked the paper towel, folding and crushing it, as she stood staring at a point across the room. 'In fact, it *should* have been anyone... anyone *but* Lawrence, because I was in love with him and sleeping with him only made me think there was a chance that he might be in love with me. God!' Dropping the towel in the bin, Caro whip-turned back to the mirror. 'What an idiot,' she mouthed. 'What an absolute idiot, Caroline Hardcastle!'

Behind, the orchestration of her mother's life support continued. Bleeps and chimes... chimes and bleeps, and always the percussion of mechanical breaths.

Caro shook her head. 'What a bloody waste of time and energy!' She walked back to the chair, falling into it as if it were water. 'It's actually embarrassing, Mum. I can't count how many times I'd go over and visit Helen. See her perfect home and her perfect kids and then go back to my flat and cry. Over what? An AGA cooker and sash windows?' With a swift movement, she thrust her chin forward to rest in her palm, elbows on knees, as she looked at her mother and said, 'Lawrence is a prick – to use Dad's favourite word. He's the most selfish man I've ever met, and I've met more than a few. How Helen's put up with him all these years, or what they've actually talked about, I have no idea. She can't have been happy. She can't... You had to look close though,' she murmured, 'to see the cracks. I mean, even I... I was probably looking closest of all, and I didn't see.'

And thinking this, she leaned her head against the back of the chair and closed her eyes. 'I'm glad she's leaving,' she said. 'She's my friend and I just want her to be happy.' Her hand came up to her chest and she breathed in, a raggedy forced inhalation that barely reached her neck. 'And I'd like to be happy too, Mum. That's why I did what I did. I thought it would be the solution and now...' Her voice broke. She forced another breath and filled her lungs and stayed silent.

Her mother lay still, the machines whirred and bleeped, and the world, of course, went on... As she would, too. She looked down and smoothed the fine rayon of her shirt. 'Helen is a grandmother now, actually. Her daughter, Libby has just had a baby.' Caro shook her head. 'She's twenty-one. Or twenty-two? I'm not sure. But it wasn't what anyone expected... Anyway,' she said and turned to the window. 'She had a boy. Eight pounds seven ounces, in two hours. As easy as that.' Smiling, Caro brought her hand to her eye and rubbed it. 'I'm happy for her, Mum. Really, I am... I mean, what does it all matter in the end?

It seems to me that the things we think we want were never real in the first place. So, yes. I'm happy for Helen… and for Libby. But …' Caro's hands fell to her lap. 'I'm so sorry for you, Mum. There'll be no grandchildren from me, and I wish you could hear me, because I want you to know how sorry I am. It wasn't what I intended, and I don't really understand how I got here…' Caro turned to look again at the window, the blue triangle between the slate grey rooftops. How did she get here? At what blind corner in the maze of her past did she make the fateful turn that would lead her here, to her dying mother's bedside, fifty-one years old, destined to spend the rest of her life alone. The current of regret that swept over her was irresistible. It coursed through, all the white water of past decisions churned up and re-hashed. *If* she could go back, *if* she could pinpoint that particular day the die was cast, she would. Caught in the flow of the moment, Caro felt that she'd change it all, let everything she'd achieved slip away, if only she could go back and stop this stain of loneliness from spreading in her heart. Because how could she have known? How could she have known at twenty-two, or thirty-two, how lonely it was possible for life to become? 'No,' she whispered, 'it wasn't what I intended. Then again, does anyone end up with the life they intended?'

From behind came a low and discreet cough, interrupting her reverie and filling Caro with a cold fear. She turned. She hadn't even heard the door being eased open, but there was her brother, Sean, standing on the threshold. Her face coloured. 'I know she can't hear me,' she said defensively.

Sean shrugged. 'I've been doing the same.'

'You have?'

He nodded.

'Actually…' He cleared his throat again. 'It's probably the only way I can talk to her. You know… properly.'

Caro opened her mouth to respond, but anything she might have said evaporated in the searing honesty of the moment, the like of which she hadn't shared with her brother since they were the smallest of children. She tried to smile, but it stuck, and tears flooded her eyes. All these years and she'd had no idea. No idea that he too might have found the familial web as difficult and treacherous to navigate as she did. She turned back to her mother, the heart monitor and the ventilator and the IV unit. The tubes and the pipes and the needles. Her mother had been such a strong person. At eighty-two she'd never had a serious illness in her life, didn't need or have help. In fact, the overriding feeling Caro took from her childhood was that her mother didn't need anyone. Not her, not Sean and certainly not their father. So it was a surprise bordering on shock to understand that Sean, in some way, had felt the distance too. And then to realise how, with his frequent visits home, he had kept trying, whereas she had, to all intents and purposes, given up.

He gave her a small sad smile, and she gave him one back.

'Why don't you eat with us?' he said. 'Before you go back?'

'I will,' she said, and she meant it. 'But I can't tonight. I'm driving home to prepare for a work thing on Monday.'

'OK.'

'But –' and there was a sense of urgency to her voice now – 'after that, I'll be back and… I thought I'd stay, for a while… Well, at least as long as I'm needed.'

Sean looked at her. 'Won't that be difficult with your job?'

'Not really. I'm due some time.' Caro threaded her hands together and looked at them. *Not yet.* She didn't have the words yet to explain all that had happened, or what *for a while* really meant. Not when she didn't know herself. 'But I mean it, Sean,' she added as she looked up. 'I'd like to come.' This much, she was sure of.

'Good. Well… When are you leaving?'

'This afternoon but –' Caro turned to look at her mother – 'I thought I'd take a trip first. I was looking through some of Mum's old photos. Us at Stonehenge.' The idea that she might re-visit the scene of that strangely happy photo hadn't formed until this moment in which she gave it voice. And although she was almost surprised to hear the words, she didn't doubt them. If she was to try and anchor herself, to reconnect with that little girl and, eventually, her mother, this was exactly where she should start.

'Stonehenge?' Sean chuckled. 'Well, it's changed a bit,' he said. 'There's a lot of rope nowadays. You can't get so close any more.'

Caro smiled. 'That's OK. I've changed too.'

And for a moment they looked at each other, brother and sister, almost strangers.

'I just have to let the nurse know I'm here,' he said. 'I'll be back in a moment.'

The door swung shut, and looking at it, Caro whispered, 'I can try, can't I? I can try and get close again.' She stood up and walked across to her mother, leaned forward and pushed a lock of her hair clear from her brow. 'Of course you could have done it,' she whispered as she bent and kissed the paper-thin skin of her forehead. 'Of course you could have gone to a university and earned a degree. It's all stardust and pretence anyway and I hate myself... I hate that it's taken me all these years to tell you that.'

20

'Oh my God, Kay!' Her head between her legs, Helen's voice was muffled. 'How many more of these am I going to find?' she said and sat upright, waving an empty packet of Maltesers.

'*That,*' and Kay glanced sideways, 'isn't empty.'

'Isn't it?' Helen turned the pack upside down and a solitary Malteser rolled into her palm, white with age. She dropped it back in, crumpled the packet and stuffed it into a carrier bag, already full of empty Maltesers packets. 'Why don't you just get it valeted?' Her voice was muffled again as once more she bent forward to scour for more rubbish under the passenger seat of Kay's car.

'I've been a little busy, Helen,' Kay snapped.

The whip-like lash of Kay's response stung and it had Helen sitting up and leaning back, the rubbish bag between her knees.

'It's not exactly on my priority list.'

'Right.' Helen folded the top of the carrier over and pushed it into the door pocket. Of course, the car wasn't on Kay's radar. She'd only just gotten her mother settled in the home and hadn't they just been talking about how that might, finally, allow her to claw a little time back? Time in which to do many things other than have a car valeted? 'I'm sorry,' she mumbled.

'What for?' Hands on the wheel, Kay did a double take.

'It was thoughtless of me. I forget how busy you are.'

'Well, hopefully it'll get a little easier now,' Kay sighed, and her shoulders rose up as she took a deep breath.

'Hopefully.' Helen leaned her elbow on the window rim. Outside, the Surrey Hills flashed past and for the ten-hundredth time in the last half hour, she picked up first her phone, then Kay's. No messages from Caro, no missed calls. *Nothing.* Despite the numerous messages and calls left for Caro. 'So,' she said brightly, 'what will you do?' And she bent again to retrieve the rubbish bag. Anything to stop the thoughts that she couldn't stop thinking, that she knew Kay could be thinking too. 'You'll have a bit more time in the evenings surely?'

'Not that much.'

'But you won't have to pop in every night, will you? Or does your dad need—' Her voice stuck in her chest as again she leaned forward, this time scooping up an empty salt and vinegar crisp packet.

'Leave it, Helen!' Kay did a double take at the rubbish in Helen's hands. 'Just leave it. OK?'

Helplessly Helen nodded. She crumpled the crisp packet and crumpled the rubbish bag and sat with the crumpled mess in her lap and stared at the road ahead. If Caro would just call or message they could stop the car, turn around and leave her to work out whatever it was she needed to work out. And perhaps they still should. Except when she'd suggested to Kay that they take a drive down to Salisbury, that after what had happened to Caro… she might be… she might need… Kay had agreed. Instantly. And if Kay thought they should go… Well, Helen didn't want to consider the depths of that. It wasn't like Caro to do anything stupid, was it? She didn't know, because if recent events had taught Helen anything, it was that she didn't have a clue what anyone might do. Libby getting herself pregnant and then ignoring the fact? Caro getting herself pregnant?

Even she herself, embarking on that wild and glorious week in Cyprus…

'Tap dancing,' Kay said suddenly.

'What?'

'Tap dancing,' Kay repeated. 'I told you. I was thinking it might help me get a bit of energy back.'

'Quitting this rubbish will help more,' Helen said and held up the bag.

'I know. But I've been snacking in the car since Alex was a baby. Think I'm too far gone to stop now. Car journey equals chocolate.'

'Understandable.'

'I just get so tired.'

'That's understandable too.'

'No, I sort of mean it, Helen.' Kay stretched her arms out and pressed the heels of her hands into the steering wheel. 'By the end of the day I am bone-weary. Finished. A little chocolate on the way home helps.'

The tone of Kay's voice had Helen turning towards

her. For years now, Kay had had only one expression: utterly knackered. 'Are you OK?' she asked.

'Fine.' Kay waved the question away. 'I'm fifty, that's all. Too much on my plate.'

In response, Helen took her seatbelt and pulled it loose so she could shift around to face Kay better. She wasn't convinced by the *fine*. Not at all. Kay did have too much on her plate. She always had had. 'The complaint at school has gone away, right?'

'It'll never go away,' Kay said wryly. 'Like your old tweets, it's there for life.'

'I don't tweet.'

'Me neither.'

'So that's one thing to be grateful for.'

'God, imagine if it had been around when we were young.'

'I can't,' Helen said seriously. 'I have thought about that and every time I do, my legs go cold.'

Kay laughed and momentarily it broke the knot of tension between them. 'All the stupid things we said and did. Imagine. Preserved forever.'

'Let alone the perms.'

'Exactly!' And now they both laughed.

And as Helen turned to the window, the laughter felt like a cushion at her spine. Caro would be fine. Of course she would. Her mother had had a stroke. That's why she'd disappeared like this. She would be fine. This was Caro! Quitting her job… well, that wasn't Caro. Burying the worry, she turned back to Kay. 'But it is over?' she asked. 'There won't be any further action?'

'As long as I attend the course, yes. It's finished.'

'Right. And your mother has her place now.'

'She does.'

'And Alex is on the list for supported housing?'

'If he survives this motorcycle race.'

'*Kay!*' Helen snapped her head around. '*Don't say that!*'

'Joke,' Kay said, raising a hand of surrender. 'Joking.'

Helen frowned. Kay's face, her rigid hunched shoulders, screamed the opposite of joking, screamed in fact *worried beyond belief*. 'Don't shoot me,' she began tentatively.

'But?'

'Alex is much more capable than I think you sometimes give him credit for. Building that bike for a start…'

And suddenly Kay's hand was at her mouth, pressing back a sob of emotion.

'Kay… I didn't mean—'

'No.' Kay shook her head. 'You're right. He is more capable, and I do need to let him go, but God it's hard, Helen. It's so bloody hard.'

Helen nodded. There was a lump in her own throat now. 'I know,' she said. 'It's hard enough when…' Her voice trailed off. What was she going to say? When they're normal? It was always so difficult to talk about Alex. The difficulties which made him *not* normal. In fact, that was the only word any of them had ever been able to fall back upon. *Difficult.* Alex had difficulties. Autistic, but high functioning. Intelligent in some ways, without an iota of common sense in other ways. He'd grown from the cutest open-faced, straightforward little boy into a heavy, clumsy, loud-voiced man, whom it was best not to engage with on the subject

268

of orchids, or *Star Wars* or any of his other pet subjects. He didn't come with a remote. He came with Kay, and if she wasn't in the room to give him a certain signal it was impossible to stop him talking not to you but *at* you. Alex, who had been Libby's best pal all those pre-school years, but whom she had left behind when primary school beckoned and there were smart, chatty girls to be best friends with. And although they had briefly met again at secondary, half a term was too much for Alex. Bullied and shunned as he was, it had torn Libby's heart out trying to protect him. And Helen's. And for fuck's sake! The memory reared its huge ugly face up so close, she actually flinched, shifted her weight and moved away from it. Because how the hell had Kay coped? If it had been hard on them, how had it been for Kay to see her boy hurt? (This was something Helen could never really think too long on, it was too painful.) Soon enough, Kay had gotten Alex moved to a lovely special needs school where he'd spent the rest of his school career and from which he'd graduated to the garden centre where he was happy. And now, this next stage. Independent living. Every move forward was a teetering precipice of worry haunted by ghosts of the future sent to torture Kay with horror scenarios of what might go wrong when she was no longer there. No wonder it was hard. No wonder she couldn't bear it. Helen turned her head to look at Kay again. Life had taken so much from her and given back so little. 'Will you please go to the doctor's, Kay?' she said. 'I'm worried about you.'

Kay glanced at her. 'Because I'm tired? I'm fifty, Helen. It's normal.'

'Because you're tired and stressed and anxious.'

'They'll give me anti-depressants. Or sleeping tablets or—'

'I know you're worried about Alex, but some of it will also be hormonal. I feel so much better than I did a few months ago.'

As if someone had pulled a string, the corner of Kay's mouth twitched up. 'I bet you do,' she said. 'Good sex can do that, as well as hormones.'

Helen smiled. 'I haven't had sex for weeks now, not since—'

'And I haven't had it for years!'

Helen laughed.

'Maybe,' Kay said. 'Just maybe, the sex was so good that the after effects are *very* long lasting.'

'Maybe,' Helen murmured. She closed her eyes. When she did this, she could still see Kaveh's copper-coloured skin and his black eyes. 'Just make an appointment,' she said. 'Promise?'

'Promise.'

'Good.' She opened her eyes in time to see signs for Andover flash past. 'Shall I call again?'

Kay nodded. 'From my phone as well.'

Moments later, Helen had let both phones drop into her lap.

'Voicemail?'

She nodded and turned to the window. 'Where are we going to start?' she said quietly. There hadn't been much point in trying to cross this bridge earlier, but surely, they'd come to it now. Salisbury was on the road signs, and the fact was that all they had was a half-remembered memory of stopping at Caro's mother's house, after their Stonehenge weekend thirty years ago. A terraced house with a blue front door, past a leisure centre if she remembered correctly. It wasn't much of an address. 'We don't actually know her mother's address.'

Kay shook her head. 'I never visited, apart from that one time.'

'Ditto.'

Helen looked down at her hands. 'Do you think she was ashamed, Kay?'

'Of her mother?'

Helen didn't answer. It was such an awful thing to accuse Caro of. 'How many times did she ever come back?' she whispered.

Kay shrugged.

'Christmases?'

'Her father's funeral.'

'When she left the day after.'

'I remember.' Kay nodded, her voice low.

'When my mother died…' Helen stared out of the window. 'I was there every day, for months.'

'Did Caro ever tell you the story of how her grandmother died?' Kay said and lowered her chin to match her voice.

Helen turned. 'Yes. The bomb shelter? How her grandmother pushed her mother in, but there wasn't room for her? That her mother waited at the garden gate for years after? Just so awful, Kay. A child, waiting at a gate for a mother that's never coming home.'

Kay nodded. 'Right. Well, she once told me that her therapist said—'

'Caro's had therapy?'

'You didn't know?'

'No… I mean I'm not surprised.' Helen wasn't surprised. In fact, the sentence made perfect sense. *Caro's had therapy.* Of course, she would have. But there was a sting in the tail. A little slap. Caro had had therapy and talked to Kay about it, but not to her? Which is exactly what she'd done before Cyprus.

Kay shook her head. 'I forgot. It was all so long ago, I forgot you didn't know. She didn't tell me at the time either, it was years after.'

'Don't worry about it,' Helen said quietly. She eased back in her seat. 'Why should she have told me, when there's so much I've never told her.' And as outside the rolling landscape of the south-west flashed by, an equally gentle truth unravelled itself in Helen. She'd hardly been truthful with herself, let alone anyone else. So indeed, why should Caro have confided anything to her. 'Go on then,' she said now, 'what did the therapist say?'

One hand on the wheel, Kay brought the other hand to her mouth and bit down on the skin at her thumbnail. 'She told Caro that her mother has been re-enacting that ever since. The pushing away.'

'Pushing away…' It was a horrible image.

'The therapist,' Kay continued, 'told Caro that it would have been such a traumatic incident, it would have affected her mother's future relationships for the rest of her life. I mean, think about it from the child's perspective, Helen. Your mother pushes you away and then never comes back? That's your pattern. That's your pattern for motherhood,

272

unless you're lucky enough to have someone to explain it.'

Helen took a deep breath, releasing the air very slowly. She was thinking of her own mother, whom she missed in some small way, every hour, of every day. With whom she had had such an uncomplicated and easy relationship. How blessed she had been to get that pattern. And how easy then to pass it on to Libby, who would pass it on to her own child. And the thought was a solid lump in her throat; at least she'd managed to get something right.

'It's funny, because Caro's always used those words, hasn't she?' Kay said. 'When she ever tried to explain it, she's always said that she felt her mother has pushed her away. Her whole life.'

'That's exactly what she says.' Helen bit down on her lip. Kay's explanation was awful and rational. Ever since she'd known Caro, back when they were just eighteen, on the brink of adulthood, she'd seen the ruthlessly independent way she'd approached life. Keeping everyone at arm's length, as if the only thing keeping her safe in life was her rock of stoicism. Which it obviously had. Because loving someone who wasn't capable of loving you back wasn't the best survival method for a young child. Zipping it up and helping yourself made more sense. She turned to Kay. 'When was Caro having therapy?'

'Just after Mike got married.'

Helen nodded. Mike was Caro's most significant ex. They had been together a decade or more. All through Caro's thirties anyway, and after they separated he'd become a father and a husband within a year. So that was when Caro had been through therapy. Right when Helen was in the thick of family life. Libby eleven, Jack eight, Lawrence climbing a mountain somewhere. 'She never told me,' she said more to herself than to Kay.

'Sometimes…' Kay didn't finish.

'Sometimes what, Kay?'

'Sometimes, Helen. And don't shoot me now… It hasn't been so easy to talk to you.'

Although Kay's voice was hesitant, her words felt sharper than a razor. Feeling the sting, Helen stared straight ahead. She might have half expected Caro to say this, but Kay as well? 'Why not?' she managed finally, but she knew why.

'Because… Because when someone's life is perfect, Helen, it's hard.'

'My life wasn't perfect,' she said.

'Well… Put it this way… you made it seem like it was.'

And how could she deny that? She had. For as long as she could remember she had spent an inordinate amount of time and energy (and money) creating and maintaining the quintessential image of a perfect existence. Lakeland catalogues, Boden shirts. Waitrose 28- day-cured ham. Homework journals dutifully signed and returned, dinner parties scheduled, pansies in spring, asters in autumn. She couldn't deny it, she'd known even as she was doing it. Smoothing over frustrations with a perfectly ironed Cath Kidston tablecloth. 'It was far from perfect,' she said, and her voice cracked.

Kay was nodding. 'I know. I know. We can see that now. But before… You never said.'

'No.' Helen nodded. She hadn't ever said. She hadn't

ever spoken of the long, lonely weeks Lawrence was away climbing a mountain or swimming lakes. And she'd certainly never spoken of her greatest fears – not that he'd die, but that she'd be left managing on her own. She'd never admitted how tedious and dull she'd found his slideshows, how embarrassing she'd found his self-absorption. Why not? This she could answer as well. Because it was too hard to admit that she'd made the wrong choice. And that was because of Caro. At university, Lawrence had picked her, not Caro. So how could she possibly have faced up to the fact that actually, she'd won the booby prize and Caro had won the main event? Because it was Caro who had gone ahead to forge an exciting and independent life, while she'd stayed home to wash socks. She'd had no choice. She'd *had* to make it sound perfect. She was Helen. The girl with the golden hair. The girl who could have had her pick. And she'd picked *wrong*?

She turned to the window. The thought made her sad. Made her feel as if she'd wasted a lot of time when there wasn't that much time to waste. Maybe if she'd opened up earlier, they could have helped. Back at university the three of them had told each other everything. When not so much as a tampon was owned and they were as equal as blades of grass under one sun. So what had changed? When did she fall for those false idols of money, status, appearance?

She stared out of the window as they sped through the Wiltshire downs – around them, ahead of them, the soft folds of chalk stretched away and away into a timeless distance. None of them had managed to escape life. Not her, not Caro, not Kay. It had crept up behind them, silent

as fog, engulfing them with responsibility, luring them
with everything they thought they should be wanting. And
honestly? It had taken turning fifty for her own personal
mist to begin to clear again, for her to glimpse new land
on the other side. Kay, who had always been able to hold
her course truer, was battling through, and would, Helen
felt sure, get there. Which only left Caro. Most vulnerable
of all. Almost certainly unable right now to see her hand
in front of her face for the thick slice of sludge life had
wrapped around her. She shivered. Caro had never spoken
of therapy and mothers pushing daughters away, just as
she, Helen, had never spoken of how deeply unhappy her
marriage had been and if she knew just one thing now, it
was this – not speaking of something doesn't make it go
away. If they got through this, which they would, because
Caro was going to be fine, she would, she determined,
spend what was left of her life honestly. Authentically. And
she wouldn't insult her two oldest friends, who were like
family, with anything less than honesty. Family. Yes, Kay
and Caro were like family. And then she remembered.
Something she hadn't thought of in years. Someone she'd
met just once, for no longer than a few minutes, who she'd
couldn't picture but could name. Sean. She turned to Kay.
'Caro has a brother.'

    Kay snatched a glance. 'She does, doesn't she?'

    'Sean. He was at graduation.'

    'I... I can't remember.'

    Helen frowned. 'Shall I Google him?'

    'Try Facebook?'

Caro's brother was on Facebook and within the space

of two minutes, Helen had tracked him down and sent a message to which he had responded.

She zipped out another message and again within a few seconds her phone pinged. Astonishing. It was astonishing. 'He's at the hospital now,' she said, and her phone pinged with a third message.

'What about Caro?' Kay flicked her indicator on, ready to turn off the A303 for Salisbury. 'If she's at the hospital as well she might not want to see us.'

Helen frowned.

'What?' Kay said. 'What?'

'She's not at the hospital.'

'Well, where is she then?'

'She's at Stonehenge.'

'*Where?*' Kay flicked off the indicator.

'Sean says she left about an hour ago. That we should try there.'

21

'Twenty quid!' Helen seethed. She turned to Kay. 'You can't even get close to the bloody stones!' With Caro safely accounted for, Helen's mood had grown lighter. Sean had said that Caro was fine and although, judging by his messages, she strongly suspected that he didn't know about the miscarriage or about Caro quitting her job, just the fact that he was able to confirm Caro's whereabouts (and yes, existence) had felt to Helen like someone lifting a stone from her chest. Added to this, the fact that Stonehenge held such a special place in her memory, it had been with a sense of quiet expectation that she'd approached the ticket desk. Stonehenge, after all these years! But twenty quid! She couldn't have been more outraged than if she was being charged to watch *Top of the Pops 2*.

'Twenty-one,' the woman behind the counter corrected. 'And that's the off-peak price.'

'We're not here to see the stones, Helen.' Kay bumped her aside. 'Two,' she said, slapping her handbag on the counter.

'I'll pay.' Helen slapped her own bag alongside.

'I've got it—'

'You paid for the petrol—'

'I've got my purse out—'

'Mummy!' chirped a small boy standing behind them. 'Why do grown ups always argue about money?' His thin voice carried high as birdsong.

'Shhh,' his mother whispered, and Helen and Kay looked at each other.

'Alright.' Kay dragged her bag off the counter. 'You get them.'

'Two then?' the woman said flatly.

'Two,' Helen repeated and stuck two fingers up.

In response the woman slid a brochure and two tickets across.

'What's this?'

'A map.'

'A map!' She turned and looked across the open vista of the visitor centre, through the thin steel rods that supported its floating roof and out to the wide expanse of Salisbury Plain where the massive slabs of stone stood, prominent and unmoved for the last few millennia. *A map?* 'Is that strictly necessary?' she said turning back.

In response, more leaflets were slid across.

'And this?'

'Safety information. It's a four-kilometre walk there and back.'

Helen's eyebrows rose up. She turned to Kay. 'I don't remember that bit, do you?'

'We were drinking cider the moment we got on the

bus.' Kay grimaced. 'I don't remember anything.'

'And we do advise,' the woman intoned, 'that you're suitably dressed, with sturdy shoes and a sunhat. And that you carry water and sun cream which you can purchase from our shop.' She indicated the shop, *the only shop*, across the foyer.

Helen's nostrils flared, releasing two tiny jets of frustration. She wanted to ask if there was a map to find the shop too.

'And just to remind you, there are no toilet facilities at the site.'

No shit, Sherlock, she didn't say. She turned to Kay and pulled as childish a face as her fifty-year-old features allowed. They hadn't seen the sun all day and menopause or not she really did believe she could hold her bladder for more than an hour. Think of all the energy saved if public institutions stopped all the ridiculous namby-pamby that seemed to be standard procedure these days.

'Why do we need sun cream when it's not even sunny?' the boy behind them asked his mother.

'My point exactly,' Helen muttered.

And once again Kay nudged her aside as she leaned into the counter and swept all the useless bits of paper into her cavernous handbag. 'Come on,' she hissed, linked her arm through Helen's and steered her away.

Outside, the pathway to the monument was roped either side. 'For God's sake!' Helen cried. 'Are they worried we're going to get lost?'

'It'll be health and safety,' Kay muttered.

'It'll be fucking ridiculous. Whatever it is.'

'Excuse me.' A white-haired couple nudged her aside, the man brandishing his phone at a speaker set in a post. *Is it working?* the woman asked, as he frowned and adjusted his headphones and thrust the phone forward again. *Is it working?* Her voice got louder.

They moved away. But boy, was Helen pissed! Ever since the visit Kay and Caro and she had made for the summer solstice, that glorious long-ago summer, with uni finished and the grown-up world only beckoning, not smothering, Stonehenge had remained a sun-filled corner of her heart and, so far, the 21st century was spoiling it. She exchanged a look with Kay and then, head down, began trudging along. Bumping and brushing against the other tourists, most of whom were dutifully wearing sunhats and carrying bottles of water. And looking around at them Helen was seized by a tremendous urge to run. Just turn and run as far away from this pageant of conformity as her legs would take her. To Acapulco or New York. Amazonas… Vegas even! Instead, like a pebble in water, she allowed herself to be jostled and rubbed along and this, she thought ruefully, is how you ended up as a doctor's receptionist for nearly a decade. Someone nudged her shoulder, a particularly sharp jab and she looked up to see a man move in front of her. She gave the back of his neck the strongest scowl she had, but the man remained oblivious, hands in pockets, elbows wide, two white snails of headphones jammed in his ears as he jabbered away. *Get it on the market pronto, bud,* she heard him say. What? Stonehenge? And looking at his hairy fat shins and his white sports socks as he plodded ahead, Helen had no doubt that yes, if it was for sale, this man would be getting Stonehenge on the market. *Pronto*. And that notched her levels of irritation up to top gear. She wasn't pissed now as much as she was furious. Who were all these people? And why were they allowing themselves to be herded, like cattle? The last time she was here, she'd been twenty-one years old in cut-off denims and a skinny-rib vest. There was no rope and no path. But there was R.E.M. on ghetto blasters and Strongbow cider and God, it had been glorious! And so much fun! They'd laughed, from morning to night, because back then it was very, very easy to laugh. She turned to Kay, her mouth a long flat line. 'It's changed.'

'*It?*' Kay answered, 'or us?'

Helen turned away. 'I don't remember ropes,' she said and took hold of one as she passed, giving it a good swing. They were really pissing her off.

Kay smiled. 'There were fences, Helen. Not ropes.'

'Fences? No!'

Kay nodded. 'The police fenced the roads. We couldn't get anywhere near the stones. Don't you remember we spent the afternoon with that group of boys from Portsmouth?' At this, Kay turned and began walking backwards. She raised her arm to point across the fields of Salisbury Plain towards the woods. 'I'd guess we were over there. You had a snog with one of them.'

Stepping aside of the flow, Helen looked to where Kay pointed. Sweet patchouli oil, sweat (he was bare chested) and a gold earring in his right ear. Instantly she was lost in the eye of a favourite, well-preserved memory. 'He was cute,' she murmured, and another photograph turned over in her mind. Swinging blonde ponytail and a narrow waist, the bumpy ridges of his back melting into the dark like a fossil buried in sand. 'Last I saw of him was when they stormed the barriers.' So Kay was right! There had been fences.

'Oh no.' Kay smiled. 'The last you saw of him was when the police started rounding everyone up. He ran away and you tried to go after him. You wanted to sleep under the stars. Caro pulled you back.'

Helen turned towards her, her mouth open with mild amazement. 'I did, didn't I? I'd forgotten that bit. She literally pulled me back. I'm not sure what she saved me from, but she saved me.'

'A police record? Devizes?'

'What?'

'They bussed them all out to Devizes in the end. Caro probably saved you from a life in Devizes.'

'Straight into a lifetime with Lawrence.'

'Half a lifetime.'

'Mmm.'

'You were happy though, Helen.'

'I was.' Helen nodded. Kay, as always, was right. That kiss and that boy she'd always remembered, but that was only because it had been kept in a safe and special place. A polished ornament of memory, spared from the gritty attrition of everyday life. At twenty-one, her impulsive nature might have led her into all sorts of dead ends far more stifling than the cul-de-sac she felt she was in now. Caro had pulled her back; she had, as usual, toed the line, gone home to resume that burgeoning relationship with

Lawrence and yes, she had been happy. But if there was one thing she'd learned in the intervening years, it was that if she ever really was going to sleep under the stars, she needed to be leading, not following. However scary that might feel.

'There she is.' Kay's cry cut through her reverie.

Helen snapped her head up. 'Where?'

'I think it's Caro. Over on the far side. Dark trousers, cream shirt.

Forgetting that there was no sun, and heavily influenced by all the floating sunhats, Helen shielded her eyes as she looked up. Sure enough, on the far side of the stones she could see a lone figure. Caro. Set apart from all the other tourists by her taut concentrated stance. Arms crossed, chin lowered, she was stood staring right into the middle of the ancient circle, under a spell seemingly every bit as powerful as any conjured by the people who built this temple.

Kay, who was already ahead, stopped and looked back at Helen, and both of them, Helen knew, were thinking exactly the same thing. Caro was not fine. Caro was not over it. Caro had not moved on.

They were only a few yards away when Kay called out.

Caro turned and looked at them and it felt to Helen as if she didn't know them. As if they were two strangers approaching. It sent a shiver of cold through her and she hung back. The last time they'd seen each other was the day she'd abandoned Caro on a stretcher outside the hospital entrance. And although she knew there was nothing about that day, or the decisions made, that Helen would or could have changed, the image of a stretcher-bound Caro, the way she walked away, was like an invisible energy force that she couldn't cross. As if she needed forgiveness to step across it. Or at least understanding.

'How did you know I was here?' Caro said, more to the stones than anything or anyone else.

'Your brother.' Kay, who was now by Caro's side, put a hand to her shoulder. 'We messaged him through Facebook.'

'And I rang Danny,' Helen added. 'Not about you but… Anyway…' Fighting to catch Caro's eye, Helen paused until she had. 'He told me about your mother. I'm so sorry, Caro.'

'Everyone's been terribly worried,' Kay said quietly.

Caro didn't speak.

Taking half a tentative step forward, Helen said, 'Danny said you've quit your job.'

'I have.' Caro didn't say anything else. She stood and looked at the stones and, a step away, Helen stood and looked at Caro.

'Caro,' she started. 'We're worried—'

Caro lifted her head. 'I switched my phone off,' she said quietly. 'That's all. I just didn't think to message, but I would have told you both. And I will… I just needed some time.'

No one spoke. Kay and Helen looked at each other.

'OK,' Kay said. 'We… we needed to see for ourselves, but if you…' She was stopped by the sudden movement of Caro swinging her handbag forward and opening it, searching, with obvious determination, for something.

'Look at this,' Caro said. She was holding a photograph.

'Is it you?' Helen leaned in. She was looking at a photograph of two small children. Bucket fringe haircuts and tiny shorts. Suntanned limbs, carefree, sitting on a fallen stone.

Caro nodded. 'I found it. I was going through some old albums.'

'When was that?'

'1976 I think,' she said. 'Before the stones got fenced off.'

Kay smiled. '1976 is beginning to have the same ring as 1876.'

'We used to come up here on day trips,' Caro continued. 'Other families went down to the coast, but this is as far as we got.' She stretched the photo away to arm's length and then drew it close again. 'When I look at this,' she said, 'I can't actually believe I'm the same person. I mean, is that really me?'

'It's you,' Kay said, rubbing Caro's back.

But Caro shook her head. 'I don't think it is, Kay. I really don't. We share the same body, but apart from that… we're strangers.' Her voice became quiet and fragile as a moth. 'Isn't that sad?' she whispered. 'How strange we become to ourselves?'

Instinctively Helen opened her mouth to speak, but over the top of Caro's bent head, she saw Kay mouth a *no*. Face burning, she turned to the stones, reaching down to grip the rope, which was warm, the fibres hairy and rough on her palms. It didn't matter. She didn't know what it was she had been going to say anyway.

286

'I'd started wondering what it...' Caro stopped. She was still looking at the photograph. 'I'd started to wonder what the baby would look like.'

Again Helen looked at Kay, whose hand was still on Caro's back. She didn't need another mouthed *no* this time. What she needed, what perhaps she'd always needed, was a tenth of Kay's intuition – Kay who, just by being present, had allowed this space to open up for Caro to step into. Kay the eternal peacemaker, negotiator, maker-of-everything-right-again. No wonder it was Kay Caro had told about her therapy. No wonder it was Kay she'd first confided her baby plans in. What bloody use would Helen have ever been with her Emma Bridgewater pottery and her selfish streak? Swallowing down the lump in her throat (because the only person allowed to cry here was Caro) Helen held herself tall, like a shield. That's all she needed to do. Be. A shield. A presence to protect her friend, struggling to find a foothold in this tortuous maze of impossible tomorrows and unrecognisable yesterdays. From somewhere very nearby and still faraway, she heard a man's voice. *Going to meet with him tomorrow, bud.* She shut it out.

'I hadn't done that since the very beginning,' Caro murmured. 'Because it felt like playing God. Picking out two people, one who I would never meet, and who would never meet each other. Using them to create a third person. That was more playing God than I'd ever dared and so after all the decisions were made, I deliberately didn't think about noses or hair colour until...' She tipped her head to the sky. 'Until in Cyprus, when the doctor treating me said something.'

Unconsciously, on either side, Helen and Kay closed ranks.

'He said,' Caro continued, 'that just carrying a baby shapes their personality. The stresses a mother has, the things she does, and the hormones released... all this starts to shape a baby's brain before it's even born. So I would,' she whispered, 'have been a mother. In some ways I really would have.'

'You would,' Kay echoed.

Caro turned to her. 'So then it didn't matter so much. It didn't matter if the baby looked nothing like me, because it would still be my child. And knowing I would have helped form it, freed me. It's hard to explain but I started to wonder about eyes. The donor, the male donor, had brown eyes.'

I always said it was undervalued, bud. From day one. That's what I said...

Helen spun round. There he was. Fat shins, white socks, snails in ears. Briefly he caught her eye and turned away, hands in pockets, jaw working.

'I saw it,' Caro whispered.

Helen spun back. She had a horrible idea that she knew what Caro meant, but she didn't want that idea to be true. She looked at Kay.

'I saw the embryo.'

Helen stared at her.

'In the kidney bowl. It had an eye, but it was black not brown.'

'*Caro.*' Kay's mouth had pinched shut, white at the edges. She kept her arm around Caro's back, her own spine hunched and shaped by the moment.

And less than half a half-step away, Helen couldn't move. Couldn't reach out to Caro or help in any way. The hour she had spent with her own stillborn son was one of the most precious hours of her life. His eyes had been closed, she never got to see what colour they'd been either, but at least she had gotten to hold her baby, to trace with her fingertip the smudge of gold that was his eyebrow, feel the imprint of his tiny body in her arms forever. *Forever.* And suddenly it all seemed so unfair. The whole universe. Because as well as her dead son, she'd held and loved two living healthy babies and now she got to hold and love a living healthy grandchild. Couldn't Caro have had one moment to hold her baby? One tiny moment?

Yep and if he'd listened to me he'd be walking away with 50k profit.

'*Would you....*' The words spewed from her mouth like volcanic lava. She twisted to Mr White Socks, strode forward and thrust a finger, rigid with rage in his stupid, stupid face. '*Take that damned phone call some place else!*'

Astonished, he stopped talking, his jaw retaining the shape of the word he was halfway through.

'We...' She had to stop and take a breath. Because her anger was out of control, a raging inferno quite capable of torching everything in sight – this man, his socks, even 5,000-year-old rocks! The inherent unfairness of life! The terrible random cruelty of it! The stupid senselessness of idiots with mobile phones. Of ropes and twenty-one quid off-peak charges despoiling her memory. Of trees felled to make brochures to tell people to wear sunhats, the roping in of common sense and spontaneity, the awful understanding of how life was tightening in on them all like a lasso… or a noose. And Caro. Dear Caro, who never even got the tiniest moment with her baby. 'We,' she started again, her chest swelling like the prow of a galleon, 'are having a spiritual moment here!' And now the tears fell, because they were. *Goddamit!* Her two dearest friends and herself, and spiritual moments in this life were few and far between. She knew this now. If there was one thing she knew, it was this! 'Stonehenge,' she hissed, 'is a spiritual place!'

The man didn't speak. He did manage to close his mouth.

And from nowhere, a tall woman dressed in a pink tracksuit appeared. 'Thank you very much, pet!' she said to Helen in a Geordie accent broader than the Tyne bridge. 'I've been saying the same bloody thing to him all day! One more —' she turned to the man — 'one more fucking call, Adam, and I'll flush that bastard phone down the toilet. See if I don't!' And she turned and stalked off, the man following behind with a last sheepish look at Helen.

Helen watched them go. She was shaking, physically shaking, and behind her all was silent. She turned to Caro. 'I'm sorry, I had to say something. I—'

But the corner of Caro's mouth had turned up, in the smallest of smiles. 'I'm fine, Helen,' she said. 'Spiritual moment is over, and… I'm fine.'

'Are you?'

Now Caro's smile grew a touch deeper. 'Yes. Today, right now, I'm fine. Tomorrow I may not be… but it will pass and…' She turned to Kay. 'It really helps to be able to say all this, if you can bear to hear it?'

Kay nodded. 'We can bear it.' She looked at Helen. 'Can't we?'

As Helen nodded the forcefield that separated them dissolved. She stepped forward, and Caro must have done so too, because before she knew what was happening, they were embracing. 'I had to go to Libby,' Helen whispered. 'You understand, don't you? I had to.'

Against her shoulder, she felt Caro's nod.

'And I'm always here. I may not have been before, I can see that now, and I'm sorry. But I am. I really am.'

'Ditto, Helen. Ditto.'

Back at the car park, Helen opened the passenger door and swung her bag onto the back seat. Caro and Kay were still talking.

'Matt has asked me to do this last conference,' she heard Caro say.

Helen turned. 'When is it?'

'Tomorrow morning. I'm heading back to the house to pick up a few things and then I'm driving home.'

'And after that?'

Caro shrugged. 'I'm coming back to Salisbury. For the foreseeable future anyway. My mother's condition is stable, but not hopeful. I can't really think beyond that.'

'Is there no hope?' Helen whispered. 'Your brother said it didn't look good.'

Caro sighed. 'No. I don't think so.'

For a long moment the three of them stood, gazing at the ground.

'Was she…' Helen started. 'Did you get to speak to her?'

Caro shook her head.

'I'm sorry,' she whispered. 'I'm so sorry.' She was thinking of own mother's last days. It was the end of September and her room in the hospice had been filled with the autumn colours of asters and gladioli, with a steady stream of visitors. Aunts, uncles, friends, cousins, Helen's two brothers, their children, her children, her parent's dog, Brodie, even the cactus that had sat on her mother's dressing table for as long as Helen could remember had been brought in and had managed to flower. Every last living thing, it had seemed to Helen, had gotten the chance to be seen and heard, to pay witness to the loving relationships that had tied them to her mother. To make peace, if peace needed to be made, apologise, explain, pay tribute or simply be. And none of it was necessary anyway, because her mother was already at peace with everyone. So why was it that once again, the most fractured relationship she knew of, that between Caro and her mother, was destined to remain so? In death, Caro's mother was going to achieve what she'd striven for in life – the ultimate pushing away.

'Helen?' Kay took a step towards her.

But tears streamed now. Suddenly she was lost in the maelstrom of grief the source of which was as untraceable as the wind on her face. Because who was she crying for? Caro? Or her mother? Or Caro's mother's mother? The grandmother who'd made the ultimate sacrifice? Or was she just crying for herself? She looked up. Caro and Kay were dry-eyed.

'Here.' Kay handed her a folded-up map.

She took it, unfolded it and blew her nose all over the ring of ancient stones.

'What are you doing!' Kay cried. 'I meant this!' And now she produced a packet of tissues.

'Helen,' Caro murmured, looking at the snot covered map. 'Stonehenge is a spiritual place.'

Slimy map in hands, Helen looked up and as she did an enormous mixed-up sob of laughter and grief escaped. And then another. 'It's the only thing it's useful for,' she said screwing the map into a soggy ball. 'A map! You can see them from space!'

'That's the Great Wall,' Kay muttered.

'Whatever!' Shaking her head and using the tissue now, Helen said, 'I'm sorry, Caro. I know how difficult it's always been with your mother. I thought... if you could have made your peace somehow.'

'I did,' Caro said simply. She pushed a lock of hair back and tucked it behind her ear. 'I really think I did. I mean I haven't been able to talk to her in the way that you mean, but I have talked to her.'

From across the plain a breeze blew in, stirring a discarded wristband that skipped and hopped across the car park to land against the wheel of a parked motorcycle. Unconsciously they turned their backs, shouldering the wind.

Caro opened her handbag and took out her wrap, slinging it across her shoulders. 'I sat for over an hour, and I didn't stop talking. I didn't mean to, but once I'd started, I couldn't stop.'

'Oh, Caro.' Now it was Kay's turn. 'I'm so sorry.'

'It's OK.' Caro batted the concern away. 'You're thinking it would have been awful?'

'I don't know…' Kay stammered. 'I…'

'It wasn't,' Caro said. 'Because when all the things I'd wanted to say had been said, there was only one thing left.

No one spoke.

'I told her that I loved her. I gave her a kiss and I told her that I loved her. Because I meant it.'

Helen took a deep breath. The breeze wasn't a warm breeze, even so she knew it wasn't the reason for the spread of goosebumps along her arm. She swallowed hard. Kay had never moved more than a mile from her mother. Love had never been in doubt there. And it was the same with her. Although she had moved away, that hadn't left space for doubt. But Caro? How might it have felt to reach the age of fifty, uncertain of whether you loved your mother? Apron strings had to be cut in life, but the bonds of love? Weren't they what held you in place? A compass, with which to explore both the world and yourself, a constant reference point? And if you'd never been shown, how were you supposed to learn to love? She thought of Caro's lost baby and a dreadful thought escaped. Perhaps it had been for the best? Because what kind of a pattern of motherhood would Caro have had to follow? Helen blinked. Her mouth turned down at the edges into a hard-upside-down U. She would, she promised herself, *never* think that thought again. *Ever.* Next to her Kay was equally silent.

'Guys!' Caro smiled. 'It's OK. There really is only so much time in one day for the spiritual, and I think we've reached the limit.'

Slowly Helen raised her head. If Caro had had any idea of what she'd been thinking…

'Thank you,' Caro continued, 'for coming to find me. I wasn't lost, but thank you anyway.'

And they stood waiting as Caro removed her sunglasses and wiped them clean.

'Where are you parked?' Helen said eventually.

Caro indicated across the car park.

Kay smiled. A beeping sound rose up from her bag. Instantly she swung it around her hip and reached in for her phone. 'It's Alex,' she muttered, then turned the phone round to show a photograph of a smiling Alex, sitting astride his motorbike. Shook standing beside.

'When's the race?' Helen asked.

'In about half an hour. Let's just not talk about it, OK?'

'OK.' Helen reached out and put her hand on Kay's arm. 'He'll be fine. He's got whatshisname with him, hasn't he?'

'Shook.'

On hearing the name, Caro leaned in to squint at the phone. 'Is that Shook with him there?'

Kay nodded. She slipped her phone back. 'He remembers you, Caro.'

'Does he?' Something passed across Caro's face, as conspicuous and unknowable as a cloud on an otherwise clear day. She reached into her bag for her keys and as she pulled them out, said, 'I nearly forgot to ask, Helen. Forgive me. How is Libby getting on?'

'Oh.' The question threw Helen off balance. 'Well…' What could she say? How wonderful everything was, when it wasn't? How difficult Libby was finding the adjustment, how she mourned the loss of her former life? How could she dangle all that in front of Caro's nose? 'She's fine,' she said.

'Good,' Caro declared, oblivious. 'I'm happy for her. Personally, I'm glad she took this chance.'

Helen blinked. Take this chance? Was getting yourself pregnant at such a young age really a chance? She made a terse unconvincing nod.

'I don't think I ever took a chance my whole life.'

Helen didn't speak. Having a baby at twenty-one wasn't taking a chance. It was a life-long, irreversible commitment. The polar opposite of the caprice-like nature of chance. Caro still didn't seem to get it!

'I mean it,' Caro continued, unaware, or ignoring Helen's tension. 'I've always been tunnel-visioned. From school onwards. The idea that there would be aspects of my life that I couldn't plan or control… It never occurred to me.' She looked at Helen. 'I know it wasn't what you wanted for Libby.'

'That's an understatement,' Helen murmured.

Caro nodded. 'Well… You asked me what I was going to do? I don't know!' And she laughed. 'When have you ever heard me say that? But I don't know. In fact, there's only one thing I've decided and that is that the second half of my life will be far less about decisions and much more about chances. Taking them. Saying yes to whatever comes along!'

'Mmm,' Kay managed.

'Mmm,' Helen managed. A laid-back, chance-taking, easy-going Caro was an oxymoron. More impossible than

Barbie's waist size.

'So.' She turned to go, stopped and turned back. 'Talking of chancers,' she said. 'How was Danny? You said he told you?'

'Umm, he's good.' Helen stumbled, and added, 'Worried about you, of course.'

'Really?' Caro's face softened.

'There's a lot to tell you,' Helen blurted. 'I've seen a flat. A new development on the river. I rang Emir initially. You know he said to ring for tips?'

Caro nodded.

'Are you surprised?' Helen asked, almost shy.

Again Caro nodded. 'Yes...' She paused. 'But it's a good move, Helen. We're all moving on, one way or another. And that's good.' She raised her hand to shield her face from the sun that had finally appeared, her gaze taking her over the top of Helen's head and across the fields to the ancient stones. 'Do you remember our trip here?'

Helen and Kay looked at each other.

'Of course,' Kay said.

'Helen wanted to sleep under the stars with that boy with the nose-ring.'

Helen frowned. An earring, yes, but a nose-ring? There was so much she didn't remember.

'Remember?' Caro turned to her.

'Yes... and no.'

'You should have,' Caro said.

'What?'

'You should have slept under the stars, but I persuaded you not to.'

'But that's not the whole story, Caro. Kay said—'

'I was wrong,' Caro interrupted.

'No.'

Caro shook her head. 'I was wrong, and you were right. Not any more. I'm going to take a leaf out of your book, Helen. I'm going to live. Take it all less seriously.'

'Is that...' Helen trailed off. Caro had already turned and with a wave of her hand was walking away. 'Give my love to Libby,' she called. 'I'll get flowers. I'm so sorry I didn't before.'

And a moment later she disappeared among the sea of cars.

22

'I think,' Kay said as she opened the driver door, 'that she's going to be OK.' She looked at Helen over the roof. 'I wasn't at all sure on the way down, but I think so now.'

'Me too,' Helen said. She looked across the car park, and saw the indicator on Caro's BMW flash orange as she turned out onto the road. 'Me too.'

They climbed in, Kay put the key in the ignition, switched it on and then switched it off. She leaned back in her seat. 'Are you in a hurry?' she said.

'Not particularly.'

'Nothing to get back for?'

Helen shook her head. What did she have to get back for? With a sense of guilt, she remembered Libby's crestfallen face that morning when she'd finished the call with Danny and come galloping down the stairs to gulp back the tea her daughter had made while explaining that she was leaving. And remembering this made her remember something else. Those yellow squares, decorating the living room. No, she had nothing to rush back for. 'Only more of Lawrence's post-it notes,' she muttered.

'What?' Kay looked at her.

'I haven't even had the chance to tell you. Lawrence has started slapping post-it notes on everything he considers his.'

Kay's lips twitched. 'And what,' she asked, 'does he consider his?'

'Oh... the commemoration medal for his Five Countries, Five Months All-Road Cycle Challenge.'

Kay laughed. 'Did he think you would take that?'

'Honestly, Kay? I really don't know what he thinks any more.' She looked down and stretched her t-shirt over her stomach. 'I'm not sure I ever did,' she added.

Kay didn't answer. She turned back to the steering wheel, her hands resting loosely at ten to two. And together they watched as the man with the white socks crossed in front of their parked car, hands still in pockets, ear buds in ears.

Instinctively Helen slid lower in her seat.

Kay was smiling. 'I don't think he's going to notice,' she said.

She was right. The man walked on, looking neither left nor right, nor in fact anywhere.

Helen watched him go. 'Why were you asking?' she said. 'If I had anything to hurry back for?'

'I was just wondering if you fancied a trip down memory lane.'

'Haven't we already done that?'

'We could so some more.' Kay leaned forward and put

the key back in the ignition. 'Shall we take a drive and see if we can't find that B and B?'

Helen stared at her. 'I haven't a clue where it was, Kay.'

'Neither have I,' Kay said. 'But it'll be fun looking.'

An hour and five minutes later, Kay slowed the car at yet another junction, another meeting point of pre-war housing, run-down commercial units and constantly flowing traffic. The back of her neck was on fire with heat and irritation. She craned forward over the steering wheel. 'This could have been it,' she muttered, 'but I don't remember that glaziers, do you?'

'I told you, I don't remember anything!' Helen covered her face with her hands. Kay, she was beginning to think, wouldn't be satisfied until they'd searched every last street in Salisbury. Which was very un-pragmatic and therefore very out of character. What on earth was wrong with her? She was the least nostalgic of all of them. 'I was twenty-one,' she wailed. 'I'd been drinking Strongbow cider all day and I honestly thought my destiny lay in the hands of a hippy from Portsmouth.'

'OK, OK...' Flushed, Kay sat back, her hand at her neck. 'Let's just try the next street up then?'

'Or let's not!' Helen sighed. 'I'm starving! And leave your neck alone. You're only going to make it worse.'

'I know.' Kay scratched. 'It's just irritating.'

'Aren't you hungry?'

'Perpetually.'

'Right then. Let's just give it up and get some food. My treat.'

'Or mine.'

'I really don't care,' Helen said and she opened her window to allow some cool air in. 'I'm ravenous.'

'Now this place,' Kay said, her mouth full of pitta bread, 'I do remember. We came in here for a fry-up before we caught the bus back.'

They were seated in the outside garden of a pub close to the city centre at a busy junction. A little distance away, over the tops of trees and less ambitious buildings, rose the majestic Gothic spire of Salisbury cathedral.

Holding her own slice of warm pitta, Helen looked around. 'Even if we were here, we wouldn't have ordered this. Not at twenty-one.' And she dipped a crust into a pot of creamy oily hummus.

'How could we? It hadn't been invented.' Kay picked up her napkin to wipe her mouth, did a double take and stumbled to her feet. 'That was Caro!' she said, stretching to see. 'I'm sure of it. The BMW there.'

'Where?' Helen pushed her sunglasses to the back of her head. She couldn't see a thing. Only the back of a large recycling lorry that belched fumes.

'She just drove past.' Kay sat back down. 'I'm sure of it.'

'She'll definitely be back before us at this rate,' Helen said and pushed the pitta into her mouth. Wiping her hands on her own napkin she nodded at Kay's phone, which lay at arm's reach on the table. 'What's the time anyway?'

Kay shrugged.

'Well, can you look?'

Kay didn't answer.

'Kay! Check the time!'

In response, Kay shuddered and pushed her plate away.

Helen stared at it. 'Aren't you having any more?'

'Lost my appetite.'

'OK. Well do you mind if...' She pulled the plate towards her, watching as Kay reached for her cardigan and pulled it on. Her face had paled two to three shades lighter and now, instead of scratching her neck, she was picking at the skin of her thumb. 'Are you OK?' Helen asked through another mouthful of pitta.

'Fine,' Kay snapped.

'You look...' And heavy as an iron bar, the penny dropped. So heavy, Helen almost sagged. Kay was fine, had been fine only as long as she'd remained distracted. Looking for and finding Caro, looking for and not finding the B and B, allowing minutes to evolve into half-hours and then whole hours. Anything to stop her thinking about Alex and the race. No wonder she was, literally, beside herself. She stretched her hand across the table, took hold of Kay's and squeezed it hard. 'Alex will be OK,' she said. 'The race is about now, isn't it?'

Kay managed a nod. She reached for Helen's wine glass. 'One mouthful?' she said. 'I'm just having one mouthful.'

'Take it.' Helen pushed the glass across. 'I'll drive back.'

Pausing for less than half a second, Kay took the glass. 'Are you sure?'

But Helen didn't get to the end of her nod before the glass was empty. She stood up. 'I'll get you one more, and then we'll sit in the sun and wait for Alex to ring.'

And she was off, returning quickly with a large white for Kay and a Diet Coke for herself. 'When he's called, we'll get going,' she said.

From behind the bowl of her wineglass, Kay nodded.

'Right then.' Helen stretched back on the bench and put her hands behind her head. The sun was out now, and the afternoon had warmed. Back at Stonehenge, sunhats and water bottles would be flying off the shelves. With Kay slightly benumbed, she wanted the space of a few moments to think about the boy with the ponytail... The one she didn't sleep under the stars with... Would she know him if they knocked shoulders on the street? His kiss had, with a fluid warmth, shaped itself into her memory, but the reality had been as transient as a breaking wave. And wasn't that the strangest thing about being human? How we all, in places wholly outside of ourselves, live forever? Like her lost child, Daniel, who remained eternal.

Behind her the traffic hummed on. People leaving or coming into the city – cyclists, pedestrians, dogs straining on leads, tots leaning out of prams – and the sun warm on her back. Moments passed over to minutes. Kay sipped and bit the skin of her thumb; Helen leaned her face to the sky. And then, just when she had started to wonder if they shouldn't get going anyway, Kay's phone beeped. Helen turned to it. 'Is it Alex?'

Kay nodded. With one hand she picked up her phone, the other she pressed against her chest as if it was needed there to keep her heart from bursting free. 'He's fine,' she whispered. 'He came ninth. Out of thirty.' And she held her phone up to show Helen the photograph.

'Kay!' Helen broke into a huge grin. 'Ninth! Is he pleased?'

'Delighted.' Kay looked up. 'Which means, of course, that he's only going to want to carry on.' The phone was at her chest now, pressed against her breastbone like a crucifix. 'I wish I could shrink him back to five, Helen,' she said. 'It's so hard. It's so bloody hard. Why didn't anyone tell us?' And in response her phone beeped three more times. She turned it around and swiped through, smiling and wiping away the rogue tears at the corners of both eyes.

'Can I see?' Helen asked after Kay had looked through. She took Kay's phone. 'This is Shook again?'

Kay was nodding.

'What did you mean earlier, when you said he remembered Caro?'

Blotting her cheeks with the back of her hand, Kay's face was as cheeky as an imp's, exactly like it always used to be. 'Between you and me,' she said, 'I think that he fancied her and...' Kay leaned forward. 'I didn't think about this until just now, but when Caro met him, before Cyprus this is, I think she fancied him too. He is quite attractive... In a weather beaten kind of way.'

'Nothing wrong with weather beaten.' Helen was thinking of Kaveh.

Kay nodded. 'He's a lovely man.'

Helen nodded. 'Well, it's probably just what she needs. A bit of fun. Romance. Maybe we should try and set them up?'

'I agree. As soon as possible.'

23

With every mile she drove Caro felt lighter. Her fingertips on the steering wheel, even the hair at the nape of her neck, everything carried less weight. As if the gravity of her world had relaxed. Trees were greener; the sky was bluer. With her elbow resting on the armrest of her car door and warm tears pricking at her eyes, she felt astonished to find herself understanding that the feeling was real, was not fading and that it really was possible she might be moving towards a happier state of being.

Cliché or not, it had helped to talk. Especially as her mother hadn't heard a word. Because with every confession made, a measure of darkness had left her soul. All the hurt and anger, the shameful envy and bitter regrets that had consumed her for so long, she had tweezered out, one by one by one. Dropping them on the floor by her mother's bedside.

She had been a jealous, tunnel-visioned, ambitious woman.

She would never be anyone's mother.

She had betrayed a friend, and not just once, because her betrayal of Helen couldn't be contained in that one night with Lawrence. What about all those times, under Helen's roof, when she had allowed herself to be used like a pawn? Returning secret smiles, standing close enough to allow his snatched and clumsy gropes. Ah, Caro. These moments stung the worst as they were finally prised loose.

And what better place than a hospital floor to leave them? Where someone would come along and sweep them away, burn them to ashes so that they could never ever be heard again?

It was over. She'd pulled out black hurt after black hurt and now she was exhausted and relieved and lighter than she remembered being for the longest time. One hand on the wheel, she ran the other hand through her hair, feeling a strand come free and curl around her fingers. Her mother hadn't heard her and never would. And the most astounding fact of all was that this didn't matter. In fact, some divine influence may have ordered it precisely so. Because the kiss she'd been able to give her mother, the whispered *I love you*, was nothing short of a miracle. All her life, *all* her life, hadn't she yearned to be able to do just that? And now she had.

She pressed the window switch and holding her hand out to let the strand of hair blow free, she did a double take. On the opposite side of the road, sitting in the garden of a pub, she thought she saw Helen and Kay. Had she? She strained in her rear-view mirror, but a lorry had pulled up close behind her blocking the view and the street was busy, with nowhere to pull over. By the time the street had widened out, with space enough to ease out of the traffic flow, the pub was long out of sight. Never mind. She'd catch up with them soon enough.

From Kay and Helen, her thoughts turned to Libby, and she frowned, idly tugging down on her bottom lip. How rude of her not to acknowledge Libby's baby. How selfish.

She followed the road out of the city centre and stopped at an out-of-town supermarket. Ten minutes later she was back in her car, with an enormous bouquet and a gorgeous pair of baby dungarees.

And yes, it stung. Badly. So bad she had to sit for a full ten minutes crying silent painful tears. But it had to be done. She had to stop by Helen's house on the way home and drop these gifts off. She started the engine and pulled away, blinking hard.

Ninety minutes later, just before six, as she pulled into the driveway of Helen's house, Caro took a moment to look around. How jealous she'd once been of this house and its occupants. Every season seemed to boast happiness and fulfilment. White lights twinkling at Christmas and butter-yellow daffodils in spring. Countless times she'd driven past, hundreds and hundreds of times, on her way back to her own clean empty apartment, her imagination over-heating with sounds and imagery she could neither hear nor see but was absolutely certain existed.

Children's footsteps, dinners cooking, voices of love and laughter and family, the sounds of a life well lived. Of Helen's life. It had been torture. Created and served to her own exact liking. No wonder it had tasted so bitter. *Ludicrous,* she whispered now and shook her head. She leaned forward and was surprised to see the front door open. Stepping out of the car, the sound hit her immediately. The sound of a baby crying.

Scooping up bag and keys and flowers, Caro hurried across the drive. She'd drop the gifts and leave. Get out of the way. 'Hello,' she called, leaning into the hallway.

No one answered.

'Hello?' she tried again.

There was a moment of silence and then the baby started up again. Wild, high cries, pitched at the same note over and over. It was distressing from this distance, let alone close up. Caro stepped inside. 'Libby?'

And from deep within the darkened interior, she thought she heard another type of cry. An adult cry. 'Help me. Someone, for God's sake, please help me.'

'Libby?' Panicked now, Caro moved quickly along the hall and into the kitchen.

There was Libby, slumped at the table, hands clamped over her ears, shoulders moving up and down as her chest heaved out great ragged sobs. And there on the floor, pushed into the corner but strapped safely into a bouncy chair, was Libby's baby, Ben. His face was purple-red and his breath was as raggedy as his mother's as he too sobbed and screamed and gasped for air.

It was a scene of such primitive and raw emotion that it stopped Caro in her tracks. Froze her in the doorway. 'Libby?' She looked from Libby to the baby and back to Libby. 'Shall I…'

Libby didn't move.

Caro took a hesitant step forward and then in the rush of an overwhelming impulse, dropped the flowers and the gift on the table, moved across to Ben, and, unclipping him, scooped him up in her arms. She pressed his tiny head to her chest with the back of her hand, softened her knees and jigged and bounced him. On he screamed. 'Libby?'

Still Libby didn't move.

'OK, OK.' Caro walked towards the window. 'OK, OK,' she whispered and suddenly Ben flayed backward, his little body spasmed in pain. Then his chin came up, his mouth opened wide and he let out an enormous burp.

With the screaming paused, Libby looked up. Her eyes were blank dark slits, her cheeks grotesquely swollen red. Snot dripped from her nose. She was unrecognisable.

And looking at her, everything about Caro went loose. Poor little Libby, such a baby herself. 'Are you alright?' she managed.

In response Libby shook her head, a choking sound coming from deep within. 'Take him,' she said in a voice so guttural it was barely human. '*Please*, Caro, take him. I can't stand it. He won't stop and I can't stand it, I can't stand it.' And she dropped her forehead to the table and pressed her hands over her ears.

Caro stood, Ben warm as toast against her shoulder. 'There,' she whispered. 'There, there.' And she looked at Libby. Briefly she thought of phoning Helen, but what could Helen do? She was miles away. And what could she do? She had no idea. Then Ben's tiny body shuddered, he threw his head back and began again with the screaming.

Same pitch, same length, again and again and it was impossible to think at all.

Caro bounced him.

Ben screamed.

And Libby yanked the hoodie of her sweatshirt up and over her head.

Soothing and bouncing and whispering, Caro turned away and walked out of the kitchen into the living room. Up and down and up and down and it took a few long minutes but eventually Ben's screams quietened and his body became still, shuddering only now and then from the sheer effort of breathing. Apart from that, the house was quiet. No one else was home. She went back to the kitchen. 'Is he hungry?' she said quietly.

Libby raised her head. 'He won't take anything. I've tried.'

Caro nodded. She lowered her chin to Ben's shoulder. He smelled so clean.

'I don't know why he won't stop.' Libby's voice was as dull as her eyes. 'Every day he does this and I don't know why and I'm so tired. I'm really, really tired. I just want to sleep.'

Rocking Ben on her shoulder, Caro stood in the doorway. 'Is there anything I can do?' she asked.

Libby didn't hesitate. 'Can you take him for a walk?'

'I...' Caro paused. That hadn't been what she meant.

'Please,' Libby pleaded. 'Mum's been gone all day and... just half an hour so I can have a bath or something?'

Caro looked down at the baby in her arms. She could feel his warmth through her blouse. Her fingers stroked the top of his head and fibres of golden hair, fine as silk, rose up like waves. An odd and terrible feeling of excitement stirred, knotting her stomach as if it were a bag of dynamite she carried, not a helpless baby. She turned, ready to put Ben back in his seat. But behind her Libby was on her feet, scooping together a bag of nappies and creams. 'Thank you,' she was saying, handing Caro the bag. 'Thank you, Caro. Thank you so much.'

Out in the driveway, Libby bent to tuck a blanket under Ben's chin. His face was still red and he had started crying again. 'He should take a dummy, when he's calmed down a bit,' she said. 'If he doesn't drop off, or if you can't take it, just bring him back.'

Caro smiled. Fresh air had banished that odd uncomfortable feeling she'd had in the kitchen. 'Don't worry,' she said and leaned into the pram. 'I've walked your mummy, haven't I? I know what I'm doing.'

'Have you?'

'Once or twice.' Caro smiled again. 'When it got too much for your mum.'

At which Libby's tears started again. 'It's really hard,' she whispered. 'I didn't know it was going to be so hard.'

'I know.' Caro waited. The last time she had seen Libby, which would have been at Christmas, she'd been radiant. Full of plans as to what she'd be doing after university, full of energy and uncomplicated optimism. Taking in her strained features and lumpy figure now, the change was astonishing and what Caro felt was a surge of pity. 'I'll keep walking until he's asleep,' she said. 'You go and take a long hot bath. Take a magazine in and don't fall asleep.'

'Are you sure, Caro? I feel—'

'Of course I'm sure.' And she was. Because it felt good being of use. Just as she had sometimes been of use when Helen and Kay's children were tiny. Auntie Caro. It was a role she'd played before and she could do it again. 'Go on now,' she said, and she turned to walk away, pram wheels scrunching through gravel.

But Ben didn't sleep. He cried all the way past the junction at the top of road and he was still crying as she reached the traffic lights that marked the beginning of the village. So she turned away from the lights and began walking in the opposite direction, where there was less traffic, more trees, the chance of silence. As she passed a bus stop, she leaned forward and popped the dummy in Ben's still crying mouth and she kept walking.

The dummy came out. Caro popped it back in. Ben spat it out. Again and again. Until finally, the constant rocking of the pram began to lull him. His cheeks puffed in and out, like a bird in song; his enormous plate eyes watched suspiciously, and with every moment that passed his crying eased. The sun slipped lower, incremental changes in light and temperature that synchronised with his eyelids, which became heavier, shelling his eyes, like fruit re-skinning itself. Eventually as Caro reached the stone sign that marked the outskirts of the village, his head fell to one side, his chest heaved a last show of resistance, his fingers splayed open and he fell into a deep, deep sleep.

Triumphant, Caro kept walking. She'd done it! She'd

gotten him to sleep. He was safe and warm and sleeping and that was because of her. A feeling of pride swelled in her chest. She sighed and carried on walking, smiling and beaming at everyone she passed. Never noticing the shift in the role she had created for herself.

The sun hadn't quite set, it was still warm and nothing, she was certain, could feel better than to be out strolling in this beautiful evening, pushing a baby in a pram.

Across the road, the wide open fields of a sports ground opened up. Caro stopped at the pelican crossing and hit the button.

A woman holding the hand of a young boy came up alongside. As they waited for the lights to change, the woman leaned into the pram, her face creasing with a smile.

'Ahh,' she said. 'How old?'

'Four weeks,' Caro replied proudly.

The lights changed and, without looking back, she stepped out and crossed the road.

24

'Arsehole,' Helen hissed, as the car on the opposite side of the carriageway overtook another car, headlights on full beam. 'Why can't they learn?' She flicked her own headlights back on and immediately the road ahead stretched out, empty and dark. Beside her Kay was scrolling through her phone.

'What's next?' she asked. Duran Duran had just finished.

'How about a little Stevie Nicks?'

'Stevie Nicks!' Kay laughed. 'You're such an old hippy.'

Helen smiled. 'She's on Spotify, I'll have you know.'

'Everyone's on Spotify,' Kay muttered. 'That doesn't make you any less of an old hippy.'

Helen laughed. What a wonderful afternoon they had spent together! After Alex's call, Kay had relaxed, and they spent another two hours sitting in that pub garden chatting and reminiscing. She'd needed it as much as Kay, who'd spoken about her mother's move into the home, Marianne in Cyprus, with whom Kay had stayed in surprisingly regular contact, and finally, the training session she was facing.

'Such bullshit!' Helen had offered, fully expecting Kay to concur.

But Kay had fallen silent and shaken her head.

'Kay! Martin's a quarter Nigerian,' she'd pressed.

To which Kay had said, 'I don't like the boy, Helen. I never have. And he's just a kid. The least I can do, as a teacher, is try to understand why.'

And once again Helen had been humbled by her friend's pragmatic, non-sentimental, zero-self-indulgent approach to life.

As the afternoon had come to a close, they'd begun, reluctantly, to think about heading back. Then, on the way to the car park, passing a Millets, Kay had come to an abrupt halt.

'Let's take a look inside,' she'd said.

It had been pointless for Helen to argue. Because hadn't she just spent forty minutes of a wonderfully sunny afternoon talking about her long-lost gap year? And the phenomenon of what was being called *a midlife trip*? Something that felt tangibly closer every time she repeated the phrase. Yes, she had to sort out the deposit for the flat first. And yes, she didn't exactly earn the kind of salary that Caro did. But once the house was sold, or Lawrence had bought her out, she'd be mortgage free and if she played it right maybe even have some left. Why not?

Yes, pointless to argue, and so they'd emerged twenty-five minutes later with a beautiful pink and grey rucksack that now sat on the back seat of her car, silhouetted like a cartoon minion. And frankly she was lucky she'd left it at that! Gorgeous hiking boots, and trousers with hidden zippers and pockets. Pocket knives, which you could practically build a house with. The cutest portable kitchens… And the tall, rugged man who'd explained how huge a thing midlife travellers were. Pointing her in the direction of several useful Instagram and Twitter handles. Which would have been great if she used either Insta or Twitter. Maybe she should start?

The unmistakable opening riff of 'Edge of Seventeen' bounced from the car speaker. Instinctively Helen's fingers drummed the steering wheel. She hadn't been seventeen when she'd first heard this, but that hadn't mattered. Stevie Nicks had leaned into her ear and sung her life.

Head bobbing, feet tapping, Helen sang along. Memories of the student flat flooding back. Friday nights, heading out of the door warm with the glow of a vodka and Coke.

As the last notes faded away, Kay bent her head. 'My turn,' she said, and within a moment, The Cure had started.

'Wait a minute.' Helen put her head to one side. 'Is that my phone?'

Kay turned the music down, and in the new silence the ringing was unmistakable and loud.

Helen frowned. 'It's probably Lawrence, ringing to ask if the lamp in the hallway is his or mine.' But a darker emotion shadowed her words. She'd been out of the house since eleven that morning, the longest time since Ben was born that she'd been away from Libby. The darkness was guilt. Which was as ridiculous as it was inevitable. All her unspoken assertions that Libby was just going to have to learn to cope, and here she was fretting that she'd gone and left her alone to do just that.

As if Kay had sensed the undertone, she turned and said, 'Where's your handbag?'

'On the back seat.' Helen concentrated on the road.

'Shall I get it?'

Before Helen could answer, her phone rang off.

Kay eased back around, opened her mouth and was silenced by it starting up again. 'I'll get it,' she said.

Helen nodded. 'I wonder what the time is?' She had been gone a long time, but surely Lawrence would be home by now.

'It's Lawrence.' Kay held the phone up.

And a wash of relief swept through.

'Shall I answer it?'

'If you have to.' He'd be ringing to ask where she was. Her absence from the house at this time of the evening being such an inexplicable occurrence, he wouldn't have been able to stop himself. What, Helen thought, is he going to do when I'm never there? How is he going to cope?

Kay swiped the phone. 'Hi Law—' But she didn't get past the first syllable before she was interrupted. 'Slow down,' she managed to interject. 'Wait…' She tapped the screen. 'I'm putting you on speaker. Helen's driving.'

'What—'

'*Helen!*' Lawrence's voice barked through the space between her and Kay, interrupting Helen across the miles.

'Lawrence?'

'*Where are you?*'

Briefly Helen glanced at Kay. She was almost embarrassed. It was none of his damn business where she was, and she was about to tell him this, about to stake one of those first markers of her newly found independence, when his voice broke through again, loaded and heavy. 'The baby is missing,' he said.

Helen felt her body temperature drop, warm to profoundly cold. The baby? Missing? That didn't make sense. Eyes fixed on the road ahead, she said carefully, 'What do you mean, *missing*?'

Next to her as a rigid dark silhouette, Kay pressed hard back in her seat, as if her body might interfere with the signal of the phone, as if she needed to get herself out of the way.

'Caro was here,' Lawrence answered. 'She took Ben out for a walk, and she hasn't returned.'

Helen's head wobbled. What on earth was this about? 'Caro took Ben for a walk?' She turned to Kay, who shrugged. 'What was Caro—'

But she didn't get any further because a keening sound rose up from the speaker. A sound that formed a word she couldn't mistake. 'Mummm. Muuuum.' It was Libby.

Again Helen glanced at Kay. 'Is Libby there?' she said, both to Lawrence and Kay.

'I'll put her on,' Lawrence said gruffly.

Now her arms were tingly and cold and her hands on the steering wheel loose as string. If Libby was at home, then Ben should be too. Caro? It didn't make any sense.

'Mum.' Libby's voice sounded strange. As strained as if there was a boot on her windpipe. Her breath was short, louder than her words, of which she could manage barely two or three at a time. *Caro,* they heard. *Took Ben… No answer… Two hours… Sorry…*

'Libby,' Helen pleaded. Her daughter was hyperventilating. 'Put your dad back on!'

But Libby struggled on, her breath more ragged by the second.

'*Lawrence,*' Helen shouted. '*What the hell is going on?*'

And a second later, Lawrence's explanation, brief and clear, tipped ice down her spine. She could not have heard right. 'What do you mean, *taken* him?'

'Exactly what I said,' Lawrence replied. 'Caro was here. She offered to take Ben for a walk, and she hasn't come back. That was over two hours ago.'

'Two hours ago? Helen?' Kay turned in her seat. 'What's happened?'

A ball of nausea swept up Helen's throat. 'I don't know,' she managed. And she flicked the indicator on, pressed the accelerator and moved out into the fast lane.

25

As Helen pulled the car into the driveway, Kay's stomach turned over. Up ahead she could see the outline of Caro's BMW, its sleek silver reflected in the moonlight. What she didn't see until she had stepped out was the outline of the other car. Parked right in front of Caro's, its blue and yellow markings were undeniable. Her heart picked up pace and her mouth went dry. The police were here. What had happened? She turned to Helen, but Helen had already disappeared through the rectangle of yellow light that was the front door of her house.

Frozen in the darkness, Kay listened to the commotion of voices coming from inside the house. Libby's voice was loudest. So young and so strained. Now Helen, and Lawrence. Everyone talking over everyone else. She managed a step forward and then stopped. She had no idea where to position herself. If something dreadful had happened – and something had happened because the police were here – should she go in? Into the heart of a family, in such distress? Because right now, Lawrence and

Helen, Libby and Jack were still very much a family. Before she could make a decision or take a step, a voice called from the doorway.

'Kay.' It was Lawrence.

Without knowing she was going to do it, Kay looked at the police car.

'She's not answering her phone,' Lawrence said. 'We had no choice.'

Confusion scrabbled her brain, like a saboteur with clippers, cutting off chain after chain of coherent thought, leaving her with the building blocks of Caro and Ben and the police. And she couldn't get any further. Her mouth opened. She looked at Lawrence, ready to try again, to try and shape some sense into the scene, but Lawrence had gone, disappearing like Helen through that brightly lit doorway. She tipped her head to the black night and the silver stars. *Where are you?* she muttered. *Where the fuck are you, Caro?*

All the way back they'd tried calling her, of course they had. Chills ran down Kay's arms, the finest cold silk pulled across the finest hair of her forearms. She turned away from the house and went back to her car, took out her bag and pulled out her phone. And in the gloom of the shadowed rose bushes, Kay listened, as she had so many times today, to the sound of Caro's phone ringing out, on and on it went. She ended the call and then immediately tried again and as she did something at the furthest edge of her peripheral vision caught her eye. A beacon, like a lighthouse through fog. Phone at her ear she walked over to Caro's parked car and there it was. Tucked away in the compartment behind the gearstick lay Caro's phone. *Kay, Kay, Kay* flashing across the screen in blue. Like a cry for help in a silent movie.

The scene that greeted her was a tableau. And yes, Kay knew that word, although drama had never been her thing. Equations, probabilities, fractions… It was, and always had been, within these boundaries that she'd been able to steer life. The sheer subjectiveness of fiction appalled her. There might be no end to the introspection. But this time there was no escaping it: what faced her was a tableau. A silent, frozen frame of a story no one yet knew the ending of.

Libby was centre, flanked by Helen. Behind, tall and erect as sentinels, stood Lawrence and Jack. Across at the far end of the kitchen, taking a detached and neutral stance, stood a policeman and a policewoman. The small distance between them and the family huge in terms of viewpoint. They were there only as impartial observers to the chaos that was unfolding.

In front of Libby, on the table, lay a carrier bag, on top of which was a pair of blue baby dungarees, the label still attached. Next to them a huge vase of flowers. Even from where she stood, Kay could read the name at the bottom of the card, propped up against the vase: *Caro.*

So that left only her. Where, she thought, as she looked around the room, should she put herself? As it was, her body decided for her. It simply refused to move. So she stayed in the doorway and did the only thing she could. She lifted her phone up and said, 'Caro's phone is in her car.'

Slow and careful, Helen turned to her.

Kay's arm fell loose. 'I just tried ringing it and…' She looked across at the policeman and woman. 'It was behind the gearstick,' she added and with her free hand rubbed at her forehead.

The policeman nodded. 'We've been ringing it.'

Kay blinked at him, unsure of how to answer. Caro's phone hadn't quite been hidden, but any rise of frustration she might have felt towards the lack of perceived effort on the part of the police had already collapsed. Swept away by the look Helen had just given her. Because for Kay, for a brief moment, looking back at Helen had been like looking at the sun. She felt blinded. Far too dazed to challenge what was being said. And wherever Caro was, whatever had happened, anger, she understood, had not been the response she'd expected walking into this kitchen. Worry, yes. A terrible, consuming panic, yes. But not the white-hot rage Helen emitted. Something had shifted. In the time between them arriving and now, Helen's mood had shifted.

Her fingers gripped her phone as she pressed it against her chest and looked across at the police. 'Shouldn't we… the hospitals? Has anyone—'

'We've checked the local A and E,' the policewoman finished the sentence for her.

At the table, Libby stifled a sob.

'They're working from the assumption that it's abduction,' Lawrence said.

'*Abduction?*'

'They think,' Helen said, without turning, 'that Caro has taken Ben.' Her voice was preternaturally calm,

Kay's blood ran cold. She stared at the back of Helen's

324

head. Caro *would not* have taken Libby's baby. That wasn't possible. Helen couldn't possibly think… But the policeman had now moved across to talk to Lawrence, so close and in such a low voice that she couldn't hear. 'I'll ring Alex,' she blurted. 'Maybe he can… maybe he can go out and start looking?'

'We have a patrol car out,' the policeman said. 'It's not a good idea to involve members of the public at this stage.'

His tone was so impassive and his jargon so practised it scared Kay. 'Alex is my son!' she cried. 'He's known Caro since he was born.'

'Even so.'

Kay swallowed and her throat was on fire. 'I'm sure,' she whispered, 'that there's been a misunderstanding…'

Now Helen turned and looked at her blankly.

'As my colleague said.' The policewoman's smile was devoid of empathy, designed to placate. 'We've made a thorough check of A and Es.'

'Like you checked Caro's car? To find the phone?' She couldn't help it. The last thing Kay wanted to do, intended to do, was let slip the smallest quantity of oil onto these troubled waters. *But this was Caro.* And Caro would not do, would not have done, what everyone in this room seemed to be thinking…

At the sound of her words, Helen stood, chair legs screeching across tiles. 'It's pitch black, Kay,' she said in a low voice. 'And Ben is four weeks old! Of course there's a patrol car out!'

Again, Libby sobbed.

'Helen—'

But Helen's hand flew up as if she might strike. '*Don't,*

Kay,' she whispered. 'Don't even try to explain it!' From under a brow that was fevered with fury she looked straight at Kay. 'Right now, unless Caro's lying dead in a ditch I don't want to know. And even then…' Helen's eyes burned. 'Even then I'm not sure I could forgive her. Look,' she hissed. 'Just look at my daughter.'

Slowly, Kay backed away. Heart pounding, she looked from Libby back to Helen. 'I'm not… I was… I'm going to get some air.'

Out in the drive, under the stars, her heart was the loudest thing in the universe. She felt sick. Split to the bone. As surely as if she'd been cleaved in two. It was disorientating to the point of destabilising. Round and around she went, spinning like a top, trying and failing to find a way to explain why Caro might take Libby's baby away like this. Unless of course they were both dead, the thought of which produced a feeling of nausea so strong she had to go and sit in the passenger seat of her car and wait for it to pass. If her phone hadn't rung, she might have sat there until the end of time, so benumbed was she.

It was Shook. Calling to say that they were back, that they had been for a while actually, and that the bike was in the garage. Alex was taking a shower. He could wait, if she thought she'd be back soon, otherwise he'd see her, probably tomorrow. The bike needed a tune…

'My friend,' she interrupted. 'Caro. The one you remember. She's missing.'

There was a small sucking sound, the sound of an intake of breath. 'Missing?'

'With my other friend's baby. Helen. Not her baby, her daughter's baby.'

Shook was silent.

'Oh God!' Kay put her hand over her mouth. 'Caro's just lost her own baby. I can't believe she'd do anything so stupid as this, but now the police are here and—'

'Kay.' Never was Shook's name more unsuitable. 'Start again,' he said, 'from the beginning.' And his voice was like a hand on her shoulder, keeping her upright.

So she did. Fact by fact, timescale correct. No assumptions, little emotion, because this was what she was good at. No drama, no histrionics. And as she explained, though it didn't occur to Kay herself, it was clear that emotion was an extravagance she'd rarely had the luxury of indulging. No wonder she was so practised.

'Will it help,' Shook said as she finished, 'if I go and look for them?'

'Can you?' she answered. Of course it would help. Whatever the police had said, it could *only* help, because all this was a mistake. An awful aberration, a one-off jolt of the slow-moving plates of their long friendship. The rupture had to be mended as soon as possible. Repaired. Rewound.

26

It wasn't that Caro hadn't been aware of time passing. How could she not have been? The scene in front of her had changed so much. All the footballers had long since gone home, grabbing handlebars from a heap of wheels and spokes, their faces flushed with the happiness of exertion. Shadows of birch trees had crept longer and then faded, swallowed up by the silent wave of darkness. And all around small pools of white had bloomed as one by one the perimeter lights had come on, clouds of gnats swirling in their glow. But she'd only known this as a movie goer knows the cinema screen. It was large and all encompassing, but that didn't mean it was real or had anything to do with her. It didn't mean that she could participate in it. No, she had been as aware of the passage of time as a stone is aware of its erosion by water. If anyone had stopped, had leaned in, and asked, *How long have you been here?* she couldn't have answered.

No one had.

Ben had slept on and on, and the desire not to disturb

his slumber had been so strong that she had simply kept walking. Past all the nearest, most recognisable landmarks until she was in an area that she barely knew, and wouldn't have recognised anyway because she had stopping seeing.

Her feet had throbbed and shooting pains travelled up the front of her shins – too many years pounding hard pavements in high heels – but these physical symptoms Caro had failed to recognise as her own. Her mind was a mirrored lake that reflected only the twilight, the rocking of the pram's suspension locking her into its rhythm, one step after another, after another, after another…

If she hadn't taken a turn into a gravelled side road she might have walked off the edge of the earth. But the gravelled side road had come to an end as it opened out into this playing field. And it was here that, for the first time since leaving Helen's house, Caro had finally stopped walking and almost woken up.

She'd become aware of a low brick building with a covered porch, in front of which were two football pitches. She'd seen that the pitches were filled with kids and the benches under the porch roof were filled with parents. And she'd seen another pram. So it had been as natural as the first turning of the first leaves for Caro to walk up, put the brake on the pram and sit herself down on the end of the bench.

Almost as soon as she had, an older woman, in sweatshirt and jeans, sitting further along had shuffled across and peered into the pram. Her eyes scrunching as she smiled.

'Gorgeous. Just gorgeous.' And leaning back, the woman had let her hands rest in her lap as she nodded at the pitch. 'That's my grandson there.'

Caro had turned to her. The woman's hands were covered in large liver spots, galaxies of freckles.

'Oh,' she said, and put a hand out to the pram to keep it rocking. 'He's my son.'

And although she had felt the tide of surprise that lapped towards her, it was very quickly over and so easily ignored. Not another word was exchanged. The woman turned back to the football pitch and, keeping a hand on the pram, Caro had leaned against the pebbly hardness of the pavilion and closed her eyes. She'd told a lie, but it felt such a soft lie that when a moment later she opened her eyes and saw that the sky hadn't fallen down on her, she allowed herself to settle into its comfortable contour. And if any kind of shape could be discerned from the swell of emotion that moved inside her, it would have been a house shape. A house in which she could sit, for a while, with her pretend baby and her pretend life. A toe in an ocean she could never be a part of.

The match had finished long ago.

Adults had stood and brushed themselves down, called out greetings and instructions. Creaked knees and flexed spines, coughed and moved through the dregs of twilight, shuffling on to tomorrow. All around like fireflies, kids had run, loose-limbed, panting like dogs, shouting and laughing and talking, the sound of their voices flutes in the air that trailed away thinner and more distant, until the last notes – *see you tomorrow* – were silenced.

And still she sat, and still Ben had slept.

'Caro?'

Slowly, Caro turned to the voice that had come through the darkness, like a sound from another dimension. In a way, it made perfect sense that there should be a voice. Just a moment ago she'd heard first a car, then a door slam, then footsteps on the pathway. But with reality still stretched paper thin, it had been easy for her to slip back across to the dream state. To turn away from those sounds and watch the black trees move silently in the night breeze.

'Caro,' the voice said again. 'Is it OK if I call you that?'

She lifted her head. The man saying her name was mostly a silhouette, but still she felt she recognised him. Something about his shadowed face made her feel that she knew him and so she didn't feel worried. In fact, she felt very safe.

'I'm Kay's friend.' The man tapped his chest. 'Shook,' he said. 'We met at Kay's. Can I sit down?' He nodded at the space beside her on the empty bench.

Caro didn't move. She watched as he walked around to the other side of her and sat down. Shook. She did remember him. He had lovely blue eyes, that's what she remembered, but when she turned to look at him it was too dark to see them. 'What time is it?' she said.

Shook leaned forward on his knees. 'It's late.'

She turned back and looked at the pram. 'I should be getting back.'

'I'll take you.'

'No need for that…'

But his hand was on her arm. 'Caro. Do you know where you are?'

Caro opened her mouth; no words came out.

'You're at the Memorial Sportsground.'

Caro was still gazing at the pram. 'What time is it?' she said again.

'Let me take you back.' Shook was on his feet.

'Libby.' Caro looked across at the dark and empty football pitch, the memory of something she'd said unspooling in her head. *He's my son... He's my son... He's my son.* And the voice, the memory of *her voice* saying those words, was suddenly so loud it deafened her. Libby could hear. Helen could hear. Everyone could hear what she'd said. How long had she been gone? What time was it? She turned to Shook, her face paper white. 'What time is it?' she said. 'What time is it? What time is it?' And with each repetition her voice grew shriller, and her panic multiplied.

27

'Got it. OK, yes,' Kay whispered. Shook had found Caro and Ben. Both fine. Ben fast asleep. No drama. *No drama*, she whispered. Still sitting in her car, where she'd been for the last forty minutes, she ended the call and looked out to the open doorway.

In the time that she'd been sat there, Helen had been out twice, pacing the drive, unable, or unwilling, to talk to her, and refusing to close the front door.

Lawrence had been out too. Surprisingly kind. Quietly he'd leaned into the car to ask if she would come back in and had agreed that he too couldn't really believe Caro would have deliberately taken Libby's baby. Which, they both said, without saying, made the alternative so much worse.

And then Shook had rung. Forty-three minutes it had taken him to find Caro while she supposed the patrol car was still looking. Was it luck? It didn't matter, it didn't matter. Caro was safe. Ben was safe.

She eased herself out of the passenger seat and clutching her phone went into the house.

The kitchen seemed even darker. The only light came from under the wall units, making floating buoys of all the faces that turned to her...

Lawrence.

Jack.

Libby.

Helen

The policeman.

The policewoman.

'He's found her,' she said. 'Shook's found them. They're OK. They're both OK.'

The policeman took a step forward, something passing across his face. A twitch of annoyance?

'He's a friend of mine,' Kay said, by way of response. 'He was out looking, and he's found them.' If he was annoyed that she hadn't listened to his *members of the public* advice... well, she didn't give a shit.

Standing at the sink, a few feet away, Lawrence folded in half, his long frame collapsing like a deckchair as he bent forward and put his hands over his head.

'I know what you said.' She was looking at the policeman. Now she turned to Helen. 'But he's found them. And he's bringing them back now.'

The policeman took the corner of his vest and pulled it towards his chin. Twisting his head, he spoke in a low voice into his radio. The response, a garble of electronic voices, crackled through the kitchen like an electric whip.

Kay looked down at her phone.

'Where?' Helen said quietly. She hadn't moved from where she sat at the table. Her face was grey.

'Memorial Sportsground,' Kay answered. 'There's a gravel track that leads down to it. Shook only went in to turn the car around and that's when he saw them.'

Behind Helen, Libby dissolved on the table in a heap of hair and heaving shoulders.

'Memorial...' Helen stared at Kay. 'What the hell was she doing out there?' And her voice was like a stone thrown into a still pond. Deliberate, precise, catastrophic.

Helplessly Kay raised her shoulders, her hand coming up to her chest to try and catch a much needed breath. She was, she realised, desperate for an anchor, a play of stay because suddenly it seemed that although everyone and everything in the room had been washed over in relief, loosened, liberated, she alone had been left out in the tumult. The police officers had turned away to consult in low voices, Lawrence had straightened up, even Jack had shifted, settling, like sand, into a chair next to his sister. Which left only Helen, and her anger.

There was a terrible thumping in her chest, a rising panic both cold and hot. Helen's question was valid. Why *was* Caro out at a sportsground, over five miles away, in the pitch black? She had no idea. She was sure of only two equally weighted certainties. Firstly, that whatever had carried Caro to this point required empathy and eventually forgiveness. And secondly, that Helen might not be capable of either. It was the end. It could be the end.

She wouldn't have called the police. But she wasn't Libby's mother and Ben wasn't her grandchild. And reasons that carried the weight of water in her hands were feathers in Helen's. Who would not be able to forgive. Because it was unforgivable. Never in all the years of knowing and loving these two women had Kay felt more alone. Thrashed on all sides, unable to find a neutral, safe shore upon which to rest. She was already exhausted, and it hadn't even begun.

Her phone rang and all the floating buoys turned once again to look at her, none of them, not one, offering up a haven.

'They're here,' she said weakly. 'They're just pulling...' And she didn't need to say any more because the crunch of wheels on gravel had everyone moving. Scraping chairs and standing and rushing past in a blur of movement so swift that no one was left to hear her finish her sentence. 'Into the drive.'

28

The one thing Helen knew she should do was the one thing she feared she couldn't. Stay in control of her emotions, remain as she was, pressed hard against the front wall of her house, obscured by night shadows. Her hands scratched against the rough render as she linked them together behind her back and leaned against them. To her right, climbing up the side of the front door, she could smell the richly sweet fragrance of jasmine, and it made her feel nauseous. But she wouldn't move. She couldn't move.

Lawrence, Libby, Jack had. Standing in the driveway they'd formed a grim welcoming party for the car that had just pulled in. Its headlights formed two columns of white light that slanted across the gravel. Helen watched as the engine of the car died and the columns went dark.

The driver's door opened and a man got out. He made an odd half-wave to Lawrence, and then moved around to the passenger side and opened the door. For a moment nothing happened and then Caro's head appeared, bent low. The man had his arm out towards her and together they moved around to the front of the car.

It was then that Helen saw Caro's head was bent low because she was holding something that she pressed close to her chest. Ben. She was holding Ben.

Her rage was instant as a firework. A spinning, sparking wheel of white fury that came from deep within and propelled her forward. She couldn't look at Caro and she couldn't look away. She couldn't speak and her mouth was full of words. She gripped her hands together, needles of fury pricking at her fingertips.

Lawrence and Libby walked towards the car, blocking any view she might have of her grandchild being handed back to his mother. Good! Because this was a memory Helen didn't want. A car-crash of a scene, loaded with damage for decades to come. Tipping her head to the stars, she bit down on her bottom lip. There wasn't an ounce of empathy she could summon up for Caro, not an ounce.

'Mum?' Libby's voice came from somewhere very close and lowering her chin Helen was almost surprised to see her daughter standing a foot away, Ben in her arms, her face shiny with tears.

Helen nodded. 'Go inside,' she whispered.

And then Libby and Ben were inside. Safe.

Still she didn't move. She remained where she was, pressed against the wall, an unseen spectator.

The policewoman had turned on the engine of the police car, so light once again flooded the driveway. Helen shrank back. All around she was aware of voices... Kay and Lawrence, the crackle of the police radio, footsteps scrunching gravel. There were seven people in her driveway, eight including herself, and three cars. It should have been easy enough to remain invisible, and indeed the general commotion made it clear to Helen that, in that moment, no one was looking for her. Except for one person.

Backlit by headlights Caro stood alone, a tall dark silhouette, like the last poppy in a slaughtered field. She hadn't tried to slip into the shadows, she hadn't moved for shelter behind the man who had brought her here. She remained apart and exposed.

And although Helen couldn't see her face, she knew that Caro was looking right at her.

Jack brushed past. He stopped on the doorstep. 'You OK?' he whispered.

Helen nodded. 'Go inside,' she said, but when she turned to him, he already had.

One less and still Caro didn't move. Helen watched as the policeman walked across to her now, his hand making soft conciliatory movements, the silver of his cap badge catching a wink of moonlight. At one point he turned and indicated the open doorway that Helen stood beside, and she felt as if she'd been scorched by a passing torch.

Now Lawrence approached Caro. He kept a foot away, arms crossed and head erect as he nodded in response to the policeman's words. Then suddenly, as if a spell had been cast from the sky above, the group broke up. The policeman went back to his car, Lawrence came brushing past her into the house… which left Caro alone again. Only now someone else had stepped up, standing much closer to Caro than either the policeman or Lawrence had. And this person's silhouette, much shorter and wider, turned to Caro and raised her arms and Helen watched, a ball of red-hot emotion at the back of her throat, as Caro leaned in to receive the embrace.

It was Kay, and Helen didn't know if she should scream or cry.

'Shook will drive you home,' she heard Kay say.

Lawrence brushed past her again, on his way back out.

'What's happening,' she hissed. The first words she'd managed to say to him.

When he turned to look at her, the expression on his face was a mixture of surprised remembrance. As if she were an important part of an equation he'd been struggling to solve.

'What's happening?'

'Umm…' Lawrence turned to the driveway, waving his hand in the direction of the police car. 'They're leaving,' he said. 'They just want some contact details.'

'Is that it then?'

Lawrence looked at her warily. 'What do you mean?'

'Is she just going to go home, and we're to forget all about it?'

'Helen.' He turned again to look across at where Caro and Kay stood, joined now by Shook. He ran a hand through his hair. 'We'll need to think about it tomorrow.'

'Is she just going home?'

'Helen—'

'Is she?'

'For now, yes. I think…'

'*What the hell were you doing?*' she raged, finally breaking free of the shadows that had bound her. '*What the fuck were you doing, Caro?*' Her voice was loud, sharp edged with emotion and shrill with bitter anger. Against the soft night air, it was a whip. And this wasn't a question. It was a condemnation.

No one spoke.

Only the condemned. Caro's arms were loose as spaghetti. 'I'm sorry,' she managed in a hoarse whisper. 'I don't know how—'

'*Sorry,*' Helen hissed. 'No, Caro. That's not going to work.'

'Helen,' Kay ventured.

'Stay out of it, Kay!' Another whip.

'Helen…' Caro took a step towards her.

'*NO!*' Helen flung her arm forward and thrust her hand out. 'No,' she said again, 'Do not come anywhere near me.'

And Caro moved back. Back to the tent of space between the open passenger door and the car.

'*Sorry?*' she hissed. 'My daughter has been through hell, and that's all you can say? *Sorry?* For stealing my daughter's baby?'

'I didn't steal him,' Caro whispered.

'Helen.'

'*KAY!*' Helen spun to Kay. '*Stay out of it.* You can't help. This time you really can't help!'

'Please, Helen.' Caro had her hands pressed together. 'I didn't steal him. I wasn't trying to take him.'

'You've been gone for hours!' Helen cried. 'You didn't take your phone! No one could get hold of you! We didn't know what the hell was going on! Do you,' she hissed, 'have any idea of what you've put Libby through?'

'I left it in my car.' Caro looked across to where her own car sat further down the drive. 'I didn't mean to be gone… I didn't mean to hurt Libby…' Her face was an oval of white.

And as Helen stood looking back at Caro, the firework inside her fizzled out, replaced by nothing at all. She felt nothing. She couldn't forgive Caro, but she no longer had the energy to condemn her, and she couldn't look at Kay because Kay might be expecting something that she knew she wasn't capable of delivering. Which only left her more numb.

'I can't… Helen…' Caro's lips shaped words that were not audible. Her face was whiter than the half-moon that sat above them.

And head down, Helen turned and walked back to her house.

In the safety of her kitchen, she stood for a long time, paralysed by the dilemma of what to do next. After long moments of ringing silence, she heard from outside muffled voices, the thud of a car door slamming, wheels on gravel. Utterly exhausted, she walked across to the table. Propped up against the vase of flowers lay the card Caro had written hours earlier. Helen picked it up, her mouth tensing as she read the handwritten message.

Congratulations, Libby. All my love, Caro.

She took the flowers and yanked them out of the vase, then with the card in her other hand, she walked across to the bin, pressed her foot on the pedal and threw everything in.

Part Four

29

Three months later

'**E**veryone has biases! Each and every one of us has thoughts we'd rather not share, naughty little opinions that we keep to ourselves. Am I right, or am I right?' Oliver (*call me Olly*), the young man leading the session, turned to the class and gave a lop-sided smirk as he showed his palms to the ceiling and shrugged.

No one answered.

'I'm right,' he answered.

The room crackled with silence.

Sitting at the far end of the front row, Kay kept her eyes fixed on his palms. They were pink, unlined, very youthful. *Wouldn't know a day's work if it walked up and slapped him in the face*, her long-dead grandad, full to the nose of biases, conscious and unconscious, would have said. She kept looking. It was about the only thing in the room she could concentrate on.

'Yes!' Olly turned, walked across to the window, stopped, stared at the floor for a moment, did an abrupt turn and walked back. 'Oh, yes!' he declared. 'We all jump to conclusions! We're always misjudging people, favouring some, making unfounded and unfair assumptions about others. I'll give you an example if I may, and I don't mind admitting it concerns me. Back when I...'

And off he went again! Striding across to the window, hands clasped behind his back now as he dipped his chin and talked into the clip-on microphone he wore. Anyone would think he was filming a TED talk. Not this; an *Unconscious Bias in the Work Place, How to Identify it, Strategies to Eliminate it, A Safe Space in which to Discuss it,* session. Run by a private company, charging God-knows-what for a bunch of adults to sit in an overheated room and be talked down to like children. *Licence to print money,* her grandad would have said... And so on. She wasn't in the mood.

'By the end of this training session ...' Olly talked on.

Kay leaned back and swallowed hard. *St Stephen's Wellness Centre,* this place was called. She hadn't even known it existed, but how ironic that today of all days she should have been made aware. Through the window she could see across the rain-lashed car park to where a huge horse chestnut stood, the magnificent spread of its foliage darkening and dying under wet November skies. Next to the tree stood a woman and a small child. The woman was wrestling with an umbrella. Every time she popped it up, it crumpled down again. The child was crying. Kay looked away.

'... and identify it in yourself and others. Now any questions?'

No one spoke.

'Great. Well let's take a moment to grab a coffee, have

a mingle and fire up a few of those assumptions, shall we?'
Olly grinned.

No one spoke.

'Refreshments in this corner,' he said, indicating the far
right-hand corner of the room, where a flask of coffee and
a tower of white plastic cups stood on a trolley.

Kay pushed her chair back. She needed a drink of some
kind. Her mouth was as parched as a cracker. In fact, every
moment since leaving the doctor's it had only gotten drier.

Determined not to get caught up in conversation, she
filled her cup and moved to the nearest window to lean
against a huge iron radiator. It was scalding hot. She inched
sideways and leaned against the wall instead, closed her
eyes, and listened to her heart pounding.

'So what are you in for?'

Opening her eyes, the first thing she saw was a large
man standing right in front of her. He wore a suit that
seemed two sizes too small, and his shoelace was undone.

'Sorry?'

'I'm just wondering,' the man turned to include a woman
who'd walked across to join them, 'what misdemeanour
brings you here?' He smiled, as if they were having pre-
dinner drinks at the office party.

'I'm a teacher,' Kay answered.

'Oh God!' The woman screwed her face up. 'That must
be a bit like treading on eggshells nowadays.'

'It's—'

'A load of rubbish!' the man finished. He waved his
hand. 'All this! I mean I don't care if you're blue with pink
dots, or red with green stripes, as long as you're buying

347

whatever it is I'm selling.' He laughed. 'You can guess I'm in sales.'

Wide eyed, the woman turned to him. 'Oh, I wouldn't say that.'

'Say what?'

'That it's a load of rubbish.'

'You couldn't!' The man laughed. 'You'd be sacked.'

Shaking her head, the woman smiled. 'Personally, I think it's going to be very useful.'

Kay closed her eyes.

'Three quid an hour useful,' the man answered. 'That's how much the parking is. Not to mention the…'

'So, *if* we could *all* take a seat again.'

The static fizz of Olly's microphone was like an electric current, shocking her back to reality. She opened her eyes and was both confused and embarrassed to see how everyone else was already back at their desks, coffee drunk, opening computers or tablets or phones.

With rubber legs she made her way back to her own seat and took out her laptop.

Olly talked on. Kay's eyes drooped. Outside, by the horse chestnut, the woman and her child had moved on. Did she ever get the umbrella to stay up? Kay scanned the car park, but there was no sign of them and suddenly it seemed important that she knew. Because suddenly, she couldn't bear it. The idea of that little boy getting wet and cold. All alone. She really couldn't bear it.

'We are on a schedule… *Kay?* It is Kay, isn't it?' Suddenly Olly was standing in front of her desk and when she looked around, everyone else had started the online test.

She nodded, lowered her head and read through the first question:

Using stereotypes is OK. Do you:

Very strongly agree, strongly agree, moderately agree, neither agree nor disagree,

disagree, moderately disagree...

For the briefest of moments, Kay almost smiled. She'd been in the classroom long enough to see stereotype after stereotype repeat faithfully over decades. In fact, stereotypes were a shorthand code in the staffroom.

She clicked. *Very strongly disagree.*

If I act prejudiced, I would be concerned that others would be angry with me.

Again, Kay smiled. Her wedding day had been as overcast and gloomy as this one. Another century, on a limited budget, with a pal of Martin's offering to do the photos. He hadn't used a flash, and as a consequence Martin's family remained amongst the pages of her wedding album barely distinguishable from the dark grey background of St Mary's C of E. Something her grandad had pointed out several times. *Can't see them, Kay. Mind, they all look the same, don't they?* How long ago was it since Martin said he'd done this very same test? She must remember to ask him if he remembered this particular question. If it had reminded him of her grandad, with whom he'd spent so many enjoyable hours watching Saturday afternoon football... And then she was going to have to tell him her news...

Sweat breaking out under her arms and at her hairline she ploughed on.

What sex were you assigned at birth? Assigned at birth? The word-salad on forms nowadays.

What is your political identity? There was no option for *No bloody idea,* so she clicked on *Prefer not to say.*

How religious do you consider yourself?

Her hand wavered.

Strongly.

Moderately.

Slightly.

Not at all.

Now her hand shook. She clicked on *Prefer not to say.*

With immense effort, Kay lifted her chin and looked around the room. Everyone else was diligently working away. And although she wanted to give this her best shot, because she did want to know, because she did understand that unconscious bias was real, and she did want to be the best teacher she could be... she simply didn't have the headspace...

Use the E and I keys. Answer as quickly as you can. E for black. I for white. E is for bad. I is for good.

A series of faces popped up on the screen, just eyes and bridges of noses. Kay clicked. *E I I I.*

Next a series of words popped up.

Love. Failure. Abuse. Disaster. Friendship. Poison.

She could feel the dressing at the back of her neck curl up and away from her skin. It itched. It hadn't stopped itching since they'd removed the mole weeks ago. A phantom itch.

Watch out! The screen said. *The keys have changed!*

E is for white. I is for black. E is for good. I is for bad.

Seven part.s

Pay attention!

The same images, the same words popped up on the screen. Eyes and noses, words. Love. Failure. Abuse. Disaster. Friendship. Poison.

Friendship.

Friendship.

Friendship.

She slammed her laptop shut and dropped her head.

She couldn't tell her father. She couldn't tell her mother. She couldn't tell Alex. The only people she could tell weren't likely to ever be found in the same room again. Three months had passed since that horrible night when Caro had taken... *not taken*... When Caro had walked for too long, stayed out far too long with Libby's baby.

'Are you OK?' From nowhere, Olly had materialised again. It spooked Kay.

She stood up. 'I can't do this,' she said, and pulled her bag from the back of the chair and walked out.

30

Even from a few feet away, Caro could see that the jasmine around the front door of Helen's house had withered to a green-black. All the white heads fallen and rotted in the autumn soil. She stopped where she was and looked down at her shoes. She felt sick. Now that she was halfway along the drive, the tremors previously confined to her stomach had spread to her legs and she felt a little weak. And she didn't know why.

There was nothing in this situation to be afraid of. She was here because she had to be here. She was here because it was the only way. Helen didn't answer her calls; she'd had to come in person.

So why was she so shaky?

She tipped her head back and took a deep breath. Nine-thirty on a November Saturday morning. The air was cold and damp, rich with the smell of organic matter, leaves and moistened soil, the slime of winter slugs and the carcases of flowerheads, stems, piles of rotting grass. It was funny, she thought as she breathed it all in, how alive the smell of decay was. She filled her lungs, pushed her hands into her pockets and walked up to the front door and rang the bell.

The house stayed silent. Caro turned to look back at the drive. Both Helen and Lawrence's car were parked there. Jack, she knew, would be away at university. Lawrence was probably out cycling. Which left Libby and Helen. *Please,* she whispered, *please don't let it be Libby.*

A moment later, the door swung back, and she was looking at Helen, whose face seemed to go through unknowable shadows of emotion.

'It's Kay,' she blurted, before Helen could say a word. 'She has cancer. She's dying, Helen, and there's nothing we can do. Nothing.'

The end.

A Midlife Road Trip

Extract

'What would you do?' Sammy persisted. 'Where would you go?'

'Where would I go?'

'Yes!' Opening her arms to the sky, Sammy threw the words out. 'For this one last chance, where in the world would you go?'

Kay looked at her, then she turned and looked across the rain-soaked car park, then she tipped her chin and looked up. And there it was. Between huge sullen clouds and a steel-grey sky, there was the silliest dream in the world. And there she was - a little girl sitting at the table playing and winning at cards with her father, a brand-new wife, lying nose to nose with her brand-new husband whispering dreams across the pillow. 'Vegas,' she said quietly, her throat closing over, because how she had let them down, those Kays and their dreams, how disappointed in her they must be.

Sammy didn't answer, but just with her silence Kay could almost calculate her astonishment.

Which she understood. Why would anyone think that

she, Kay, five foot three and almost as wide, would belong anywhere like Vegas. She turned back to Sammy. 'I was meant to go years ago with my husband. Even bought the jacket.'

'But?'

'We got divorced instead.'

'Vegas?' Sammy whispered.

Kay smiled. 'I'm good at cards. Always have been.'

Sammy was nodding, her eyes alive with amusement. 'It's not what I expected you to say,' she laughed, 'but it beats my eighties weekend in Blackpool any day.'

'Well … ' Kay sighed. 'It's not going to happen. I mean money wise it's out of the question.'

Also by Cary Hansson

**"Bridget Jones crossed with Shirley Valentine" –
Cup Full of Books**

**"A fantastic page-turner filled with humour, life
lessons and enlightenment." – Readers Favorite**

Helen Winters worries the walls are closing in. With her children
grown and her husband literally climbing Mt. Everest on her
fiftieth birthday, she regrets not taking the more daring paths she
dreamed about in her youth. So when a well-meaning gift reveals
a depressing image of her future, she takes a leap of faith and jets
off to Cyprus for a vacation with her two lifelong friends.

Basking in the glorious sunshine and crystal-blue waters while
enjoying the attention of handsome European men, Helen starts
to feel truly alive. But one of her best friends isn't in Cyprus for the
sunshine, and when Helen learns the true reason, tensions threaten
their lifelong bond leaving Helen to wonder if she can she shake off
years of disappointment and claim her well-deserved happiness.

Find out more and get hold of Cary's other books here:

www.caryjhansson.com/books

Follow Cary here:

facebook.com/profile.php ?id=100083965671063

twitter.com/JohanssonCary

instagram.com/caryjhansson/

Acknowledgements

Thanks to my team, Emily and Mary. Berenice, Amy and Andrew.

And to my lovely ARC team, you know who you are!